HECATE'S HEIR

THE CROSSROADS KEEPER SERIES BOOK 1

SAMANTHA BLACKWOOD

BARGHEST
PRESS

This book is dedicated to my husband Bill, my biggest supporter and fan, and to my dogs, each of whom has given me permission to include them in this and other upcoming works of fiction. They tell me life is stranger than fiction, anyway
... and they are right!

Join my VIP Readers Club for news about upcoming releases, behind the scenes details about book characters, and more. Visit my website at www.samanthablackwood.com to sign up for my newsletter and join the VIP reader club.

Get links to other books in this series and learn about new series coming soon on my Amazon Author Central page at www.amazon.com/author/samanthablackwood.

Check out the *Literature and Living with Dogs* Facebook group, which features all things dog, including books that have a strong canine character—or two. Readers are invited to join the group and immerse themselves in canine conversations with me and other like-minded dog lovers.

A life without dogs ... is there such a thing? If so, it isn't for me.

— SAMANTHA BLACKWOOD

PIECES & PARTS
PROLOGUE

onor lay on the cobblestone path at the edge of the Crossroads, covered in sweat, groaning softly. His body writhed in a tangled mass of limbs, his skin bare and human in some spots and covered with thick fur, black as midnight, in others. While his throat was now human enough to groan instead of whine, his snout was still present, with razor-sharp teeth very much in evidence.

My, what big teeth you have, thought Vinnie. He hesitantly touched the soft fur on Conor's back haunch, wrinkling his nose at the overwhelming smell of dog, human sweat, and the magic of the shift. "You alright?"

From ingrained habit, Vinnie hid his concern, so his question came out sounding like an accusation. Of what, he didn't know. This was the third time today that Conor had shifted involuntarily into his Barghest form. Each time, the transition back to human took longer and was more painful.

Vinnie realized they needed to find the Crossroads Keeper soon. If they failed, Conor would soon remain in Barghest form, lose his humanity, and go rogue. No Barghest could maintain their sanity or humanity without a Keeper to focus and control the flow of magic from the Crossroads, to which the Barghest was bound as a guardian.

Conor's mouth was now human enough for speech. "You're not getting your teeth on my veins anytime soon, you bloodsucker." As his transition back to human form finished, Conor rolled to his side, wincing as he shook off the last remnants of the shift. His Hellhound ancestry helped, but it wasn't enough. If they didn't find the Keeper soon, he had a few weeks, or even less, before Vinnie would have to end him. With a pained breath and several muttered imprecations, he climbed to his feet.

Vinnie placed his arm under Conor's and helped him up, but kept his face turned away, so Conor wasn't obligated to acknowledge his assistance.

Once Conor regained his balance, Vinnie took a step back and pulled out an expensive French cigarette, rolling it between his fingers. He couldn't smoke any more, since his turning, but holding a cigarette was a habit he'd never broken.

Voice laced with concern he couldn't hide this time, Vinnie spoke. "We need to find the new Crossroads Keeper soon, or this Crossroads will go rogue, along with you. Does Maia have any ideas? Or is Alexandria's location still protected by that damned magic wall?"

"You think I don't know we need to find her?! And no, Maia says she still can't get a fix on her location, but the wall is weakening." Conor picked up the clothes he'd shed when he realized another shift was imminent and quickly dressed.

Vinnie stared intently at the cigarette rolling smoothly between his fingers while Conor dressed, then watched as the Barghest shifter tied his shoulder-length midnight-black hair in a loose ponytail, the thick, wavy strands protesting the confinement by fanning out across his shoulders.

Conor gave his friend a grim smile before turning away and striding toward the small stone temple in the middle of the Crossroads, his pained amber eyes intent on something covering the smooth stones of the courtyard near the steps leading up to the pillars guarding the temple's entrance.

Vinnie's keen gaze got there ahead of Conor and his nose picked up the metallic scent of blood, along with a whiff of something burned. He saw something—or someone. Or parts of someone, anyway, scattered across the stones. He winced, wondering if Conor was already half rogue, before following Conor over to the body parts. The powerful scent of copious amounts of blood on the ground did nothing for the vampire. He preferred his blood from living donors and served in expensive whiskey glasses, thank you very much.

Conor crouched down and scanned the body parts, carefully avoiding the shining crimson puddles of blood. His tall, leanly muscled form kneeling at the edge of the blood pool, he murmured, "One leg, one arm, and a head this time."

"What do you mean 'this time?' Have there been miscellaneous body parts lying around at the Crossroads before tonight?" Absently, Vinnie put the cigarette back in his pocket and looked more closely. The ends of each body part were clean and even. "They did this with a knife or something similar," he said. *Not Barghest teeth,* he realized. He released an internal sigh of relief.

Conor slid his eyes to Vinnie and grinned. "You don't have to say it. I can tell what you're thinking. I can't control my shifts right now. Unlike my Hellhound ancestors, however, I *can* control my Barghest form's craving for fresh meat." Conor wrinkled his nose. "Besides, humans taste like shit, and all those zippers and buttons get stuck between your teeth."

Vinnie smoothed back his straight, black, and heavily pomaded hair. "I don't want to know how you know about the flavor and culinary difficulty of eating humans. Since we have established that YOU didn't leave part of your dinner here, where the fucking hell did these body parts come from? And how come I'm just now finding out that this isn't the first time?" Vinnie spied several small piles of ash scattered across the ground around the body parts. "Ugh, this place smells of smoke, and there's ashes everywhere. Have you taken up smoking again?"

"I never smoked, and you know it. I'm not stupid enough to smoke, knowing how sick it makes those with magic." Conor snickered and added, "unlike a certain vampire I know."

"Fuck you."

The two stood in amiable silence and studied the scattered body parts, both sets of eyes drawn to the lone head amongst the carnage. Conor absently poked the head with his foot, causing it to roll unevenly across the cobblestones, picking up gray flakes of ash as it rolled, until it stopped, face-up. "I found a few pieces of someone two nights ago after a shift. Just an arm and a foot. I didn't want anyone jumping to the same conclusion you did, so I buried them."

Vinnie froze when the head rolled over, his eyes laser-focused on the face, his body still as death, obscured by the night. He bent over, nostrils flaring, and sniffed the blood on the head.

"Fuck. Fucking fuck. Fuckity fuck. We have a big problem."

Conor's eyebrows rose. "Well, that was an eloquent swear session, even for you, for whom 'fuck' serves as a major prop to your severe lack of adequate language skills."

"Fuck you very much."

Conor toed the remains again, and a severed hand flopped out from under a leg. "So, what's the big problem we have, besides the obvious body parts and ash littering the Crossroads? And don't think I'm going to clean this mess up by myself. I did my part by cleaning up last time."

Vinnie snorted. "It's *who* those body parts belong to that's the problem." He hesitated and pursed his lips before jerking his chin at the head. "That's Big Paulie."

Conor's questioning gaze swung between the body parts and Vinnie. "Who? So, you know him then?"

"I knew him." Vinnie frowned in confusion. "Big Paulie was head of the Carbone crime family back in the day. The Gatti Family whacked him in 1985. I never did like John Gatti after he used one of my family's restaurants as the scene of the hit. I told my kitchen staff to be sure to spit in his food whenever he came in to eat."

Conor snickered. "You sure you didn't drink some spiked blood tonight? If this mob guy died almost forty years ago, I'm assuming in New York since that's where your, ah, Family had its base of operations, why are his fresh-looking body parts lying here?"

Vinnie realized he was again rolling the cigarette in his fingers. The smooth feel of the paper and potent aroma of tobacco were soothing counterpoints to his unease. He didn't remember taking the cigarette out of his pocket. He almost put it between his lips, then remembered. Bad idea. After his turning, he tried to smoke a cigarette and was violently ill for days. Couldn't even smell or taste blood for an entire month. If you couldn't appreciate the complexity and nuances of the blood you drunk, especially when it was the *only* thing you were able to ingest, it made for a miserable existence. He lost many things when he lost his humanity, but he missed cigarettes the most. And good New York pizza. Fuck.

"Oh, it's him. Or at least part of him. I once punished him for whacking one of our guys by taking him on a little blood vacation." Vinnie smiled in remembrance. "His blood, my vacation. Anyways, I never forget a blood donor. His blood was quite memorable. You could taste the evil in it. It's him. I can smell it. I don't know how it's him, or what he's doing looking like he hasn't aged a day with his head rolling around on our Crossroads, but I have some theories. And you won't like them."

Conor grimaced in pain as he rose from his crouch next to the body parts. The involuntary shifts were hell on his human body. Of course, he mused grimly, there was the distinct possibility he wouldn't have to worry about a human body for much longer. He put that thought aside. He wasn't the only one in mortal danger if they couldn't locate the new Crossroads Keeper soon.

Maia's niece, Alexandria, was the next Keeper, her life force inextricably bound to the Crossroads, her duty to protect it and to guide supernaturals using the Crossroads as a traveling point, whether they were traveling across the world, across realms, or even across the border between this life and the next. She was a nexus. As a Keeper and a priestess of Hecate, the goddess of Crossroads, they desperately needed her here to stabilize the Crossroads. And to save his sanity, and his life, of course. In fact, now her aunt Maia, the last Keeper, was dead, Alex's very life depended on being here and bonding with her Crossroads—even if she didn't know it yet.

Conor stared bleakly at the body parts littering the cobblestones, his nostrils quivering at the lingering drifts of smoke and ash in the air. "I may not like your ideas, but I need to hear them. We need to get this sorted out. There's enough to worry about, trying to manage this Crossroads without a Keeper in place. We can't afford for anything to interfere with finding Alexandria and getting her bonded to the Crossroads before it's too late."

Vinnie aimed a vicious kick at the cobblestone holding the head in place. "Hopefully, Alex doesn't run the other way when she rediscovers the supernatural world and her role in it. She's got to feel abandoned by her aunt. I'm damn sure her mother told her some fucking shit about how she took custody back from Maia and how her aunt didn't want to see her anymore. She has *no* idea of how truly needed—and loved—she is."

MAIA SIGHED IN EXASPERATION. If she still had living fingers, she could better manipulate the Tarot cards on the table. As it was, her ghostly fingers were limited to one card at a time. Shuffling them was out of the question.

Sorrow at her recent death filled her, not for the first time. She remembered a moment of terror as a strong magical force with ill intent seized her. Then nothing. Nothing for a long while. As consciousness returned, she realized she was sans physical body, but thankfully, she still had her mental faculties. Some ghosts went mad and turned into mindless ghouls, endlessly replaying the moment of their death. Especially if they were murdered, as she suspected she had been.

She used her psychic energy to turn over another card. She *must* overcome her sister's magical block and discover the location of her niece, Alexandria. If she failed, the Crossroads would fail, and Conor would go rogue. If not bonded with the Crossroads soon, Alexandria would wither and die, and she would never know why. Maia couldn't have that on her conscience, any more than the whole situation already was. She grimaced as the old thought pattern repeated in her head. *How could she not have realized her sister, Helen, would resort to kidnapping Alexandria to prevent her from inheriting the Keeper heritage that she felt should rightfully be hers?*

The card she turned over revealed the Angel of Judgement, making her ghostly form flinch. She should have tried harder to find Alex after Helen kidnapped her fifteen years ago, when Alex was still so young—just twelve. Helen may have been Alex's biological mother, but Maia was her legal guardian. Alex was her responsibility, and she had failed her. She had failed the Crossroads, Conor, and the Council by dying before she found Alex and trained her for her destined role as the next Crossroads Keeper.

No point in crying over spilled milk, she thought, shaking her head to dispel her negative thoughts. Too much depended on her breaking through the magic wall and finding Alex before it was too late. A faint thread of soul connection assured her Alex was still alive. As a senior Keeper in the Athenian line, Maia would have felt her niece's death. Plus, she would likely have been the one to guide Alex's spirit through the Crossroads if Alex had died before her. She turned over another card. Death revealed his skeleton grin. "Well, fuck," she muttered.

"Vincent's foul language habit is wearing off on you," Conor said as he stepped into the room.

Maia wheeled around, startled. "Don't creep up on me like that! You scared me to death!"

Conor chuckled, and Maia realized the humor in her last sentence.

"Sorry. I didn't mean to startle you, Keeper. My apologies."

"My Keeper role ended at my death, as you well know." Maia peered closely at Conor's face. "What's up? You look like you've seen a ghost. Oh shit. I did it again. *Of course,* you've seen a ghost. Me. I mean, you look upset. Has something happened at the Crossroads?"

"Oh yeah. Something's happened alright. Ever heard of Big Paulie Carbone?"

"No. Should I have?"

"Probably not." Conor shook his head as he strolled up to the table, where the tarot cards told a tale of trouble. "He was a gangster in New York back in Vinnie's time. Head of the Gambino crime family until he turned informant for the FBI. We just found him, or rather parts of him, at the Crossroads. Vinnie identified him from his days in New York as head of his own, ah, Family."

Maia tried to take a deep breath to clear her mind, then remembered she didn't have the ability do that. This whole ghost thing really was a bummer. Fuck. Maybe Vinnie's predilection for profanity was rubbing off on her just a little. "So, how did he die? And what do you mean 'parts of him?'"

"We found a head, a leg, an arm and a hand, plus a few other bits and pieces. Looks like someone cut them off with a sharp knife. Based on the amount of blood, this happened in situ, at the Crossroads. Recently."

Feeling herself go white ... well, whiter, Maia asked, "So, someone cut him up and left him at the Crossroads? Why? Don't the New York crime families like to keep things 'in house' so-to-speak? Why would they kill him here in San Antonio? I was at the Crossroads yesterday to welcome a couple of ghost guests. Oh, and a werewolf. I saw nothing. They definitely killed him after that."

Conor tapped nervous fingers on the table. "Well, that's the thing. Big Paulie died in 1985. A rival crime family whacked him. His body is buried in New York. Well, at least, it was ..."

Maia's stomach sank. Well, not really, since she no longer had one, but it sure felt like it. "But how can that be? Are you sure it's him? Maybe he didn't die in 1985. Perhaps he's been in the Witness Protection Program? Maybe relocated to San Antonio? Maybe bad guys he ratted out finally located him and came down here to take him out."

She knew she was grasping at straws and sounded like a character on one of those crime shows she still liked to watch—when someone took pity on her and turned on the TV. That damned little 'On' button still resisted all her ghostly efforts.

Conor sank down into a chair at the table and toyed with the Tarot cards, shuffling and reshuffling them. "Nope. Vinnie said his face hasn't aged a day since the last time he saw him alive, in 1981. And, as head of a crime family himself back then, they informed him of the details of the hit and allowed him and other Family heads to view the body. He says the Families do that to erase any doubt about the need for a successor to be appointed."

Maia eyed Conor and sat, hovering her form over a chair opposite him, envying his ability to shuffle the cards. "So, how can Vinnie be sure its him? Maybe it's someone who just resembles him?"

Conor shook his head and put the cards back on the table. "Nope. Vinnie and Paulie had some 'history.' Paulie disrespected Vinnie's Family over something, and Vinnie 'punished' him by turning him into a vampire's pincushion. Vinnie says he never forgets the taste or smell of a donor. It's him."

With effort, Maia slid the top Tarot card off the newly shuffled deck and turned it over. The Tower appeared, sitting ominously on a hill, with lightning spearing the battlements. Disaster was coming.

1

A BLAST FROM THE PAST

Alex maneuvered her car into the small parking lot behind the restaurant and counted herself lucky to snag the last parking space. She turned off the car and rested her head on the steering wheel, blowing out a stressed breath.

Why did her co-workers feel the need to throw a going away party for her? And why, oh why, had she agreed to attend? She'd only worked at the museum for six months and always kept a personal and social distance from those she worked with.

She did her job and did it well. She helped where needed and stayed out of office politics. If only it had been as easy to stay away from her department head, whose hands did the talking for him— typically by being placed in inappropriate places on his female subordinates' bodies. When Alex hesitantly mentioned it to an attractive young co-worker, she shrugged and said, "That's the price you pay for working with one of the most brilliant minds in Medieval European History. Most of us stay just long enough to burnish our resumes, then leave for another museum or university job."

What the hell happened to the #MeToo movement? Alex wondered. Then again, museum work culture progressed as slowly as the shift from Medieval Times to the Enlightenment.

Considering Dr. Hanson's Medieval History specialty, Alex thought, his opinion of women as objects made for his pleasure made more sense.

Of course, Alex, being a product of the 21st century and never one to think before speaking, did not react well to Dr. Hanson's 'hands on' approach with his female staff. The last straw for her was waking from a fainting spell to find his hands on her shirt 'checking for a heartbeat.' On her boobs. Both of them. That scene did not end well, and, for once, she didn't regret her tendency to talk first and ask questions later.

The female staff had all clapped as she gathered her things and walked out—after telling Dr. Hanson exactly where he could put his hands next and advising him it wouldn't be much of a stretch, as his head was already occupying the same space.

THE FATIGUE and headache plaguing Alex for several weeks had gotten worse lately, dragging her down, making her mental processes slow, and lowering her emotional defenses. And then she fainted at work. Maybe she could blame illness for her harsh words and ask for her job back? Nah, she didn't regret them at all and couldn't blame not feeling well for her smart mouth, as that had been getting her into trouble for years.

A sigh escaped as she checked her makeup in the rear-view mirror. Her large green eyes stared back, dark circles staining the light olive skin underneath them. She pulled her long black hair into a messy knot and fastened it with a jeweled clip. That would have to do, she thought, before grabbing her purse and heading through the parking lot toward the front of the restaurant, mentally girding herself for a girl's night out, which was *so* not her thing.

Alex didn't do close relationships. She'd experienced too much loss to open her life or heart to anyone else. She'd loved her aunt, who raised her, with her whole heart. When her aunt died just before Alex hit her teenage years, Alex had grieved deeply.

Upon her aunt's death, Alex's mother briefly returned from her travels, moved Alex from the only home she'd known, her aunt's sprawling estate in sunny, warm San Antonio, to an elegant river-front condo in frigid Connecticut. Her uncaring mother stayed just long enough to install a live-in babysitter and a housekeeper before re-embarking on her working international travels, sourcing antiques for her high-end antique store in Westport.

Her mother had remarried when Alex was fifteen, and light came back into her life in the form of her warm and caring stepfa-ther, who treated her as his own daughter from the beginning. When her stepfather passed away during her college years, breaking Alex's heart yet again, she hung a 'closed for repairs' sign on her heart and kept her distance from people. She was happiest when alone. Or at least that's what she told herself.

As the door to the restaurant closed behind her, Alex gave her name to the hostess, a tall, elegant woman in a black sheath dress that looked like it cost more than Alex's entire wardrobe. *Probably does*, Alex reflected glumly.

"Follow me," said the hostess, smiling and looking both snotty and welcoming at the same time. She turned and led Alex toward a large booth in the back of the bar area.

Boy, tonight is sure going to be a lot of fun—not, Alex thought, trailing after the hostess toward her oh-so-fun going away party. Ears ringing from the pounding of music from a pretty decent live band mixed with the buzz of dozens of conversations, Alex's nose wrinkled as the smell of fruity drinks and fried bar food wafted from the tables she passed. She spied the booth filled with her former coworkers up ahead, took a deep breath, then approached the already laughing group.

After the second expensive, fancy cocktail, Alex admitted to herself the farewell party wasn't horrible. The women in the booth surrounding her had really let their hair down, included her in their group gossip, and were dishing dirt on Handsy Hanson, their nickname for her former boss.

They gave her a farewell gift that was both embarrassing and potentially useful: a canister of pepper spray snuggled tightly in a bright pink rubberized holder, complete with a neon green reflective wrist strap.

As Alex tipsily bid farewell to her former colleagues, she realized she was in no shape to drive, so she called an Uber, hoping she remembered the location of her car when she woke up in the morning.

Maybe the alcohol would keep the nightmares at bay tonight, and she'd actually get a good night's sleep. Yeah, right.

ALEX HIT the alarm button again and blearily realized her efforts were having no effect at quieting the strident noise disturbing her sleep. Her head pounded with a vicious headache and traces of darkness remained from the familiar nightmare that haunted her dreams. She peeled open one eye and peered towards her nightstand, where her phone bounced along the surface as it continued to ring. Oops, not the alarm clock then, but the phone. To stop the ringing, which was piercing her aching head, she accepted the call and croaked a sleepy greeting. "Hello, Alexandria Blackwood here."

A tinny voice with a deep and very Southern drawl asked, "Oh, did I wake you, Miss Blackwood? I figured you are on Connecticut time, so it's an hour later there—"

Irritated and in pain, Alex snapped at the caller. "It's seven thirty in the morning here, so this better be good. If this is a telemarketer, I'm going to curse you and all your male progeny to eternal itchy balls."

"Oh! Oh, ma'am, I'm so sorry to have got you up with the roosters!" Alex heard an audible swallow at the other end of the line.

Probably thinking about those itchy balls, she mused, smiling at the thought.

Alex yawned and stretched, her limbs aching with a fatigue that no amount of sleep cured. "Well, I'm awake now, and I'm assuming you have a legitimate reason for calling." She peered at the clock on her nightstand, confirming that, yes, indeed, it was the ungodly hour of seven thirty. Considering she didn't crawl tipsily into bed until after two o'clock in the morning and had the old familiar nightmare when she did, she was severely sleep deprived, hung over, and more than a little cranky. She might just curse the caller and his progeny, whether he was a telemarketer or not.

"I apologize again, ma'am." Regret and sadness filled the caller's next words. "But I'm afraid that I'm the bearer of sad news. Your aunt Maia passed away several weeks ago, here in San Antonio. She—um. She had no emergency contact listed, and so it wasn't until the police reached out to me last week, after finding my name in her personal records, that I learned of her passing. My name is Alan Allman. I'm your aunt's attorney, and the executor of her will."

Pain deepened the man's voice. "I'm also a long-time friend of your aunt. You may not know this. In fact, I'm fairly sure you don't, but she loved you very much. Also, you are her sole heir."

Alex pulled the phone away from her ear and peered at it in pained confusion. She then put the phone back to her ear and took a deep, shaky breath. "But ... my aunt died fifteen years ago. My mother and I moved to Connecticut after her death. How could she still have been alive all this time?"

A mournful sadness at losing the woman she thought of as her 'true' parent, her heart-mother, filled her thoughts. Her childhood, spent at her aunt's verdant estate in San Antonio, had been idyllic. Her mother was an infrequent visitor during those years. Scenes of books read together with her aunt, tea parties under the weeping willow by the koi fountain, kind words, comfort cooking, and hearty hugs hello and goodbye swept through her until the familiar pain of a migraine pounded the memories away, as it always did. Only, this time, the pain was muted, leaving her with the pleasant memories, instead of the need to bury them to avoid the blinding pain she usually experienced whenever she thought of her childhood. Alex glanced at the partially open blinds. The first blush of dawn shafted rosy light through the slats. Sun rose late in the fall and winter months in Connecticut.

Her aunt's attorney cleared his throat. "I'm so sorry my dear, but I'm afraid your aunt has been alive and well these past years. She never stopped searching for you after your mother took you and fled. I'm so sorry your mother told you your aunt had died. Maybe she thought it was for the best. However, by taking you from your aunt, who had primary custody of you, she made an unfortunate decision that has affected your life. Your aunt loves— loved you so much. She made a home for you here, where you were—are wanted and needed." He hesitated and murmured so softly Alex almost missed it. "More than you know."

"Hold on a minute. I need to think." Alex padded into the bathroom and splashed her face with water in a vain attempt to wake up and wash away the shock of Alan's words. The cold water just made her face wet and ran down to dampen her nightgown. Legs dragging with tiredness, Alex sighed, shuffled back to the bed and sank down on it, her hand to her still-aching head.

She eyed the phone on the nightstand with trepidation and considered hanging up. But that wouldn't make the revelations of the last few minutes go away, though, so she picked up the phone with a sigh. "Hello again. Sorry about the delay."

"Oh no worries, dear! I'm so sorry to be the bearer of this news ...."

"Yup. I get it. Moving on—I knew my aunt had custody of me. I was told this was because my mother traveled so much for work. So, my mother lied? My aunt didn't die and leave me with my mother?" Alex realized that sounded bad. Dying hadn't been her aunt's fault, but she realized she had felt abandoned afterwards. Yes, she had her mother, but there was never the same connection there, not even after all these years. And the nightmares she suffered ever since moving to Connecticut as a child were all about loss and abandonment. Go figure. A deep well of anger rose at the lies her mother had told her and the impact they had on her life.

Alex drew in a deep breath and slowly let it out, trying to think through the piercing sense of loss. The pain was as fresh as it had been fifteen years ago when her mother visited San Antonio while her aunt was away and shattered her world. "Your aunt is dead." Her mother's voice was flat as she explained. "I guess you'll have to come live with me in Connecticut. I'll be hiring a live-in sitter, so you'll have company when I'm away."

Mind racing in time with the pulse of her headache, her eyes closed in pain and grief. Alex's world shattered and reformed, the broken pieces not fitting together as before.

"So, you say that I'm my aunt's heir? And she just died recently. Are you sure? Of course, you're sure. Oh, wait, is there anything I need to do regarding her funeral? Can I do it from here, or do I need to come to San Antonio? What am I saying—of course, I need to come there, at least for the funeral and, uh, the reading of the will. I'm sorry, I'm still not awake. This is all a bit of a shock. And I'm not feeling well." *Hung over,* Alex thought wryly. A massive, freaking huge shock. And boy, did she need to have a serious talk with her mother.

Alex had a fiery temper at the best of times. She knew she hadn't inherited it from her emotionless mother and wondered, for the hundredth time, if she got it from her father, her aunt, or another relative. How many other family members had her mother kept from her? Alex pounded her fist into the bedcovers, startling her dog awake. Larry yawned and stretched, then his long, pink ears perked as he realized trouble was brewing.

With barely controlled anger, Alex asked, "What do I need to do next?"

After a slight pause, the attorney responded. "Again, I'm so sorry for your loss, Miss Blackwood. I understand your anger at discovering the truth this way. I took the liberty of arranging for a funeral home to collect your aunt's body from the morgue. I'll text you their contact information, so you can speak to them directly. I will tell you, though, that your aunt left specific instructions about her funeral rites. Perhaps it would be best for you and me to meet in person, so we can go over everything before you make funeral arrangements. I know this is likely an inconvenience, but the sooner you can travel here, the better."

The anxiety in the attorney's voice set tiny alarm bells ringing in Alex's mind. It sounded as if he not only wanted her to travel to San Antonio immediately but needed her to do so. Strange. Good thing she quit her job a few days ago. Alex smiled slightly, the memory of telling her boss where he could stick it after one too many handsy 'accidental' boob touches flitting through her mind. Well, one was too many, but she put up with his behavior longer than she should have because she had really needed the job. After quitting as manager of her mother's antique shop six months ago, she still hadn't found her niche, despite her master's degree in Medieval European Studies with a minor in Business Management.

Alex hadn't told her mother about her latest job loss. She didn't want to listen to her ask snidely if she was ready to come back to work at her 'real job' yet. *I'll eat Larry's dog food before I go back to work for my mother at her fancy-ass antique shop,* Alex vowed.

Overwhelmed, Alex collapsed back onto the bed as her vision narrowed. Her headache pounded again into migraine territory. She'd always been in reasonably good health. Lately, however, tiredness and fatigue, along with frequent, incapacitating migraines, plagued her.

Larry's head nuzzled under her hand, as if offering comfort and a loyal, if rather small and furry, shoulder to lean on. She absently stroked his soft, curly fur.

Alex heard Larry's deep baritone voice in her mind. *"I'm up for a plane ride, but don't put that ridiculous rhinestone collar on me for the trip, or I'll poop in your shoes. Again."*

A smile curved her lips at Larry's gruff demand. She gave him a last pat, then rose from the bed before speaking into the phone again. "Well, I'm between jobs at the moment, so I can arrange flights within the next few days, if that works?"

"Oh, that would be wonderful," Alan said. "If you like, I can arrange your flights for you and cover the cost from your aunt's funds. It's no trouble! You can, of course, stay in your old rooms in the carriage apartment at the estate while you are in town."

Again with the enthusiasm, she thought warily. Not one to look a gift horse in the mouth, especially considering her current bank balance couldn't feed said horse more than a bag of carrots, she responded, "Sounds great! Thank you. Just text me the flight details, and I'll be there."

As she hung up, Alex thought about her aunt, risking the painful, deep headache that attacked whenever she did so. Why had her mother lied? Pain spiked through her head. That was her last conscious thought as she fell back onto the bed and into a well of darkness.

ALEX WOKE to her rescue dog, Larry, aka Larry the Kibble Guy, hater of rhinestone collars, licking her face. She scrunched up her lips so Larry couldn't put the 'French' in French poodle by licking inside her mouth. Yuck! She knew he did it on purpose. He'd told her so the first time he did it when she'd taken him to the car after adopting him from the animal shelter where she volunteered. Yep. He literally told her so, in words delivered straight to her mind. She'd thought she was going crazy. She knew dogs could *not* talk, er, communicate in words, mind-to-mind or otherwise. So, why the hell had she heard the ball of fluff smirking at her from the passenger's seat say, *"I'm a freaking French poodle now, so I figured French kisses are the way to go? No?"* The conversation went downhill from there.

She smiled at the memory of 'hearing' Larry's first words in her mind as she stroked Larry's pink ears. "Hey, boy, I know you said you would be up for a plane ride. Have you ever been on a plane? Here's the deal. I'll bring you with me and I promise, no rhinestone collar if you agree to no French kissing. Oh, and no pooping in my shoes. Again."

Paws crossed daintily on the duvet; Larry considered the offer. *"Gotta put a time limit on the 'no French kissing' requirement and the 'no pooping in your shoes' one, too. I never make open-ended commitments. Let's say, no Frenchies or shoe poos for one month. How's that sound?"*

Alex laughed out loud, then winced as the pounding in her head returned with a vengeance. "Okay, no French kissing or shoe pooping for one month, in exchange for me not making you wear the rhinestone collar. But I honestly don't see what's wrong with it. At least it's blue." She snickered. "Velvet."

Larry curled his lip and revealed a very sharp-looking, sparkling white canine. *"You freaking know I'm a pit bull inside, where it counts. It's bad enough they permanently dyed my damn poodle ears and tail pink. I keep telling you, inside I'm rough and tough, a real junk-yard dog, and not a prissy poodle, but do you listen?! NO! I might as well be talking to the wall."*

He jumped nimbly off the bed and trotted into the hallway, nose in the air. *"If you don't feed me soon, I'm going to starve literally to death."*

Alex watched Larry prance out of the room with amusement. "I know you're a pit bull at heart, bud. Give me a sec and I'll be down to feed you a pit-bull-sized portion of kibble."

She knew Larry's comments were meant to distract her from her anger at her mother and fresh grief over her aunt's passing. She took a deep, cleansing breath and turned her thoughts to preparing for her trip. Uh oh, she forgot to mention to her aunt's attorney that she'd be bringing a dog. She'd keep the *talking* dog part to herself. She hoped it wouldn't be an issue.

2

MOTHER DEAREST

After feeding Larry breakfast and getting dressed, Alex huffed out to her parking space, prepared to take on her mother. No car. Shit. Then she remembered leaving it at the restaurant the previous evening after drinking way too much and having fun with a group of coworkers she got to know better in one night than in the six months prior. Alex sighed and called an Uber. *So much for stalking straight over to her mother's house to demand answers,* she thought. She had a stop to make to pick up her abandoned car before she could get her huff on again.

Later that afternoon, Alex sat in her car in front of her mother's condo. The scudding gray clouds overhead matched the raw wind buffeting her small Honda. She shivered. She hadn't seen her mother face-to-face in six months. Not since she'd caught her mother in a lip-lock with Alex's now very much ex-fiancé.

Her hands tightened on the padded steering wheel as she realized that the anger and betrayal she harbored toward her mother the moment she caught her kissing the man who had proposed to Alex only the week before was the strongest emotion she'd felt concerning her mother in a long time. Perhaps ever. She snorted and shook her head. Well, at least until now. Discovering that her mother stole her as a child from her loving aunt, told her that her aunt had died, and then brought her to this cold condo in icy Connecticut definitely topped the fiancé kissing thing—by a thousand miles.

Gray and black shadows writhed at the edge of Alex's vision, and she gasped as a sharp pain pierced her head. There was more to her mother's lies about that time, but her mind shied away, not ready for the pain the memories of her time in San Antonio brought with them.

Alex's thoughts traveled back to her childhood when she first arrived in Connecticut at twelve, after her aunt's supposed death. Her mother's distant personality, combined with her long absences, caused several lonely years. Alex realized, even then, that her preference for being alone was a safety mechanism based on her fear of loss. She had fended for herself emotionally since she was an adolescent. On the plus side, she reflected, it had made her fiercely independent. On the minus side, it had made it hard for her to open herself to close relationships of any kind.

Memories of her stepfather surfaced, and she smiled sadly in remembrance. When Alex was fifteen, her mother surprised the hell out of everyone, Alex most of all, by remarrying. She had never understood why her loving, lively, and loyal stepfather had married her emotionless mother. When she saw them together, she watched as her mother slipped on a mask of pleasantness. But she knew that's all it was—a mask. One of many. Why couldn't her stepfather see that? She never told him that, though. He had accepted Alex and treated her as his own daughter right from the start. He stayed home with her while her mother traveled. When her mother would leave on yet another trip, he'd smile at Alex and say, "Well, Shorty, now we can have some fun." And they always did.

Tears slipped down Alex's face as she sat in the chilly car with her memories. She had loved her stepfather fiercely and would never have hurt him by asking him what he saw in her mother. She sighed as she realized she hadn't wanted to disturb the status quo. As an awkward teenager, she finally had the love of a true family member again, which had been missing since her aunt died. She had realized then that she feared doing anything to mess that up.

Several years later, her stepfather's cancer had robbed him of his health. Alex's love for the man who helped heal her heart again after the childhood loss of her aunt forced her back into her mother's spacious condo, where she acted as his primary caregiver until he passed away. Tears filled her eyes as she remembered his last words to her. "*Shorty, remember that family isn't about blood, it's about heart. And my heart has always belonged to you. You are the daughter of my heart. My heart-family.*"

Alex moved out of the condo the day after his funeral. The same day the moving vans her mother arranged arrived to take everything that had belonged to her stepfather away to give to the charity shop.

She had hated her mother then. And not for the first time—or the last.

She vowed to herself then never to open her heart to anyone again. The pain of each loss was just too great. Her aunt. Her stepfather. Her only heart-family. Both left her way too soon.

Alex shook her head, wiped her eyes, and sniffed up her emotions. Feelings did no good when dealing with her mother, as she had none that Alex had ever seen.

Cold fingers of autumn chill reached for her when she climbed out of the car. She wrapped her coat more tightly around herself, then headed up the flagstone path to her mother's front door.

ALEX POUNDED her fist on the deep burgundy door, ignoring the highly polished brass knocker in the shape of a cat. No answer, just like the ten times she had tried to reach her mother by phone. Since early that morning, she'd left six increasingly agitated messages, with no call back. Once she picked up her car, she drove straight over to her mother's luxury Saugatuck

River waterfront condo. She pounded on the door again. No answer.

Perhaps her mother was around back. She trudged down the narrow path, then poked her head around the side of the condo. The icy wind off the river scoured her face, as she spied the yacht moored at the dock, tightly covered in its blue cold weather shroud. She'd already peered in the garage window and knew that her mother's sleek Jaguar was nestled inside. Her mother hadn't asked her to water the plants and feed her Siamese cat, Choy, so she couldn't be away.

Determined, Alex rapped on the front door again. Still no answer. Her mother was home, she was sure of it.

She was ignoring Alex.

What. The. Fuck.

Alex slapped the front door hard, making her hand sting. "I know you're in there, Mom! Why did you lie to me about Aunt Maia? We need to talk! Now!"

Still no response.

With one final rap on the door, Alex stalked away. She threw a final angry look toward the condo and saw a shifting shadow at the top-floor window that belonged to her mother's bedroom. Her mother's cold eyes were watching her leave. As she climbed back into the car, she shivered, and not from the frigid air.

Alex was going to get answers about what happened fifteen years ago, when her mother lied, her aunt supposedly died, and the nightmares and headaches started. One way or another, she'd find out what happened to the woman she thought of as her heart-mother. If she had to travel to San Antonio to get those answers, so be it.

3

WHAT'S YOURS IS MINE

Her calculating ice-blue eyes narrowed in thought, Helen watched her daughter stalk away. She stroked Choy's soft fur as he purred and stretched under her hand. Helen realized the lies she told Alex about her sister's death all those years ago were now exposed. Now Alex was aware of them, she wouldn't stop until she discovered the whole truth about what happened back then.

Several weeks ago, Helen felt it when her sister, Maia, had died, as anyone in the Keeper family line would—as any twin would. She knew then that change would be coming.

A strangled breath escaped her as a familiar agony pierced her soul. She had lived with this pain ever since the morning of her twelfth birthday, when Hecate chose her twin sister, Maia, as the next Crossroads Keeper instead of her. She had been *so sure* the goddess would choose her. Her own mother had encouraged her in this belief. "Helen, it'll be you," her Keeper mother told her as she stroked her long, blonde hair just before the choosing. "You may be the oldest only by a matter of minutes, but the goddess *always* chooses the oldest daughter. *Always.* Plus, you have the strength of character needed. Your sister takes after her father. She's weak."

Helen's life plans ended that day when the goddess Hecate had turned to her sister Maia with a smile. The rest of her childhood went by in a jealous blur. She had tried more than once to end her sister, always being careful to make sure it would look like an accident. Accidents happened, right? But that damn Barghest, Conor, had thwarted her every time. He had protected Maia and kept her safe, as was his duty as the Guardian of the Crossroads and Protector of its Keeper.

On an unseasonably cool and overcast morning in August, just after her eighteenth birthday, Helen had left the estate for an Ivy League university across the country, determined to put the Crossroads behind her. There, while enrolled in her master's program, she met her first husband, knowing him as a strong magical force the day they met.

Helen smiled in reminiscence. Talon had been a powerful mage, tall, dark, and deadly handsome. He was a popular professor, and she his graduate student, but she'd made sure he fell for her. They married less than a year later, right after her graduation.

Choy let out a yowl as Helen's hands clenched in his fur. Despite Talon's depth of power, his magic couldn't conquer the Crossroads—couldn't make her Keeper. He'd died trying. Oh well, she'd thought after his death, as she stroked her toddler's silky black hair. Talon's child, Alex, would have both his magical power and hers. She'd have another chance at her destiny, through her daughter.

Painful memories of that time flooded back. Helen remembered how, upon Talon's death, the Council had turned on her. They accused her of instigating Talon's attack on the Crossroads. Of trying to steal the role of Keeper from her sister. She denied it, of course, but she knew they didn't believe her. They had no proof, though. She'd made sure of that.

With a bitter smile, she recalled her last appearance before the Council. The words of the Council Elder who'd read out her judgement echoed in her mind.

"Defendant Helen Grimby, while we cannot prove your

involvement in this terrible attack, neither does that absolve you of it. Your Keeper ambitions have been clear since you were a child. But it was not to be. Hecate and the Crossroads made their choice, and it wasn't you—will never be you. Do you understand?"

Helen discarded her denials, as they both knew them to be untrue. "I understand. May I go now?"

"I haven't finished, defendant," the Elder chided. "Our laws differ from human ones. We don't need to prove you guilty 'beyond a reasonable doubt' to mete out punishment. That said, the Council rules you guilty by association, if not in fact. You are hereby convicted of attacking this Crossroads and attempting to overthrow its rightful Keeper."

Helen gasped in outrage. "You can't—"

The Elder raised her head high, her black eyes cold as she studied Helen. "Oh yes, we can, young lady. And we will." Taking up the parchment in front of her, she read off the punishment. "You will hereby relinquish full physical custody of your daughter, Alexandria, to your sister, Maia, from this day and henceforth. You will be allowed one supervised visit per month. You will immediately remove yourself from the vicinity of this Crossroads by at least a thousand miles and remain at that distance. The monthly supervised visit with your daughter must be arranged in advance and will require written permission from your daughter's guardian prior to each visit. Lastly, you shall not be allowed at this, or any, Crossroads for the remainder of your natural life."

The Elder flourished a quill pen and signed the judgement, holding it and the pen out to the clerk to be brought to Helen for her signature in acceptance of her punishment. With a hostile glare, the Elder asked, "Does the defendant understand and agree to these terms?"

Realizing she had no choice but to agree and sign in acceptance of her punishment, Helen nodded her understanding. Besides, she reflected with an inward smirk, it would save her from years of childcare. She could 'reach out' to her daughter once she was old enough to understand. Once Alex's magic flowered, Helen could use her daughter's magic to take her rightful place as Keeper of this Crossroads.

Helen happily handed Alex to the care of the court and left without a backward glance at the screaming toddler.

With her newfound freedom, Helen travelled the world, biding her time until Alex's twelfth birthday, when she would again attempt to gain the Keeper heritage through her daughter's sacrifice.

HELEN FORCED her thoughts from events of the past. She grimaced and turned away from the window and the cold, dark weather it revealed—and from the memories of her first failed attempt to gain her rightful heritage.

Her second attempt had also failed. If her plans for that choosing had worked, the goddess would have accepted her adolescent daughter as a blood sacrifice and chosen Helen as the next Crossroads Keeper. Unfortunately, things had gone disastrously wrong. Apparently, contrary to all her arcane research, Hecate did not accept human sacrifice. In fact, the goddess got more than a little pissed at those who thought to offer them. She had been incredibly lucky to escape with her life—and with Alex.

Upon her return to Connecticut with a grieving Alex in tow, she'd done what she could to cover their tracks. Helen had planned to bide her time until Alex's magic emerged. Her disappointment when Alex's magic did not manifest was intense. At first, she thought her daughter a late magical bloomer. But, as the years passed, with no sign of latent power budding, Helen lost hope. Her burning need to take her rightful place as Keeper had dimmed, the embers banked. The desire to take her rightful place as Keeper still burned, though. Waiting. Biding its time.

Velvet slippers shushed across the thick carpet as she paced in front of the bed, memories of her multiple failures looping through her mind. Choy watched her warily, his diamond-blue eyes narrowed to slits.

Helen touched the pendent at her neck as she remembered her earlier efforts to make the Crossroads accept her as the rightful heir and Keeper. After the plan to sacrifice her adolescent daughter had so spectacularly failed, she improvised. She told Alex her aunt had died, then spirited her away to Connecticut. She paid handsomely to have Alex's memories magically covered. Helen was patient, willing to bide her time until her daughter reached adulthood and gained her full powers.

In the meantime, Helen hid them both from the searching, vengeful eyes of her sister and the goddess. They would never give up searching for Alex, but the wards she'd purchased hid them well. They had also shrouded Alex's memories of her childhood. It wouldn't do for her to go in search of her roots.

The pendant clutched tightly in her grip, Helen sighed heavily. The magical protection and memory block it contained was weakening. The pendant hid both her and Alex from Maia's searching. It also served as a magical lock on Alex's memories of her aunt. Helen had purchased the pendant from a powerful witch at an extremely high cost fifteen years ago. It contained a small amount of Maia's blood, which tuned its magic to the Crossroads. The magic in the pendent created a magical barricade against all seekers. It also obscured Alex's memories of her time in San Antonio.

A cruel parody of a smile stretched Helen's lips as she lost herself in memories. It hadn't been hard to give the witch a sample of Maia's blood. She'd bloodied her often enough when they were children. And, knowing the magical properties inherent in blood, even as a child, she'd hung on to it.

As long as Helen wore the blood-magic pendant and fed it small amounts of her own power, it blocked the Crossroads power to call to its own. Maia's search would be in vain if the power in the pendant remained strong. Even the goddess Hecate could not penetrate magic bound by a living Keeper's blood.

But with Maia's death, her blood no longer held magic, so the power in the pendent was weakening and would soon wither. The Crossroads would once again able to work its own magic. With Hecate's help, and Maia's searching, The Crossroads would bring her daughter, the chosen Keeper, back to it. She couldn't fight that, but perhaps she could take advantage of it.

Patience Helen, she counseled herself. She'd always known her plans to use Alex to gain the Keeper role were a long game. It might be time to enlist some competent help this time, though. She'd wait to see how things played out this round. No harm in making some plans for the future, though.

4

COMING HOME

L anding gear on the plane thumped into place as it approached San Antonio's airport. As the plane banked into the sun, the headache plaguing Alex for the past several weeks reached migraine status as the stark sunlight pierced her eyes. Her fatigue forced her to sleep for most of the flight. Alex took a deep breath of the dry, stale cabin air and stretched her arms over her head, yawning deeply. *At least the flight was comfortable,* she reflected. Her aunt's attorney had arranged for a First-Class seat on the plane. *Nice.*

The final landing message burbled softly over the plane's speakers. "Tray tables up, chairs in an upright position."

A disgruntled Larry eyed her from the soft-sided crate stuffed under the seat in front of her. *"Oh, look. She awakens. I thought you would never stop drooling and catching flies. My legs are asleep. If I don't get to stand up and stretch soon, they're going to fall off. Then you'd have to carry me everywhere like one of those stupid pocket dogs."*

Alex returned Larry's surly stare with one of her own. *"You've complained this whole trip. If you don't stop whining, I'll cut your legs off myself. I'll get a little skateboard, strap you on it, and wheel you everywhere."*

Larry sneezed violently, splattering dog snot all over her shoes.

Alex sighed and wiped at her one pair of good shoes with a tissue. Well, at least he hadn't pooped in them. Probably because he couldn't. Yet. Alex sighed, jet-lagged and irritable.

After a whirlwind of packing and preparation, she was minutes from landing in a city she hadn't visited in half her life-time. She looked out the small window and saw the rolling Hill Country fields give way to tiny houses and streets as the plane approached the city.

Familiarity settled in Alex's heart and a pleasant buzz stirred her blood. Her fatigue and headache receded. This trip to San Antonio felt like coming home, even though she hadn't been here for over fifteen years. She was a grieving adolescent when she left the city at twelve years old. Her mother had flown in on what Alex thought was a normal visit. A few days into the visit, her mother told Alex that her aunt, with whom Alex lived, would not be returning from her vacation in France, as she had died in a car accident on the winding roads of the French Alps.

When Alex broke down in tears at the loss and asked her mother if she would stay in San Antonio now, she merely looked annoyed.

"Of course not, Alex. You're just a kid, so you'll have to come live with me in Connecticut. I can't leave you here by yourself, and I'm not moving back to this godforsaken backwater." When Alex asked why, her mother responded with pinched lips. "Because I said so."

The way her mother looked when she uttered the phrase had so scared Alex that she never asked again. Her mother had NEVER used that phrase or tone with Alex, her parenting style being more 'let's just be distant acquaintances' than 'because I'm the parent, and I say so.' So Alex had shut up, and packed up, mourning her aunt, her heart-mother, with every breath. Then she'd flown away with the woman who gave birth to her.

Sharp spikes of pain pierced Alex's pounding head. She drew in a pained breath, then forced her thoughts to the present. The headaches attacked any time she thought about that chaotic and grief-filled time in her life. And the nightmares followed. *It's no wonder the memories are hazy and painful, and better left in the past,* she reflected.

The plane touched down with a firm bump and a hard reverse thrust of the engines. As it rolled toward the distant terminal, Alex winced at the sounds of passengers prepping for a quick departure, her head pounding in time with the slam of the overhead compartments.

A wave of sadness and apprehension washed over her. With her one human connection in this town dead, her duty now was to arrange a funeral for someone she'd mourned a long time ago. So why did it feel like she was coming home?

5

FAMILIAR, YET NOT

A lex collected her luggage from the carousel, tightened her grip on Larry's leash, and looked around for the Arrivals signs and arrows, hoping they would lead her to the exit.

Larry sneezed with gusto. *"Good god, what a disgusting mélange of smells in this place. It's almost worse than on the plane. I have no idea what that kid sitting behind us smashed into my fur with his grubby little hands during the layover, but I need a bath. Maybe a massage, too. And find me some grass, pronto, or there'll be a yellow puddle on that nice lady's shoes in a minute."* Long muzzle opened in a doggie smile, pink tongue hanging out, Larry looked with longing at said lady's expensive shoes.

Tugging Larry away from the target of his shoe-peeing fetish, Alex sighed. Larry was *not* a good traveler. Who would have thought? A talking poodle with pink ears and tail who thought he was a pit bull inside. No wonder he had issues.

As she exited the Arrivals tunnel, a line of faces appeared, many peering anxiously for the familiar form of their friend or family. Mixed in were bored-looking limo drivers holding signs with names, waiting for their fares to find them. Alex did a double take. There was a sign with her name on it. A very non-bored looking tall, lean, dark-haired man, whose bright amber eyes met hers with recognition and some heat held the sign. A small smile hovered on his lips as he gave her a quick nod, then strode forward and reached for her luggage.

Alex took a hasty step back, hauling her luggage and an annoyed Larry with her. "Wait, how do you know it's me, er, I mean, how do you know I'm the person named on your sign? I've never met you before. I don't think."

Good god, I sound like a moron, she thought, as the warmth of a blush swept over her face.

Mr. Tall, Lean, and Handsome deepened his smile. "Are you sure we haven't met? Darn, that sounded too much like the 'you look familiar, do I know you?' pickup line."

Alex's blush deepened and a pleasant warmth settled low inside. "Um, should I remember you? Do you—I mean, did you know my aunt?"

The man straightened with an apologetic grimace, then rubbed his hand across his mouth, his desire to start the conversation over obvious to Alex.

"My apologies. My name is Conor, and yes, I knew your aunt. I was her Prot—friend. We were best friends. I met you several times when you were a child. It's okay if you don't remember me. I understand." Conor grinned and held out his hand for Alex to shake.

A jolt of energy thrummed when her hand met Conor's. She jerked her hand back quickly, shaking it to ease the tingling in her fingers. Lord, she'd better get a grip. She had just left one long-term relationship with a man whose good looks and marriage proposal did not make up for his total scumminess. She discovered this character after their engagement, when she found her fiancé with his tongue down her mother's throat, upon arriving unexpectedly at the antique shop she managed for her mother. Other than stopping by later that day to collect her things and tell her mother she quit, Alex never discussed the matter with her. After that romantic disaster, it had seemed politic to swear off men, at least for the foreseeable future. *Okay, at least until now,* she mused.

Damn, she shouldn't be thinking about getting it on with her late aunt's best friend. Wait, how old did that make him? He didn't look a day over thirty-five, which would mean he was in his late teens or early twenties when Alex last lived in San Antonio. Was Conor her late aunt's boy toy?! What *was* it with the older women in her family? Gross. Better stop this mental conversation right now. Moving on ....

"Uh, okay. Nice to meet you, Conor. I'm assuming my aunt's attorney, Mr. Allman, asked you to pick me up? That was thoughtful of him. And you." *Okay, Alex, time to shut up, let him have your luggage and get the ride to the estate over with so you can hide in embarrassment under the soft covers on the big bed in your childhood room in the carriage apartment.* With amazement, Alex realized she remembered that bed and the apartment clearly, and with no ensuing migraine, for the first time in years!

Larry sniffed Conor's leg and growled softly. *"If this guy doesn't get a move on, I'm going to pee on him. Maybe I'll just pee on him right now, anyway."*

"Larry! No!" Alex jerked out of her reverie and tugged hard on Larry's leash, pulling him away from his pant leg pee mission. "Poor guy has been holding it since we left JFK. Is there some grass we can get to quickly, so he can do his business?"

Conor gave Larry a hard stare, then grabbed the handle of Alex's suitcase and led her to the exit door. "There's a small patch of grass at the end of the concourse here. Will that do?"

Alex shot Larry a glare. "Yep, it'll do, right, Larry?"

Larry grinned, hanging his pink tongue so far out of his mouth it was even with his long, pink ears. *"It'll do. If you can just put your tongue back in your mouth and stop drooling at Mr. Man here, we can get a move on before my bladder bursts."*

Alex snorted and pulled on Larry's leash before following Conor's broad shoulders out of the terminal and toward Larry's potty opportunity.

THE COMFORTABLE SEAT in the expensive black Mercedes cradled Alex in a soft embrace. She subtly stroked the supple, black leather. She sniffed. The vehicle still had that new car smell. Conor slipped into the driver's seat and closed his door with a firm thud. The sound drew Alex out of her car envy.

As Conor guided the car smoothly into traffic, Alex asked, "Is it far to my aunt's house from here? I don't remember the drive ...."

Conor threw her a quick glance before returning his full attention to the road. "Not too far. We'll be at the estate in about thirty minutes."

Alex stared out of the window at the changing scenery as Conor merged expertly onto the highway. There were more cars than she remembered. Lots more. The highway intersections, with swooping lanes arching gracefully above and below the roadway they traveled on, both confused and delighted her. From the highest of the arches, Alex saw the San Antonio city skyline stretch out in all directions. Everything appeared bigger, brighter, and more vibrant than her memories. Or her nightmares. Alex shook off that thought and concentrated on drinking in as much of the city as she could see from her window.

Larry shifted on her lap, where he had insisted on sitting for the drive, his unique doggie scent wafting up and reassuring her. *"I think I'm going to be sick. He's racing up and down these highway ramps and changing lanes like a race car driver. A bad one. That crashes."* Larry licked his lips then rubbed his muzzle against the window, leaving a smeared nose-print on the clean glass.

Alex pulled Larry away from the window and apologized to Conor. "I'm sorry, Larry is smearing up your window with his nose. He says, um, he's acting like he doesn't feel well. He doesn't travel well. Will we be arriving soon?"

Conor threw Larry a narrow-eyed glare and issued a verbal warning. "If you get sick in my car, mutt, I'll make you regret it."

Larry gave Conor stink-eye, turned around once, and then laid down in Alex's lap before heaving a huge put-upon sigh.

Alex could swear that Larry understood every word Conor said, and, judging by Conor's quickly smothered grin, that Larry had mind messaged him a few choice swear words in return.

The luxury car glided smoothly onto the exit ramp. Conor glanced at Alex and winked. "Sometimes you just have to be firm with fluffy tyrants like Larry."

Alex felt Larry's low growl vibrate under her hand. She grabbed his scruff and shook it gently. "Umm, perhaps we should change the subject. Larry is getting irritable, and that's always a bad thing."

"Getting? Is he *ever* in a good mood?"

Larry's growl intensified, and Alex had to use firm pressure to keep him on her lap.

"Okay, sorry, that was uncalled for. I'm not acquainted with Larry. For all I know, he has a sunny disposition hidden under all that poufy fur," Conor said.

Alex blew out an exasperated sigh. It was like both the man and the dog were in a virtual pissing contest to see who could push the other's buttons more. "Okay, you two, I'm tired and getting irritated. Can you both just shut up and be nice, at least until we arrive? You don't have to be besties, but a little politeness goes a long way."

So much for her initial attraction to Conor, Alex brooded. If he and Larry didn't get along, any chance of a relationship was doomed, as Larry was heart-family first.

Larry peered sideways at Conor from behind his fluffy pink ear. Conor peered back. After what seemed like a long time, but couldn't have been more than a few seconds, Conor shifted and turned his gaze back to the road. The tension in the car dropped several degrees and Alex sighed with relief.

With a soft snort, Larry put his head under Alex's hand, demanding pets. *"Don't worry, Alex. We've called a temporary truce. We'll work out the details for a more permanent one later. I told him that if he hurts you, he'll have me to answer to and that while I may be small in this stupid poodle body, I'm mean. And sneaky. I'll bite his ankles bloody, then I'll crap in every one of his expensive shoes if he breaks your heart."*

Alex smothered a snicker. *"What did he say in response? He can't break my heart, as I don't have one anymore, remember? Wait just a damn minute, can you mind-talk to him? I thought you could only do that with me."*

A cheeky grin curled Larry's lips as he smeared another wet nose-print on the window. *"He and I have, ah, a few things in common, so yes, I can mind-talk to him. I'll let him explain what those things are."* The annoying poodle would not say any more on the topic for the rest of the drive, despite Alex's pleading. He simply curled up in her lap and pointedly went to sleep.

POWER BUZZED IN HER BLOOD, vaguely at first, as if she'd just knocked back a triple cappuccino. As Conor drove ever closer to the estate, energy flooded Alex for the first time in weeks. In forever. In fifteen years. The headache and fatigue that dogged her recently completely disappeared. As her mind cleared, memories of the estate, of her aunt, came flooding back, and sudden tears pooled in her eyes. She blinked rapidly to dispel them before they fell and completely embarrassed her, then rested her head on the cool glass of the window and stared out at the alien, yet achingly familiar, landscape slipping by the car.

A wispy cloud passed over the sun, darkening the brilliant blue of the sky for a moment. Alex felt a chill, despite Larry's warm body on her lap. She remembered so much, but there were shadows writhing in the corners of her mind. There was so much more to remember. She was sure of it.

As Conor turned onto the estate's private road and the ornate wrought-iron gates came into view, Alex sat up and strained against her seatbelt, trying to take in everything at once. The gates opened and the sleek car drove through them, before following the driveway through the stands of live oaks and palm trees, alongside colorful flower beds, until the mansion came into view.

She gasped as the beautiful architecture and stucco and brick walls of her familiar childhood home came into view. Her heart contracted, then expanded. The heart she thought she no longer had grew so big that it filled her vision, raced in her blood, and poured into her mind, until nothingness took over.

ALEX CAME AWAKE SLOWLY and realized she was lying on a soft comforter stretched across an enormous bed. She opened her eyes and gazed at the ornately carved bedposts, which rose to the burgundy-colored canopy over her head. Her hand slid across the familiar nubby silk of the dusky rose comforter. She was in her childhood bed in the carriage house. It wasn't really a carriage house, she remembered, but a separate apartment on the second floor of the main residence, reached by a colorfully tiled outside stairway.

Larry's muzzle rested on her chest. She reached down to pet him. He placed a paw on her other arm where it rested on the bed. *"So, Sleeping Beauty awakens."*

"How did I get up here? The last thing I remember is driving through the estate gates and feeling overwhelmed." Alex gasped. "Oh god, don't tell me. I passed out, didn't I? Did ...did Conor carry me up here? I'm so embarrassed! How am I going to look him in the eye again?"

Larry licked her face and settled back on his haunches. *"I don't think it's his eyes you keep ogling, you perv. But yes, you passed out. Conor carried your ungainly form up here and placed you on the bed. He wasn't looking at your eyes, either, I'll have you know. That hound ... er, man needs a good peeing on!"*

Alex sat up and swung her legs off the bed. Her head spun with a wave of dizziness, but it quickly passed. The strange energy that infused her as she approached the estate still buzzed in her veins. She felt great for the first time in weeks. Months. Fifteen years.

Larry jumped off the bed and shook himself as Alex stood and took stock of her childhood room. Nothing and everything looked the same. The last of the daylight filtered through the palm trees outside and spread dappled spots of brightness on the familiar, worn Oriental rug. Her desktop was clean, with the comfortable office chair her aunt had purchased especially for her pulled up in front of it. Her luggage rested in front of the large, ornately carved wooden armoire that hulked along the far wall.

As she unpacked her clothes into the strangely empty armoire and the bureau next to it, Alex reflected on her years away from the estate. The last time she'd been here, both pieces of furniture were full of her favorite clothes. Not that they'd fit anymore or be in fashion. It just felt strange, like the gap of fifteen years since she was last here was both longer and shorter than she remembered.

She showered in the familiar rose-colored bathroom, where the sharp scent of the lavender and lemon shampoo brought back pleasant memories of her childhood. No painful headache steered her mind away from them, as had always been the case since leaving the estate with her mother after her aunt's supposed death. Alex grimaced and amended her train of thought to incorporate recent information—or rather, since her mother kidnapped her from the estate, taking her away from her home and her heart's true mother.

Once dressed, Alex strode out of the apartment and trotted down the stairs, more determined than ever to get answers. She had a feeling she wouldn't like most of them—maybe more than most.

6

UNEXPECTED ANSWERS

The sun had set while Alex showered and changed, but the heat of the day still radiated from the wrought iron rail under her hand as she descended the carriage house stairs. Low lights broke the darkness on the pathways that spread out before her, some leading toward the gardens, others to the raised pond and fountain in the courtyard. Determined to get answers, she took several steps on the path leading to the front of the mansion, then stopped, considering. Would she find him there? She wasn't even sure he lived on the estate grounds. *Damn. Now what?*

Larry, walking calmly at her side, suddenly froze and let out a rumbling growl. Then she heard it. A low, pained whine came from deep in the gardens, down the dimly lit path in the opposite direction from the main house. Larry took off like a shot, heading toward the tortured sound. Alex wheeled around and jogged after him. Larry had a sixth sense about danger. She doubted he'd be leading her into it.

The pained whine came again, this time ending in a hair-raising howl. Maybe Larry's sixth sense wasn't working, Alex worried, although she continued at speed toward the source of the sound.

Alex heard scuffling ahead and slowed as the narrow garden path opened into a large, open area, surrounded by tall trees and thick undergrowth.

Larry's white fur stood out in the darkness as he ran toward the center of the open space where two wide, cobbled paths met and formed a courtyard in front of a small stone structure. Several graceful stone columns fronted the building, soaring two stories to the tiled roof. Alex spied large ornate wooden doors in the shadows of the portico between the columns, marking the entrance to what she could only call a Greek temple. The doors stood ajar, but the entrance itself remained in shadow. Low stone walls edged the paths leading off the temple's courtyard and arced off into the darkness. *Pathways to nowhere ... and everywhere,* thought Alex, feeling a stirring of familiarity in her chest.

Larry drew her attention, his long muzzle nosing a jumbled pile of torn clothing on the ground at the edge of the courtyard in front of the temple. The pile of rags had Larry's intent interest. As they moved, Alex realized with a shock that the messy pile was alive. The nightmare creature on the ground growled and whined, swiping out at Larry as he pranced nimbly out of the way.

Larry barked urgently at Alex. *"Stay back. I don't know how much control he has right now."*

Alex reached the edge of the courtyard and peered at the writhing figure laying prone on the cobblestones. The almost full moon shone on a jumble of fur and bare skin covered with scraps of cloth. The creature turned its head away from her and growled. "Get away, Alex. Go back to the house."

Never one to listen to commands, Alex was always more likely to do the opposite when given one. Even though fear caused her steps to slow, she approached the creature and crouched down, placing her hand on the soft, thick fur on its haunch. "What can I do to help? You seem to be in pain."

The large, shaggy head turned to face her, and she gasped in shock as she saw Conor's agonized amber eyes staring at her out of a face that was eerily his, yet not.

"I warned you to go back to the house. My control isn't good right now. I don't want to hurt you." As he spoke, his muzzle receded and his face became more human, causing Alex's memories to stir again and the fog covering them to lighten.

"You won't hurt me." Alex didn't know how she was sure of that, but she was. The nightmarish creature in front of her was Conor, stuck in between his Barghest and human forms. Alex's hand, still unconsciously stroking the thick fur on Conor's leg, froze in shock. How did she know that? And what the hell was a Barghest? And why was she petting him?

She yanked her hand back and scrambled away from Conor. He let out a deep groan as his limbs and body tightened, back arching in agony, as he reshaped into fully human form. Fully naked human form. She pulled her gaze from below Conor's waist and focused on his weary face, which, although covered with sweat and lined with the remnants of pain, wore a sardonic grin.

"You don't listen very well, do you?"

"Um, no. It's not one of my strengths." She pulled off her over-shirt and handed it to Conor, leaving her in a thin tank top.

Conor used her offering to wipe his face instead of covering his groin, then sat up and draped the shirt over his lap.

Good, thought Alex, with a trace of disappointment. *At least that was one less distraction.*

The dark, misty corners of her mind filled with secrets were giving them up at a rapid rate. Overwhelmed by the barrage of surfacing memories, Alex scrunched her eyes closed, then shook her head.

"You're a Barghest, a type of Hellhound shifter. You serve as the Guardian of this Crossroads, and you are—were the Protector of the Keeper. My aunt. You protected her as she managed the Crossroads." Alex stated it as fact, nodding once to confirm her words.

"So, your memory of the supernatural is returning, then. You remember this estate holds a Crossroads, and that your aunt served as its Keeper." Conor eyed her with caution. "Do you remember anything else?"

Alex shook off her shock and stood. She glanced toward the temple at the center of the Crossroads. The temple's stone columns shone white in the moonlight while the open door they guarded remained shadowed in darkness. Her thoughts writhed and twisted, darting in and out of her conscious mind as the fog in her brain shifted and fought back. She paced the courtyard, trying to get a grip on her memories, until a sharp pain lanced through her skull. With a frown, she ignored the pain, expelled a frustrated breath, and answered Conor. "I think that's enough memories for one night, don't you?"

Distracted by Conor's concern and her racing mind, Alex found herself at the top of the temple's steps. She approached the gleaming stone columns and peered toward the enticing entrance they framed.

Conor jumped up and ran toward her, shouting, "NO!"

Alex didn't hear him, though. As she reached the massive columns guarding the entrance to the temple, an urge she didn't understand made her reach out and touch a carving on the left-hand pillar. The carving showed a woman in Greek robes holding aloft a torch. A large black hound accompanied her.

As her fingers brushed the cold stone folds of the woman's robes, a powerful energy force radiated from the dark entrance between the columns. The magic enveloped her, pulling her forward into the temple, then further, straight into the blue flames flickering on an altar at the center of the sacred space. The pain from the flames was sharp and swift, quickly burning straight into Alex's soul. She screamed as her nightmare came to life around her.

∾

THE ROOM she found herself in was as familiar as her own bedroom. After all, she had spent enough nightmares in it. A vaulted ceiling arched overhead. Stone walls were barely discernible in the gloom. The flickering light from a massive fireplace burned orange, then blue. As in her nightmares, strong cords bound her to a column which, now she thought about it, looked suspiciously like the one she had foolishly touched moments before.

Alex felt the familiar fear deep in her bones as she struggled to free herself from the column. She glanced toward the fireplace, expecting to see the dark figure from her nightmares tending the flames while sending an inky black smoke swirling towards her, smothering her, but the fire burned a clean, bright orange, interspersed with bright blue flickers, and the dark figure was nowhere to be seen.

Okay, this is different. The nightmare memories ebbed, making coherent thought possible, and she remembered the ties that still bound her to the damn pillar. Not everything about the dream had changed, then.

Alex took a deep breath and tried to analyze the situation. She realized she didn't feel the same desperate need to escape the ties that bound her to the pillar as she usually did in the nightmare. This was probably because the smothering black smoke wasn't wafting toward her, reaching her, causing her to retch and cough, then awake back in her bed, covered in sweat, chest heaving in fear. Her breathing sped up in sympathy with the memory of the nightmare's darkness as her back pressed into the warm, soft stone of the pillar. Wait, warm stone? Soft stone? In her dreams, the stone of the pillar was cold and hard. The ties that bound her to the column suddenly fell away, and she dropped to her hands and knees, scrabbling away from the column in fear.

She put her back to the smooth surface of a wall, as far from the fireplace as she could get, then closed her eyes. *Get a grip, girl. Time to pull up your big girl panties and look at the nightmare's column.* Nope. *Not yet,* she thought, *maybe not ever.* She'd just hang out here in the corner until she woke up. Wait, damn it. This time she wasn't asleep. She clearly remembered finding a half-shifted Conor, then touching the stone robes of the carved woman on the column and being drawn into this place. Instinctively, she realized the scene before her was real, while her previous nightmares were just distorted memories, mere dark echoes of it.

A voice came from the direction of the pillar, and Alex realized she'd better stop theorizing and pay attention. She reluctantly brought her eyes up to the column and gasped. "Holy shit!"

In front of the large stone column, seeming almost a part of it, stood a woman in robes. She was tall and graceful. As she moved, the robes draped about her figure swirled in gleaming golden folds. The woman's hair and eyes were as black as night, her body carved in strong, elegant lines, but with the warmth of living skin instead of cold stone. Her beautiful olive-skinned face was solemn, but there was a gleam of wicked humor in her gaze as she approached Alex, who still cowered by the wall.

The regal figure reached down and drew Alex to her feet. "Welcome home, child."

Long fingers squeezed Alex's hand in a firm grip and the woman's commanding voice echoed from the stone walls. "Alexandria, my priestess and heir, I hereby bind you as Keeper to this Crossroads. Now that you have returned to accept your inheritance and take up your duties, it is well and good. This Crossroads is in danger, as are those bound to it. The evil that is threatening this place you can feel, I know. Now is the time to fight it, to save this Crossroads, your heart-family, and yourself—before it's too late."

A wave of raw magical power flowed through the woman's hand and into her, where it entwined with her soul. Alex realized her world had just changed irrevocably. Her throat tight with fear, she swallowed, then gathered the courage to reply to the awe-inspiring woman before her. "That's, uh, that sounds like a big job, being Keeper. Don't you, like, interview for it? Choose the most suitable candidate? At least a willing one? Who are you, anyway, um, if you don't mind my asking?"

The golden dark woman chuckled deeply as a fleeting look of sympathy crossed her face. She squeezed Alex's hand once more before letting go and turning away. With a regal wave, the woman gestured toward a short-legged round table with low, backless couches positioned on either side, positioned in front of the merrily burning fireplace. Food and wine filled the table's surface. "Come, my priestess, let us sit and refresh ourselves."

The furniture and food hadn't been there a minute ago. Alex was sure she would have seen it. Whoever this woman was, she was a powerful supernatural, perhaps even a goddess. Ah, who was she kidding—this memory, turned nightmare, was real. She suspected who this woman was, and even where she was. Shrugging off the tangled memories, Alex gingerly approached the closest couch and sank down onto its plush surface.

The woman sat smoothly on the other couch and reached for the wine. "Would you like a glass? It's Etruscan, their best vintage."

Alex nodded wordlessly and took the full wineglass in shaky hands. She took a sip, then spluttered, choking on the sharp, rough edge of the beverage, which wasn't wine by any stretch of the imagination. "This isn't wine, at least not like any I've ever had." A memory surfaced and an awful thought struck her. "Crossroads ... we're in the Underworld, aren't we? Oh, no ...."

A sharp, amused laugh burst from the woman. "No, my dear, this isn't pomegranate juice or any magical food that might trap you in the Underworld. In fact, this isn't the Underworld at all, but a place between the worlds called a Crossroads. All Crossroads exist in the In-Between." After a brief hesitation, the woman queried Alex. "You have been here once before, as a child. Do you remember?"

Alex couldn't hold back her curiosity any longer. She didn't sense danger, although she could feel the woman's immense, innate power. Unable to suppress her desire for an answer, she voiced her question. "Who, exactly, are you?"

The woman's wise, knowing gaze confirmed Alex's suspicions even before she spoke. "My name is Hecate. I'm the goddess of the Crossroads, among other things. My priestesses and heirs, the Keepers, such as yourself, stand sentinel in my stead at the meeting of these pathways. Your job is to guard this Crossroads and guide travelers between the realms, along the web of the ley lines that meet at this place. Your powers, child, are unique, and they are so needed right now."

Alex's head spun, and it wasn't from the wine. She admitted to herself what she already suspected. She was having a freaking fireside chat with an actual goddess. A goddess who was calling *her* a priestess with unique powers. A Keeper, she realized, like her aunt. More of the gray fog cleared from the recesses of her mind, and a fresh memory surfaced.

The morning of her twelfth birthday, Hecate had called her to the Crossroads and drawn her into the In-Between. She remembered sitting in this room as a child. It was the same room that had haunted her nightmares for years afterward. The regal goddess she was now sitting across from had told her then that she was the next chosen Keeper and would be her aunt's successor. She remembered being so proud, honored—and scared.

Alex recalled the childish plea she'd made to her aunt after her conversation with the goddess. "Aunt Maia, I don't know if I can do this. It's a big thing and a huge responsibility. I don't know if I'm strong enough or good enough."

Her aunt had stroked her hair and smiled fondly. "Alexandria, you are the strongest, best person I know. You will be a great Keeper. One of the best. I'll teach you all I know, but I'm sure you'll go even further in knowledge and power than I. Next week, I'm going to travel to the Crossroads in France to discuss extra tutoring for you with a good friend. She is the Keeper at the Crossroads outside of Grenoble and is one of the most powerful and knowledgeable Keepers amongst us. I'm sure she'll agree to help me ensure you get the type of training that will match and challenge your unique powers."

Sorrow pierced Alex's heart at the next memory. Her aunt had never returned from that trip. She had died on the winding roads of the French Alps. Wait. No, she hadn't. Her mother had lied and told her that when she came for her. She'd also told Alex she wasn't a Keeper but an ordinary human. Eventually, Alex had believed her. She closed her eyes against the painful knowledge. It must have been her mother at the fire during her nightmares, fanning the flames and covering her memories with smothering smoke. There were other dark memories from that time lurking under the fog. Instinctively, Alex recoiled from them, knowing she wasn't ready for them all. Yet.

ALEX'S THOUGHTS jerked back to the present as Hecate shifted and rose to her feet, holding her hand out for Alex to take. Alex shook off the memories, both light and dark, and rose, slipping her hand into Hecate's. "I'm so sorry, goddess. My mother—"

"I know." Hecate squeezed her hand. "It wasn't your fault. Your mother stole you away from your heritage, jealous, once again, that it couldn't be hers. But you are here now, and we can work together with your aunt to ensure you get the Keeper training needed to help you defend and protect the Crossroads against the coming darkness."

Hecate hesitated. "As I mentioned before, Alex, your powers are ... unique. You will eventually need more training than your aunt can provide, but that's an issue for another time." The goddess led Alex toward the stone columns. "Come now, I'd better get you back to your Barghest before he damages himself. He's been throwing himself at the gateway between the pillars since I brought you through them."

Alex demurred, her voice firm. "He's not MY Barghest. He is— was my aunt's Protector. Not mine."

The goddess shook her head and chuckled knowingly. "The Keeper position isn't all you inherited from your aunt, my dear. I'm sure she'll explain everything when you see her."

Fresh pain jolted through Alex at the loss of her aunt, and irritation welled at the goddess's cavalier words. "Wait, you said my aunt will help me learn my Keeper duties and mentioned 'when I see her,' but she's dead." Accusation rang in her voice. "I thought you'd know that, being a goddess and all."

Instant regret, sprinkled with fear, filled her. *Oops, did I just tell off a goddess? Hopefully, I live to tell the tale. Damn this mouth.* Sigh.

As they reached the columns, Hecate pushed Alex between them, causing her world to spin and darken. The last thing she heard the goddess say echoed, as if spoken from a great distance. "You'd better talk to your Barghest about your aunt. It seems he's been rather lax in his duties."

Nausea rose, so she closed her eyes as her body and soul traveled both too far and not far enough. After a discombobulating moment in transit, the magical momentum transporting her from the In-Between ceased. She opened her eyes and squinted at the brightness of the moon slanting between the columns on the portico of the temple. A wave of dizziness led her to press her hand against the closest column for support. Just as she fingered the carved surface under her fingers, an arm slid around her waist, and she let go, sliding toward the cool marble floor in a dead faint.

7

BURNING BRIGHTLY

Helen realized the moment Hecate bound her daughter as Keeper of the San Antonio Crossroads. She felt the wrench deep in her soul, but more practically, the heat and light generated by the deep red ruby set in the pendant she wore confirmed it.

Memories of the powerful dark witch she had paid handsomely to create the pendant filled Helen's thoughts. The witch headed a coven with a terrifying amount of power. Over the years, the pendant had served its purpose well. It had clouded Alex's memories and hid both of them from the seeking magic of the Crossroads, the goddess Hecate, and her Keeper sister, Maia.

The witch had imbued the gemstone with Maia's blood, linking it to her life force, giving the stone its true 'blood red' appearance. The powerful blood magic blocked Maia's Keeper magic. Through her, it had also blocked the power of the Crossroads, and even that of the goddess. The pendant's power deflected their gaze and defeated their efforts to find the next chosen Keeper—her daughter, Alex.

The pendant had worked well for the purpose over the years, but Helen admitted to herself it was now taking on a life of its own. Instead of cooling when Maia had died, as its magical power drained away, it had warmed several times over weeks since her death. Since Alex had banged on her door two days ago, demanding answers about the past that Helen was not prepared to give, the magic in the pendent had become even more unstable.

As Helen reeled from the knowledge that Hecate had bonded her daughter as the next Crossroads Keeper, the gemstone lit up and heated to a painfully burning point. The pendant's searing light reflected in her feline Familiar's bright eyes. Helen ripped the red-hot pendant from her neck and screamed in anger, pain, and frustration. Choy ran. He knew better than to be around for one of Helen's rages.

Normally, Helen maintained icy control of her temper, leading many to believe she didn't have one, but that was incorrect. Her temper, and the rage that generated it, burned fiery hot underneath her cold exterior and had ever since the goddess awarded another a heritage rightfully hers. A heritage that her mother had assured her would be hers. One she knew in her heart would soon be hers, even if she needed to take matters into her own hands. Again. And this time, she had no intention of failing.

A final groan of frustration echoed in the high-ceilinged room as Helen cast the burning pendant into the fireplace. The stone burst into deep red flames that burned brightly, then winked out as normal orange flames replaced them.

The pendant left a deep, weeping burn on Helen's chest. She went in search of Choy, who, as her feline Familiar, could help her work enough magic to soothe and heal the wound.

Helen realized her plans, long dormant, required new action. She'd need help, and this time vowed to ensure her collaborators had stronger magic and more knowledge than her late husband, Talon. She vowed the San Antonio Crossroads would ultimately be hers, no matter the cost.

8

WHAT DO I KNOW?

Alex heard anxious voices arguing over her prone form and felt Larry's rough, wet tongue licking her face. Ugh, so she had fainted. Again. Conor must think she was a hot mess, fainting at the drop of a hat. He'd definitely bulk up his lean muscles if he kept carrying her up to her room. Not that she minded the muscles—or the carrying part, if only she could be awake for the process. *Hmmm*, she considered.

Not able to pretend unconsciousness any longer, Alex let out a breath and slowly opened her eyes. Hard, cold points of light winked in the night sky while the moon hung amongst them, gazing down on her with indifference. She felt the smooth marble of the temple portico under her back and realized she was still at the Crossroads. Okay, if Conor carried to her room this time, at least she would enjoy ... er remember the process.

Larry's cold nose nudged under her hand, demanding pets. She obliged while she considered her return to consciousness.

A deep, dry voice commented. "I think she's finally done with her nap."

The sardonic words cleared Alex's mind. She sat up and felt Conor's arm wrap protectively around her shoulders, while Larry stood sentinel by her other side.

Alex glared at the speaker as she took in his familiar appearance. He was a very well-dressed, very pale, stocky man with a badly reset nose, crooked from many breaks. In what appeared to be an unthinking habit, the man ran his fingers through his thick, black hair slicked back in a style reminiscent of the 1950s. The diamond in the signet ring on his left hand glinted in the moonlight as he twisted an unlit cigarette through his fingers, and another corner of her mind cleared of gray fog.

Her voice shook with shock at the memory the fog revealed. "Uncle Vinnie? Is that really you? I remember you! Why are you being rude? You used to be such a nice man. Well, okay, not really nice, but you did always give me pizza whenever I called you out for saying something especially obnoxious." Alex snapped her mouth shut before she could get it, and herself, in any more trouble. *I really should think before I speak,* she mused. *One can dream.*

With a wicked twinkle in his dark eyes, Vinnie reached down, grabbed her hand, and hauled her to her feet. He enveloped her in a firm, if slightly chilly, hug as he gently patted her back. "Mia cara! It's so good to see you again! Look at you, all grown up and so beautiful."

At a low growl from Conor, Vinnie quickly released Alex and stepped back, squeezing her hand and chuckling merrily as he let her go.

Conor put his hand under Alex's elbow, as if worried she might keel over at the slight breeze that riffled the night air. Then he yelled at her. "What were you thinking?! I told you to stop, but NOOOO, you had to prance over and touch that damn column. You disappeared into the temple. I tried to follow, but the doors slammed shut. I couldn't get in. You were just gone. Don't you ever think before you act?"

Since Alex knew that not thinking before acting was one of her shortcomings, Conor's words touched too close to home, sparking an angry defensiveness. "What I do, or don't do, and when I do it, is really none of your damn business. You can't tell me what to do!"

Alex rubbed a hand over her tired eyes and thought, *good god, now I sound like a toddler.* In a slightly less argumentative voice, she continued. "Anyway, I'm back from, uh, where I went, and I'm perfectly fine. Well, except for the fainting part. But I'm okay now, so can we just drop it?" She stepped away from Conor's supportive arm.

Conor's gazed sharpened, his amber eyes intent on her face. "Back from where? Where were you? In all the times I stood sentinel on the temple portico for your aunt while she worked Crossroads magic, the temple doors never closed. She never disappeared into thin air. I could always see her inside the temple as she carried out her duties. I can't protect you if I can't see you!"

Vinnie and Larry's eyes fixed on Alex, in addition to Conor's accusing ones, everyone silently demanding an answer. "Um, I'm not sure I'm supposed to tell you all where I was, or with whom." She palmed her face in remembrance. "Oh, wait—yes, I am."

Eyes narrowed in anger at Conor, Alex issued a blunt statement. "Hecate told me to tell you that you are being 'lax in your duties' and you need to explain something to me about how my dead aunt is going to help me learn my Keeper duties."

Damn it. She sure blew trying to keep secret her time in the In-Between, living her nightmare, and chatting with Hecate all to hell. Now they would know the goddess had bound her to the Crossroads as Keeper. Alex heaved a sigh as she glanced between the men ... and dog ranged across from her. This really wasn't something she wanted to deal with right now. Or at all if she was honest.

The best defense is a good offense. Alex fixed Conor with an accusing glare. "So, what was Hecate talking about when she told me to ask you about my aunt helping me? I thought my aunt is dead. Really dead this time, not dead fifteen years ago, like my mother told me. Is she ... not dead ... this time, either?" Alex grimaced in disgust. "Boy, she really does 'not die' a lot, doesn't she? And it seems you lie a lot, if you are in on this whole 'dead but not dead' charade." Oops, there she went, running off at the mouth again.

A hunted look entered Conor's eyes, and he avoided her gaze.

"Cat got your tongue?" Alex grinned wickedly, knowing that a Barghest, with its canine roots, would absolutely HATE the feline reference.

"Girl, you haven't lost your smart mouth, that's for sure." Vinnie's lips curved in amusement as he gestured to Conor. "Since it looks like Conor is currently wrestling with a lack of words, allow me to be the bearer of both bad—and good news. Bad news is yep, your aunt really did kick the bucket this time. Good news is that she may be dead, but she ain't gone. Her spirit didn't cross over. Your aunt's ghost still hangs out here at the estate. Says she still has a job to do. I know she can't wait to see you."

Vinnie rubbed his hand over his face and huffed out a breath. "You know, Mia never stopped searching for you after your mother kidna—er, took you to live with her. She told me earlier this evening that she wanted to let you settle in before she came to see you. She didn't know how much you remembered of your childhood, and about the supernatural, and didn't want to appear as a ghost and scare the shi—er, crap out of you."

Alex's heart fell, then leapt at Vinnie's words. Her aunt was dead. The hope that Hecate had kindled when she said her aunt would help train her in her Keeper duties fizzled. But her aunt's spirit was still here, as a ghost, so she'd at least get to talk to her and tell her how much she had missed her all these years.

So many questions and concerns tumbled around in Alex's mind. Feeling disorientated, she leaned against the closest stone column and pressed her head against its cool surface. How could a ghost train her in her Keeper duties? Duties she wasn't at all sure she wanted anyway, so maybe it didn't matter. Maybe the Council could send over an experienced Keeper and give her a pass? Now she had most of her memory back, she remembered that Keepers typically trained from childhood so they could safely handle the complex and powerful magic required to manage and protect a

Crossroads. They also had a dedicated team to help them learn and handle the job, including a magical Familiar and a Barghest Guardian, plus mentors, trainers, etc. How was she expected to handle the job with no training or experience? How was she supposed to keep her commitment to emotional independence when working with a team to protect the Crossroads was a job requirement? Being a Keeper was a calling, a lifetime commitment. It wasn't something you learned 'on the job.' Especially not when a Crossroads was in danger, as Hecate had warned.

ALEX BANGED her head lightly against the hard stone of the temple's column, trying to stop the vicious round of thoughts from overwhelming her.

"Well, I've about had enough surprises, fireside chats with goddesses, and being yelled at tonight. I'm going to bed. I'll see you all in the morning."

Vinnie raised his hand in farewell. "Until tomorrow night, mia cara. Sleep well."

Oh yeah, of course, she thought, *Uncle Vinnie's a vampire.* She wouldn't see him again until the sun set on the new day. A day which, judging by the position of the moon and a faint lightening of the sky in the east, wasn't all that far away.

With a half-hearted wave, she turned away and trudged through the gardens until she reached the stairs leading to the carriage house, Larry trotting at her side. She sank down on the bottom step and put her head in her hands.

Larry nudged her hand aside and touched her cheek with his cold, wet nose, before swiping a lick from her chin to her brow.

"Ugh, Larry, we talked about this. I thought you promised no kissing."

"I promised no French kissing, which is an entirely different thing, as you well know." Larry gave her face one final lick, before settling on the step next to her and pressing his warm body into hers.

Alex brushed her hand over Larry's soft fur. "What am I going to do, Larry? I didn't sign up for this crap, any of it. I don't know anything about being a Keeper, and I certainly don't want to have a 'team.' I don't want to lose my independence. My heart is an island and all that, remember?" She heaved a disconsolate sigh. "Maybe it would have been better if my memory didn't come back, and I stayed in Connecticut."

"*That's bullshit, and you know it,*" Larry stated. "*You were living a half-life in Connecticut, not knowing your true nature or heritage, not realizing the enormous amount of power and potential within you, separated from your heart-family and from your destiny.*" Larry snapped his jaws in exasperation. "*Why the hell do you think you have a talking dog? I'm not just an oddity, I'm your magical Familiar! Most Keepers have one, as I'm sure you've figured now that your memory is returning. And I'm yours!*"

Alex nodded in acknowledgement and sighed wearily. "It's been a long day—and night. Can we please head upstairs and go to bed, Mr. Familiar? I'm done with the heavy destiny and relationship shit for the night."

As Larry snored next to her, Alex's mind whirled, racing through a maze of conflicting thoughts and impulses. She came to San Antonio to grieve and bury her aunt, then fly back to her normal, independent—and not lonely, she chided herself, life in Connecticut. Her arrival at the estate earlier in the day opened a window into a world that she hadn't known existed until the day's events uncovered her childhood memories. She'd flirted with a Barghest and reunited with her Uncle Vinnie, the vampire. A goddess had transported her to the In-Between for a fireside chat. Said goddess also bonded her to the Crossroads as its Keeper, she grimly recalled.

The memories, the knowledge and weight of new responsibilities and new-old relationships, weighed on her mind and heart.

She thought longingly of her original plan: to grieve her aunt, settle her estate, and skip town, back to being alone, and happily independent, in cold, boring Connecticut. The thought that she could stick with that plan flashed through her mind. She sighed in relief, then wondered why the thought of returning to Connecticut filled her with a cold emptiness.

She lay awake until the first golden light of a new day shone around the edge of the heavy curtains, before slipping into sleep.

9

THINGS THAT GO BUMP IN THE NIGHT

L arry's head popped off the bed when a firm knock
      sounded at the door. Alex pulled the covers over her
      head. "Go away!"

The knock sounded again, louder and longer this time.

Alex heard Conor's muffled voice on the other side of the door.
"Time to rise and shine! It's almost noon, and your aunt asked me
to ask you to join her for lunch in the main house."

Alex's stomach growled. Food sounded good. She couldn't
remember the last time she ate. Larry, the traitor, jumped off the
bed and skittered to the front door, whining and wagging his tail.

"I thought you didn't like Conor?" Alex groused.

*"I don't, much. But I like food, and I'm dying for a pee. Unless you'd
rather I pee on your shoes?"* Larry scratched at the door and stuck his
nose in the crevice at the bottom.

The knock came again, more of a pounding this time. "Alex, I
know you're in there!"

Alex dragged herself off the bed and stumbled groggily toward
the door. She raised her voice in annoyance. "Don't get your tighty-
whities in a knot! I'm coming. Larry needs to pee, so I'd suggest
moving away from the door, or he'll run you over." She opened the

door and Larry darted out, barreling past Conor on his way down the stairs.

Conor eyed her, nonplussed. "I guess I woke you up."

Alex rubbed her hair, realizing it was a total rat's nest. "No shit, Sherlock!"

"Um, well, okay. Sorry. I'll let your aunt know you'll be about a half hour."

Alex moved aside as Larry came bounding back into the room, having checked and left his messages on the shrubbery at the bottom of the stairs.

"I'm starving! Where's the dog food you brought for me? It's only kibble, but it'll do for starters." Larry cocked his head and eyed Alex critically. *"You might want to look in a mirror before you answer the door next time."*

Connor glanced at Larry and smothered a grin before sobering and meeting her gaze. "So ... half an hour? I'll stop back by and show you the way in case you don't remember."

"Make it forty-five minutes," Alex said, just to be contrary. And because she hadn't had her caffeine fix yet. She was *so* not a morning person at the best of times, and she'd been up most of the night. She closed her eyes and groaned as the memories of the night before surfaced.

"Okay, I'll see you in forty-five minutes," Conor agreed. "Oh, and I'd suggest wearing something dressy. There'll be a few guests at lunch who are old-fashioned. They prefer formal attire for mealtimes." He muttered, "Even if they don't actually EAT the meals."

Alex frowned, puzzling over Conor's last statement as she shut the door. Oh! If her aunt was a ghost, perhaps the other lunch guests were ghosts, too. No food required for them. Hopefully, the kitchen staff wouldn't forget to provide some noshes for the living guests ....

After a nice, long shower, Alex dressed in a sleek sundress printed with huge, yellow sunflowers. *Not very formal, but the best I can do,* she thought. She had purchased the dress the previous year on vacation in Aruba, while on her first trip away with Sean-the-scumbag-ex-fiancé. Alex shook her head to dispel the, thankfully no longer painful, image of Sean and her mother kissing up a storm behind the old-fashioned cash register in the antique store her mother owned.

Speaking of old-fashioned things, Alex wondered idly just how old the ghost guests she'd be meeting at lunch were. She grabbed her purse and stepped toward the front door just as a heavy knock sounded.

"I'm back Alex. Are you ready?"

She swung the door open abruptly and narrowed her eyes at Conor. "What! Are you implying that, as a woman, I'd inevitably be late getting ready?"

Conor took a hasty step back, startled surprise and wariness etched on his face.

With a small sigh, Alex apologized. "Sorry, I didn't mean to snap at you. I know you're only trying to help. It's just—last night was a lot, you know?"

Conor's face softened, and his gaze heated as he eyed her dress appreciatively. "Yes, I imagine it is. Having your memory magically suppressed for fifteen years, then coming back here, getting your memory back, and receiving a crash course in the supernatural, and your role in it, all in one day, must have come as a shock."

"You can say that again." Alex muttered as she shut the door behind her and started down the stairs, Larry at her heels.

Conor led her around the front of the mansion and through the main doors into the grand foyer, where the ceiling soared two stories above their heads. The heels of Alex's sandals made clicking sounds on the smooth, cream-colored marble floor as they crossed what seemed like a mile of tiles. Alex glanced around as they walked, taking in the graceful curve of the staircase leading to a gallery on the second level. Huge paintings and tapestries jostled for wall space with mounted swords and other weapons, piquing Alex's educated eye with their ancient beauty and undoubted value.

"Lunch is being served in the library today," Conor said, before adding, "It's Friday, so the normal crowd is here for the weekly poker game."

Alex turned her head and squinted at Conor as they passed under the massive oak staircase, then took a left and headed down a long corridor lined with massive carved oak doors. "Poker? My aunt hosts a weekly ghostly poker game. Why am I not surprised?"

Conor grinned. "They play for haunting rights at the bar that's part of Vinnie's Italian restaurant. Vinnie doesn't mind since it gives him bragging rights as the most haunted bar in San Antonio. It's even on the haunted ghost walking tours, and it sure brings in the tourists."

"Okay! That's interesting." Alex couldn't manage any more than that, as the idea of ghosts, let alone ones playing poker for haunting rights, boggled her mind a bit. It seemed her aunt hadn't told her everything about the supernatural community surrounding the Crossroads when she lived at the estate as a child. "And what other surprises am I in store for at lunch? Poltergeists? Goblins? Demons?" Alex gasped as a scary thought struck her. "Oh god, please tell me they're not playing Strip Poker!"

Larry, trotting at her side, snorted a laugh. *"Can you imagine?"*

"Unfortunately, I can," Alex whispered with a grin.

Conor stopped outside a highly polished and intricately carved oak door and knocked lightly, giving her a sideways smile. "Ghosts have excellent hearing. Kind of like vampires. To answer your questions, poltergeists, no. Not usually, anyway, unless Crazy Jack shows up. Goblins, yes, just one. Demons, no. They hate poker."

"Okay, great," Alex muttered under her breath. "Are they going to have a problem with Larry being here? Goblins don't eat dogs, do they?" Alex shuddered.

Larry, standing to attention at her side, gave her a disgusted look. "*Put on your big girl panties, woman. Don't show fear to the ghosts, don't meet the goblin's eyes, and be careful not to walk through any ghostly apparitions. They hate that. And, for the record, I can handle a goblin with one paw tied behind my back.*"

The door swung open silently, and Conor ushered Alex into the room. Larry pranced at her side with his tail held high.

AS ALEX STEPPED into the room, she tried to take in everything at once. The room was vast and elegantly decorated. High above her head, a filigreed wrought-iron balcony surrounded the room, seemingly floating halfway to the ceiling. Alex realized it was a second floor. Both floors featured floor to ceiling bookshelves filled to the brim with books, the far wall broken only by tall windows streaming with light. Alex thought she'd love to spend an afternoon in the room browsing the titles and curling up in a comfortable chair with a stack of books.

She realized she was procrastinating regarding the primary reason for her presence in the room and being rude to her aunt and the gathered guests, so she shifted her focus to a large, round table in the middle of the room. Speaking of floating, most of the chairs were 'occupied' by translucent figures hovering a few inches above, or into the chairs ranged around the card-strewn table. All eyes in the room were focused on Alex. The motion of the game ceased as the players appraised the new arrival.

The pause ended as one of the translucent figures rose and approached Alex. She recognized the familiar form of her aunt. The casually elegant blouse and trousers she wore complimented her aunt's trim, if translucent, figure. Alex's heart contracted as a montage of happy childhood memories of time spent with her aunt flashed through her head. As the ghostly form of her aunt reached her, she could swear she smelled her aunt's signature perfume, remembered from the many hugs they shared during her childhood. Her aunt had been a hugger. Alex decidedly was not, but she remembered those loved-filled hugs with a sad pang.

"Alex, my dear, it is so good to see you!" Her aunt's hand reached out to caress Alex's cheek, sending a chill through her skin. "Oh, I have missed you so much! I'm so sorry that I didn't do a better job of protecting you! I've been searching for you ever since ... never mind. Now's not the time to speak about such things."

"Aunt Maia!" Alex exclaimed, as unwilling tears leaked down her cheeks. Desolation at her stolen childhood warred with joy at seeing her beloved aunt again. "Mom told me you had died, and that's why I had to go live with her. I mean, I know you're dead *now*, but I thought you were dead *then*, when she took me. Was it really a kidnapping? I mean, she is my mother."

Maia's lips tightened as her gaze filled with regret and a snap of anger. "Yes, Alex, I'm afraid your mother stole you away illegally. I had full custody of you, legally, both in the human and the supernatural world's courts. The Council judged your mother unsuitable to raise you. After she took you, she had a powerful witch place a shielding spell on both of you. No matter how much I tried, even with Hecate's help, I could never locate either of you. The witch linked the spell to my life force and my magic, which powered it until my death."

The ghost of her aunt smiled slightly. "Once I really died, the spell weakened enough that we could pinpoint your location." Maia waved off further explanation. "We can talk more later. For now, come and meet our current residents! Most have been vacationing with us for quite a while. The staff will bring lunch for you and Conor, as I know you must both be hungry."

Larry nudged her leg with his cold nose. *"Tell her not to forget food for your Familiar, namely, me. I'm starving."*

Alex shook her head in confusion and reached down to stroke Larry's soft topknot to assure him she heard his hungry demand. It was all a lot to take in. She decided she'd process the information her aunt had provided later. And ask her questions. Lots of questions.

As Maia led her closer to the table, Alex interjected. "Aunt Maia, could we get some food for my, uh, dog Larry, as well?"

"Of course, dear," her aunt said as they reached the table. "I've already ordered something I'm sure Larry will enjoy. Conor mentioned him to me when you arrived. I'm so glad your Familiar found you in Connecticut, so you're already magically paired. It'll make things easier."

Make what easier, Alex wondered, as she studied the ghostly assembly spaced around the table. Oh, and the goblin. How she had missed him when she first entered, she didn't know. He crouched in a child's booster seat on a chair next to her aunt's. The size of a chunky toddler, his thick, pale green skin and dark green hair served as counterpoints to the green baize felt covering the card table. His protuberant eyes studied her with a childlike, but fierce and slightly feral, curiosity.

Pointing to the goblin, Maia said, "This is Grenoble. He followed me home from the trip to France I was taking when you were abducted, and he's been staying here ever since. Grenoble is really very sweet, but he does like his meat raw, so I'd keep Larry well away from him."

Grenoble nodded at Alex, and in a slightly insulted voice, rumbled, "I'd never eat a Keeper's Familiar." He cast a derisive glance Larry's way. "Besides, he's got way too much fluffy fur. I'm sure it'd get stuck in my teeth." The goblin smiled, showing off an impressive set of extremely pointy, if slightly green, teeth.

Larry stood tall, tail pointing straight up, and let out a low growl. *"He can try to eat me, but it wouldn't end well for him. It would be HIS flesh between MY teeth, not the other way around."*

Alex glanced down and met Larry's gaze, saying aloud. "Behave, Larry. We are guests here. No shenanigans." She added a last admonition in mind-speech. *"And no crapping in anyone's shoes."*

Larry smiled big, hanging his tongue out as far as it would go while eyeing the goblin appraisingly. The goblin returned Larry's appraisal with one of his own.

Alex turned to Maia and apologized. "I'm sorry for Larry's attitude, Aunt Maia. And for not mentioning that I was bringing a dog for my stay. I hope it's alright."

"Larry is your Familiar, dear. Of course, it's alright." Maia gave Larry an amused look. "I wouldn't expect you to travel without him, nor, I'm sure, would he let you do so."

Larry side-eyed Alex. *"Can we talk about this later? I'm so hungry that I'm going to start gnawing on that goblin if we don't see food shortly."*

Alex flicked Larry an exasperated glare, then turned her attention back to her aunt, who proceeded with introductions of the ghostly guests. "Alex, this is Seth, Wilbur, Connie, and Elizabeth. Everyone, may I introduce my niece, Alexandria. She is our newly bonded Crossroads Keeper."

As the ghostly guests nodded and murmured in greeting, Alex noted their wide-ranging attire. There were several time periods represented. The Regency elegance of Seth's finely tailored cutaway suit jacket contrasted with the blue workman's overalls worn by Wilber and with Connie's very 1950s pink sweater twinset and poodle skirt. Her eyes widened as they reached the last guest. This ghost was less translucent than the others; in fact, her body appeared almost solid. She even had rich color infusing her face and clothing. The ghost hovered over a chair, as did the other ghosts, but her rich multitude of long velvet and brocade skirts covered the whole lower portion of the chair, hiding it completely. Her back was stiff, and her bust prominently displayed in a tight-fitting, beautifully embroidered bodice. A giant ruff surrounded her neck, making it look as if her head sat on a round white tray. The ghost's deep red hair hugged her head in an intricate series of curls and braids, on top of which sat an impressive, jeweled crown.

Larry's sarcastic words in her mind pulled Alex out of her fascinated study of the regal ghost. *"Your mouth is open and catching flies."*

Alex promptly shut her mouth, tore her gaze away from the Renaissance era ghost, and looked a question at her aunt.

Maia eyes twinkled with merriment. "That's Queen Elizabeth the First, dear, but she prefers Liz."

Okay, thought Alex, *we have a Queen of England in residence. Interesting.* Now that her childhood memories of the estate were filtering back, Alex rifled through them. They didn't include ghosts or goblins, or even poker. She realized just how much about the estate and her Keeper duties her aunt hadn't shared with her as a child. The overwhelmed pressure she experienced the previous evening returned in force. A deep, cleansing breath helped relieve some of the stress. Larry pressed his warm body against her leg reassuringly. That helped even more.

Her aunt pointed to a ghost dressed like an Old West cowboy, right down to the chaps, spurs, and bolo tie, who was currently hanging upside-down from the second-floor railing. "Last, but not least, that's Jack, but he prefers Crazy Jack."

Crazy Jack cackled and waved his Stetson hat. "Welcome home, girlie!" With a wild hoot, he released the railing and swooped down to circle the massive, glittering chandelier hanging high over the table, before settling himself amongst its gleaming brass branches.

Conor, who Alex had completely forgotten about once they entered the room, spoke from her side, startling her. "We apologize for interrupting your poker game, Maia. If you'd like to finish your current hand while I see about getting lunch served?"

"No worries, Conor. We just finished our last hand. Liz won. Again." Maia's mouth curved in a reluctant smile. "She now has haunting rights at Vinnie's bar for the next three weekends! The rest of us are going to get rusty at our haunting skills if we don't start winning soon."

Grenoble grunted in agreement. He hopped onto the table, collected the cards and poker chips, then jumped nimbly down and scurried over to a carved oak sideboard. After putting away his bounty, he brought out a stark white damask tablecloth, quickly covering the table with it before hopping back into his booster chair strapped to the seat next to Maia. The little goblin patted his protuberant stomach and smacked his thick, green lips. "What's for lunch today, Keeper Maia? I'm starving!"

Maia smiled indulgently at Grenoble before returning her warm gaze to Alex. She patted the open chair on her other side, motioning for Alex to sit.

Conor took a seat beside Liz, greeting her as an old friend and laughing at something she said, sotto voce.

Larry jumped up on the only spare chair on the other side of Conor.

"Git yer fluffy ass off my chair, you mangy cur! *Nobody* sits in Crazy Jack's chair." The cowboy ghost extricated himself from the chandelier, then swooped down and planted his translucent form in the chair, right on top of Larry.

Larry quickly jumped down and shook himself, before trotting over to Alex. *"It was worth a try,"* he said. He blinked innocently, before sitting casually at her feet, as if the cursing ghost meant nothing to him. Alex saw the chill in his eyes, though, and knew her furry Familiar was a little unnerved at finding himself 'inside' a ghost.

The door opened, and several servers entered. They carried huge round steel platters on stands, which they placed in the center of the table. The rich, garlicky, cheesy scent of New York-style pizza tickled Alex's nose, and she inhaled deeply.

Maia grinned at Alex and gestured at the fragrant platters. "Your Uncle Vincent instructed his restaurant staff to bring over pizza with your favorite toppings for lunch today." She pointed at the iced bucket that a server placed next to the pizza. "There's your favorite soda, Dr. Pepper, too."

The pizza smelled wonderful, and Alex helped herself. Her heart softened knowing that Uncle Vinnie had indulged her love of pizza and even remembered her favorite childhood toppings. She hadn't had Dr. Pepper in fifteen years and wasn't a big soda drinker anymore, but she accepted a can, opened and proffered by an attentive server. After a long sip of the frothy beverage, bubbles tickling her nose, Alex's mind filled with memories of her childhood. No migraine accompanied the pleasant thoughts. Progress.

Larry nudged her leg. *"Hey, how about a couple of pizza bones down here, please, before I expire from hunger?"*

Alex discreetly slipped a crust under the table to Larry's waiting mouth. *"You already ate a full bowl of kibble, you glutton, so don't act like you're starving."*

A stately older man with silver hair, dressed in a butler's elegant outfit, paused next to Alex's chair. He placed a china plate filled with fragrant chopped meat on the floor in front of Larry and said, "Your meal, Sir Larry."

"I could definitely get used to this," Larry mumbled as he tucked ravenously into his lunch, not even sparing a glance for the butler.

Alex thanked the man Larry's behalf. "Thanks. I appreciate you preparing something special for my furry companion."

The butler gave a stiff nod. "You are quite welcome, ma'am." After giving Alex a polite smile, he marched around the table to Grenoble and placed a similar plate on the plastic tray attached to the goblin's booster seat.

Alex watched in fascination as Grenoble bent over and buried his face in the meat, chomping and slurping messily, his hands gripping the tray tightly, as if afraid someone would snatch his food away at any moment. She started as a sharp voice penetrated her study of the greedy goblin.

"What we would like to know, Alexandria," Liz asked in a distinctly posh and regal English voice, "is what you are going to do about the body parts that keep appearing at the Crossroads. We can't have random bloody arms, legs, and heads just turning up willy-nilly. It's very unsightly—and likely a symptom of something nefarious, which we just cannot have."

Everyone stopped talking and gazed at Alex expectantly.

Alex frowned at her pizza. Her appetite gone, she placed the food back on her plate, eyeing Liz with annoyance. *The arrogant ghost's 'queen' was definitely showing,* she thought. "Uh, body parts?

At the Crossroads? This is the first I'm hearing of them. And what, exactly, makes them my responsibility?"

Liz peered down her nose at Alex, which was quite a feat, considering she wasn't much taller than Grenoble. "The goddess has bonded you as Keeper of the Crossroads, has she not? That makes anything that happens at this Crossroads your responsibility."

Maia made a shushing motion toward Liz, then turned Alex with a worried look that she quickly covered with a smile. "We can talk about all that later, dear. Let's enjoy our conversation while you eat your lunch."

Sure, Alex mused, as she played with the half-eaten slice of pizza on her plate. *Let me just enjoy my food while envisioning bloody body parts.* Not for the first time, she wondered how she found herself in this mess ... and how she could extricate herself.

"You gonna eat that?" Larry's familiar voice in her mind distracted Alex from her gloomy thoughts. *"If not, can I have it?"*

With a sigh, Alex lowered the rest of her lunch under the table to Larry.

10

WHAT THE HERITAGE!

W hen the luncheon broke up, the gathered ghosts said their farewells to Alex and Maia before drifting off through walls and ceiling. Alex wondered where they were going, before recalling her aunt's words. These ghosts were guests, residing on the estate as an 'extended vacation'—even if some of their stays stretched centuries. *I guess they're off to do whatever ghostly stuff ghosts do on vacations,* she mused.

Sudden movement on her left startled Alex out of her reverie. She realized Grenoble had vacated his booster seat and was crouching a few feet away from Larry, who stood stiffly at her feet, returning the goblin's stare.

Alex reached down, intending to pick Larry up onto her lap, but he moved away. *"Grenoble and I were just mind-talking about going for a walk,"* said Larry, without breaking his stare-down with the goblin.

Alex mind-spoke back. *"Is that a good idea? Going off with a raw-meat eating creature who might think of you as a snack?"*

Maia rose to her feet and asked, "What is it, dear?"

Alex stood up and turned her back on the Familiar/goblin staring contest. She leaned close to her aunt's translucent ear and whispered her concerns. "Uh, Larry wants to go for a walk with Grenoble. I'm not sure that's such a good idea."

"Don't worry, dear, Grenoble never breaks his word. He's already told you he never eats a Keeper's Familiar. Honor is very important in goblin culture. Larry will be perfectly safe with him." Maia patted her arm and floated toward the door, gesturing for Alex to follow her. "Why don't we two have a nice chat in the kitchen?"

Alex shook her finger at Larry and frowned in warning. *"If you get eaten, I'll never forgive you. Run if he looks hungry."*

Larry grinned at her, then fell into step with the goblin. His parting words as they walked away provided small reassurance. *"Never fear, Alex. You won't get rid of me that easily. Plus, like I said, I could take this guy with one paw behind my back."*

Alex watched Larry's tail swish out the door as he followed his goblin companion. Sometimes she worried that Larry would one day bite off WAY more than he could chew. *Well, on his own fluffy head be it.*

"Alex? Are you coming?" Maia's voice drifted in from the hallway.

As she hurried after her aunt, Alex realized it was time to ask some questions. Okay, a lot of questions. Hopefully, her aunt would have answers—and be willing to share them with her.

ALEX FOLLOWED her aunt's floating figure down several increasingly familiar hallways until they emerged, at last, into a kitchen large enough to cook for an army. An enormous stone fireplace sat empty while modern appliances and custom-made oak cabinets with marble countertops lined the walls. Someone had extensively remodeled the kitchen since Alex had last been here. For some reason, that saddened her.

Childhood memories washed over her. The kitchen filled with her aunt's love and laughter while they mixed cookie dough in a ceramic bowl as it snicked on the tile counter. The scent of just-baked cookies cooling on racks. Her aunt's light slap on her hand as she attempted to steal a too-hot cookie. Alex teared up, loneliness settling deep in her bones. Her stepfather. Her aunt. The only family she had ever loved with her whole heart, and who had loved her in return, were gone. *It's better to be alone,* she reminded herself, *than risk having my heart broken again.*

Maia paused next to a large, square, scrubbed-pine table surrounded by sturdy pine chairs painted in bright Fiesta colors. The table and chairs lit a spark of recognition in Alex. She remembered sitting at this table doing homework while her aunt bustled around the kitchen making dinner. Her favorite chair had always been the purple one.

Maia gestured toward the purple chair in invitation, causing Alex's heart to warm. Her aunt remembered her favorite chair. Alex sat and felt the woven seat creak, as if welcoming her backside back. She smoothed her hands over the satiny surface of the table, remembering, as the scent of beeswax wafted up, its sweet fragrance familiar and comforting.

In a semblance of sitting, Maia hovered above a chair across from Alex. She gazed at Alex sadly. In a rush of earnest words, her aunt explained. "Alexandria, I never stopped loving you or searching for you. I'm so glad I finally found you and have you here with me again. You may not be my blood daughter, but you *are* my heart-daughter, my dear."

The years apart fell away. Alex leaned her head on the smooth pine table and cried for all the years with her aunt she had lost. She felt the light touch of her aunt's chill hand as it stroked her hair. "I felt so alone after Mom told me you died. I was so mad at you for leaving me. Mom was no help. You know how cold and detached she is. Don't get me wrong. She paid for live-in sitters, provided clothes, the best schools, but I know she did it out of duty, not love. Even as a child, I knew that."

Eventually, Alex raised her head from the table, took the tissues that hovered from her aunt's ghostly grip, and wiped her eyes, before continuing her tale. "When Mom remarried a couple of years later, I was glad. Her new husband, my stepdad, Ben, was so nice to me right from the beginning. He talked to me as if my opinion mattered. We did things together—sailing, hiking, just talking. He was my heart-dad. When he died, I had my heart broken a second time. First you, then Ben. I swore I'd never care for anyone like that again. And I haven't. I can't. Do you understand?"

Alex dashed away her remaining tears, glaring fiercely at her aunt. "I came here to plan your funeral and settle the estate. I wasn't expecting Conor, Vinnie ... you. I sure as hell wasn't expecting the goddess Hecate or being bonded as a Crossroads Keeper. It's all too much. I'm not ready for relationships again. I can't be what you all want. I haven't trained, I have no experience, no power. I can't be a Keeper or build a team to protect the Crossroads. Hecate must be mistak—"

"Don't you dare say that! Any of it!" Maia shouted, her ghostly figure vibrating with anger and becoming more solid, with color flowing in to fill out her pinched features. "Your Uncle Vinnie. Me. Even Conor. We are your heart-family. We never left you or stopped loving you. Your heart has been broken too many times, but it's not dead, no matter what you think."

Maia clasped her hands and visibly tried to calm herself. Color leached from her cheeks as she again faded into translucence. "As for your heritage as a Keeper, it's in your bloodline and has been your destiny since the goddess chose you as a child. Training, knowledge, yes, it would have been best if you were raised as a chosen Keeper. Your mother took that from you, just as she took you from me. Don't let her take your destiny away in a sea of doubts."

The ghostly form of her aunt rose from her seat and drifted around the table, stopping next to Alex's chair. A chill hand covered Alex's warm one as she spoke truth. "You are so powerful, my dear, even more powerful than I. That's why your mother took you. She was jealous of your power, as she was jealous of me being chosen as the Keeper instead of her all those years ago. Helen always thought the Keeper position was hers by right, and our mother encouraged her. When she wasn't chosen, your mother became bitter and spiteful."

Maia grimaced in remembrance. "Let's just say you weren't the only one with an unhappy few years growing up, at the hands of Helen the Cold-Hearted." The ghost patted her hand and murmured encouragement. "Don't let your past determine your future, my dear."

Maia's words pierced Alex's heart. She hadn't realized she was still angry with her aunt for dying and leaving her to be raised by her uncaring mother. Not until the early morning phone call from her aunt's attorney, only days ago, had she known that her mother had lied to her for years. The discovery that her aunt, her heart-mother, hadn't died, and that she had missed all those years with her because of her mother's actions and duplicity, devastated Alex.

"I'm so sorry, Aunt Maia. I don't blame you for anything that has happened. I'm so used to loss, to being alone, and guarding my heart. My experiences have made me a loner, and very independent. I haven't been able to rely on anyone, so I'm used to setting my own course. I'm not sure I can change that now. I like my apartment, my volunteer work at the animal shelter, my life in Connecticut." Even as she uttered the last sentence, Alex felt its ring of untruth.

She turned her thoughts away from family matters to concentrate on her supposed destiny. "I don't know exactly what happened with the goddess last night." Another untruth. "Okay, I do know what happened. I also know that Hecate, and you, both feel I'm the chosen Crossroads Keeper, but I really don't think I'm cut out for the job."

Alex heaved a frustrated sigh. "Damn it, I don't even know what the job actually IS. I'm not prepared. Plus, there's the danger to the Crossroads Hecate mentioned. And what's this Queen Elizabeth, I mean Liz, mentioned about body parts being found at the Crossroads and me being responsible for figuring that mess out, too?" Alex gave her aunt a mute look of mingled defiance and defeat.

Maia took a deep breath—or at least appeared to. Alex didn't think she really needed to breathe. She mused, momentarily distracted, *do ghosts breathe?*

"Alexandria, dear, I know this is all a bit more than you are prepared for, and I'm sorry about that. But I'm afraid there's more. This danger the goddess mentioned, she warned me of it several months ago. Conor and I were investigating it when I died." After a brief hesitation, Maia continued, her voice serious. "Here's the thing. My death wasn't natural. Someone murdered me, and I think it was because of the trouble brewing at the Crossroads."

Alex reared back in her chair in shock. "What!? Murdered?! Do the police know? Are they investigating? Do you think it's about the body parts?"

After patting Alex's hand one last time, Maia returned to hover over her chair on the other side of the table. The ghost met Alex's eyes straight on. "My death was by magical means. The killer made it look like natural causes, so no, the police are not investigating. The body parts are a new wrinkle. They didn't start appearing until after my death. The first parts appeared last week. Conor found them and buried them without telling me. A few days ago, a second set of body parts appeared while Conor was at the Crossroads, experiencing a bad shift. Vinnie heard Conor's groans and went to help. They found the latest parts together. I'm not sure how Liz found out about them, but she has been in residence a long time and has her ways." Maia subsided with a sigh, a pensive, sad expression resting on her translucent face.

A small splinter on the side of the table drew Alex's attention. She picked at it distractedly and spoke in a flat voice. "Liz said it's my responsibility as Keeper to sort out the situation with the body parts. I'm assuming she is correct?"

"Well, technically, yes. She's correct." Maia paused before continuing. "As I mentioned, before I was murdered, Conor and I were attempting to discover the reason behind the darkness infecting the Crossroads." She shrugged. "I'm sure my murder is connected to these body parts, as it's too much of a coincidence otherwise, wouldn't you say?"

Alex inhaled deeply, pursed her lips, and blew out a breath. Then she did it again, trying to steady herself. She couldn't process what her aunt was saying about being murdered, even though she knew in her gut something connected it to her investigation of the trouble at the Crossroads. Instead, she concentrated on the immediate issue. "So, if I help Conor investigate the problems with the Crossroads and figure out why the body parts are appearing, will that help?" She knew what she was really asking, although she didn't give these thoughts voice: *would that satisfy her aunt, would it appease the goddess? Afterwards, could she relinquish her Keeper role, avoid letting anyone into her heart, and head back to her old, very normal, very independent, if lonely, life afterwards?*

Maia nodded slightly, her face pensive. It seemed she heard, or at least suspected, the unspoken words reverberating in her niece's head.

"Let's take it one step at a time, Alex. First, let me tell you about the investigation so far and what the goddess told me about the darkness infecting the Crossroads..."

Light had long since faded from the sky as her aunt's words finally slowed. They sat in weighted silence for several minutes, both exhausted by knowledge, torn by powerful emotions, and yet enjoying each other's now silent company.

Alex pushed out her chair and stood, knees creaking with disuse. "Well, that's a lot. Obviously. We can talk more in the morning. Now, I'm going to find Larry and head to bed if that's okay."

Maia's reply cut off when the back door flew open, and an agitated Conor and Vinnie burst into the kitchen.

Fresh blood splattered Conor's face and clothes, and he was

panting with exertion. "We have a problem. More body parts, a lot more, have appeared at the Crossroads. Looks like parts from multiple people. There's also a ton of ash floating around."

Alex stared at Conor for a beat. "What do you mean body parts 'just appeared?' Don't you mean you just found them? They can't have appeared out of thin air in front of you."

A silent Conor glanced at Vinnie, then back at Alex, his eyes flat.

Vinnie, nose wrinkling as he scrubbed at a bloodstain on the sleeve of his jacket with a once-white handkerchief, answered for him. "In fact, that is *just* what he fucking means. The parts did, indeed, appear out of thin air. One minute, Conor and I are enjoying the night air at the Crossroads, sitting on the temple steps and shooting the shit, and the next minute, arms, legs, blood, and ash are flying at us from fucking nowhere."

Everyone froze and stared at each other. What. The. Hell.

11

THE SCENE OF WHAT CRIME?

The grandfather clock in the front hall struck the hour, its resonant chimes reverberating down the hallway into the kitchen. The rich, deep sound brought everyone back to life after the moment of shocked surprise following Vinnie's announcement that yes, the newest body parts at the Crossroads *had* just appeared out of thin air.

Everyone spoke at once in a jumble of voices. Finally, a sharp whistle returned the room to silence.

Alex glanced at her aunt, who was lowering her hands from her mouth. "Wow, you can still whistle?"

"I'm dead, not useless," Maia retorted.

Conor cleared his throat and spoke. "I think everyone needs to see the scene, including you, Alex. If we have a hope of figuring out what's going on, everyone needs to be on the same page. It isn't pretty, and there's a lot of blood, so prepare yourselves." He glanced at Alex, apology showing in his eyes, before plodding toward the open back door, his ponderous pace evidence of his reluctance to revisit the nightmare scene.

"I'll meet everyone at the Crossroads. I want to get a few supplies together, so we can begin figuring out what the hell is going on," Vinnie said. He gave Conor a small smile. "I told you a couple days ago I have some ideas about what's going on. I'm thinking tonight's the night to share them ... if I'm correct." With vampire speed, Vinnie shot out of the door and disappeared into the darkness.

Nothing like getting thrown in at the deep end, mused Alex. *If I need to get this solved before getting my life back, now is as good a time as any.*

Maia interrupted Alex's dark musings. "Alex, dear, why don't you change out of that pretty dress into some older clothes? You can meet us in fifteen minutes by the entrance to the path leading to the Crossroads." Maia turned to Conor and asked, "Can you please round up some flashlights? Some of us can't see well in the dark, and we don't want to miss any clues."

AFTER CHANGING INTO JEANS, a t-shirt, and her running sneakers, Alex headed down the stairs to the courtyard, pausing at the bottom to get her bearings so she could head in the right direction. It was well past dark, the only light coming from the dim landscape lighting edging the paths through the courtyard and from the silvery light of the moon. The scent of flowering night jasmine and the deep chirrups made by the frogs splashing in the fountain teased her senses. In this beautiful place, the horror waiting at the Crossroads seemed a million miles away.

Admitting she was delaying, Alex started walking across the courtyard toward the gardens and the entrance to the path leading to the Crossroads. As she approached the fountain, she heard a gravelly voice she was sure belonged to Grenoble, the goblin.

"Ha! I absolutely beat you in that last round! Did you see that frog fall off the wall into the pond? I *know* I hit him! I've got perfect aim."

Alex called out, her voice urgent. "Hey, you, stop whatever it is you're doing." She hurried toward the voice, fearing something bad was happening to the poor fountain frogs. *What the heck was wrong with this place? Body parts falling from the sky, frog abuse. What's next,* she reflected grimly.

As she rounded the last bush, the fountain came into view. Spotlights strategically placed in the surrounding live oak trees lit the area, revealing two short figures lounging by the raised stone wall of the fountain pond. She squinted as she hurried across the paving stones and realized the culprits were Grenoble—and Larry! They gave each other a loaded look, before peering at her approaching form with a nonchalant insouciance. *'Nothing to see here, lady,'* their poses reflected.

Alex crouched down on the flagstone path and glared at Larry, meeting his slightly guilty gaze. *Stern voice,* she told herself. "Have you two been tossing rocks at the frogs? Why would you do something like that? I know Grenoble might want to, uh, *eat* the frogs, but what's your excuse?" She turned her scolding gaze to Grenoble. "And even if you *do* want to eat the frogs, it's not polite to play with your food before eating it. You know that, right?"

What is my life becoming, Alex mused in despair. Just a couple of days ago, she was safe in her ordered world, wondering if she should take the barista job at the local coffee shop she normally frequented to tide her over until a better paying, if boring, job came along. Now here she was, hip-deep in the supernatural—a bonded Crossroads Keeper on her way to investigate flying body parts, telling off a goblin for playing with his live food before killing and eating it. *Life was a crap shoot, that's for sure.*

Larry hopped up on the wide stone rim of the pond and adopted a wheedling expression. *"We weren't throwing rocks at the frogs, Alex. Grenoble wouldn't eat Maia's fountain frogs. Well, not anymore, after getting royally told off last time."* He shot Grenoble a doggie grin, then went back to stating his case. *"We were, uh, just playing with the frogs."*

Alex rolled her eyes and huffed her annoyance. "Don't lie to me, you fluffy felon. I distinctly heard Grenoble say he 'hit' a frog."

A low growl rumbled from Grenoble's curled lips. It raised the hair on Alex's arms and a caused a primal fear to clutch at her heart. Goblins were definitely predators, she realized.

"Do not insult my friend, Keeper, or I may make an exception to my 'no Keeper's for dinner' rule," Grenoble ground out, his round-eyed gaze fixed intently on her face.

Larry hopped off the fountain wall and paced over to Grenoble, placing his body between Alex and the angry goblin. *"Grenoble, my friend. I ask that you forgive her the insult to me. She's a new Keeper and doesn't understand the supernatural world yet. I'm doing my best with her, but training a Keeper takes time."* He threw a worried glance at Alex before finishing his plea to the goblin. *"Alex is my friend, in addition to being my Keeper. I ask that you agree not to eat or otherwise harm her, as I'd miss her."*

Alex listened to Larry's mind-speech with growing dismay. She realized Larry had shared his plea to Grenoble with her so she understood the gravity of the situation. *Good Lord,* Alex thought, *am I really being defended by my dog?*

Grenoble cast an appraising eye over Alex, as if deciding if she'd make good eating or not. After a tense moment, the goblin fixed Larry with a serious gaze. "Larry, you are my friend, so I will do as you ask. I will consider Alex a friend-of-my-friend, and therefore, permanently off the menu."

With a dark glare at Alex, Grenoble instructed her, "But you had better apologize to your Familiar, Keeper. The role between the two of you is one of magical equals and demands mutual respect."

Larry's eyes glinted with merriment as Alex met his gaze, as if he knew how hard this would be for her. "Alright, I apologize, Larry. I'm learning about this whole Keeper thing. But I still want to know what you two were up to out here." She sighed in despair. Damn, she really couldn't keep her mouth shut if she tried.

Larry shook his head, then his whole body, making the tags on his leather collar jingle. *"Apology accepted. As to what we were doing, we were, ah, having a peeing contest. We're about the same height, so we figured we'd see who had a longer ... I mean, better aim. The first one to hit five frogs wins."*

Alex closed her eyes and counted to ten. She found herself doing that a lot since Larry came prancing into her life. "So. You're telling me you two were doing some weird male bonding thing and measuring the size of your dicks? It's not only human males who do that?"

Huh, who would have thought, Alex mused, before deciding not to go any further into analyzing male psychology, human, canine, goblin or otherwise, and just let it go.

"Okay, you two, I don't know who was winning your pissing contest, but you'll have to figure out some other way to decide who wins." Alex eyed Grenoble warily and added, "If Maia doesn't want you eating the fountain frogs, it's a good bet she doesn't want you peeing on them, either, don't you think?"

Grenoble hung his head and scuffed his hairy bare feet on the flagstones while Larry looked down, considering the chipped blue polish on his claws.

Alex remembered with a shock her original grim mission and turned to hurry along the path toward the Crossroads. She threw an explanation over her shoulder. "In case you're interested in helping, they found more body parts at the Crossroads. We're going to investigate so we can solve the issue." *And so I can get back home before I become any more attached to either the estate or its inhabitants,* she promised herself silently.

ALEX HURRIED through the gardens and soon reached the head of the path leading to the Crossroads. She realized she was slightly out of breath and acknowledged she really needed to resume her exercise routine.

She spied Conor waiting a little way down the path.

He turned at the sound of her footsteps and frowned at her. "There you are. We were wondering if you got lost. The others went ahead to the Crossroads. I agreed to wait here for you and start searching for you if you didn't show up soon." Conor peered around her and spotted Larry and Grenoble bringing up the rear of her strange little parade. "Why do they both look like they've been up to something?"

Alex smiled grimly. "Because they have. That's what held me up. These two yahoos were measuring their dicks by having a pissing contest in the fountain pond. The good news is that now they are best friends and Grenoble has promised not to eat Larry and, more importantly from my perspective, me."

Conor glanced at the two chagrined creatures, huffed out a laugh, and turned away, still chuckling, to lead the party down the path toward the Crossroads.

Impatient to reach their destination so she could get on with the investigation, but dreading what she'd see there, Alex quickened her pace. An avid fan of TV detective shows and murder mystery movies, she realized that seeing blood and gore on-screen would not at all be the same as seeing it in real life. Her stomach roiled in response, and she rubbed it gently, asking it to bear with her.

As they approached the Crossroads clearing, Alex heard a strident British voice complaining. "So, where is the girl, then? If she gets lost in the estate gardens on a simple nighttime walk, how will she be able to handle her duties as Keeper and find out who made this appalling bloody mess?"

Conor gave Alex an apologetic shrug. "Liz can be a bit abrasive. She's—she was a queen, so tact really isn't her strong suit. But she's a lot of fun once you get to know her."

"Right. A lot of fun," Alex muttered. She ran her hand over her face and across her hair, then put on her game face before stepping onto the cobblestones of the courtyard and approaching the temple.

Vinnie's squat form stood out, black and shadowed under the moonlight. The ghosts of Maia and Liz hovered to one side. Both appeared more solidly human than at the house. Alex wondered if proximity to the Crossroads powered the ghost's presence. She realized she was avoiding looking at the wetly shining jumbled mass of human body parts scattered across the slick cobblestones in front of the temple, so she sucked it up and gazed at them.

Her stomach heaved. She closed her eyes, breathing in deeply, before holding her breath for several beats. The acrid scent of smoke and ash made her cough. Steeling herself, she opened her eyes, and this time forced herself to look more closely at the scene.

"Grenoble, no!" Maia shouted at the wayward goblin. "The body parts aren't snacks!"

Despite herself, Alex chuckled. *Didn't the detectives at a TV crime scene make macabre jokes over the murder victims?*

Conor appeared next to Alex, startling her out of her reverie. "Are you okay?"

"Yep, I'm just peachy," Alex sniped. "Sorry, that was rude. I get sarcastic when I'm stressed."

"True that," Larry added as he sniffed and pawed at a pile of ash on the ground.

Alex gave Larry a quelling glare, then asked Conor to shine the flashlight he held at the closest body parts. The light made the fleshy pieces appear very white against the dark trails of blood surrounding them. The gray ash scattered around the scene glinted in the flashlight's bright beam.

"We counted," Conor told her. "There's three hands, seventeen toes, two full legs from the knee down, one nose, and what looks like a spare kneecap. No heads this time, so no way to identify the victims. From what we can tell, there are parts from at least three individuals."

"Okay, thanks for the report." Alex submersed herself in her role as a detective, soon forgetting about the gruesomeness of the scene. She took the flashlight from Conor and knelt near the largest grouping of parts. The beam's bright light played over the assorted hands, legs and toes, then followed the whiplike strands of blood trailing away from each piece. The clean, almost surgical slices at the end of each body part puzzled her.

"From my limited knowledge of TV forensics," Alex stated, "it looks as if someone severed these pieces from the bodies with a very sharp object. The parts were tossed or thrown away, perhaps by the force of the blow that removed them."

Intrigued by the incongruity of the scene, her nausea receded. "It looks like a team of ninjas with scalpels came through here. Did we find any weapons in the area that could have done this?"

Vinnie joined her, crouching next to her and studying the parts impassively. "I agree with your conclusions, Alex, although I doubt your ninja theory is the answer." Her uncle smiled approvingly and patted her on the shoulder. "Very good idea about the weapons, though! And yes, we looked but didn't find any. I brought back some large plastic tubs from the restaurant to gather up the parts once we're done with examining them. I'll send over some of my staff to finish cleaning up once it gets light out."

Not seeing anything to be gained from continuing to kneel on the rough cobblestones, Alex rose to her feet. She glanced at those gathered around before focusing on Vinnie, who was using a crisp white linen handkerchief to wipe ash off the knees of his tailored trousers as he stood. "Uncle Vinnie, did you or Conor see or hear anything when the body parts flew at you?"

Vinnie glanced at Conor and shook his head firmly. "Nope. Didn't see or hear a damn thing. Which, when you think about it, is pretty fucking weird. As supernaturals, both Conor and I have preternatural senses. We *should* have seen or heard something. The parts appeared out of thin air, along with the smell of burning and drifts of ash." He toed a small pile of ash, which puffed into the air, gray flakes glinting in the moonlight.

Alex sighed. This would not be quick or easy. Not like those detective shows where everything wrapped up in an hour, including time for commercial breaks.

Glancing over at her aunt and Liz, Alex asked, "Why don't you two go back to the house? Conor, Vinnie, and I will stay and look into things some more."

Maia threw Alex a sharp glance, before turning to her friend.

"Liz, how about that game of *Go Fish* you promised me?" Before leading the reluctant Queen away, Maia reinforced her earlier order to Grenoble. "Leave that stuff alone now, you hear? I'm sure Alex or Larry will rat on you to me if you don't!"

Grenoble grunted and scurried after the departing ghosts, muttering, "No point in hanging around if snacks are not on offer."

AFTER SEVERAL MORE HOURS SPENT SCOURING THE area around the Crossroads and conferring with Vinnie and Conor, Alex admitted defeat, at least for now. Other than the body parts, blood, and scattering of ash, nothing unusual jumped out at her. "We need to come back in the daylight to discover any more about this."

Vinnie reminded her, "I'm outta here before sunrise, doll. I gotta be back in my apartment soon. Besides, Conor and I can see as well at night as you can during the day. There's nothing here to explain what happened." Hesitating, Vinnie cleared his throat, looking distinctly uncomfortable before voicing his thoughts. "As I've mentioned before, I might have an idea about what's going on. But it don't really make sense—yet."

Conor grumbled in annoyance. "Spit it out, man. You have alluded to having a clue several times. Let's hear it, then."

"I think the body parts are coming from the In-Between." Vinnie glared at the entrance to the temple as he rolled a cigarette absently in his fingers. "I think undead, unnatural creatures are being created in the Underworld, and their creators are trying to get them to Earth. Why, I don't know, but judging from the fact that at least one, my old 'friend,' Paulie Castellano, was a criminal in real life, I'm sure whatever the plan is, it ain't good. The only good thing right now is that they don't seem to be having much success with the 'getting them to Earth' part of their plan." Vinnie tucked the abused cigarette back in his pocket, glanced between Conor and Alex, and shrugged. "At least, that's my theory—for what it's worth."

A dark worry settled over Conor's features. "Unfortunately, it's a good theory and I agree with you." He shook his head in bemusement. "First time for everything, I guess. And yeah, I don't think their plan involves sending the bodies over in pieces for assembly later. Still not sure how this helps us, though."

Everyone exchanged perplexed looks, then glanced down at the body parts still strewn across the cobblestones, silently demanding answers from them they each knew wouldn't be forthcoming.

With a sigh, Alex realized she was going to have to do something she *really* didn't want to, and that was to consult with the goddess Hecate. She suspected that by enlisting her help, she'd be getting more deeply entangled in the web of heritage and duty that surrounded her new role as Crossroads Keeper.

Her hope of escaping her supernatural role and returning to her normal life dwindled. She'd cross that bridge when she came to it. She had promised her aunt she would help with the current situation, and she always kept her word. Plus, natural curiosity, along with the grief of discovering her aunt died because of her own investigation, fueled Alex's determination to get to the bottom of things.

There was nothing for it, she'd have to figure out how to arrange another fireside chat with Hecate.

12

HECATE'S CHARGE

Alex convinced Vinnie to leave the Crossroads and return to his apartment, but Conor and Larry wouldn't budge. They both reiterated that watching over her was their job, and they would not leave the Crossroads if she insisted on seeking an audience with the goddess.

Not sure where to begin, Alex retraced the steps she unwittingly took the night before, which had resulted in her initial fireside chat with Hecate in the In-Between.

Larry and Conor were still arguing about which of them would accompany her into the In-Between as she climbed the steps to the temple and approached the stone columns that seemed to mark the entrance to the Crossroads portal. Alex laid her hand on the smooth stone of the nearest column and muttered a quick prayer. "Goddess Hecate, I humbly request a meeting to talk with you about how I can help with the danger to this Crossroads."

After finishing her entreaty, the same awful disorientation she'd felt the first time she travelled to the In-Between filled Alex. This time, however, the feeling was momentary, and no nightmare images intervened. She soon found herself in the same dimly lit stone room where she had last met Hecate. A fire burned merrily in the hearth and the atmosphere felt welcoming. *Progress,* Alex reflected, *no fainting. And no nightmares.* She released the column, unsure of her next move.

The goddess emerged from the darkness beyond an open archway. She inclined her head and beckoned Alex forward, gesturing to one of the comfortable couches by the fire. "Welcome back, Keeper," Hecate said, smiling slightly and settling onto the couch opposite Alex. "I understand the situation at this Crossroads is getting more dire. I can feel it, too." The goddess shook her head and huffed in frustration. "Just when I think I'm approaching an answer, the view becomes shrouded, and time turns away from me."

Alex frowned in thought. "Do you have any idea where I can start? As you know, being a Crossroads Keeper is new to me. Forgive me for saying so, but if *you* can't figure out what's causing the darkness and the flying body parts, how am I going to, as a newbie Keeper?"

Hecate pursed her lips and speared her with a narrowed-eyed glare. "I chose you for a reason, Alexandria. You are the right Keeper for this Crossroads—for more reasons than you are ready to know. Your mother's meddling caused a regrettable absence that has resulted in a woeful lack of training, it's true." The goddess softened her gaze, but her next words were implacable. "However, Keeper, that's really your problem to solve, not mine. Your mother's interference has delayed your training, but I know your supernatural powers, along with diligent effort, can help you make up for lost time. Talk to your aunt. Ask her to outfit you for your Keeper role and to begin your training immediately. There is no time to be lost. Our foe is powerful and getting closer to the dark results he ... or she desires."

The blazing fire in the hearth drew the goddess's attention. Hecate stretched her hands toward it, as if needing its comforting warmth. The goddess appeared tired, her shoulders bowed, weighed down with worries.

The red and blue glow of the fire cast flickering shadows on the stone walls, light and dark, in a spiral dance. Alex sat quietly with the goddess, both mesmerized by the fire, for what seemed like hours but was likely only minutes.

Rousing from her fireside trance, Alex broke the silence. "Um, can you at least tell me, are we looking for human bad guys or supernatural ones? We just need to know where to begin our investigation."

Hecate turned her gaze from the flames and gave Alex a grave look. "There must be a god or goddess involved in this, likely a Titan, as they are the only ones who surpass me in power and can block themselves from my view. I would wager they have both human and supernatural accomplices."

A determined expression settled on Hecate's regal features. "I will work from this end to delay the darkness, but I fear time is short, Keeper. I see more darkness and more bloodshed ahead. No matter how I try, I cannot see the outcome of this battle."

The goddess rose and placed a gentle hand on Alex's shoulder. "Listen to your aunt, work hard at your training. I think my powers, and those of my sisters, can give you a moon cycle, maybe a little more, to prepare. Get ready, then we get to work. This Crossroads, and those dependent upon it, need both of us in order to survive this battle."

～

ALEX LAID her hand on the column, warm under her touch from the fire in the hearth. The now-familiar pull began and soon she stood in the dim pre-dawn light of the Crossroads.

From her place at the top of the temple steps, Alex saw Larry and Conor hurrying toward her across the courtyard. Conor, with his long, lean legs, reached her first. "I thought I told you not to disappear on me again!"

Conor exchanged a frustrated glance with Larry, then visibly gathered his control. "How can we help you if you go haring off on your own? I know you don't know enough about your supernatural role, or ours, so let me explain it. I'm not just the Crossroads guardian, I'm *your* Guardian and Protector. You and the Cross-roads are one and the same to me, Alex. And Larry is your magical Familiar. His job is to stay by your side, protect you, and help you focus and amplify your Keeper magic."

"He's right, you know." Larry peered worriedly up at her. *"Strong magic binds us to the Crossroads, and to you. If this Crossroads fails, so do we. I'll live to fight another day, in another body—preferably NOT a poodle body."*

Larry snorted and edged away from Conor. *"And, for your ears only, if we fail, if this Crossroads falls, Conor may live to fight another day, but it won't be as a shifter with a human form. He'll go Barghest permanently and likely go feral and have to be, what's the euphemism you humans use? He'll be 'put to sleep.'"*

Alex gasped, gazing at Conor in concerned horror.

"I'm assuming the mutt told you my situation," Conor said with a dark smile. "Please don't pity me. I know what my purpose is and what my fate will be if we don't succeed. But this isn't about me. It's about the sanctity and well-being of this Crossroads and the community linked to it, and, by extension, all other Crossroads on Earth, as well."

Conor took a deep breath, then put words to the extent of the danger facing them. "If one Crossroads falls, the rest will be vulnerable to the same fate. If all the Crossroads fall, the resulting chaos will bring bloodshed and war, not only to the supernatural communities, but to the human world, and beyond."

Terror filled Alex's mind and quickened her pulse. Not only did the fate of the Crossroads hang in the balance, but so did the lives of many others.

Larry was the furry love of her life, but she'd always consid-ered him as 'just' a dog—loyal to the end, even if he had the unusual ability to mind-speak with her. Now she thought about it, she wasn't sure why she hadn't questioned that ability further the first time Larry's surly voice first entered her head. She shook her head. Now was not the time to analyze that. But Conor was at least half human. Even though she had sworn never to let another person close enough to cause her pain if they left or died, she knew from the pang in her heart at the danger of Conor going feral that she was perilously close to losing her aloneness, her independence.

Alex sank down on the low stone wall at the edge of the Crossroads and buried her head in her hands, overwhelmed by the changes wrought in her life since that phone call from her aunt's attorney only a few days before.

Larry rubbed his head against her leg, and she absently reached down to pet him. After giving Alex a half-hearted tail wag, Larry's familiar voice entered her mind. *"Grenoble told me the cook always gives him scraps if he gets to the kitchen early enough in the morning, so we have a 'date' to meet for a begging contest before breakfast. I'll see you back at the room later."* He fixed a gimlet eye on Conor and growled low, issuing a warning he shared with Alex. *"Remember what I said about hurting Alex."*

Conor grinned and patted the air. "Yeah, yeah, you'll bite my ankles bloody and crap in all my expensive shoes."

"That's the least of it, Barghest. I may be stuck in this damned poodle body, but I pack more supernatural power than you think."

Sobering, Conor replied, "I don't doubt it, Larry. Grenoble makes mincemeat of weak supernaturals." He grimaced. "And I mean that last comment quite literally. If he has offered you friendship, then you definitely pack some serious magical power in that furry little body."

His nose in the air, Larry issued one parting shot to Conor as he pranced away. *"I'll take that as the back-handed compliment it was and let you live, Barghest. This time."*

THE GOLD of the impending sunrise suffused the horizon. Conor settled beside Alex and tentatively placed his arm around her shoulders. Weary and overwhelmed, Alex didn't fight the comfort he offered. She laid her head on his shoulder and heaved a sigh.

"How am I going to do this? Two days ago, I thought I was a regular human, living a boring, but normal and independent life. It's what I knew, it's what I still want, at the end of all this. I have no idea how to be a Keeper. I'm pretty sure it's not something I could learn in a lifetime, let alone a month—which is all the time the goddess gave me."

Conor stroked her tousled hair. It had long ago fallen out of the pert ponytail she put it in for her lunch date with her aunt, what seemed like a lifetime ago.

"What exactly did the goddess say? And what happened fifteen years ago, when your mother took you?"

Conor's quiet question broke down the last of Alex's defenses. She told him all of it. She spoke of the grief she felt when her mother told her that her aunt had died. In an emotionless voice, she explained her grief-filled journey to Connecticut, where she lived a lonely life with her distant and often absent mother, in a cold and empty house. Her voice broke when she told him about her stepfather and the joy he brought into her life, only to have it snatched away by his death a few years later. She told him about her long-ago vow never to open her heart again, knowing she could not survive another heart-family loss.

Even though there was so much more she could tell him, Alex ran out of steam and lapsed into silence. They sat quietly for a while, watching the sky turn gold, then red as the sun peeked over the horizon, sending its still-weak light across the sky.

Conor rubbed her arm, bringing her out of her reverie. "Didn't you ever wonder why there was no funeral for your aunt or why your mother never brought you back to visit your homestead? After all, if your aunt had truly passed away, either your mother or you, as her closest living relatives, would have inherited the estate."

Lips curved in a sad smile, Alex spoke. "At first, I was too wrapped up in grief to wonder about those things. My mother put me in counseling, which helped a lot. The grief over my aunt's death didn't hurt so much. I stopped pining for the estate and those left behind here, like Uncle Vinnie—and you. In fact, after a while, it was like a shroud covered my childhood memories." She frowned in remembrance. "That's when the headaches started. And the nightmares."

Conor's arm tightened around Alex's shoulders. He ground out several abrupt questions. "Shroud? Headaches and nightmares?"

Alex patted his arm where it rested on her shoulder, his hand rather close to her breast. *Just a few more inches*, she mused, then mentally slapped herself. She couldn't lust after Conor. Just could not. Besides, he still loved her aunt. Right? Now was *so* not the time to be thinking with her libido. She straightened and pulled away, hunching her shoulders, and lowering her gaze to her lap.

Conor got the message and removed his arm from her shoulder, instead leaning back on the wide stone wall upon which they sat and eyeing her intently.

"After about six months in therapy, my therapist said she'd done all she could, and the rest was up to me. By that time, I had grown used to the gray fog that smothered memories of the past and actively avoided thinking about it, as when I did, the headaches and nightmares came." Alex shrugged and turned her head away to avoid Conor's penetrating gaze. "The years passed. The headaches and nightmares lessened as I stopped trying to remember and let the fog cover my memories."

Alex lapsed into silence, absently rubbing at a seam in her jeans. The memories came flooding back—this time without the pain that had always accompanied them in the past.

She shook her head to clear it of both light and dark memories in order return to the present and continue her story. "The headaches and nightmares returned in force about two weeks ago. I also began feeling really fatigued, which I thought related to not getting enough sleep. Patches of memory surfaced, but I didn't understand them without context, and it still hurt too much to remember, so I didn't try."

"That bitch!" Conor snapped the words out, making Alex jump. "Sorry. Keep going with your story."

"Umm, okay. After one particularly rough night, I fainted at work and subsequently lost my job—not because of the fainting, though. That's a long story for another time." Alex eyed Conor nervously. His face was thunderous.

Conor inhaled a deep breath and rearranged his features into a supportive smile. "Sorry again. Go on."

Alex hesitated. "I was just about to break down and go see a doctor when my aunt's attorney, Alan, called and gave me the news that my aunt had just passed away. That's when the holes in the fog shrouding my memory started getting bigger, I think. Once I arrived back at the estate, things started falling into place. When I saw you shifting, the fog pretty much cleared, and I remembered mostly everything. The supernatural, Uncle Vinnie being a vampire, you being a Barghest, the Crossroads, and Aunt Maia being a Keeper."

With a start of surprise, Alex realized something else. "I haven't had a headache all day, and I didn't have a nightmare last night. I'm tired now from being up all night, but it's a normal tired. The overwhelming fatigue is gone, too." Alex had the sneaking suspicion there were still a few dark surprises lurking under the remaining wisps of fog, still curling ominously in the corners of her mind. She resolved to deal with that another time.

Conor pounded his fist against the unforgiving stone wall. He closed his eyes and drew in a deep breath, then another, reaching for control. He fixed a sad, knowing gaze on Alex and explained his anger. "You're feeling better, and your memory is returning because the spell your mother had that dark witch cast when she took you has finally broken. It started weakening when your aunt died several weeks ago. Maia suspected after your kidnapping that her blood, and the magic inherent in it, was likely the focal point used to weave the psychic wall around you and your memory and to obscure your whereabouts. A few days ago, once the blocking spell lost enough of its potency, she was able to divine your location. That's when she asked me to have Alan call you and arrange for you to travel here."

Still stuck on something he said earlier, Alex queried. "Witch? What witch? My mother had a spell cast on me? That bitch!"

"Yep, she's a bitch alright. Always has been, and I've known her since she was a child." Conor nodded in agreement, then his eyes narrowed in anger. "I'm pretty sure the woman your mother told you was a therapist was actually a powerful dark witch. She must have used blood magic to shroud your memories and hide both you and your mother from us. It's the only reasonable explanation. We've all been searching for you ever since we returned from our trip to the French Alps and discovered your mother had taken you."

A deep remembered pain filled Conor's amber gaze. "Maia still feels guilty about leaving you here while we took that trip—as do I. None of us thought your mother would do something like that. I do not know what her long-term plan was in taking you." He smiled grimly. "Although, I imagine she had one, and still does, and it likely isn't good."

Thoughts of her mother made Alex shiver in imagined cold. "My mother probably just wanted to keep me from my aunt, whom she knew I loved with all my heart. She's a bitch like that. I'm sure she thought taking me would cause both my aunt and me pain. I don't think she had, or has, any long-term plans. The Keeper role was never meant to be hers, no matter her long-held desires."

Alex shrugged. "She probably knows I'm bonded as the new chosen Keeper now, though, so what can she do?"

"I don't know what she can do. But you can be sure she's planning something." Conor bit his bottom lip and shook his head.

So sexy, Alex's wayward mind wandered, her gaze on his white teeth grazing his full red lip. *Enough with the flaming hot thoughts,* she counseled herself sternly.

Conor's nose quivered as he sniffed the air, then his face lightened. "You *do* know Barghests can smell arousal, don't you," he asked with a wicked grin.

Alex blushed to the roots of her hair, hoping the still-weak morning light hid her flame-colored face. She hopped off the low stone wall and faced the now-congealing mess of body parts still strewn across the cobblestone courtyard in front of the temple. Time for a change of subject. "So, what are we going to do with this mess? I don't think there's any more to be learned from it, so we should probably clean it up."

Alex considered her last words with dismay. So, she'd rather clean up a disgusting mess of bloody hands and toes than flirt with the sexy Barghest? *Yep, she would.* And she thought Larry had issues. She had more, for sure.

THE MURMUR of distant voices startled Alex out of her revealing reverie. She realized a small group of men were approaching from the tree line by the path to the gardens. *Oh goody, a distraction.*

Conor smirked at her. "This conversation isn't over, sweets. But I'm a patient man. And persistent."

The promise in his words stirred her to the core. She took a deep, cleansing breath, and shook herself roughly to release the sexual tension growing between them.

"Looks like the workers Uncle Vinnie said he'd send over are here."

Conor tacitly agreed to the change of topic, hailing the approaching men and waving them over to where they stood.

Upon their arrival, Alex realized the men were all extremely good-looking. *Not vampires,* Alex considered. *The sun's out. But probably part of a vampire's blood harem.*

The group drew up and stopped in front of Conor, respectfully dipping their heads. They all wore backpacks, and some carried shovels.

The tallest man stepped forward. Fine wrinkles lined his chiseled face, while gray threaded his blond hair. He addressed Conor, his deep voice laced with a slight New York accent. "Hello, sir, I'm Abel. Vincent sent me and the crew over to clean up the mess at the Crossroads." Abel glanced over at the bloody scene impassively and gestured at the workers to get on with the job.

Alex realized that, as senior harem member to a powerful vampire like Vinnie, Abel had probably seen worse—and had often been the one to clean it up. She idly wondered if Abel had been one of Vinnie's bagmen during his tenure as the head of one of the most powerful mob families in New York, back in their 1980s heyday. Abel didn't look a day over forty, but he would have to be much older if he had indeed been an associate of Vinnie's before his turning, almost 40 years ago.

Abel focused his incredibly blue eyes on her, startling her from her musings. "Hello, ma'am. Welcome back to San Antonio, and congratulations on your bonding as Keeper. I know Vinnie is happy to have you home."

"Uh, thank you," Alex stuttered, blinded by the gorgeousness that was Abel.

Conor stepped between her and Abel and issued a sharp instruction to the other man. "Thank Vincent for sending you. Please oversee the cleanup." He gestured pointedly at the camera slung around Abel's neck. "Get lots of pictures before you start and send them to me as soon as possible."

Taking her arm, Conor steered Alex away from the group and toward the path leading away from the Crossroads.

She smiled and peered up at Conor. "Jealous much?"

Conor snorted. "I have nothing to be jealous of. I know you're attracted to me. I can smell it, remember? I may be 250 years old, but I'm not senile yet. I can still tell when a woman is flirting with me."

Alex swallowed the wrong way, coughing until she could catch her breath. Conor whacked her firmly on the back until she stopped choking.

"You're *how* old?" Alex exclaimed, her eyes wide in disbelief. "I mean, I know you've been the Guardian here for a long time, but I didn't realize it had been centuries. Geeze."

Alex shut up before she talked her way into any more trouble.

Talk about being attracted to an older man, she reflected, wryly. A deep blush tinted her cheeks. "Sorry. I didn't mean to insult you."

"No worries. I don't insult easily." Conor laughed as he guided her into the garden and through the courtyard until they both stopped at the bottom of the stairs to the carriage house apartment.

Conor bent down and brushed his lips along her cheek, setting fire to her skin in the path of his mouth. "Get some sleep, sweets. I'm going to supervise the boys doing clean up. I'll see you later."

Alex stood there, stunned, as she watched Conor's tall, lean form lope away until hidden by the lush foliage of the courtyard. She touched her cheek as she trudged up the stairs, her tired legs making slow work of the long trek up the steps leading to her much-needed bed.

As she opened the door at the top of the stairs, she heard a light pattering of paws behind her. Larry squeezed past and darted into the apartment ahead of her. *"So, I hear when Keeper's fall, they fall hard,"* he chuffed, grinning like a furry idiot, his tongue hanging all the way out.

"I have no idea what you're talking about." Alex sniffed in disdain at Larry's insinuation, before heading into the bathroom to change for bed. Since hearing Larry's voice in her head for the first time on the day she adopted him from the animal shelter where she volunteered, Alex could never really think of Larry as 'mere' dog, even though she tried. He could freaking talk, for goodness' sake! Even if it was only in her mind, and that of other supes. In her opinion, Larry was a guy, even if a short, furry canine one. She couldn't disrobe in front of him, so the bathroom had become her changing room from the first night he wormed his way into the bedroom, leapt up on her bed, and curled up to sleep.

"I'm still going to keep an eye on him." Larry's voice echoed in her head through the closed door. *"I've told him more than once not to break your heart, or he'll suffer the consequences."* Larry snorted a laugh. *"But what happens if you break his?"*

"Oh, shut up, you jerk," Alex said, as she left the bathroom and headed for the bed.

Smiling, she pushed Larry gently over to one side of the huge, soft mattress. "And move your furry ass over. You can't always sleep in the middle. I'm tired of hanging off the edge all the time."

13

A DIVINE HISTORY LESSON

Alex ate a quiet lunch in the kitchen later that day, after waking from a deep and dreamless sleep. A stocky, red-faced chef named Henri, whose French accent was so strong that Larry had to translate for her, provided the food. He had apparently gained experience in understanding the chef's thick accent during his marathon kitchen-begging session with Grenoble the night before.

When Alex asked who won the begging contest the previous evening, Larry gave her a disgusted stare. "Grenoble won, of course, but only because he speaks French." He snorted and shook his head, his pink ears flapping against Alex's leg. "I'm pretty sure he cheated and bribed the chef."

Alex snickered and went back to her admittedly delicious lunch. She ate every bite, both because the food was obscenely good and because she figured she'd need the fuel, as she planned to begin training right away, even if she didn't know what training she needed. The sooner she prepared for the dangers ahead, the sooner she could get back to her normal life. If she was successful. *If I'm even alive after the danger comes to a head,* she mused glumly as she mopped up the last of the delicious meal with the last of the homemade bread. *I'll have to ask*

Henri if he'll come back to Connecticut with me, so I can continue eating like this.

A CHILL HAND settled on Alex's shoulder and she started, almost losing her grip on the glass she held, narrowly avoiding spilling the last of a truly great homemade lemonade on her t-shirt. She drank the rest, put the now-empty glass down, and watched as her aunt cornered the table and hovered above a chair across from her.

"I'm sorry to startle you, dear." Maia met Alex's gaze with a worried frown. "I thought you'd be able to sense my presence. Keepers always know when a ghost is close."

"Yeah, well, we've already established that I have absolutely no training, and likely no aptitude, for this Keeper role." Immediately feeling guilty for snapping at her aunt, Alex apologized. "I'm sorry, Aunt Maia. I know it's not your fault that I'm not ready for this Keeper gig. I'm just a little stressed."

Maia drew herself up and used Alex's full first name. *Uh oh,* Alex's eyes widened in alarm, *I'm about to get a talking to.*

The stern tone Alex remembered from her youth filled her aunt's voice. "Alexandria, your heritage is *not* a 'gig.' You are one in a very long line of priestess Keepers chosen over the millennia by the goddess Hecate for their magical power to guard and protect the Crossroads. Our family is of the Athenian line, one of the oldest and most distinguished of the priestess lines. You are aware that my middle name is Persephone, in honor of the goddess Persephone, correct?"

Not waiting for an answer, Maia squared her ghostly shoulders and fixed Alex with a narrow-eyed gaze. "I think it's time for a brief history lesson, niece, before we begin your training. I'd suggest you pay close attention, as there might actually be a quiz later." With a thin-lipped smile she added, "Oh, and your life may depend on it."

Alex straightened in her chair and leaned forward. "Okay, shoot." She grimaced. *Uh, maybe not the best analogy, considering.*

Maia fixed Alex with a sharp schoolteacher glare. "We'll start at the beginning, shall we? Millenia ago, Hades kidnapped my namesake, the goddess Persephone, and took her to the Underworld. The only deity who agreed to help her mother, Demeter, rescue Persephone was Hecate. Once Persephone was returned to her mother, the three goddesses formed a magical triune, their power amplified when working together. The three agreed that no god should have the power to take others unwillingly and bind them to places not of their choosing, whether in the Underworld, here on earth, or anywhere else in this dimension or any other. They combined their power and wove an extremely powerful magic. Using Hecate's power over the In-Between, they formed links between all existing ley lines. To facilitate ley travel, the triune also formed a Crossroads at each convergence of three or more powerful leys."

Maia paused and raised her eyebrows in enquiry until Alex nodded to show she was paying attention. "The original purpose of the Crossroads was to provide the gods with free passage, enabling them to travel anywhere connected to the ley lines. To protect ley travel from inference, Hecate formed a tribe of priestesses to manage and protect the Crossroads. She obtained the Hellhounds, from which she created the Crossroad Guardian Barghests, from Hades himself."

Alex realized her mouth was hanging open and snapped it shut. Both fascinated and slightly terrified by her aunt's tale, she asked, "But how did Hecate convince Hades to give her the Hellhounds ... I mean Barghests?"

Maia snickered, then burst out in delighted laughter. Once she had recovered enough to resume her tale, she explained. "Even the gods can be bargained with—and fooled." She sobered and added, "Mind you, such shenanigans are best left to the gods themselves. It never ends well for humans or supernaturals who try to bargain with the gods."

A snort came from under the table. Larry's voice, for once free of its usual snarkiness, reinforced Maia's words. *"You got that right, sister. Never, ever mess with the gods or their emissaries."* Alex briefly wondered what Larry done to fall afoul of a divine being and decided she'd press him for details later. There *had* to be a story there.

Alex turned her gaze back to her aunt and repeated her question. "So, how did Hecate get the best of Hades and get the Hellhounds from him?"

"Hecate is more than a divine being, dear. She's a female, and very adept at handling the male of her species." Settling further into her seat, her translucent form sinking below the surface of the cushion, Maia resumed her story. "Once Persephone was returned to her mother, Hecate traveled to the Underworld and asked for a quiet word with Hades. She told him she knew the truth—that he had lied to Persephone, and everyone else, about the binding powers of the pomegranate seeds he gave to Persephone to eat." Maia's lips curved in a conspiratorial grin. "The thing is, those seeds actually *have* no binding powers, so Persephone had no obligation to return to the Underworld for half of each year. Hades, of course, didn't want that information getting out, which made him amenable to a bargain with Hecate—and so he handed over several score of his most prized battle Hellhounds."

Alex frowned in disapproval. "But what about Persephone? It wasn't really fair of Hecate to make a deal to keep quiet about Persephone's lack of obligation to spend six months of the year in the Underworld playing footsie with Hades."

A smug smile curved Maia's lips. "Do you really think Hecate would have bargained with Persephone's freedom? Hecate told Persephone the truth about the pomegranate seeds as soon as she discovered it. Persephone then shocked the heck out of Hecate by explaining she had been in on the 'kidnapping' from the start. She said she quite liked it in the Underworld—away from her mother's overbearing ways. Hades' pomegranate seed lie was not news to her, and she was quite happy to go along with it. To this day, Persephone gets a free pass to travel six months out of every year, once she makes an obligatory stop in the Underworld for a dirty weekend or three with Hades. And her mother, Demeter, is none the wiser."

Both women stared at each other for a moment, then burst into gales of laughter. Eventually, their laughter quieted to giggles, and they wiped away mirthful tears. Or rather, Alex did while Maia dabbed a translucent tissue under her eyes, forgetting they could no longer shed tears.

ONCE THEIR SHARED MIRTH ABATED, Maia heaved an unnecessary sigh and her expression sobered. "There's more. And this next bit explains the continued importance of the Crossroads, their Keepers—and their Hellhound Barghest protectors.

Over the course of the millennia, as with any creation of significant magical power, the Crossroads' purpose grew. Scattered and beleaguered supernaturals, many descending from or created by gods even older than the Titans, found they could travel the Crossroads in the same way as the gods. Ghosts powerful enough to refuse the call of the Underworld and remain on Earth could also use them to travel—something they had never done before. Until the formation of the Crossroads, ghosts who refused the call of the Underworld were bound to the location of their death, memories of which would slowly drive them insane and turn them into poltergeists, their souls full of anger and hate. Traveling the leys and staying at Crossroads enables ghosts to avoid that terrible fate."

Alex thought of Crazy Jack, the angry ghost at lunch the previous day, and asked, "Is that what happened to Crazy Jack? Is he a poltergeist?"

Maia smiled. "If Jack were a poltergeist, he wouldn't be welcome here. No, Jack is just plain old crazy, as he was in life. But he's harmless." She hesitated before adding, "Relatively."

Her aunt's caveat didn't reassure Alex, and she resolved to stay far away from Crazy Jack, just to be on the safe side.

"Now, to the very last part of the history lesson, Alex, and where you and I come in," said Maia. "Crossroads don't just provide safe passage for travel. They also offer 'safe' places to stay. Over the millennia, the ley junctions have become gathering places—for gods, for ghosts, and for supernaturals, where all can be sure of a welcome and a place of safety. Communities soon formed close to each Crossroads. Because of the ease of travel between Crossroads, agreements of mutual aid formed between these communities; warlords and despots of the divine or super-natural variety were destroyed. A political structure solidified, which has for centuries assured the neutrality, equality, and well-being of all supernatural Crossroads communities."

Maia's voice filled with pride. "Hecate's original creation has grown beyond all recognition and is now critical to the continua-tion of supernatural society as we know it. Many have tried over the years to conquer a Crossroads and subjugate the surrounding supernatural community. All have failed. The community, the Council, the priestesses, and the Barghests have remained strong and have always prevailed—with Hecate's help."

Worry edged Maia's words. "This brings us to the present situa-tion. We know Hecate can feel the encroaching darkness infil-trating this Crossroads in the In-Between and that it is inhibiting her power. In the past, isolated threats usually originated and were suppressed here on Earth and have always involved disgruntled humans or supernaturals. That's why the current situation presents a big problem. If, as Hecate suspects, a god or goddess is involved, we may be in trouble. If this Crossroads falls, the others will follow. You are the Keeper of this Crossroads and thus at the forefront of this battle. You are the only one who can win it."

Alex listened to her aunt's explanation with a growing sense of horrified understanding. Her breath quickened and heart rate soared as the walls of heritage, duty and responsibility grew ever higher. So much for walking away once the current danger was over. It would *never* be over for her. She pushed away from the table and jumped to her feet, chair clattering to the floor behind her.

Larry scurried away from Alex's side as her anger burst forth in a spray of denial and entreaty. "Well that's just fucking wonderful, Aunt Maia. Let's put the survival of a millennia old Crossroads network on the shoulders of someone brand new to the supernatural world who doesn't know what the hell she's doing! Can't we bring in support? There's got to be another, more experienced Keeper who can step up and take the lead here … or just plain take over?!"

"Language, dear." Her lips pursed in disapproval; Maia chided her niece. "Just a few days back and you are once again picking up Vinnie's foul mouth. Do you remember what happened last time you used that word in my presence?"

Alex's mouth puckered as a memory surfaced. "You made me shot glass of lemon juice," she recalled, remembering her ten-year-old self knocking back the small glass of sourness, slamming the glass on the table and asking defiantly for more. This very table. She cast her gaze over the smooth pine, feeling a mix of emotions. Surprise registered at the audacity and anger she had displayed as a child, when faced with her aunt's displeasure. Alex was grateful for the memory, despite the sadness it brought—as it was a memory she didn't have access to just two days previously.

"I couldn't stand the sight or smell of lemonade for years afterwards," she murmured. Her shoulders drooped. With a resigned sigh, Alex picked up the chair and sank back into it, absently petting Larry's soft fur as he pressed close to offer comfort.

"Well, I'm an adult now, so I can use swear words if I want. Besides, you've put the weight of the Crossroads survival on my shoulders. I think a 'fuck' is the least I'm entitled to."

A distinct chill emanated from across the table. Alex glanced at her aunt through downcast lashes and backtracked. "Okay, okay, I'll try to keep the swearing to a minimum." *At least around the house,* Alex added softly.

"I heard that," Larry snarked. *"What do I get for not telling on you?"*

Alex grabbed Larry's pink fluffy ear and tugged gently on it as she mind-whispered her response. *"You get to live, you furry little blackmailer."*

Maia made a show of checking her ghostly watch. "Conor told me about your conversation with the goddess. We only have a moon cycle to prepare you, so I'll start your Keeper training this evening. Please bring Larry and meet me at the old stables at sunset." The ghost's translucent form drifted toward the door, where she paused to issue her parting shot. "Conor will be in charge of your physical training, dear, which starts at sunrise tomorrow."

"Well, fuck." Alex swore under her breath.

"I'm telling." Larry chortled.

"Alexandria." Mia scolded Alex from the doorway. "I thought we agreed not to use that word."

"You agreed, I didn't," Alex said, wincing as she remembered Conor's warning that ghosts had exceptionally good hearing.

"I think I'll go back to my room and get some rest now, if I'm going to have a late night tonight and such an early morning tomorrow." Alex eyed her aunt peevishly. "I'd like to take some time tomorrow afternoon to go into San Antonio and do a little shopping. I didn't bring enough clothes for an extended stay."

Maia gave Alex a kindly smile, backed with an iron glare. "Sorry, dear, that won't be possible." She surveyed Alex's casual attire with a moue of distaste. "In fact, I do hope you brought something suitable to wear, as you have an appointment tomorrow afternoon in Sylvan City to meet with my attorney to discuss the details of my will. After that, the funeral home is expecting you, so you can give them guidance concerning my funeral. I've asked Conor to drive you, as you aren't familiar with the area and wouldn't find your way to Sylvan City on your own."

With that last parting shot, her aunt gave her a triumphant grin and swept from the room.

"Damn, she may be dead, but she sure ain't gone," Larry said, admiringly.

Alex threw him a filthy look before rising to shuffle tiredly back to her room and get some rest before her first Keeper training session at sunset.

Larry skipped along at her side, annoyingly energetic, chattering the whole way. *"You'll love Sylvan City. Grenoble says it's the best Crossroads town of all, and he's traveled to most of them, so he'd know."* He licked his lips hungrily. *"I hear they have great restaurants, where magical Familiars are welcome inside ...."*

Alex paused with her hand on the doorknob to the carriage house, then glanced down at her furry companion. "You are *not* coming to Sylvan City tomorrow. I'll be busy with the attorney and the funeral home, so there won't be time to eat out. And since when do you listen to everything Grenoble says? You two are thick as thieves."

Larry shuffled his paws on the colorful tiles of the landing and gave her a shifty side-eye. *"I don't know what you've heard, but we had nothing to do with the missing steaks, or the broken window in the conservatory."*

Alex huffed an exasperated laugh and opened the door, ushering Larry through before entering herself. "'Thick as thieves' is just an expression that means you've been hanging out together a lot." Reconsidering, she added, "But I suppose it does imply a criminal partnership, so no wonder you feel guilty. No more stealing or breaking things, capisce?"

"Scout's honor," Larry said.

"You were never a Boy Scout, so that doesn't mean much, does it?"

Larry sniffed and changed the subject. *"Hey, can I get some kibble? A mid-afternoon, pre-nap snack?"*

Alex emptied a small portion of kibble into Larry's bowl before curling up on the bed for her own nap. She vaguely felt the dip of the covers as Larry joined her, then she fell into a deep sleep.

14

THE HEART OF THE MATTER

The creeping black edge of a nightmare seeped into Alex's unconscious mind. She tried to wake herself up, and panic set in when she realized it was too late. Dread filled her as a menacing gray fog swirled ever closer. Sensing evil, she turned and ran, tripping and stumbling over a rough surface she recognized as the cobblestone path near the Crossroads. She ran on the endless path but couldn't reach the Crossroads, couldn't outrun the evil approaching. The remaining light faded and darkness came, while the gray fog coiled closer, its chill grip encircling her legs. As she fell, the fog overtook her, reaching with soft, gray hands to cover her body and darken her mind. As she fell into the darkness, Alex cried out to the goddess. "Hecate, are you there? I need help!"

～

"ALEX? ALEX! WAKE UP!" Large hands shook her roughly. She turned her face aside from frantic doggie licks. Both helped bring her back from the nightmare.

Groggily, she reached up and pushed Larry's worried face away. "S'okay, bud, I'm awake now. No more kissing, please."

Forcing her eyelids open, Alex met Conor's worried gaze. He stopped shaking her and began smoothing his hands up and down her arms instead.

Conor moved his hands to her shoulders, lifting her gently. "Let's get you sitting up. There, that's better." He held a drink to her lips. "Here, sip this, slowly."

Alex took a sniff and wrinkled her nose. "It smells awful."

"I promise, it tastes better than it smells. Please, drink some. It'll help you feel better, I promise."

Alex reluctantly sipped at the foul-smelling concoction as Conor tipped small amounts into her mouth. It did taste better than it smelled, but not by much. *Ugh.* She sat up further and pushed the glass away, coughing. "No more, please."

Now that she was waking up, Alex's mind flashed back to the nightmare. She shivered in reaction to the evil intent she felt smothering her while in its throes.

"It was just a nightmare," she said, not sure if she was trying to reassure herself or Conor.

Belatedly, it occurred to her to ask, "How did you know I was having one anyway? And how did you get in here?"

Conor glanced at Larry, who sat stiffly on the bed, his worried chocolate-brown gaze on Alex's face. "Larry sent out a mental alert and called to me. He said you were in trouble. I had already sensed it and was heading here anyway, though. I have a master key, so when I heard you screaming, I let myself in."

Pulling up a chair, Conor ran his fingers through his hair and took a deep breath. "That wasn't a normal nightmare, though, was it? It felt evil, and it was emanating from the Crossroads. I'm sure it was seeking you out."

Conor pounded his fist on the arm of the chair. "Damn it! We need to get a grip on this and figure out what darkness is infecting the Crossroads. And where the hell was Hecate? I heard you call out for her. She should have sensed the disturbance in the In-Between and dealt with it before it ever reached Earth—and you."

Alex's brain finally engaged, the effects of the drink restoring her to full consciousness. Dread filled her and adrenalin drove her off the bed toward the door. She threw open the door and bolted down the stairs, shouting over her shoulder as she ran. "Come on! I think Hecate's in trouble, too!"

With Conor and Larry on her heels, Alex raced toward the Crossroads.

When the temple came into view, Alex's worry spiraled. A wispy gray fog hung in the air, weakening the late afternoon sunlight. Without hesitation, Alex ran through the mist and up the steps to the temple. She reached for the closest stone pillar and rubbed it rapidly, as if the carved stone was a magic lantern, and she was making a wish. "Hecate? Hecate! Goddess, can you hear me? Can we please meet? Please bring me to the In-Between! Now!"

Conor latched onto Alex's arm just as she closed her eyes and started the now-familiar fall into the In-Between. Moments later, she opened her eyes. Realizing she was still rubbing the column frantically, she stopped, threw Conor an embarrassed grimace, then patted the column with gratitude before withdrawing her hand.

An unnatural gloom smothered the room's normal cozy atmosphere. The typically brightly burning fire in the hearth was almost out. A few red-white coals still smoldered, but a thick, gray mist obscured them.

Heart pounding in horror at the scene, Alex ran toward the hearth, almost tripping over a prone form sprawled on the stone floor. Hecate lay still and silent as the gray mist writhed snake-like over her body. Instinctively, Alex fell to her knees and thrust her hand through the chill mist until she felt the fine linen of Hecate's robes under her seeking fingers.

"Conor, help me move her!"

"Grab her arm and pull, Alex." Conor grunted in effort as he did the same on Hecate's other side.

They slowly dragged the comatose goddess toward the hearth.

While Alex tugged and pushed the prone form, an irreverent

thought flitted through her mind. *Apparently, goddesses are extra-heavy. Either that, or I'm waaayyy out of shape,* she admitted to herself.

Once they reached the hearth, Alex helped Conor place the goddess on the thick wool rug spread in front of the fire.

Alex grabbed the bellows and squeezed them repeatedly, forcing air into the guttering fire. "We need to get this fire going. Now." Somehow, she knew a roaring fire would push back the malignant gray mist—and save the goddess.

Conor placed kindling on the now-glowing embers and stacked wood on top. Alex continued to work the bellows with fearful gusto. The gray mist wrapped itself around the dry logs, as if attempting to prevent the fire from reaching them.

Alex worked the bellows harder and pursed her lips, blowing futilely on the embers. She chanted a profane prayer. "Light, light, light, you fuckers, light! Come on! Come on! Light!"

At last, the flames accepted the kindling and whooshed up to kiss the dry logs, crackling and sparking, dissolving the gray mist as the logs glowed red. The fire grew brighter as the mist receded.

Alex dropped the bellows in shock as bright blue flames erupted from the middle of the now merrily burning fire and reached for Hecate, laying still and silent on the hearthrug.

Conor pulled Alex back, away from the sentient fire. They both watched in horror and fascination as blue fingers of flame encircled the goddess. The fire writhed and flickered as it gradually burned off the gray mist. Finally, the last of the eerily glowing blue fire sank gently into the goddess's body, leaving her clothes and skin untouched.

Hecate heaved a breath as her eyes fluttered open. She gazed in dazed confusion at Alex and asked, "Why are you here, Keeper? I don't remember calling you."

Alex offered the goddess her hand and helped her to stand. "It's a long story, Hecate. Why don't we sit down and talk?"

As the goddess lowered herself onto her usual couch, she

scowled at Conor. "Barghest, how did you get here? Your duty is to guard the Crossroads in the human realm."

Conor settled himself on the raised hearthstone and fixed Hecate with an enigmatic gaze before answering. "Hecate, earlier this evening, your Keeper was in serious trouble. A gray mist with evil intent was dragging her into an unnatural nightmare from which I fear she may not have awakened without help from her Familiar and myself. We woke her, and once awake, she realized the gray mist was emanating from the Crossroads. She feared for you and hurried here. I followed to protect her, as is also my duty."

Conor placed another log on the fire before resuming his explanation. "Your priestess was right to come here, goddess. We found you unconscious and the Crossroads fire almost extinguished. A thick gray mist, which seemed sentient and suffused with ill intent, covered both you and the fire."

Barely checked anger radiated from Conor. His amber eyes glowed, while the beginnings of a muzzle contorted his face.

Alex laid her hand gently on Conor's fisted one, stroking it gently until he relaxed his grip and took her hand in his.

After a final soft squeeze, Conor released Alex's hand and stood. The set of his shoulders still showed angry tension, but his words to Alex were reassuring. "I've got my Barghest under control now. Thank you, Alex."

He stalked toward the goddess, towering over her seated form. "Goddess, with all due respect, I'd highly suggest thanking Alex instead of castigating her. I'm pretty sure she just saved this Crossroads. And maybe even you."

Hecate paled and sat back, her hand picking at the gold braid lining her robe. "The gray mist," she murmured. "I have caught glimpses of it approaching before. After a while, I've seen it leaving. I'm not sure what happens in between."

The goddess rubbed a hand on her forehead and across her disheveled hair. The regal woman looked tired, worn and distinctly ungoddess-like.

"It is as I feared. There are gods involved in this attack on the

Crossroads." Hecate met Alex's surprised gaze and apologized. "Alexandria, I'm sorry. You were right to fear for the Crossroads and to come here to defend it. You are a worthy Keeper. I owe you a debt of gratitude."

Alex's cheeks reddened at the goddess's praise. "Uh, thank you, Hecate. I did what I had to. What about you, though? You were unconscious." A thought struck Alex. "You told me the first time we met that you have been 'losing' time, and that you suspected a god is likely involved in the threat to the Crossroads. I'm assuming both relate to the gray mist that just attacked us?"

"Smart lady," Conor said to Alex before turning his penetrating gaze to the goddess. "Now is not the time for goddess-like cryptic answers. What, or who, is it you fear is bringing danger to the Crossroads?"

Hecate stared into the flames of the hearth for a long moment, as if searching for answers within its blue and red flames, before rousing herself and regaining her regal composure. With a firm voice and direct words, she explained. "You are both right. The gray fog is sleep, with a side of nightmare. It causes an unnatural sleep, and yes, it can be dangerous. The fog is certainly life-threatening to you, Alex, although it likely would not be fatal to a goddess."

Chagrin flitted across the goddess's face. "Of course, the damned fog shouldn't even be able to affect me to this extent. Which is how I know who the culprit is, and yes, it's a god. His name is Morpheus, the god of dreams. His father is Hypnos, the god of sleep. Morpheus is one of Oneiroi, divine triplets, brothers who govern the world of dreams and nightmares. He is the only one strong enough to use his powers to affect other gods, though, so it has to be him."

Hecate dropped into silence, her gaze once again fixed on the fire, as if answers could be found within its flickering flames.

Conor prompted her. "So, we need to find Morpheus and 'convince' him to stop."

The goddess let out a wry laugh. "I fear Morpheus would need more 'convincing' than anyone here could provide, including me. He may be the gray glove of sleep being used to cloak this nefarious plan, but within that glove is another hand, manipulating Morpheus for her own ends. I suspect which goddess would dare, but I need more evidence before accusing her."

Alex huffed in annoyance. "Well, if you know who is behind this whole thing, can't you just go to the God Council or whatever and get a restraining order? I mean, even you people... uh...gods must have rules about right and wrong."

Head thrown back, Hecate issued a huge belly laugh that relieved much of the tension in the chamber. She laughed until tears streamed down her face before finally subsiding into giggles.

Conor and Alex exchanged a confused glance, then settled their eyes back on the amused goddess.

"My dears, have you not studied classical mythology? The gods do not have a moral system that is at all comparable to that of humans. If we had a motto, it would sum up as, *'every god, or goddess, for themselves.'* Weaker deities, supernaturals, and yes, humans have always suffered for the amusement of the strongest of the gods." The goddess tipped her head to one side and shrugged casually. "Things have gotten better in the past millennia. The gods now mostly leave humans and supernaturals alone and confine their games within their own realms, but there is still no rule of law amongst divine beings."

Hecate paced in front of the hearth, her robes backlit by the dancing flames. She looked every inch the powerful goddess again. "No, I'm afraid this is going to be on us to sort out using what I think you in the human world call 'rough justice.' We will need reinforcements, so I'm calling in some IOUs and will bring in my heart-sisters, Demeter and Persephone, to help me protect the In-Between and reduce the threat to the Crossroads."

Alex squared her shoulders. "What do I need to do? Can we bring in reinforcements on the earth side of things, at the Crossroads? Maybe a more experienced Keeper?"

Hecate glowered at her, and Alex wilted, knowing the answer

before Hecate spoke. "Alex, I'd suggest you train well over the coming moon cycle. As Keeper of this Crossroads, the duty falls to you to protect it. I will help, of course, as will your aunt and the rest of this community. However, I'm afraid there is no one else with your unique qualifications. Are you suggesting I chose unwisely when I bonded you as Keeper?"

Alex knew there was only one answer to that question. "No, ma'am. You know best, I'm sure. I'll do my best to learn what I need to in order to help protect the Crossroads."

Nodding at Alex as if that was a given, Hecate turned her intense gaze to Conor. "Barghest, I authorize you to activate Sylvan City's paranormal posse to aid you in protecting the Crossroads."

An enthusiastic gleam in his eyes, Conor nodded at the goddess. "Yes, ma'am."

Hecate hesitated before adding a final instruction. "I suggest placing a guard on Alex's aunt, Maia, as I suspect she may be a target. Her knowledge is key to preparing Alex to fight this battle."

"Will do." Conor promised.

With a clap of her hands, Hecate ended the strategy session. "Let's get on with things, then. I'll see you out."

The next thing Alex knew, she and Conor were standing on the rough cobblestones outside the temple in the gathering gloom of dusk.

Larry rose from his position on the stone wall bordering the path and hurried toward Alex. He nuzzled her legs. She smiled affectionately and reached down to ruffle his ears.

"Sylvan City has a paranormal posse?" Alex queried Conor.

Conor grinned, his eyes lighting with excitement. "Yep, and it hasn't activated in over fifty years, so the gang will be thrilled." He guided Alex toward the path leading back to the house. "But I'll have to fill you in later. You have a Keeper training date with your aunt tonight at sunset, remember?"

"Oh, shit!" Alex gasped as she broke into a trot. "I'm going to be late!"

"And don't forget, we have physical training tomorrow at

sunrise," Conor called after her. "Wear jogging clothes and meet me by the fountain at first light."

"I think that deserves a fuck." Alex muttered several more while she and Larry hurried toward the old stables.

THE AFTERNOON'S grim events filled Alex's thoughts as she wound her way along the path leading to the stables. She admitted to herself that, since her return to the estate, she'd been dealing with events using her head and not her heart. She had been so sure she could 'think' her way to a solution: find out where the danger was coming from, figure out the mystery of the body parts, and solve her aunt's murder—all as an exercise in mental gymnastics. Her goal, to let events wash over her and plod onward, to solve the situation on her own, always keeping her plans in mind. Her desire remained to return to what she thought of as her 'happy place,' her 'real' life in Connecticut. No commitments, no relationships, no emotional connections, safe from the deep emotional hurt a severed connection with a loved one could cause.

Just short of the entrance to the old stables, realization hit her like a ton of bricks. Her heritage as a Keeper meant her connection with and obligation to the supernatural world wasn't something she could 'solve' with her mind, like a particularly hard puzzle. Relationships with those around her, her aunt Maia, her Uncle Vinnie, even, and perhaps especially Conor, were simply not something she could continue to fight.

With a pained sigh, Alex acknowledged her heart was already involved, whether she liked it or not. Her new-old heart-family had already bull-dozed through the brick walls built around her emotions and grabbed hold of her heart, bringing it, reluctantly and painfully, back to life.

As she placed her hand on the barn door's handle and prepared to begin her magical training, Alex understood that her heart was now irrevocably in the game, not just her head.

When Alex entered the stables, a strident voice echoed out of the gloom. "You're late."

"Sorry, Aunt Maia. Conor and I were in the In-Between, talking battle plans with Hecate." Alex suspected that talk of the goddess and battles might distract her aunt from her tardiness, and she was right.

Maia's translucent form materialized in front of Alex, an eager look on her face. "You met with the goddess? What battle plans?"

"Well, it's like this ...."

15

CONOR'S BOOT CAMP

Alex collapsed on a bench by the fountain, breath heaving, sweat pouring down her face. "My aunt didn't tell me that training included running five miles with a heavy pack on my shoulders. I don't imagine I'll be running after the bad guys, trying to beat them off with my backpack."

Conor leaned over and grabbed his ankles. His post workout stretch gave Alex a superb view of his exceptionally fine ass. He didn't look a bit out of breath. *Damn Barghest genes,* mused Alex.

After finishing his stretches, Conor plopped down on the bench at her side. "I'm in charge of your physical training, which includes getting you in shape, as you know. You might not need to wield a backpack, but you *will* need physical strength to wield the Keeper staff." He frowned, considering. "And maybe a sword or two." Then he grinned. "Plus, if all else fails, it'll give you the speed and stamina to run away from the bad guys."

Alex's lips curved in a grudging smile. She slapped the back of her hand against Conor's shoulder in reproof. His very hard and muscled shoulder. She resisted the urge to leave her hand in place. *No, nope, not going there,* she reminded herself. What the heck was up with her libido today? She wasn't about to make the same mistake twice. She winced in remembered anger at discovering her mother in a passionate embrace with her fiancé, Sean-the-scumbag. With a few terse words, Alex had dumped both her fiancé and her mother on the spot. The looks on their faces as she stomped out still gave her a gleeful and wholly justified sense of satisfaction. With a sigh, Alex closed off thoughts of her previous failures in love and family and returned her mind to the present.

Conor had been the Crossroads Guardian since at least her aunt's bonding, Alex remembered. *Had they been more than magical partners,* she wondered. She suspected so. She shook her head, making sweat fly from her soaked hair. There was no way she could settle for either her mother's *or* her aunt's lover leftovers. No thanks. Her relationship with Conor needed to remain in the friend-zone only.

Unaware of Alex's internal dialog, Conor met Alex's eyes with his warm amber gaze. "While I'm in charge of your physical training, your aunt is in charge of your magical Keeper training. How'd your first night go, by the way?"

Alex hung her head, sweat dripping from her face onto her running shorts. "Not so good. My aunt outfitted me in the latest Keeper gear." Her lips curved in a reluctant grin. "Black leather and knee-high boots—which is really cool, by the way. Plus, she gave me a magical pendant and told me to wear it at all times." She glanced down and fingered the pendant hanging from a silver chain, admiring the crescent moons that represented the triple goddesses who created and still protected the Crossroads. The large moonstone in the middle caught the sun with a magical sparkle.

"Uncle Vinnie was there, trying to help me 'merge with my magic,' as he put it. Larry was also trying to help, but with no success." Alex huffed a frustrated sigh. "Aunt Maia had me hold the Keeper staff during the training session, but so far, it's just a stick for me. I had trouble feeling the staff's magic or channeling my supposed magic into it, let alone doing anything with it. I suppose I could hit the bad guys over the head with the staff," she muttered darkly. Worry creased her forehead. "We don't have much time before I need to be ready to defend this damn place."

"Patience, Alex." Conor patted her sweaty arm. "You'll get there."

I better, Alex reflected with a sense of desperation. She had to work with her heart-family and the supernatural posse to stop whoever was behind the flying body parts, figure out the connection to the gray mist and the dark gods troubling the goddess, and defend the Crossroads from the current danger. It was her only hope of returning to her old, slightly boring, but independent life. A life with no magical staffs, no lethal swords, and no five-mile runs. A life with no ghosts, no weekly supernatural poker games, no paranormal posses, and definitely no Barghests. That's what she still wanted. *Right?*

Conor's voice interrupted her morose thoughts. "That reminds me, we need to shower and grab some lunch before heading into Sylvan City for your meetings with Alan and the undertaker."

Sunk in her mental musings, Alex almost missed Conor's reminder. "Alan? Oh, you mean Mr. Allman, my aunt's attorney. Yes, I know I need to meet with him to discuss my aunt's Will and go to the funeral home to make the funeral arrangements for Aunt Maia's mortal remains." She ran a hand over her sweaty, messy hair and frowned. "It feels weird to be arranging a funeral for my aunt when I can go up to the main house and talk to her whenever I want."

"You can talk to her ghost." Conor reminded her gently. "Her mortal body is dead. Murdered."

Alex sighed in defeat. "Yeah, I know. This whole thing is just so hard. It's not what I signed up for, at all." She picked at a splinter on the bench and sniffed hard, trying not to let the welling tears fall.

Conor leaned back on the bench and stretched out his long legs, before casually crossing them at the ankle. "I've got some time if you have any questions about your aunt's ... your ... estate before you meet with Alan."

ALEX TOOK Conor up on his offer to listen. She couldn't very well ask her aunt about her own funeral, and she wasn't comfortable seeking information from her about the estate and the full details about her inheritance, either. Plus, there was one other thing niggling at her from her first conversation with Alan the other morning, what seemed a lifetime ago, when he called to inform her of her aunt's passing. She *had* to ask someone about it. The niggling thought blossomed when her aunt mentioned the attorney yesterday. Her aunt's face had softened, pain pinching her lips. She'd been too busy since yesterday to visit with her Uncle Vinnie and ask him about it, and Conor was right here and offering his ear.

Shifting uncomfortably on the bench, Alex put some space between her and Conor. She took a deep breath, met his eyes, then spoke quickly, before she could chicken out. "So, what's the deal between Alan and my aunt? Were they, like, an item?"

Alex hesitated, unsure how to phrase her next query, but the words just tumbled out. "I thought you and she were a thing. Were you both romantically involved with her? I mean, not that there's anything wrong with seeing more than one guy. I don't blame my aunt at all, really, as long as both of you were aware of the other . ..."

Face burning with embarrassment, Alex equivocated. "I mean, I checked out Alan's picture on his law firm's website. You are both extremely good-looking guys ...." She grimaced, wishing for the thousandth time she could engage her brain before opening her mouth. That all sounded *so* lame. And judgy. Sigh.

As Alex reached the end of her monologue, she realized Conor had gone completely still, face blank, eyes hooded. Once she finished, words trailing to a stop in a welter of embarrassment, Conor shocked Alex by bursting into laughter. He laughed so hard and for so long, he had trouble catching his breath. Tears of mirth streamed down his face.

Confused and angry at Conor's cavalier attitude, Alex pulled her legs up onto the bench and put her arms around them, both for something to do and so she didn't punch Conor's smug, laughing face.

Finally, when Conor's laughter had subsided to mere chuckles and wheezing, Alex straightened. She blew out a breath to cool her anger. "I'm not sure what's so funny. I don't appreciate being laughed at. You did offer to answer my questions, after all. It's just that Alan sounded really broken up when I spoke with him on the phone about my aunt's death, and my aunt looked so sad when she mentioned him yesterday, so I thought ...."

Conor took a deep breath, wiping his hands over his red face to remove the last remnants of his mirth. He turned apologetic amber eyes on her. "I'm sorry. I'm not laughing at you, at all. Okay, maybe a little." He chuckled again, briefly. "Alan and your aunt have had a romantic 'thing,' as you put it, for the past fifteen years, since right after your abduction. He is a family law attorney, in both the human and the supernatural worlds. She consulted with him immediately upon her return from France after finding you missing and realizing your mother had kidnapped you."

Alex's face heated in mortification. "Oh, I didn't realize."

"No, you didn't realize, and you also don't know as much as you think you do about the relationship between Maia—your aunt, and me, either. I am the Guardian of this Crossroads. My duty is to protect both this Crossroads and its Keeper, and I've done both for over a century. I've known Maia since she was born. Once the goddess chose her as the next Keeper, I took over her training." Conor's lips twisted in a grim smile. "Hesia, your Keeper grandmother, wasn't interested in training her younger daughter as Keeper. She had already decided her older daughter, your mother, Helen, would be the next Keeper and had been preparing her for that role since childhood. When the goddess chose your aunt as Keeper, both your mother and your grandmother were incoherent with rage. They even questioned the goddess's choice."

Alex gasped. She knew little about the supernatural world, but even she realized a goddess's decision should *never* be questioned. Intrigued, she asked, "What happened?"

After a derisive snort, Conor replied. "*That* conversation didn't go well. I don't know what happened, as your grandmother requested I not be present for her 'debate' with the goddess, but I do know that she withdrew into herself after that meeting. She did the minimum required to keep the Crossroads functioning, and refused to train the next Keeper, your aunt, Maia. So, I stepped in and did the best I could."

Conor met her eyes, his a deep well of emotion. Anger, regret, grief, and remembered affection all swirled within. "I loved your aunt, yes. Like a daughter. Like a best friend. I—we were never an 'item,' as you so crudely put it."

Alex wished the earth would open up and swallow her. She closed her eyes and ducked her head in embarrassment. Here she was worrying about whether her aunt had been sleeping with Conor and feeling jealous of her relationship with him. All the while, he was grieving the loss of someone he thought of as his daughter and best friend. She realized she was still carrying way too much emotional baggage from the debacle involving her mother and her fiancé six months before. *Projection much?* She sighed, unhappy with her musings, and with herself.

Hesitantly, Alex placed her hand on Conor's arm. "I'm so, so sorry for your loss. And I'm sorry for thinking your relationship with my aunt was something it wasn't, when in fact, it was so much more. You must mourn her loss greatly. And here I come bumbling in, a clueless new Keeper, acting like a jealous idiot and assuming things not in evidence. I can only say, in my defense, that I have some history with my bitch of a mother and my scumbag fiancé."

Conor raised his face to the sky, then heaved a breath and shrugged, as if to shake off the seriousness of the conversation. He stood up quickly, grabbed her hand, and pulled her to her feet before casting a glance at the midday sun. "I'm starving," he said. "Let's head back to the house and shower, then we can head over to Vinnie's restaurant for some lunch before leaving for Sylvan City."

ALEX TRUDGED AFTER CONOR, her thoughts a jumble of confusion. *Isn't he going to respond to my apology? Is he still angry with me? If so, why the offer of lunch? Wait, is that a date?*

Ahead of her, Conor turned around and walked backwards, grinning mischievously at her. "So, you were jealous of your aunt? That means you like me, right? I mean, I realize you're attracted to me. I can smell it, remember? But liking me enough to be jealous, now that's a whole different thing."

Alex snorted and threw up her hands. "Is that all you got out of my abject apology? That I'm jealous of your relationship with my aunt? Men!"

"So, you do like me then—at least a little." Chuckling softly, Conor slowed and turned to walk at her side. His gaze slanted at her, eyes narrowed. "And what's this about a fiancé? I'm assuming he's out of the picture, since, reading between the lines of your cryptic comment earlier, you caught him doing something he shouldn't with your mother. Want me to beat him up? Want me to beat your mother up?"

Alex laughed and found the pain of her mother's betrayal hurt less than it had for the first time in months. "No beating anyone up, you knucklehead. And yes, I dumped my fiancé after I walked in on him in a passionate lip-lock with my mother."

With a wry smile, Alex explained further. "I dumped my mother, too. I immediately quit as her business manager. She owns a swanky antique store in Westport and travels most of the time, collecting items for the store. She raised me to run the shop so she could resume jetting all over Europe once I took over—even sent me to Yale for degrees in business management and European art history."

Alex's lips curved in an evil grin, and she smiled in satisfaction.

"I know for a fact she's having a hard time finding someone qualified to take my place. She hasn't traveled in the six months since I quit."

"Vindictive little thing, aren't you?" Conor smiled grimly. "Not that your mother doesn't deserve it, and more." After a moment, he asked, "You sure you don't want me to beat her up?"

"Nope. Once I'm finished with my training, *I'll* beat her up." Alex sighed. "She took so much from me..."

Conor's hand reached out, taking hers in a firm, comforting hold. The sun shone, reflecting off the fountain as they passed it, on their way back to the house.

Despite everything, Alex's heart felt lighter than it had in months. She could do this Keeper thing with the help of her rediscovered heart-family. She realized she had been letting the actions of others, especially her mother, control her life for too long. Alex wanted her power back, and she knew just how to get it.

"Lead on, kind sir. Let's get that pizza. Then, I have an estate to inherit and a funeral to plan."

16

A CROSSROADS COMMUNITY

After a delicious lunch at Vinnie's restaurant, Conor returned Alex to the estate so she could change into something appropriate for her afternoon meetings.

As she strolled to the main house after changing clothes, Alex smiled in remembrance of her aunt's stern voice telling her to dress for the occasion.

The simple black dress she'd packed for her aunt's funeral would have to do, Alex reflected, as she sat on the front steps waiting for Conor to bring the car around. The heat of the afternoon sun penetrated her bones, and she drowsed in its radiance. San Antonio's warm weather was a pleasant change after the chilly temperatures of late fall in Connecticut. The smooth rumble of Conor's car heralded its approach and brought her fully awake. Reluctantly, she left her comfortable perch on the mansion's front steps and slipped into the car with Conor, where the icy blast of air conditioning after the afternoon heat made her shiver.

Conor slanted a glance at her before putting the car in drive and gliding smoothly up the driveway. Before reaching the main gate, he steered the car onto a small, paved road that paralleled the estate's high stone wall. "Not bringing Larry today?"

"I wasn't sure he'd be welcome at the lawyer's office or funeral home, so I left him at the main house." Alex's lips curved briefly in amusement. "Last I saw, he was arguing with Grenoble about who could run down the large sweep of stairs in the front hall the fastest."

Alex suspected her face reflected her dour mood. When she changed clothes earlier, she realized she had been blaming her aunt for the current situation. She'd mourned the woman dearly as a child when she'd been told of her passing. Several days ago, she had been devastated all over again when she learned during that fateful phone call from Alan that Maia had been alive until a few weeks ago. The weird dichotomy of simultaneously mourning her aunt's death a second time while fighting with her ghost about her Keeper heritage and responsibilities bewildered Alex. She'd have to apologize to her aunt when she returned from planning her funeral. Damn, this was all just too weird.

"A penny for your thoughts." Conor's voice broke into her dismal introspection.

"Oh, they aren't worth even that," Alex replied. "I guess I'm dealing with the fallout of mourning my aunt. Again. And now I've got to meet with the attorney about her estate and the funeral home to plan her funeral, knowing all the while that her ghost is back at the house and expecting a report on today's meetings. Plus, I realize I've been acting like a baby about the whole Keeper thing. I know it's not my aunt's fault, or anyone's really, so I owe her an apology on top of everything else." Alex sighed despondently.

Conor chuckled and flicked her a sympathetic glance. "You're right. It's a lot, but I think you are handling it admirably, considering."

Alex summoned a smile. "Sorry to be such a drag. I didn't mean to unload on you."

"No worries. I can handle it. If you ever need to talk, come find me." Conor slowly steered the car through a gate barely wide enough for it, then gathered speed on the smooth, but still narrow, road outside the estate walls.

"Thanks, Conor." Alex touched his shoulder lightly to emphasize her thanks before withdrawing her hand quickly, self-conscious about the intimate gesture.

Sensing her embarrassment, Conor quirked his brow and gave her a sly smile. "You can touch me anytime, sweets, and not just on the shoulder."

Face burning, Alex turned away and gazed out the passenger window, pretending to watch the scenery as it slid silently by. "Uh, thanks, but no. I'm really not interested in a relationship."

"Sure, you are, sweets. I can smell arousal, remember."

"That's a natural bodily reaction I can't help." Alex sniffed in disdain. "It doesn't mean I want to hop in the sack with you."

"Sure, it does, sweets."

"Oh, shut up. And nobody in this century uses the term sweets."

"I do."

Somehow, Alex knew Conor wouldn't let her have the last word in this conversation. *Best to change the subject,* she reasoned.

"Before you used it just now, I didn't know there was a back gate to the estate. I've not seen this area before. Are we almost there?" *Good goddess,* Alex grimaced. *I sound like a toddler.*

Alex watched Conor's long fingers grip the steering wheel as he slowed and took another curve on the narrow road. They were now driving through a close-packed forest of trees, their branches almost brushing the glossy black doors of the car.

She lowered her window, and the moist, earthy scent of verdant woodland assailed her nose. A massive monkey screeched and swung from a branch before launching itself through the air and over the car before grasping a branch on the other side of the road. Alex smothered a shocked gasp at the sight of the monkey, more than slightly freaked out. *A monkey?* Her memories of San Antonio's flora and fauna were spotty, but she was pretty sure the list of native wildlife didn't include monkeys. Especially not ones as big as small cars.

"Did I just see a ginormous monkey swing across the road, or am I going crazy?" Alex asked the question with a calm that she did not feel. *Toto, we're not in Kansas anymore,* she counseled herself in a slightly hysterical whisper.

"Oh, that's just Oscar. He's a monkey shifter." Conor slowed for another sharp turn in the road that cut through the thicket of trees. "He must be on gate duty today."

Alex peered over her shoulder at the monkey, who grinned at her from his perch half-way up the tree on the far side of the road, before another turn of the road hid him from view. "I didn't see any gate. Have we passed it already?"

"The gate is magical, not literal, and we passed it a while back," Conor explained. "We'll be in Sylvan City in a few minutes. Alan's law firm is on Main Street. Parking can be tough to find, so we may have to park and walk to his office."

Alex eyed the impenetrable greenery crowding the car on either side. "So, Sylvan City is big enough for a main street? I thought, by the size of this road and the surrounding woods, that we were heading into the countryside."

"Your aunt never took you to Sylvan City as a child?"

"I don't think so. I'm sure I'd have remembered this drive, and I never knew there was a back road off the estate. No wonder she said I'd never find it and had you drive me." Alex shrugged, chagrined.

"We actually only just left the estate grounds," Conor said. He glanced over at her before turning his gaze back to the narrow road. "The estate property ends at the magical gate to Sylvan City lands."

"Oh, I didn't realize the grounds extended this far outside the walls," Alex murmured.

Conor cleared his throat and threw her a sideways glance. "Uh, I'm not sure if your aunt has given you a Crossroads history lesson yet ...."

A wry chuckle escaped Alex. "Oh yeah, she gave me a loooong history lecture yesterday. She started back in ancient Greece with

Hades' pretend abduction of Persephone. Now that I think about it, told me that supernatural towns have grown up near many of the Crossroads. Is that what Sylvan City is?"

A thrill of understanding and excitement caused Alex's mood to shift, and she bounced a little in her seat. "Oh, that's so cool! And that explains Oscar-the-monkey-shifter, too!" Relief that there was a normal, if supernatural, explanation for Oscar and the unnaturally lush landscape they were driving through filled her.

Chuckling, Conor gave Alex an amused grin. "You are bouncing around like a kid being taken to the circus. Excited much?"

"Nope, not me," Alex said, trying not to smile. "Okay, that's a lie. Yes, I'm excited. It's my first visit to a supernatural city. Do they have fairies? What about unicorns?"

Conor smiled at her enthusiasm. "Yes, there are fairies, but I advise you to steer clear. They are dangerous creatures. No to the unicorns, not in the city anyway. There is a herd living in the woods on the outskirts, though." He frowned a warning. "They are also dangerous. In fact, much of the supernatural world has its dangers. Until you understand a bit more about it, I'd suggest treating every creature you meet with caution, and respect. Mutual respect and equality are important in Crossroads cities. That's one reason they exist."

The car crested a small rise and Alex gasped as she took in the spectacular view. The forest fell away sharply on either side before climbing the slopes of low hills on either side of a long, wide valley surrounding a large, narrow lake. Sunlight glittered on the deep azure blue of the water. A low-slung town hugged the length of the near side of the lake, bustling with activity. Houses, shops, and streets stretched out from the shore and continued the length of the valley. Low warehouses and other businesses edged the town and extended to the foothills. There were no high-rise buildings jutting into the sky, just a pleasant jumble of prosperous two-and-three-story red brick, stone, and colorful stucco buildings laid out in a carefully plotted example of excellent urban planning. On the far side of the lake, Alex noticed farms and vineyards dotting the verdant land.

"We really aren't in Kansas anymore," Alex murmured, entranced and already half in love with the supernatural city spread before her.

Conor grinned. "No, we're still in Texas, but a part of it most will never see. You are right about Sylvan City, though. It is a supernatural enclave, created by travelers who arrived via the Crossroads. For many centuries, Sylvan City was a quiet backwater outpost visited mostly by native shamans using the Crossroads to travel between tribes. Over the last three centuries, both humans and supernaturals fled Europe in droves, with a desire to start a new life in a new country. The immigrant supes, who arrived in San Antonio via our local Crossroads, carved Sylvan City out of this land almost three hundred years ago. Once the human cities in this area grew enough to reach the outskirts of Sylvan City, the town's leaders had the area magically shielded by powerful spells. They used the power of one of the Crossroad's ley lines to attach the city to the In-Between. Most humans cannot see or travel to the city."

"But we drove here." Alex protested. "How can we be in the In-Between?"

As he drove down the road leading into the supernatural city, Conor explained. "This place isn't actually IN the In-Between, nor is it fully in the real world any longer. It's kind of in-between the In-Between and the human world." He raised his eyebrows and threw her a quizzical glance. "Does that make sense?"

Alex grinned. "Not in the least. But that's okay. I don't need to understand it to know that I'm about to enter a magical place." She bounced a little in her seat again, unable to quell her excitement. Despite her determination not to get attached to anyone or anything while in San Antonio, the desire for her old life in Connecticut receded slightly. She quickly shut off that train of thought and fixed her mind on her goals: get the estate settled, get her aunt buried, get the mystery of the body parts sorted, and save the Crossroads and, by extension, the supernatural world. *Normal superhero stuff*, she reflected, wryly. Then get out of town. Both towns. Whatever.

17

BEGINNINGS & ENDINGS

A thrill of excitement coursed through Alex as she gaped at the town in wonder. She watched as what looked like a satyr mom pushed a stroller filled with two baby satyrs across a side street. A tall, slender man with silver hair and lavender skin bent down and helped the mother maneuver the stroller up the curb on the far side and onto the sidewalk. Alex saw the satyr wave a thank-you to the purple man as she clopped away.

Creatures of myth and fairytale filled the streets. Alex had always secretly wished they were real. *Well, they are real—and here they are*, Alex mused, as her eyes darted around. Besides the supernaturals who resembled those in familiar fairy tales, there were several so strange looking she could only guess at their species. Interspersed amongst the supernatural beings were many very human-looking residents. Alex decided she'd question Conor later about the range of species inhabiting the town.

Conor expertly pulled into a curbside parking space just vacated by a car belonging to the purple man Alex had seen assisting the satyr with her stroller. She turned to Conor with a questioning look.

Understanding her mute query, Conor explained. "That's

Chris Fernwood. He is a type of Dark Fae." An unhappy twist of his lips gave way to a frown. "Dark Fae get a bad rap, but most are more civic-minded than their Light Fae brethren. Chris is a good guy. He's a helper."

Alex nodded as Conor exited the car and walked around the hood toward her door, his intention to open it for her clear. Determined not to take part in such an old-fashioned tradition, Alex hurried to open her door and step out before Conor could reach her. As she turned from closing the door, she promptly tripped, unsteady on unaccustomed heels, and would have landed on her face if Conor didn't block her fall with his leanly muscled body.

Embarrassed by her antics and unbalanced by the unexpected full-body contact, Alex quickly pulled away and placed herself at a respectable distance. *There is no respectable distance where Conor is concerned,* Alex mused wryly. Just seeing his tall, lean form from a distance made her libido sit up and whine in anticipation. *Down, girl.*

Conor suppressed a grin and turned away, before pointing toward a large burgundy door several yards away. "That's Alan's office. Come on, he's expecting us, and we'll be late if we don't hurry."

After brushing imaginary lint off her dress, Alex gathered the remnants of her dignity and followed Conor down the sidewalk. She turned the conversation toward the purpose of their visit. "I've never been to the reading of a will before, but I've seen several on TV. Will there be other beneficiaries present?"

When he reached the deep red door, Conor grasped the elegant brass doorknob and turned it. "Other than a few small bequests, you are your aunt's sole beneficiary, so no, there won't be anyone else at today's meeting." He opened the door and stood aside, gesturing her to enter first, his smirk informing her that he knew why she'd hurried out of the car earlier—and almost landed on her ass.

Alex huffed an annoyed snort, then swept by him to enter the gleaming marble and dark wood reception area of the law firm. Perusing her surroundings with raised brows, Alex concluded the lobby looked exactly as law-firm-like as she imagined one would in the human world. Then she spotted the witch at the reception desk. *Definitely not in Kansas,* Alex reminded herself, as she eyed the purple smoke drifting from a small black cauldron perched atop the reception desk. A smoky sage scent wafted from the cauldron, tickling her nose. She stifled a sneeze and turned her attention to the witch perched behind the reception desk.

"Hello, dear. You must be Alexandria. Welcome. My name is Mabel. I'm Mr. Allman's receptionist." The outlandish woman reached up to straighten the monstrously huge black velvet witch hat perched precariously on her silver-purple hair. "You look just like your aunt described. I've known your aunt for many years, and I know how glad she is to have you back where you belong."

"Uh, thanks?" Alex stuttered. "I'm just here for the reading of the will and to plan my aunt's funeral, then I'll be returning to Connecticut."

"Of course, dear. Whatever you say." With a sweet, but disbelieving smile, the older woman gestured them toward elegant chairs ranged against the far wall. "If you'll please have a seat, I'll inform Mr. Allman you have arrived." Instead of picking up a phone, Mabel hopped spryly off her office stool, then trotted up a curving staircase, before disappearing down a corridor at the top.

Alex settled herself a safe two chairs away from Conor, hoping her disorientation wasn't too obvious. "Does everyone in town know my aunt?" *And my business,* Alex wondered, silently.

"As the Keeper of the Crossroads, the community definitely considered your aunt a VIP. After all, without the Crossroads, Sylvan City wouldn't exist." Conor nodded in agreement with his next words. "Plus, she sits on the Town Council."

"You mean 'sat' on the Town Council. Now she has passed, I'm assuming the Council will appoint someone else." A panicked thought struck her. "Oh goddess, don't tell me positions on the Council are hereditary, too? Am I now on the Town Council?" Alex had trouble catching her breath as the twining tendrils of heritage and responsibility tightened further around her body and soul.

"A seat on the Town Council is one thing you don't have to worry about." Conor gave her an understanding look, as if sensing her panic. "Your aunt still holds her seat on the Council, as death doesn't bar Council membership. As long as she meets the attendance requirements, she's still got her Council position, for as long as she wants it." He grinned. "Maia enjoys having her fingers involved in everything in this community, so I don't see her stepping down anytime soon."

Alex heaved a sigh of relief, the bonds constricting her chest loosening, if only a little. Hurried steps sounded, and she looked up to see Mabel tapping down the bare wood of the stairs, followed by a tall, distinguished-looking older man. His silver hair glinted in the light from the overhead chandelier, while his strong profile contained signs of an interesting life. The wrinkles bracketing his mouth and eyes evidenced a surfeit of past smiles.

Recognizing Mr. Allman from the picture on his law firm's website, Alex blinked in surprise. *He's even more handsome in person,* she appraised. She stood as the man reached the bottom of the stairs and approached her.

The attorney smiled and held out his hand in welcome. Alex winced slightly as she reached for his hand, remembering her threat, during that early morning call, to shrivel the balls of the attorney's progeny. Oops.

"Hello, Alexandria, I'm Alan Allman, your aunt's attorney. Please, call me Alan." Alan enveloped Alex's hand in his large one and shook it gently, his light brown eyes twinkling mischievously down at her, a small smile playing on his lips.

Alex realized Alan was also remembering her ball-shriveling threat during that fateful phone call. Double oops. She smiled and spoke to cover her nerves. "Please, call me Alex."

The attorney spoke in a deep, rich baritone. "Welcome to Sylvan City, Alex. I hope your flight was okay? The carriage house is suitable for your needs? Have you spoken with your aunt?"

When Alan showed no signs of releasing her hand, seeming to have forgotten he still enveloped it within his much larger ones, Alex pulled hers gently away.

"The flight was great, thank you. I've never traveled First Class before. Larry enjoyed the meal the flight attendants prepared especially for him. He said to say thanks." Larry hadn't really offered his thanks to the attorney. He had considered the special meal his due for the inconvenience of flying.

Alex took a calming breath when she realized she was babbling. "Everything is fine with the carriage house, thanks. And no, I don't need anything else at the moment. I have spoken with my aunt, as well."

She couldn't help adding a slight rebuke. "Why didn't you tell me she was still at the estate, as a ghost? When you called and told me she had been alive all these years and just recently died, I thought I'd missed the chance to say goodbye to her." She grimaced, wishing she could take back her chiding words, but she was tiring of everyone keeping things from her. She wasn't a hot mess that would break down when told things straight. *Was she?*

"My apologies, Alex. Conor told me your aunt specifically requested I not mention her ghost was in residence at the estate when I called to inform you of her death. I assumed she wanted the opportunity to speak with you, er, in person, as it were." The attorney looked uncomfortable for a moment before asking, "How is she? Maia, I mean. How is she, um, handling things?"

Conor spoke from Alex's side, startling her.

"You haven't spoken to Maia recently, Alan?"

"Uh, no. After her death, I saw her ghost only once, when she asked me not to come to the estate, at least for a while." Alan hung his head, the picture of dejection.

A lightbulb flashed in Alex's head as she remembered Conor's confirmation that Alan and her aunt had been an item for years. She placed a consoling hand on his arm. "I'm so sorry for your loss."

Alan gave her a tremulous smile. "Thank you, my dear. I

surmise you have discovered that your aunt and I were ... intimately acquainted. We've been seeing each other for over a decade." He mustered a dry chuckle. "We both knew marriage wouldn't suit either of us, so long-term dating was our status quo, and a lovely one, too."

A confused frown darkened the attorney's features. "That's what I don't understand. Why can't things go on as they were? I'd just be happy to be with her. I don't care that she's a ghost now."

Now I can add supernatural relationship counselor to my Keeper resume, Alex mused, with a reluctant sense of belonging. "I'll talk to her. I'm sure she thinks she's doing what's best for you by giving you the opportunity to move on."

"I don't want to move on." Alan grumbled his grievance. "I just want to spend time with her, like always."

"I'll talk to her," Alex said, grimly determined to fix this rocky relationship, as the poor man seemed heart broken.

"Thank you so much, dear." Alan turned his head away and surreptitiously wiped his eyes. "I just miss her so much. She's ... she was the love of my life."

"Well, we'll just see about bringing that love back into your life." *Even if she's very much dead,* Alex added silently to herself. *But who am I to judge true love?* She considered, knowing she'd never really experienced it.

Alan cleared his throat and issued a heartfelt apology. "I'm so sorry, my dear, for burdening you with my affairs."

A small smile and the returning twinkle in his eyes informed Alex that Alan realized the double meaning of his words.

The attorney gestured toward the stairs. "If you will please follow me to my office, we can commence with the reading of your aunt's last will & testament."

Alex nodded, then headed toward the stairs. Behind her, Alan addressed Conor. "Conor, if you will please accompany us? Maia requested you be present for the reading, as well."

Alex glanced back and met Conor's confused gaze. He

shrugged, agreeing to Alan's request with a tilt of his head, then followed Alex toward the stairs.

ALEX TOOK a seat in the beautifully embroidered armchair in front of Alan's desk. She brushed her hand admiringly over the silky-smooth, carved wooden arm of the elegant chair. The neatly arranged office was stuffed full of books and files. She absently noted the quality of the vast mahogany desk filling the space in front of her. *English, mid-eighteenth century, probably from the home of a nobleman*, she appraised, before shaking her head to bring her mind back to the task at hand.

Conor covered her hand with his, massaging it gently. She realized he was attempting to smooth her hand, where she maintained a death grip on the carved lion's head on the arm of her chair.

She released her nervous grip on the chair and gave Conor a grateful smile. "Sorry, I was strangling the poor lion, wasn't I?"

After one last encouraging squeeze, Conor released her hand. His attention shifted; his enquiring gaze now fixed across the massive desk at the now-seated attorney. "I'm not sure why Maia requested my presence, but I'm glad to be here, if it helps Alex."

Alex realized she was delaying by continuing to study the stunning desk. With a sigh, she looked up and focused her gaze on the attorney. Surprise filled her at the transformation had taken place in Alan's demeanor. The grief-stricken and lovelorn man from downstairs had vanished. In his place sat a sober and businesslike attorney. His sympathetic eyes still hinted at the kind man underneath, though.

Two overfilled legal folders occupied a corner of the desk. Alan shuffled the folders closer and handed one to Alex before opening the other. He patted the pile of papers, now exposed. "If you'd open your folder to the first page, Alex, we can begin."

Alex opened the folder and saw the words *Last Will & Testament* sprawled in elegant script across the top of the heavy, cream-colored paper. Her eyes blurred with tears when she saw her aunt's name printed neatly underneath the grim header.

"Alexandria, as I mentioned on the phone when we first spoke, you are your aunt's heir and, except for several small bequests, her sole beneficiary. Her entire estate is now yours. The papers in this folder include details of the extent of her holdings. I don't want to immerse you in too many details right now. We can meet again, as often as needed, to go over the specifics, but suffice it to say that your aunt's estate is extensive. It includes the manor house and grounds, along with all personal property thereon, including outbuildings, vehicles, furniture and household items, and the Keeper Collection of jewels and weaponry, both mundane and magical."

"Jewels? Weaponry?" Alex murmured the question in dismay.

"Your aunt inherited the Keeper Collection when bonded as the Crossroads Keeper. It's an extensive collection of jewels and weapons gifted or purchased over the centuries by the Keepers of this Crossroads. Many of the pieces have magical qualities, and all assist the Keepers in their role as protector of the Crossroads. I'm sure your aunt will introduce you to the Collection when the time is right."

"Okay," Alex said in a small voice, fingering the triple goddess pendant around her neck and wondering if it was part of the Keeper collection. She'd bet anything it was.

"Her financial investments, holdings, and liquid assets are also extensive." Pointing at the stack of papers in her hand, Alan instructed her to turn to the list at the back of the pile. "That's a summary of her financial assets and includes a list of all funds held in local, national, and international financial institutions and investment funds."

The names of several dozen banks and investment companies, along with the large numbers listed under each, overwhelmed her, so she turned to the last page. Eyes round, she gasped in shock. "This says there's over a hundred million dollars in these accounts!"

Alan nodded gravely. "Yes, that's correct. That chart summarizes the portion of your aunt's portfolio invested in cash, mutual funds, and stocks. It does not, however, include her real estate holdings, which are also extensive." Quickly flipping through the papers in the folder, the attorney referred her to another set of papers in her own file, entitled Real Estate Holdings.

"Besides the estate and grounds on which the Crossroads sits, your aunt's real estate holdings include full or part interest in residential and commercial buildings and land both here in Sylvan City and in San Antonio and the surrounding area. There are also several international properties, listed on the last page." Referring to the papers in his hand, the attorney mentioned another astronomical number as the worth of her aunt's real estate holdings.

Now mine, it's all now mine, Alex realized, with a growing sense of disbelief and a sharp stab of anxiety.

Professional, but kind eyes fixed on hers, and the attorney summed up. "So, my dear, as you can see, the estate your aunt left in your hands is quite extensive. It will take me several weeks, perhaps longer, to familiarize you with everything so that you have a working knowledge of the depth and breadth of your inheritance, which is one reason I requested you travel to San Antonio."

With a sly look and a self-deprecating chuckle, the attorney added, "Oh, another reason, of course, is so that the goddess could bond you to the Crossroads as its Keeper, in order for you to protect it, and Sylvan City, from the encroaching darkness."

Alex snorted in disbelief. "Well, thanks for that. Not."

Nodding in acceptance of her sarcastic comment, Alan leaned forward with an earnest expression. "Your aunt's concern for you, of course, is the last, but certainly not the least, reason, I requested your presence in San Antonio. Once Maia discovered where you were, she desperately wanted to see you, to assure herself of your health, and to apologize for not being able to stop your mother from stealing you away all those years ago."

He finished his speech with a kindly glare, "Alex, you are wanted, loved—and needed—here, more than you know."

"Well, fuck." Alex slapped her hands on the carved wooden arms of her chair as the bonds of duty, love, and obligation tightened further around her. "You all want to tie me so closely to this damn place, and to all of you, that I can never leave."

She pushed out of her chair and stalked to the door, throwing an apology over her shoulder. "Sorry about the swearing. My aunt says Uncle Vinnie's foul mouth is rubbing off on me again. But I'm pretty sure my swearing is all my own. I need some air."

She hurried from the office, Conor's quiet words to the attorney stoking her temper and quickening her pace.

"I'll catch up with her and ensure she doesn't do anything rash. Can you send these papers over to the estate? I'll have Vinnie sit with her to go over them once she's calmed down."

Alex stomped down the stairs, barely sparing the witchy receptionist a glance as she steamed toward the front door. A hand reached around her and grabbed the brass knob, turning it to open the door in front of her.

An inelegant snort escaped her. "I had a huge lead on you, Conor. How did you reach the door at the same time as me?"

"Supernatural speed. Barghest here, remember?" Conor replied with a grin, as he ushered her into the bright sunlight outside the law firm.

Shielding her eyes against the glare with her hand, Alex looked up to meet Conor's calm, amber gaze. "I'm sorry for the scene back there. I—it's just a lot, you know?" She chuckled darkly. "I seem to say that to you a lot, don't I?"

Conor took her arm to steer her past a goblin taking up more than his share of the sidewalk, before commenting. "Yes, you do. And it's okay. It *is* a lot. For anyone, let alone someone separated from the supernatural world and kept ignorant of her place in it for half her life. But you're strong, smart, and brave. I think you are handling things pretty damn well, all things considered."

Cheeks reddening at Conor's words, Alex shrugged away the compliment. "Thanks for your kind words, but I'm not so sure you should have so much confidence in me. I'm not feeling very strong or smart right now." Shoulders hunched and head down, Alex trailed along in Conor's wake.

~

AFTER A TEN-MINUTE WALK and a thorough study of the different surfaces of Sylvan City's sidewalks and roads, Conor's hand on her arm jerked Alex out of her despondent thoughts. She raised her gaze from the sidewalk, and her eyes fell on an elegant purple sign in the shape of a coffin that swayed from an iron bracket attached to a tall stone building. The sign's flowing golden script exclaimed *O'Connor & Daughters Funeral Parlor.* They had reached their next destination.

"You okay?" Conor asked. "You totally missed the unicorn carriage, as well as the giant squid."

"Unicorn carriage? Giant squid?" Alex shook off her melancholy. A faint stir of her earlier excitement at seeing Sylvan City for the first time returned. She turned wide eyes on Conor. "I missed a unicorn carriage—and a giant squid?"

"Yes, to the unicorn carriage, and no, to the giant squid." Conor chuckled. "I made the squid up. Well, not totally. The lake houses a giant squid, but he almost never comes into town."

"Almost never, huh? But aren't squid saltwater creatures?" Alex frowned in confusion. "Wait, what am I saying—this city is magical, so the lake must be, as well. I imagine a supernatural giant squid could live in the lake if he wanted to."

"Billy the Squid is fifty or sixty feet long and at least several centuries old. No one, not even your Keeper aunt, knows how he made his way from the ocean to the lake, or how he survives in a fresh-water lake." Conor shrugged. "But you're right, it probably has something to do with the magic in this place."

Alex's mind caught on the squid's name, disbelief vying with amusement. "Billy the Squid? Really? Now I know you're just pulling my leg. Right?"

Conor gave her a lopsided grin as he knocked on the bright

purple door of the funeral home. "I'd never lie to you, so no, I'm not making Billy, or his name, up. I'm sure that hasn't always been his name, though. He's an ancient creature. As for the origin of his current moniker, Billy *loves* TV Westerns and country music. He *will* turn up at any Western-themed or country music event held in Sylvan City." He smiled, eyes crinkling in amusement. "And that's probably why no one even mentions Westerns or country music around Billy, or holds events featuring them within the city limits, and hasn't for the last fair few decades. Nobody wants a sixty-foot squid crashing their party."

While Alex digested details of a TV Western and country music loving supernatural squid named Billy, the door underneath the coffin sign flew open, causing Alex to start and swerve her gaze to the opening. At first, she thought magic opened the door, as she didn't see anyone in the doorway. Then she glanced down as an impatient, querulous voice rose to her ears.

A squat, orange-skinned woman with frizzy yellow hair and unnaturally large green eyes glared up at them. "You're late. I'm Greta, the funeral director and general dogsbody around here." Grunting in annoyance, she complained. "How am I supposed to get Mr. Walker ready for the viewing if I have to wait around for you lot? He's going to take an age to get right."

The orange creature shifted her short bulk so they could enter the building, then gestured abruptly for them to follow her to a door on the right side of the well decorated and airy lobby.

Alex and Conor shared an amused glance at the woman's muttered words as she hustled them through the foyer. "I still can't find his left leg. What am I going to tell his wife?"

Grumbling Greta, Alex dubbed her with a secret smile, as she followed the angry orange woman through a doorway into a cluttered office. The cramped space contained a human-sized desk, flanked by chairs of all sizes and shapes.

Greta climbed onto a tall chair behind the desk, settling herself with a final grunt. She gestured vaguely for them to take a seat wherever, then fixed Alex with a stern gaze.

"So, here's the thing. About your late aunt, Maia, I already have a list of her wishes for the funeral. Her attorney sent it over last week. I've got everything in hand, including a choir for the chants, a pavilion tent, catering, and a band for the after-party. So, all I need you to do is pick a coffin and a date."

Mind whirling from Greta's abrupt words, Alex cleared her throat and clarified. "So ... a coffin ... and a date."

After rifling through untidy stacks of paperwork, Greta pulled out a file with unerring precision and slapped it down on the desk with an impatient snap.

"I'm thinking the Dreamwood 750 coffin. It's hand-carved by wood trolls in the forest north of town. Elegant, yet understated. Of course, there's also the Dreamwood 1000, but I think that's a bit too much. Your aunt might object to the gold-plating on the lid and the emerald-encrusted handles." Greta wrinkled her forehead, then nodded decisively. "Seeing as I'm sure her ghost will be in attendance at her own funeral, I don't want to listen to her complain about the 1000 model being too ostentatious. So, it's the Dreamwood 750, agreed? I have one in stock, so that'll work nicely."

With a concerned glance at Alex's stunned face, Conor cut in. "Perhaps you could show us the coffins, Greta, so Alex can decide what her aunt would prefer?"

Alex nodded in agreement with Conor's words. "Yes, please, I'd like to do at least this one thing for her."

Greta hopped off her chair with a huff of frustration and grouched a terse reply. "Alright, but don't say I didn't try to help. There're so many coffins to choose from it'll make your head spin. Could even take you days to decide," she added cryptically.

The woman's short legs hurried them through a narrow door at the back of the office. "I don't have all day. As I already mentioned. Here's the coffin showroom. How about I leave you in here for a bit while I get back to work on Mr. Walker? The coffins are all priced and have descriptions on the tags. Once you've made up your mind, just say so, and I'll be back in a tick."

Greta hurried from the large room before Alex could gather her thoughts. The door to the office slammed shut behind them, and the doorway disappeared, a smooth blank wall in its place. Concern about the disappearance of the exit waned as Alex stared open-mouthed around the huge warehouse-sized space, lined floor to rafters with coffin-sized cubbies, each containing a unique and beautiful coffin. From tiny coffins barely large enough for a doll, to coffins large enough to hold a horse, the high-ceilinged room heaved with hand-crafted body boxes, in styles from plain to pretentious.

The lemony smell of polished wood floated in the air. Dust motes glinted in shafts of light coming from several small, dusty windows high on the far wall. The meagre light from the windows did little to reduce the shadowy gloom filling the vast, coffin-filled space.

Conor fingered a small coffin covered with gemstones, then shot Alex a lop-sided grin. "Now you've done it. Greta doesn't like to be questioned about her expert opinions. We'll be in here until it's time for us to be needing a coffin of our own."

Defensive at the implication she'd intended to insult the orange-haired termagant, Alex sniped a reply. "I wasn't questioning her knowledge, merely attempting to assert some amount of control over the process." A hint of childish petulance laced her last words. "Besides, you asked her first, so *you* actually started it."

Alex eyed a medium-sized coffin covered with carvings that she could swear were moving. "I thought there'd be more to do in the way of planning the funeral. Not that I mind that Aunt Maia took care of almost all the details. It's just that planning the funeral was one of the main reasons for my trip to San Antonio."

Conor gave her a thin, knowing smile. "Both your aunt and Alan are very crafty, in case you haven't already figured that out. They wanted ... needed you here and told you what you expected to hear to make that happen."

"No shit," Alex murmured, distracted by a highly polished oak coffin covered with beautifully carved scenes depicting woodlands and what she recognized as the Sylvan City lake. Then she spotted the carving on one end, which depicted the Crossroads and the graceful temple occupying the cobblestone courtyard at its mid-point. Alex smoothed her hand over the carving with reverence, awed at the lovely craftsmanship.

"This is the one. Aunt Maia will love it." She turned over the tag attached to the handle and snorted in disgust. "It's the Dream-wood 750. Greta was right, damn her." Sighing, Alex groused. "I'm tempted to pick another, just so she doesn't have the satisfaction of knowing she was right. She's going to gloat; I just know it."

Conor joined her in front of the coffin. "But you won't choose a different coffin just to spite Greta, as that would be childish, right?"

Alex nodded her head in defeated agreement. "My aunt will love this one. I can't wait until she sees it. And I so wish I didn't have to choose it—or any other."

Conor called out into the gloom of the coffin room. "Greta, you were right about the coffin! We bow to your greater wisdom. We'll take the Dreamwood 750."

With an amused side-eye, Alex murmured, "Grovel much?"

"I'll do what it takes to get me out of this place before I start feeling the need to measure myself for my own coffin," Conor whispered.

A loud pop sounded from behind them. Startled, Alex whirled around in fright.

Greta appeared in front of them, a triumphant smile wreathing her face. "Told you so." Behind her stood the doorway leading back into her office ... one that hadn't been there only moments ago. She gestured for them to follow her out of the coffin room.

The door to the coffin room closed behind them with a heavy thud. Greta resumed her seat behind the desk. A small, satisfied grin still curved her month.

Alex suspected the impatient woman had enjoyed giving them both a scare by locking them in the coffin room.

"So, last thing I need from you is the date for the funeral. I've got the Friday or Saturday at the end of the month available. The chorus, band, and catering crew are all available for either of those days. Otherwise, it'll be at least another two weeks after that until everyone is available again." Greta eyed Alex with a disgruntled air, her impatience for an answer obvious.

Alex glanced from Greta to Conor. "Uh, I suppose the Saturday evening would work." The date for the funeral was over two weeks away. So much for a quick turnaround and dash out of town. Sigh. She queried Conor, "What do you think? We should have time to notify everyone before then, right?"

"No need to worry about that." Greta reached into the untidy mess on her desk with unerring precision and pulled out a pen and a large, leather-bound appointment book. "I'll put the funeral announcement on the Magicnet. Everyone will have the date and time of the service by this evening. And anyone who is anyone will be there that Saturday." Greta threw Alex an enquiring glare, her pen hovering over the large appointment book, now open on her desk. "Seven o'clock work for you?"

"Uh, that's fine, thank you. Is there anything else I need to do? I mean, besides show up?" Alex devoutly hoped not.

Greta threw her pen down and snapped the appointment book closed. She hopped nimbly off her tall chair and quickly ushered them to the exit. "Nope. I have it all under control. Be here at six o'clock on the day of the funeral, so I can introduce you to the choir and run through procedures with you."

She eyed Alex's short black dress critically. "Make sure you ask someone about appropriate funeral attire for the next Keeper. What you've got on tells me you don't have a clue."

ONCE THE DOOR to the funeral parlor closed firmly behind them, Alex met Conor's gaze and blew out a relieved breath. "I'm so glad that's over. Greta may be incredibly rude, but she seems extremely competent. I'm happy to leave everything to her."

Conor chuckled as he steered Alex up the street. "A wise choice. Most people leave everything to Greta, including her father and sister. It's not surprising that she's a little grumpy, having to run the funeral home mostly on her own."

"A little grumpy?"

"Okay, a lot."

"That reminds me," Alex asked, "I'm assuming it's not polite to ask a supernatural their species, correct? It just seems like it would be rude. That said, what species *is* Greta? And, for that matter, what is Alan? Is he human? He looks it, but I guess you never know."

They drew to a stop in front of a shop window filled with a display of gleaming swords and daggers. Conor perused the deadly display for a few minutes before replying.

"Greta is a river troll. They are a semi-aquatic species and always choose to live near a large body of water." He gave Alex an approving smile. "You are right about Alan, though. He's more than half human. His grandmother was a Light Fae, so he's got some magic and will live a very long time, but he chooses to live as a human." He murmured cryptically, "Mostly."

Alex decided not to press Conor on his last comment. Instead, she asked, "Do you see anything you like?" She blushed furiously when she realized how risqué that sounded. "I mean, in the shop window, you know, the swords and daggers." Her face completely on fire, she realized she was just digging herself a deeper conversational hole. "I'll just shut up now."

Conor burst out laughing, then shook his head at her with a grin. "Alex, you are a joy to be around. I never know what you're going to say next."

"Neither do I," Alex muttered.

"In answer to your question, I have no need of swords or daggers." A feral gleam entered Conor's bright amber eyes. "My claws and teeth, in Barghest form, do the job just fine."

I just bet they do, thought Alex with a visceral shiver.

Conor led Alex toward several interesting-looking shops. "Greta's right. You probably don't have anything appropriate to wear for the funeral. Time to make you very happy and do some clothes shopping. I imagine your wardrobe is rather sparse, since you weren't planning on being in San Antonio for more than a few days, so feel free to go wild."

Alex pursed her lips and shot Conor a disapproving frown. "It's sexist to assume shopping makes a woman happy, Conor. However, considering two things, I'll overlook the blatant misogyny in your remark."

With a nervous side-eye, Conor asked, "What two things?"

"Well, first, since you are an old man—at 250 plus years old, a *very* old man, I'll give you a break because of your age. Being a historian, I'm fully aware sexism was rife two-plus centuries ago."

Conor winced and dramatically clutched his heart. "Ouch, that stings. You're right, but it still stings." He gave her a mock-hurt look. "Besides, I like to think I've moved with the times. I renounced sexism a long time ago."

"When? Ten years ago ... fifteen?" Alex sniggered.

"No, actually, it was the summer of 1798, in Scotland, when a coven of witches outsmarted me, tied me to their altar, and were about to slit my throat as a sacrifice to their dark goddess."

Sobered, Alex asked, "So, how did you get away?"

"My Crossroads Keeper galloped in on her trusty steed and single-handedly handed the witches their proverbial asses." Chagrin and reluctant amusement vied for dominance on Conor's face. "Once she finished laughing at my ignominious pose, she untied me and helped me off the altar. I rode back to the Cross-roads slung across her horse."

Alex giggled at the image of Conor as an opposite-gendered damsel in distress, having to be saved by a dashing, and very female, hero. "Oh, that's hilarious! I can see where that quite punc-tured your ego and undermined your misogyny."

"It did that." Conor chuckled wryly. "Ever since then, I give women all the power and respect they are due. Always." He hesi-tated, giving Alex a nervous side eye before asking, "What's the second reason you're willing to overlook my sexist comment about women and shopping? Or do I not want to know?"

Her lips curved in an evil smile. Alex hooked Conor's arm with hers and pulled him toward the brightly lit shops. "Because *this* woman happens to enjoy shopping. It makes me happy, especially now that I can afford it. So, let's go."

18

MAGICAL BOOT CAMP

Conor steered the car through the estate's small back gate just as the sky darkened toward sunset. A grueling afternoon of shopping, then a light dinner in a cute little Sylvan City cafe called Soups & Sips left Alex dozing in the front seat. She startled upright at a light touch from Conor.

"We're home, sleepyhead."

After helping Alex carry her many shopping bags up to her room, Conor retreated, saying he needed time to plan her physical training in the morning.

Just great, Alex mused glumly, *a magical beating tonight and a physical one in the morning.* She hurriedly changed into workout gear, then trotted toward the old stables for her evening of magical Keeper training with her aunt.

A pattering of poodle feet sounded behind her. Alex sighed in relief, then smiled down at her canine companion when he joined her on the path.

"I'm reporting for Familiar duty." Larry explained. His muzzle opened in a doggie smirk. *"Had a delightful afternoon in town with your Barghest?"*

"Once again, he is *not* my Barghest, you furry pain in my—"

Larry interrupted. *"I wouldn't finish that sentence if I were you. Not unless you want me to—"*

Alex groaned. "I know, I know, you'll crap in my shoes. But you promised not to do that for at least a month, remember?"

Larry sniffed. *"Circumstances change."*

As ALEX APPROACHED THE STABLES, the murmur of many voices reached her ears, signaling a sizeable audience had gathered to watch her embarrassing attempts at magic. "Well fuck," she whispered under her breath.

"I heard that." Larry grinned his taunt at her. *"And if I did, I can guarantee that your aunt did, as well as everyone else inside. Supernatural hearing, remember?"*

Alex resisted the urge to swear a complete sentence. She realized the desire came from frustration at her lack of magical aptitude. Sighing, she stepped through the barn door into the large open space once occupied by an equine training ring. The arena still smelled faintly of horse and sweat.

She paused in surprise, then peered nervously at the supernatural crowd arrayed on the viewing benches around the arena. As one, they greeted her. "Hello, Keeper!" Several waved hands, claws, or tentacles in greeting.

A massive luminescent blue squid sprawled his long tentacles along one entire wall of the arena. Alex eyed the huge supernatural creature in awe. So *that's* Billy the Squid, she mused, suppressing a delighted grin. The human-sized cowboy hat perched precariously on top of Billy's enormous head made his presence less intimidating than it might otherwise have been.

Someone waved wildly at Alex from the back of the audience arrayed on the bleachers. She raised her hand to return the gesture. With a start, she realized the enthusiastic waver was Chris, the Dark Fae she saw on her first visit to Sylvan City. He had been helping a satyr mom with a stroller across the street. She recalled

Conor's earlier words. 'Chris is a helper. He's a nice guy.' Judging from the bright smile he was wearing as he continued to wave a welcome, Alex agreed with Conor's assessment of the Dark Fae.

Alex turned her wave to Chris into a general wave to encompass the entire audience. "Uh, hi, everyone. Nice to meet you all." Her awkward greeting to the assembly complete, Alex fixed her gaze on the familiar trio gathered in the center of the training ring, a sharp question in her eyes.

Conor nodded to his two companions, then stepped forward. He met Alex's irritated gaze, his amber eyes dark with an unspoken apology.

"Uh, hi, Alex. Maia, Vinnie, and I thought it might help if you met the supernatural posse sooner rather than later. Almost everyone here is a member of the posse. They are all dedicated to protecting the Crossroads and its supernatural community. We haven't had to call the posse together for half a century. In case you don't remember, Hecate asked me to call the posse to duty to help us—and you fight the danger we now face."

"Nice speech." Alex couldn't keep the sarcasm from her voice. "Thanks for giving me a head's up about meeting the posse tonight when I saw you half an hour ago. You know, when you told me you'd see me in the morning."

Vinnie stepped up to Conor's side, a placating hand raised toward her. "Alex, Maia, and I asked Conor not to tell you about meeting the posse tonight. We thought it might make you nervous if you knew in advance."

Alex narrowed her eyes and growled. "So, you thought it would be better just to blindside me with everyone at once? What, were you afraid I'd turn tail and run back home to Connecticut?"

When Vinnie winced and shared a pained look with her aunt, Alex regretted her harsh words, but she didn't apologize. That would let them off the hook for throwing her in at the deep end of the supernatural. Not just tonight, with the posse, but from the first moment of her arrival. Vexed, she realized she resented her heart-family for their assumption that acceptance of the supernatural world would come naturally to her. Everyone seemed to take for granted that her physical return to the Crossroads, and the unblocking of her memory, meant she was ready to throw herself whole-heartedly into the supernatural world and take up her Keeper duties.

Alex glared at the now decidedly nervous-looking trio. "I'm here now. And, as I've told you before, I'm committed to helping you all defend the Crossroads against the current threat. After that, we'll see." With a small smile, she gave a queenly wave of her hand. "Shall we get on with the training?"

Conor appeared at Alex's side, startling her. "Would you please not do that? I'm going to put a bell on you if you keep it up."

"Sorry, sweets—um, Alex." Connor dipped his head in apology, gazing up at her from beneath his thick black lashes.

"And don't do that, either. Cute looks won't get you anywhere with me." Silently, Alex admitted to herself that they just might, if she wasn't very careful.

"Apologies again," Conor said with a grin and a wink. He took her arm and steered her toward the viewing benches. "Since you're here now, and so is the posse, why don't we make some introductions?"

They drew to a stop in front of the closest group, and Conor began the introductions. "I'm sure you remember Greta from the funeral home. Seated behind her is Chris. You might remember him helping Stella, the satyr sitting next to him, with her baby stroller earlier today?"

Conor took Alex's nod as a signal to continue and introduced another dozen supernaturals. Alex promptly forgot the names of most. She was never good at remembering people, but a few individuals stood out. Abel, the leader of Vinnie's blood harem, was there, his blue-eyed gaze intense enough to feel. Other members of Vinnie's harem and staff were also present. Each dipped their head respectfully when introduced. Alex smiled at the attendees of the ghostly poker game, who formed a tight group, hovering above narrow wooden benches toward the back of the risers.

Queen Elizabeth bestowed a regal nod on Alex. Crazy Jack cackled and waved wildly before swooping up to perch on a rafter high above, still waving maniacally. Grenoble the goblin gave her a blank stare, then a slow tip of his chin, which unnerved her slightly.

As they approached the enormous squid ranged against the far wall, Conor's amused gaze met hers. "And, last but certainly not least, this is Billy the Squid."

While giving a small finger-wave to the huge squid, Alex eyed the cowboy hat perched ridiculously on his massive head in fascination. Before she could stop it, her mouth ran away from her. Again. "Love the hat." *Can't stop that mouth for nothing,* thought Alex with an inward cringe.

Billy bent his massive head, regarding her solemnly from one huge, round chocolate-brown eye. One of his tentacles reached up and gently nudged his cowboy hat, tipping it at an even more rakish angle. A deep voice resonated around the arena, seeming to come from nowhere and everywhere. "Thanks, Alex. It's my lucky hat. Figured we might need some luck."

No shit, Alex thought, as she nodded to acknowledge the squid's words. *Luck would sure as hell come in handy right now.*

Conor murmured in her ear. "The posse is expecting a few words from you."

"I can think of a few words for you lot blindsiding me like this."

"Not those words."

Fuck. Alex closed her eyes and drew in a deep breath, trying to calm and center herself. She hated public speaking. Always had.

"Time to pull up your big girl pants and address the posse, Alex. There's no popcorn at tonight's performance, so the crowd deserves at least a few words from the star attraction." Larry's snarky comment filtered into her mind.

Strangely, her furry Familiar's words fortified her. Alex turned to face the assembled posse, who sat attentively in their seats, their collective gaze fixed on her face. "Hello everyone. Thank you all for coming. I'm not sure how much Conor and company shared with you about the current danger, but we need your help, or this Crossroads may not survive. Hecate tells me we face one or more gods who wish to use the Crossroads for a nefarious purpose. She is working in the In-Between to discover who they are and what they plan, but in the meantime, we have to do some investigating on our end."

Alex drew in another deep, steadying breath, took the time to meet everyone's eyes directly, then finished her impromptu speech. "We also need to protect this side of the Crossroads, figure out why random body parts are appearing here, and find out if my aunt's murder-by-magic relates to her investigation of the current situation. It's a lot, I know. I ... we would really appreciate your help, so we can get to the bottom of this mess and fix things."

Heads nodded, accompanied by murmurs of agreement. Alex realized most of those present were already aware of the danger facing the Crossroads. A wave of appreciation and thanks flowed through her as she realized Hecate had been right to ask Conor to activate the posse. She needed all the help she could get if she was going to get out of this alive, much less be able to return to her independent, if lonely, life in New England.

Alex admitted to herself the strange dichotomy of being glad to have a team of helpers now, only to want to abandon them once the current danger passed, but she couldn't help her conflicted feelings.

A LOUD THUMP by her leg startled Alex out of her confused reverie. The Keeper staff now lay on the ground by her feet. Alex bent down and grasped the smooth wood of the staff, unintentionally caressing it as she straightened. She held the staff horizontally in both hands and spread her feet, planting them firmly on the packed dirt of the ring, and waited for the first attack of the training session.

"Let your magic connect with the magic in the staff." Maia's voice rang out, echoing off the walls of the huge arena. "Feel the staff communicate your next defensive move and make it."

Sure, Alex mused glumly, *like it's easy to mind-meld with a wooden stick that talks.* She concentrated on the staff, trying to sense its energy. Nothing. Damn it.

Larry's deep voice in her mind encouraged her. *"Just relax and feel the hum deep inside your belly. That hum is your magical energy. I'll amplify it so you can use it to connect with the staff."* Larry leaned supportively against her leg, a golden glow surrounding his body.

Alex shivered. Larry's magic scratched against her skin as it sought a way inside. She closed her eyes, attempting to feel the hum Larry spoke of, reaching deep down inside, but finding nothing within which equated to her concept of magic. Her knuckles whitened as her grip on the Keeper staff tightened. Frustrated, she wondered if she could choke the damn thing into submission by squeezing out the staff's magical power.

Just as she was about to give up yet again, her feet left the ground. Panicked, her eyes flew open and fastened on the huge blue tentacle wrapped around her waist. She choked a scream as her body dangled in mid-air. Billy's tentacle tightened, leaving her gasping for air as he raised her even higher.

Alex glimpsed Crazy Jack roosting on a rafter below her and realized Billy's tentacle had raised her almost to the roof of the tall structure. If she didn't die from the fall, she reflected grimly, getting her head battered on the roof would do the trick. *Then* she'd fall.

The web of rafters below her filled Alex with a wild hope. Maybe she could grab onto a rafter on the way down—if she could get Billy to release his ever-tightening grip.

Desperate, Alex took unthinking action. She pointed the head of her staff at the cowboy hat perched on Billy's head far below and imagined power streaming out of the crystal set between the ornately carved tips of the crescent moon. Enough power to shock Billy into releasing her.

A red flame of magic came roaring up from her very soul, causing a searing agony that almost made her lose her grip on the staff. Alex screamed as she felt answering blue flames flicker from the head of the staff. The red and blue flames met, danced, and joined, creating another flare of pain as the power arced between her hands and the staff. It took all her dwindling reserves of strength to point the flaming staff at Billy's ridiculous hat and issue a command. "Stop! Let me go!"

A flare of red-blue fire shot from the end of the staff, streamed through the air, and hit Billy's cowboy hat dead center. A bright flash of flames consumed the hat. The last thing Alex remembered was a booming voice echoing in her head. "She smoked my lucky hat!"

ALEX AWOKE SLOWLY. Soft voices murmured above her head. *Do you think she's okay? Boy, that was a lot of power! Yes, but can she harness it? She's going to be sore in the morning.* A gentle hand touched her cheek, and a voice she recognized as Conor's asked, "Alex, can you hear me? Are you alright?"

Gingerly, Alex peeled her eyelids open and squinted at the bright lights above. Conor's worried face hovered above her, and she frowned in confusion. "I can hear you. I think I'm okay, but I haven't tried to move anything yet, so that may not be my final answer. What happened? Last thing I remember—oh, shit!" Her memory came flooding back, and she jerked upright.

Her eyes darted around wildly. "Is Billy okay? I didn't light him on fire, did I? How did I not fall ... or did I fall? How did I not break any bones? Or die?"

Before Conor could answer, the surrounding crowd parted, and a huge blue form hove into view. Tentacles fanned out on the ground around the creature. Several of the squid's huge appendages waved slowly in the air over Alex's head. Billy focused an excited chocolate-brown eye on her, and, if a squid could grin, then Billy was grinning madly.

"It worked! I figured you might need to feel you were in danger in order to access your powers for the first time. Humans call it the fight-or-flight reflex. Billy's deep, gleeful, laughter caused the ground to rumble. "I made you fight while taking flight—and you found your power!" The squid's huge brown eye peered down at Alex in pleased satisfaction. "Oh, and don't worry about flaming my lucky hat. Gives me an excuse to buy a new one I've had my eye on for a while."

Alex took a deep breath and counted to ten, then did it again. Once her anger cooled, she fixed Billy with a determined glare. "Thanks for being understanding about your hat, Billy." But if you ever tentacle me again, we are going to have words—and maybe more flames."

Conor edged between Alex and Billy, giving the squid a meaningful glare before holding out his hand to help Alex up from the dirt of the ring. As Alex got shakily to her feet, Conor speared Billy with a withering look. "There was probably another way we could have helped Alex access her power, instead of scaring her half to death, Billy."

"You're right, but my way was quicker." Billy rumbled, a hint of nervousness entering his gaze as he eyed Conor. "And it's done now, so how about we let bygones be bygones. We could even—"

Alex interrupted, including both Conor and Billy in her forceful response. "Yes, let's all do that. But first, how did I get back down to the ground in one piece? The last thing I remember is being up near the roof, which has to be thirty or forty feet high."

Billy gave Conor a wary side-eye before answering Alex's question. "Besides toasting my hat, your power gave me a good jolt, Keeper, but I held on to you long enough to get you close to the ground before releasing you."

"How close?"

"About five feet."

Alex gingerly stretched and tested each limb, thanking the

goddess when she encountered a general soreness, but no actual pain.

"Okay, Billy." Alex pinned the giant squid with a narrow-eyed glare. "I'll agree to let bygones be bygones. Just, please, no more tentacle rides, alright?" She hesitated, realizing a thank you was due, even if a grudging one. "And thank you for helping me access my power, even if your method leaves a lot to be desired."

The squid hung his giant head and shuffled his tentacles sheepishly along the ground. "No more tentacle rides, Keeper. I promise. And you are welcome."

Conor glanced over at the rest of the posse. They huddled together near the arena door, whispering amongst themselves. "Okay, that's enough for tonight, everyone. Greta and Chris, can you two stay behind? Everyone else, let's meet again tomorrow night, same time."

As the rest of the posse disbursed, Greta and Chris joined the group in the center of the arena.

Greta and Chris moved to join them, carefully threading their way through Billy's writhing tentacles. Once they reached the group, Greta spoke first. "I take it we have first watch at the Cross-roads tonight, Barghest."

Chris nodded acceptance of his role on first watch with Greta. "We'll inform you immediately if anything happens."

"Yes, thanks you two. Vinnie and I will relieve you in four hours." Conor looked up at Billy. "If you could keep an eye on the gate into Sylvan City tonight, I would appreciate it."

"Will do. I can see the gate and the road leading into the city clearly from the lake. I'll alert you if I see anything suspicious."

Bone weary, not having words left for anyone, Alex moved to exit the arena, planning to trek back to her room at a slow shuffle. A slight breeze wafted behind her before Conor's powerful arms whisked her off her feet. Her first impulse was to fight to be put down and insist on walking back to her room on her own, but fatigue overcame her desire to assert her independence, and she sank down into Conor's embrace, closing her eyes with a sigh. "Thanks, Conor."

"No problem, sweets. I'm sure you must be exhausted after using so much power." Conor strode up the path toward the carriage house, carrying her weight effortlessly.

As Alex slipped into sleep, lulled by the smooth cadence of Conor's gait, she could swear Larry snorted in amusement.

THAT NIGHT, the gray mist came for Alex again, only this time she had help fighting it before it could pull her into a nightmare land from which she suspected she might not escape. Conor's arms wrapped tightly around her, and his insistent voice called her back. "Alex, honey, come back to me. It's okay, it's going to be okay. Fight it, Alex. Wake up! Please!"

The gray mist attacked Alex every night after that. Conor moved a cot into her room and slept there each night. Members of the posse took turns guarding the Crossroads around the clock.

The mist came for Hecate each night as well. Posse members took turns guarding the In-Between. At least two posse members remained there with Hecate at all times. The goddesses, Demeter and Persephone, both spent time there, as well, strategizing with Hecate while discreetly providing protection in triple goddess numbers and power.

The nightmarish gray mist approached Alex's aunt several times. However, the ever alert and powerful posse guard assigned to her had powerful defensive magic and were able to block it each time. The irate ghost maintained she had no need of such babysitting and grew ever more irritated with the posse's protection.

Groggy from lack of sleep, terrified that her slowly developing skills and power would not be enough to win this battle, Alex doggedly continued her training.

She ran and swam and practiced martial arts with Conor during the day. She worked magic with her aunt and the members of the posse each evening. Her control over her magic became more balanced, and her connection with the Keeper staff consistent. She may have scorched another one of Billy's cowboy hats and burned a hole in Greta's cape, but she hadn't hurt anyone. Yet.

OVER THE COURSE of the next two weeks, Alex realized she was growing stronger, both physically and magically. She might not be quite ready for the coming battle, but she was heading in the right direction, and faster than seemed natural.

After a grueling bout of Krav Maga in the estate's gym, during which Alex pinned Conor to the mat, if only for a few seconds, she gathered her courage to ask for his opinion. As they both lay gasping and sweating, she asked, "I feel like I'm making progress much faster than is normal, or am I just giving myself too much credit?"

Conor hesitated, staring up at the metal beams over their heads for several seconds before turning his head to meet her gaze. "Alex, I'm aware that you like to think of yourself as human, as that's the way you were raised after you were … taken from here, but you're not. Keepers are a type of supernatural, just like Barghests, goblins, trolls, even vampires. Some of us look more human than others. Some even pretend to be more human than they are, but we're not. You're not. Your supernatural heritage gives you faster reflexes, faster healing, powerful magic, and so much more."

Conor gently brushed Alex's hair back from her forehead, then settled his hand on her shoulder. "Maia's history lesson surely taught you that Hecate created Keepers millennia ago to act as her emissaries on Earth. Remember, back when the Crossroads were first formed, gods were the primary users. Do you really think a mere human could act as a ley line guide and Crossroads Keeper for the gods?"

Alex's mind rebelled at Conor's words. "But I thought. I didn't know that I—that Keepers, aren't human. I've always thought of myself as human. I don't know how not to." She sighed in dismay.

"I understand. It's got to be difficult for you. But you need to come to terms with your supernatural heritage and master your powers." Grimly, Conor added, "You will need all of your supernatural strength if we are going to win this battle."

19

PASSING THE TORCH

The day of her aunt's funeral, Alex arrived at the funeral home early. Greta's stern glare implied she was late as she hurried them through the huge white pavilion tent set up behind the funeral home.

The large, covered space heaved with busy workers. Greta paused to issue last-minute instructions to the caterer, giving Alex time to stare in awe at the elaborate preparations for the after party.

Greta's sharp voice penetrated Alex's reverie. "Pay attention, Keeper. The food's made to your aunt's specifications. It will be served here in the pavilion directly after the funeral service. Once the funeral is over, you will lead the procession up the bank from the lake to the pavilion. Don't trip, and don't go too fast, so we don't have anyone breaking a leg on the way."

A sharp poke from Greta's bony finger urged Alex forward. "Let's go. We need to get down to the stage by the lake, so I can introduce you to the choir and show you where to stand for your part in the service."

Alex held her sword scabbard against her leg to prevent it from banging painfully against her knee and concentrated on not tripping on the long, draped robes she wore as they speed-walked down the gentle slope to the lake shore. She silently reviewed the instructions Greta had issued, then her brain caught up with Greta's last words. "Wait, what part in the service? No one told me I'd be doing more than attending. I thought Conor was going to give the eulogy."

Greta gave Alex a harried glare. Her curt reply cut off when Alex tripped on her long robe as they stepped off the gravel path onto the uneven ground of the lake-side field. The powerful river troll grabbed Alex's arm just in time to save her from face-planting in the lush grass of the field.

Alex realized she needed to stay on Greta's good side if she had any hope of getting through her aunt's funeral without embarrassing herself. Or her aunt. "Thanks for saving me from that fall, Greta. I appreciate it. And I really am paying attention. That's why I asked you about my part in the ceremony."

"Can't have the star attraction with a broken ankle or grass stains all over her robes, now, can we? Pay attention, Alex. And try to stay on your feet from here on out."

Greta rolled her protuberant eyes and snorted in frustration. "Of course, you have a major part in the ceremony. You are Hecate's next chosen Keeper now that your aunt has passed away. The goddess bound you to the Crossroads several weeks ago in a private ceremony, however, you are Keeper of more than just the Crossroads. The supernatural community of Sylvan City is under your care, as well. Of course, there must be a public ceremony, both so the town can bid farewell to your aunt's mortal remains and so you, as the new Keeper, can receive the Charge of the City."

Greta shook her head and mumbled under her breath as she led Alex through rows of chairs arranged in front of a large stage, which was set up next to the lake shore.

As they approached the stage, Alex noticed stairs leading from the stage to a floating pier, which jutted out into the lake's placid surface. Bobbing next to the pier was a low, wide, raft-like wooden boat. Ornately carved dragon heads rose gracefully into the sky from each curved end, fore and aft. Carefully stacked logs filled the bottom of the vessel. Strapped to the top of the log platform sat what Alex recognized as her aunt's Dreamwood 750 coffin.

What the hell, Alex thought. Aloud, she asked Greta, "So, this is going to be like a sort of Viking funeral, where my aunt's body— um, the deceased—floats out into the water on the burning boat?"

They left the many rows of chairs behind, then approached the stage. Alex craned her head to view the top of the platform and saw supernaturals in choir robes milling about, chatting quietly amongst themselves while eyeing her curiously.

Greta led Alex around the side of the stage, then pulled her to a stop next to a set of steep steps. "Where do you think the Vikings got the idea for ritual fire-funerals from, Alex? This ceremony stretches back millennia, right to the creation of the Crossroads, when funeral pyres were commonplace."

"Oh." Alex rubbed her forehead wearily, frustrated by her lack of knowledge of the supernatural in general, and Keeper lore in particular. As she followed Greta up the wooden steps and onto the stage, she reflected with dismay that, since her arrival back in San Antonio and reintroduction to the supernatural, she'd never felt both so out of place and at home at the same time.

A sharp whistle shocked Alex out of her reverie. She swung her gaze to the source of the sound.

Greta lowered three fingers from her mouth and grinned at Alex. "Your aunt taught me to whistle like that. Comes in handy when trying to organize supernatural funerals."

The river troll raised her voice to address the choir, now standing in orderly rows on the stage. "Alright, everyone, time to get to work. This here is Alexandria, our new Keeper. I'm going to talk her through the ceremony, but I'd like her to hear the first few bars of your chant first, so she can get an idea of your volume, since she'll have to talk over it in some parts."

The members of the choir nodded their heads respectfully at

Alex, then collectively drew in a breath. The choir conductor raised her hands, then sharply pulled them down. A low, whispered collection of voices tickled Alex's ears. As the conductor continued to gesture, the choir's volume rose and dropped in an Otherworldly harmony unlike anything Alex had heard before. The hair on her arms rose, and her skin broke out in goosebumps as the unearthly chant reverberated in her bones. *Home*, she thought—and felt.

The chant broke off abruptly when the choir director moved her hands in a slashing motion. She turned around, eyes fastened on Alex for approval. Alex realized with a start that the director was the satyr mother she'd seen having trouble with a baby stroller on her first visit to Sylvan City.

"Hello, Keeper. My name is Stella. I am honored to meet you." The conductor fingered the long robes hiding her goat-like legs and hooves, her liquid eyes filled with sympathy. "We are all so sorry for your loss. Most of us were acquainted with your aunt and mourn her passing."

Alex nodded her thanks, then opened her mouth to offer a reply, but Greta cut her off. The troll propelled her toward the front of the stage, where a beautifully carved wooden podium sat facing the chairs in the field. A long altar table stretched behind the podium. Upon an intricately embroidered altar cloth sat candles in tall brass holders, along with a chalice and several other ritual implements Alex didn't recognize.

Greta pointed to the top of the podium. "I've taped a cheat sheet right here, so you know what to say, and when to light the altar candles and do the other ritual stuff. I'll signal when it's your turn to come up on stage."

A recess on the podium's polished surface featured a crystal vase containing a single stark white lily. Greta pointed at the vase. "Speak directly into the lily, Keeper. It's enchanted and will work to amplify your voice to the crowd."

After whipping Alex through a brief explanation of the items on the altar, Greta directed her attention to a set of steep stairs on the far side of the stage. "Once you've said your piece, lit the candles, and done the rest of the ritual stuff, it'll be time to light the funeral pyre. Those steps lead to the pier. There'll be helpers ready on the pier with a torch for you. Once the pyre is burning well, they will push the boat out into the lake. You'll remain on the pier as the boat burns while the choir performs the Parting Chant." Greta finished her lecture with a firm nod. "Got it?"

Alex mutely nodded back.

Greta led Alex back toward the funeral home, explaining it was now time for her to greet the arriving guests. "Just be yourself," Greta counseled. "Nod a lot. Shake hands, paws, tentacles, whatever, and keep the line moving. We're expecting most of the town to attend, so we'll be on a tight schedule."

THE NEXT HOUR went by in a blur as Alex nodded her head and shook the various offered appendages. She accepted a multitude of condolences, but knew she'd never remember half of them. Words and faces all blended together in her tired mind.

"You alright?" Conor asked. He had stationed himself at her side once the first guests appeared. His solid presence comforted her as she interacted with more individuals in one night than she ever had in her life. Her mind boggled at the variety of supernaturals she met, as well as the many humans in attendance.

"I'm fine, thanks. I think the last of the guests have arrived, so that's good. Will you be with me for the funeral service, too?" Alex asked in a hope-filled whisper.

Conor smiled and shook his head. "Sorry, sweets. I'll get you to the stage, but you're on your own for a major part of the service. As the new Keeper, town residents must see that you're to handle the ceremony on your own."

"Right," Alex muttered with barely contained sarcasm, "it's all on me. *Again*."

Two short figures, one furry and one green, raced inside the door just before Conor closed it. Ragged breathing testified to their hurried journey from somewhere.

Conor eyed the two latecomers, his brows lowered in annoyance. "Larry, Grenoble, glad you two could make it."

Larry pranced to Alex's side. He leaned his warm, furry body against her leg, panting heavily. Alex reached down and petted the soft, curly fur on his head. "You okay, furball?"

Larry nodded. *"Yep."*

Grenoble faced Alex, then executed a small, rather formal bow. "Keeper Alexandria. I am sorry for your loss. Your aunt was a true Keeper. I mourn her passing. I now formally recognize you as the new Keeper of the San Antonio and Sylvan City Crossroads and offer my full allegiance."

"Uh, thank you, Grenoble." Alex stuttered her reply, touched by the sincerity of Grenoble's words.

Larry's breathing had evened out, and he nuzzled Alex comfortingly. "We only came to offer our condolences. We have first watch at the Crossroads, so we'll be heading back there now. I'll see you after the funeral, at the after party. I hear the food is going to be amazing."

The two unlikely friends left as quickly as they had arrived. Alex met Conor's gaze and sighed. "I hope those two don't get up to any mischief."

Conor quirked a brow. "Surprisingly enough, Grenoble is a great watchman. I'm sure he'll teach Larry well. No promises on their behavior at the after party, though."

All heads turned toward the back doors as a sharp whistle cut through the air. Greta finished her whistle, then issued instructions to the crowd. "Okay, everyone, time to head down to the lake for the funeral ceremony." She directed the flow of bodies with skill. "This way. No crowding now, but let's hurry up and get down there, so we can get the ceremony underway."

The assembled supernaturals and humans followed Greta's

direction, filing obediently out of the wide French doors and onto the path leading to the lakeside venue.

Alex heaved a deep breath, set her shoulders, and followed at the back of the line.

"You better get a move on." Maia's familiar voice spoke from beside Alex as her translucent form took shape. She chuckled when Alex started at her chill touch. "Come on, dear. I'll walk down to the field with you, but let's hurry." With an inelegant snort, her aunt added, "I don't want to be late to my funeral."

The next hour passed in a blur for Alex. She did what Greta directed her to do, sitting, standing, speaking, and conducting the ritual on queue. Her aunt's ghostly presence, which hovered over a seat reserved for her right in front of the stage, was a comfort. Alex spoke the ceremony's ending words into the white lily on the podium, smiling in relief and accomplishment when her aunt nodded in approbation.

The choir began the song preceding the Parting Chant. Alex dreaded the next part of the service. Reluctantly, she trudged toward the wooden steps leading to the pier. Before descending, Alex observed the scene below. On the pier stood three very tall, blue-skinned men, each clad in leather and metal armor. Each held a large torch topped with dancing yellow-gold flames. The funeral boat bearing her aunt's coffin bobbed gently in the water, its near side bumping up against the tires edging the pier.

Tears welled as Alex descended the steps, momentarily blinding her and causing her to hesitate on the last step. Maia floated onto the pier ahead of her. She paused next to the closest warrior and gestured for Alex to join her. "Come, dear, it's time for all of us, including me, to bid farewell to my earthly body."

Alex nodded, then dashed away her tears and joined her aunt. "It's the smoke from the torches, I couldn't see for a moment."

Maia gave Alex a searching look before turning to the closest warrior, who bowed his head and spoke in a rough voice. "Keeper Maia, we grieve your loss."

"Thank you, Tyre. You have been a good friend and an able ally. I ask that you give my niece your allegiance in my stead."

The warrior's eyes met Alex's, his a well of grief. "Keeper Alexandria, we honor you as Hecate's chosen priestess. You have the allegiance of the Indigo Fae."

A blue wisp of magic wove around each of the men before twining around Alex. The crescent moon pendant around her neck warmed and glowed faintly blue. The warriors' grief at the loss of her aunt pierced her soul. She gasped at the sudden psychic connection. Yet another magical bond snapped into place.

Alex took the flaming torch Tyre held out, raising it aloft as she stepped to the edge of the pier near the middle of the boat. The warriors on either end of the boat mirrored her movements.

"Now!" Tyre gave a guttural yell, ending on an ululation echoed by the other two warriors.

As one, Alex and the warriors touched their torches to the kindling under the logs stacked under Maia's coffin. The dancing yellow gold flames lit the kindling immediately, then hungrily reached for the logs above.

The dark water under the boat roiled as a massive tentacle appeared and coiled itself around the wooden dragon at the stern. Gently, the tentacle pulled the burning boat away from the pier, toward the middle of the lake. Golden yellow tongues of fire licked at the coffin atop the funeral pyre and reflected on the lake's surface, making the waves in the boat's wake appear aflame.

Alex wept for her aunt's loss a second time, as she had as a child. She watched the flames consume the coffin and, finally, the boat on which it sat. The Parting Chant sung by the choir reached a crescendo, then broke off abruptly, as the boat broke apart in a shower of golden red sparks.

The blackened pieces slipped beneath the water, and the waves settled into stillness after consuming the boat's last flames. Darkness again covered the lake's surface.

Alex was halfway along the pier, heading to the stairs leading up to the stage, when an urgent shout shattered the air. The call came from the top of the bank, near the white shadow of the party pavilion. "Attack! We're under attack!" The voice cut off with a scream of pain before going silent. On the bank above, pounding footsteps accompanied cries of anger and pain. Sharp explosions shattered the air, accompanied by the percussion of gunshots and the whizz of arrows.

The battle had arrived.

20

A NIGHTMARE BEGINS

Alex pounded up the stairs and back onto the stage so she could see the battle and prepare to join it. The Indigo Fae warriors followed close behind, then ran past her before leaping off the stage and running up the slope toward the fighting.

The choir huddled together at the back of the stage, faces slack with shock and confusion. Alex ushered them down the steps. "Take cover, folks. Or if you have the skills, join the battle."

A heavy thud, followed by the sound of claws scrabbling on the wooden planks of the stage, sent Alex's heart into overdrive. She unsheathed her sword and spun toward the sound, then expelled a sigh of relief at the sight of an enormous black dog.

Alex met Conor's familiar amber eyes, now set over the muzzle of his Barghest form. Growling, Conor positioned himself between Alex and the fighting raging around the pavilion near the funeral home.

A much smaller white dog with very pink ears rocketed onto the stage, claws scrabbling as he tried to halt his momentum. Larry slid into Conor's furry flank, which stopped his graceless slide, but toppled him onto his back.

Conor growled in irritation at the furry projectile. "What are you doing here? You're supposed to be guarding the Crossroads. Where's Grenoble?"

Larry scrambled to his feet, panting. *"Sorry, Conor. In a hurry. Got news. Bad guys made it through the Crossroads."*

"No shit?" Alex flicked a glance at the fighting. The battle was moving down the slope toward the field. And the stage.

"Report, Familiar. What happened?" Conor snapped at Larry.

Larry stood to attention, his four paws evenly placed, his head high, then he mind-spoke his report. *"Grenoble and I were on first watch back at the Crossroads. We spotted movement, then saw a crapload of dead-but-not humans appearing out of thin air in front of the temple. Most of them were bleeding."*

Lip curled in disgust, Larry added, *"Judging by the non-attached body parts accompanying them, many of them lost a body part or two on their way through the In-Between. They attacked as soon as they saw us. The Fae guards held them off so Grenoble and I could get here and warn you. Grenoble can use the ley lines, so he transported us to the Sylvan City gate, then we hoofed it here. These idiots beat us here, some-how. They're really freaking fast—for dead guys."*

Alex studied the melee of supernaturals and attackers fighting outside the pavilion. Confusion fought with dread in the pit of her stomach. "They sure as hell don't look dead to me. They fight like wild things, even with missing parts."

"We can argue about this after we win the battle. Once they are really, truly dead."

Extending her arm, Alex called her Keeper staff, hoping like hell it responded. She'd done this successfully only a few times in training. She heaved a sigh of relief when the hard wooden length of the staff smacked into her hand.

The podium, Alex thought. She strode across the stage, then pushed her face up to the fragrant lily on top, praying its ampli-fying enchantment still worked, grateful when it did.

Most of the funeral attendees had risen from their seats. Some hid behind chairs, clutching their children, while others pulled their weapons, preparing to fight.

"Everyone, we're under attack by beings who traveled here through the In-Between. Some are wounded from their journey, and, ah, they may actually be dead, but they can still fight like hell. We need all posse members and others who can fight to work together and destroy these things. Can someone round up the children and infirm and get them somewhere safe? Everyone else, please head up toward the pavilion with whatever weapons and magic you have."

A tearing, rending crash pulled Alex's gaze to the pavilion. She watched in horror as one corner collapsed, causing the tables filled with food to crash to the ground. Screams filled the air. Fighting flowed away from the pavilion and spilled down the slope toward the lake.

Crunch time, Alex thought, as determination filled her. *Time to put these new Keeper skills to the test.*

GRETA HOPPED ONTO THE STAGE, her short legs pumping fast, her body barreling toward the podium. She shoved Alex roughly aside, brought her face close to the lily and shouted an order. "Everyone, herd the attackers towards the lake! Billy and the river trolls are hungry!"

Hooves pounded along the lane behind the funeral home. Alex's eyes widened in shock as a herd of beautiful white horses appeared. Each animal featured a single deadly horn on their forehead. The herd galloped past the collapsed pavilion, their many hooves pounding a fighting rhythm into the earth as they charged the attackers.

Unicorns! Alex gasped in awe. *Badass ones.*

The majestic creatures waded into the battle. Their wickedly sharp horns slashed at the attackers as they herded them slowly toward the lake. Alex watched as members of the posse helped the unicorns surround the attackers. Working together, the posse and unicorn fighters pushed the undead creatures ever closer to the lake shore. Explosions of magic shook the ground. Showers of sparks in all the colors of the rainbow spiraled in the sky before heading back to earth. Shots and screams rang out. Arrows whizzed overhead.

Alex got her first good look at the attackers when two tall men bounded onto the stage. One man clutched a shotgun in a bloody grip, both his hands missing several fingers. The other leveled an arrow at Conor. Blood dripped down his face from where his nose used to reside.

Conor growled and lunged at the man with the shotgun as he took aim at Alex. She left Conor to deal with Bloody Shotgun Man as she swung the point of her staff toward No-Nose Arrow Man. A scream ripped out of her as she channeled magic into her staff. Flames of raw red power poured from her hands, then merged with the blue flames raging along the staff. It responded hungrily, ready for battle.

Just as the arrow flew from the bow toward Conor, a blazing stream of red-blue magical energy surged from the staff, destroying the arrow in mid-flight. The staff's magic continued its journey, arcing toward the man who loosed the arrow. He dropped his bow with a strangled cry and grimaced in agony as the destructive stream of magic pierced his chest. Alex watched in horror as the man's scream cut off abruptly and his body dissolved into gray ash, the smoky flakes drifting toward the stage floor like dirty snow.

"Well, that's one way to do it." Larry's grim snicker sounded in her mind.

Alex spotted Larry at the edge of the stage, where he was biting savagely at the ankles of another undead attacker. "One way to do what, kill someone?" She whispered in anguished horror. "I've never killed someone before."

Larry gave Alex a stern, if concerned, side-eye as he continued to savage the undead's legs. *"I'd get used to it, quick, if I were you. There's gonna be more killing before the night's over. And we want it to be the bad guys dying, not us. Besides, they're already dead, remember?"*

Conor's huge, black, furry body appeared behind the man Larry was chewing on. His leap brought the man crashing to the stage. With a savage bite and a swift twist of his head, Conor tore open the man's throat. Both Conor and Larry coughed and sneezed as the man's body turned to ash in their mouths.

Alex eyed the waves of battle. The supernatural posse and unicorns had corralled most of the undead creatures and were pushing them onto the smooth pebbles of the lake shore. The attackers were not going easily. Sounds of gunfire, arrows, magic, and shouts of pain and fury filled the air on both sides of the conflict.

As the first of the attackers fell into the lake, pushed there by the weight of the mob, the dark water roiled and parted. Huge tentacles surfaced and arrowed toward the bodies in the water, where they wrapped roughly around a torso here, a neck there. The undead creatures screamed and thrashed as they disappeared under the waves. Seconds later, an oily gray pool of ash surfaced in place of each scream.

A haunting melody hung in the air as dozens of squat bodies swam rapidly toward the shore. The Otherworldly song cut off abruptly when the swimmers emerged from the water.

Faster than Alex could see, the river trolls swarmed the undead crowded onto the beach. The cries of the undead cut off abruptly as the trolls dragged them into the lake, disappearing under the surface with their prey. Alex grimaced as she realized no pools of ash were rising from where the undead went under, clutched tightly in the powerful arms of the river trolls.

Larry curled his lips, revealing blood-covered ivory canines. *"The trolls aren't killing them. Well, not any deader than they already are. They're taking them back to their dens to feed their families."*

"Too bad they'll get nothing but a mouthful of ashes when it's time for dinner," Alex replied with a wince. She resolved to ensure the river trolls received as much fresh meat as they wanted after this was over. *Animal meat—cows, sheep, and so on,* she amended to herself, *not humans. Not even dead ones.* A shudder ripped through her.

Movement in the water caught Alex's eye. She realized some of the undead creatures pushed into the water had avoided both tentacles and trolls and were swimming toward the pier.

Gripping her staff tightly with one hand, Alex felt for the sword fastened to her side with the other. The sword slid smoothly, eagerly, from its leather scabbard. A tang of delighted anticipation resonated from the sword.

Conor had positioned his Barghest body between Alex and the battle. His amber eyes regarded her with concern.

"Back off, fur-face. This is my fight, too. I'm the freaking Crossroads Keeper, remember?" Alex pushed past Conor and hurried toward the steps leading to the pier. "Some of the undead bastards got away from Billy and the river trolls, and they're heading this way. I've got work to do."

Alex heard the padding of two sets of paws follow her down the steps and onto the pier. She grinned when she heard Larry and Conor grumbling unhappily to each other about her determination to get herself killed.

Her blood-thirsty sword swung low, beheading the first undead to reach the pier as he tried to heave himself onto the wooden boards. As the ash from the creature's disintegrating body puffed into the surrounding air, Alex grunted and darted a glare toward her companions. "No plans to get myself killed, guys. You both taught me well. Besides, Swordy McSword-Face here is eager to draw blood. Now, let's get to work."

ALEX WATCHED grimly as the last of the undead on the pier puffed into ashes under Conor's teeth, while Larry bit brutally at his ankles. She thought she recognized the man, but no way could Charles Manson be that dirty gray pile of ash on the pier. Denial, mixed with more than a touch of horror, congealed in her stomach. *Manson died years ago, in prison. Right?*

Larry spat out the last of the ash with a barking cough. *"Yeeech! Those things taste awful! No self-respecting canine likes the flavor of dead meat. And the ash chaser really sucks!"*

Exhausted, her adrenaline rush long gone, Alex climbed the steps from the pier and shuffled onto the wooden planks of the stage. Conor and Larry padded behind her.

Conor's amber eyes fixed on Alex. Head tilted, his lips curled in a doggie smile. His pink tongue hung down between extremely sharp canines. *"Time to go human. Want to watch?"*

Alex snorted and turned her back, ostensibly to observe the last of the battle in the field below, but really to hide the fiery blush tinting her cheeks. *Yep,* she thought with chagrin, *I do want to watch, but nope, not going there.*

The view from the stage revealed the supernatural battle was over. Half a dozen undead were left 'alive.' They huddled together on the grassy bank above the beach. Bands of blue magic held the creatures in place as the Indigo Fae warriors guarded them.

Boards creaked behind her, alerting Alex to Conor's approach. Almost afraid to turn around, Alex hesitated. She wasn't sure she'd be able to keep her eyes from wandering.

"Don't worry, Alex. I'm dressed. Sort of. At least, I've covered all the really important bits." Conor's voice hinted at suppressed laughter.

"I'm not worried." Alex turned around and grinned when she saw Conor's makeshift attire. The narrow, but long, embroidered cloth that previously graced the altar wrapped around Conor's waist like a towel. *No drooling,* Alex chastised herself.

"Uh, I love the look, Conor. I've never seen an altar cloth double as a towel before." *A very short towel,* she mused, her eyes admiring Conor's muscled legs. She mentally slapped herself and forced her eyes rise to meet his.

Conor's merry gaze met hers, his lips curved in a suggestive grin. "Well, the items under this altar cloth *are* sacred—to me, at least."

Larry snickered. *"More like an abomination, if you ask me."*

"Nobody asked you." Conor's foot snaked out, aiming a gentle swipe at Larry's legs.

Alex sighed, exhaustion sweeping over her. "Okay, guys, how about a verbal truce? We should head down to the field and find out what the hell happened."

The trio climbed off the stage, then walked through the fallen chairs and torn funeral programs toward the supernaturals milling around the field.

"At least we now know where the body parts have been coming from," Conor said. "Judging by the smoke and flakes of ash we found after each previous body part episode, I'm assuming this lot were the first ones to make it through the Crossroads in one piece."

Larry hacked another cough before correcting Conor. *"Well, mostly in one piece. In case you didn't notice, most of the attackers here tonight were missing a minor body part or three."*

Conor threw Larry a grim look. "They were whole enough this time that the few missing pieces didn't immediately ash them, though. And they could damn sure fight."

Many of the supernaturals were ranging over the site, helping clean up the aftermath of the battle. A group of burly, very tall men with miles of bulging muscles were dismantling the pavilion.

"Giants." Conor murmured in answer to Alex's questioning look. He pointed at a smaller pavilion at the edge of the field. "That's the medical tent. Fae healers are working on survivors."

Alex spotted Chris, the Dark Fae, directing the team of giants working to remove the collapsed pavilion. He must have felt her gaze, as he stopped to wave at her, before returning to his task.

Her gaze returned to the field. She tried not to stare at a group of tall, slender females with seaweed green hair and hauntingly beautiful faces. They strode across the field, gathering the attacker's weapons and dumping them in wooden barrels covered in runes. Alex couldn't help another questioning glance at Conor.

"The runes on the barrels will deactivate the weapons so no foe can wield them against supernaturals or humans again." Conor moved closer, then whispered in her ear. "To answer your other question, the ladies gathering the weapons are mermaids. I wouldn't stare if I were you. They have vicious tempers and are rather self-conscious about their human legs when on land."

"Soooo. They have tails when in the water? Do they live in the lake? Of course, they do. Duh." Alex answered her own question about the mermaids, feeling out of her depth. Again.

Conor smiled. "Yes, the mermaids have tails when in the water. Their pod lives in a cove at the far end of the lake. They've been here for as long as I can remember. Fortunately, they leave the boaters alone. Mostly."

"Mostly."

"Yep. As long as the boaters stay away from their cove, and don't over-fish the lake, things go swimmingly."

Alex snorted in amusement at Conor's terrible pun, then she spotted the unicorns. Her heart skipped a beat at their fierce beauty. The herd ranged by the lake, placidly munching on the oat grass edging the pebbled beach. Alex surreptitiously studied the magical equines. Snuffles of pleasure had replaced their ferociousness in battle. Fairytale creatures, come to life. *Maybe the supernatural world had some positives, after all.*

"Hail, Keeper." The deep voice startled Alex from her reverie. She realized they had reached the trio of Indigo Fae who were guarding the remaining attackers.

Wracking her brain, Alex remembered the speaker's name. "Hello, Tyre. Thank you for guarding these, uh, men." She eyed the undead with revulsion. "And for keeping them mostly in one piece. We will need them to get some answers."

A familiar hand touched Alex's shoulder. She turned to see her Uncle Vinnie. The anguish on his face sent Alex's heart plummeting. "Who? Who did we lose?" Eyes wildly surveying the scene, Alex shouted, "Larry! Grenoble! Where are you?"

"It's not them. They're both fine. We lost six supernaturals, but no one you know. There are over two dozen wounded." Vinnie's voice broke, his anguish obvious. "Including your Aunt Maia."

Alex's mind went blank. Blackness crept along the edge of her vision. Conor's arm wrapped around her just as her legs buckled, his strong grip preventing her from sinking to the ground. The warmth of Larry's furry body pressing against her leg helped ground her, and the blackness receded.

"But my aunt is a ghost! She's already dead. We just burned her body, for goodness' sake. How can she—her ghost—be wounded?"

Vinnie shook his head sadly, then took her hand, leading her slowly toward the healing tent. "The healers aren't sure what's wrong with her. Her ghostly spirit is still present, mostly, but it appears to be in a deep sleep." Sighing, he added, "She is more transparent than I've ever seen her."

Alex prayed to Hecate. *Goddess, please hear me and grant my appeal. Please heal my aunt's spirit. Please help her wake up and return to me. To us.*

She dropped Vinnie's guiding hand; her own clenching into fists as she approached the healing tent. *This was why you don't let people into your heart,* she thought, her heart aching with desolation. Again. *Too late now, though.*

"I can't lose her now. Not after just finding her again."

Maia's translucent form lay prone on a cot set up in a corner of the tent. She made no indent in the covers or pillow but seemed somehow to be resting on them. Her eyes were closed, her face blank in sleep. A dense cloud of gray smoke writhed within her translucent form, filling her chest with tendrils of darkness. Alex stroked her aunt's hair, the chill of death icing her fingers as they touched the prone form.

"Aunt Maia? It's me, Alex. Please wake up if you can. We need you. I need you." A sob escaped as she slid to her knees beside the cot.

A silvery voice interrupted Alex's weeping. "She's in a deep sleep, Keeper. We've done what we can, but it's not much. There's a powerful magic at work here, and we don't know how to counteract it. Her spirit is still here, but not fully."

Alex glanced up at the willowy woman standing at the end of the cot. "What do you mean?"

"We aren't sure, mind you, but we think part of her spirit has passed through the veil. Not willingly. Based on our conversation with your uncle, we think the Oneiroi, particularly Morpheus, are using their powers over sleep and dreams to pull her spirit into the Underworld." The Fae woman's face softened as she met Alex's gaze. "Your aunt's spirit is strong, and she's fighting it, but I'm not sure how long she can stand against the gods."

The soft sound of murmuring voices penetrated Alex's grief. She looked up from her spot beside her aunt's bed to see Greta, Vinnie, and Conor talking quietly near the tent's entrance. Conor seemed to feel her gaze. He met her stare, grief and determination fighting for dominance in his eyes.

Alex removed her hand from her aunt's pale form and stood. Tears fell as she regarded the still body on the cot. The resilient woman who raised her was fighting a battle with the gods for her spirit. Her aunt couldn't win the battle on her own, Alex knew. She heaved a deep breath, then counseled herself. *Time to put on your big girl panties, girl, and fix this.*

She joined the trio standing at the entrance to the tent. "So, what's the plan? How do we find the gods behind this, get my aunt's spirit back, and stop these undead creatures from using the Crossroads to get here? This crap has to end. Soon."

Greta narrowed her eyes and gave Alex an appraising look. "You're the Crossroads Keeper. You tell us."

Conor cut in. "Alex, you're right." He speared a warning look at Greta. "We—all of us need to do those things. But we can't go in without a plan, or more intel. We need to get the posse together and have a strategy meeting, as well as talk to Hecate and the other goddesses to see what they have learned."

Vinnie fixed the disgruntled river troll with an inflexible glare. "Greta, can we leave you in charge of cleanup here at the funeral home while we gather the rest of the posse at the old stables on the estate to discuss the way forward? Dawn is only a few hours away—"

"Yes, vampire, I get it. You have to get back to your lair for your beauty sleep soon." Greta sniffed and threw Alex a peevish frown. "The posse and the townspeople will help you, Alex, but you are the Keeper, and the responsibility for the safety of the Crossroads and Sylvan City rests on your shoulders. Time you got serious about your commitment."

No pressure, Alex thought as she watched Greta pound down the path, barking orders and sending those in her path scurrying to do her bidding.

"What would you like us to do with the prisoners, Keeper?" The strange voice echoed in Alex's head, disorientating her. She realized it belonged to Tyre, the Indigo Fae warrior who was guarding the surviving undead. Grimacing, she closed her eyes in dismay. *So now I've got another voice in my head. Boy, it sure is getting crowded in here.*

"Conor, Tyre is asking what to do with the prisoners."

"Tell him to bring them to the old stables." Conor pushed aside the canvas covering the tent's exit. "I'll round up the posse, and we'll head over there, too. Time to get some answers and plan our next steps."

21

DEAD BUT NOT

A lex plodded down the narrow road leading out of Sylvan City. Conor walked silently beside her. She was about to give in and ask the perennial childish question, 'Are we there yet?'

Before she embarrassed herself with the query, Conor pointed to a narrow track that arced away from the road.

"The town gate and ley line are this way. Follow me, but be careful. The path is uneven and there's a sharp slope." When they left the funeral home for the estate, Conor had told Alex they would take the ley line back to the estate, to save time.

"Why didn't we take the ley line the first time you brought me to town, for my meetings with the attorney and the funeral home? Why the long car ride through the woods?" Alex realized her tone was testy. Her spirit was weighed down with a mixture of grief, exhaustion, and the burden of responsibility.

"I brought you in the car so you could view Sylvan City from the hill above the lake. I wanted you to be impressed with the beauty of the valley. It was your first time seeing the city that's part of your heritage."

Conor gave her an understanding smile, then echoed Alex's own earlier words about her Keeper role. "I know, it's a lot."

"Damn right it is," Alex grumbled. "It's a shitty job, but some-one's got to do it."

Conor laughed at her grumpy response. "And you are just the woman for the job."

"We'll see about that." The walls of duty and responsibility grew taller and thicker around Alex. She hardened her heart, reminding herself she'd promised to help with this crisis, but no more. Then she would take herself back to her emotional island in Connecticut, where grief could not follow. She was almost certainly lying to herself, she admitted, but she wasn't ready to give up her dream of a return to emotional independence yet.

Conor touched her arm, startling Alex from her dismal thoughts. They stopped just before a clearing of scrub brush spread under the twisted limbs of a circle of live oaks. "Now that you are linked to the city, when we cross into the clearing, you will feel the pull of magic from the city gate. The ley line station is just past the gate."

"What gate? I don't see anything. And I sure don't see any station," Alex queried, her mind filled with the huge, busy, and bustling image of Grand Central Station in New York.

Conor chuckled, then led her forward. "The gate is right—"

Alex gasped as waves of magic hit her. The hair on the back of her neck rose and a tremor traveled from her head to her toes. Almost as quickly as the magical power wash over her, it receded, leaving her shivering in its aftermath. "Wow, that was intense," she marveled. "So, that's what the gate feels like."

"Not everyone will feel it as intensely as you. This evening, when the city accepted you as its Keeper, your magic became keyed to the gate. From now on, the gate will exchange magical power with you every time you pass through it."

"Okay, sure. Sounds terrific," Alex sniped, decidedly testy as another magical brick joined the already towering wall of her Keeper commitment.

"It's your heritage, sweets. Nothing I can do about that, other than inform, guide, and protect you." Conor took her hand and reached toward the gnarled trunk of the nearest live oak. "Brace yourself. Your first ley line trip might come as a bit of a shock."

As Conor's fingers touched the tree, Alex felt her body snatched away into a maelstrom. Her ears popped as the rushing wind snarled her hair. Dizzy at the kaleidoscope of colors and shapes rushing past, she felt as if she was traveling in a speeding car, with the top down, as scenery sped past in a blur.

Before her senses fully processed the experience, all sound and motion ceased. Her eyes were closed to shut out the disorientating sensations. She opened one eye slowly, then the other, fighting the wave of nausea that filled her stomach. She swallowed the sourness in her mouth, breathing deeply and slowly to reestablish equilibrium.

Conor's hand rubbed circles on her back. Alex moved away when she realized his hand felt good. Too good. *Nope, not going there,* she reminded herself, although with a lot less assurance than the previous times she'd uttered the mantra.

The last of her disorientation finally past, Alex muttered, "Well, that was ... interesting."

"Don't worry, you'll get used to it. The first time is always tough. Pretty soon, you'll be able to travel the line yourself."

Alex's eyes widened. "Me? I'll be able to use the ley line, without help?"

"You're a Crossroads Keeper, so of course you will."

Despite herself, a stirring of excitement at the idea of mastering ley line travel filled Alex. The places she would go. Or could she? Would her responsibilities keep her physically, as well as psychically, tied to the Crossroads? Well, damn.

"We have likely beaten everyone else to the estate. If you want to go back to your room and change, you have time."

A white blur came at Alex at speed, skidding to a stop in front of her. Larry squinted at her torn, ash-covered clothes and wrinkled his nose. *"I'd take him up on the offer to clean up, Alex. You look like you've been dragged up a chimney backwards."*

"Thanks, Larry, for that visual." A rush of affection for the furry little despot filled Alex, and she bent down to scoop him up for a cuddle.

Larry skittered out of her reach, wrinkling his nose in disgust. *"Oh, no, I don't want undead ash all over me, thanks. You can hug out your cuddle urge once we hit the sack. After you've showered several times, of course. Then, I wouldn't be averse to a belly rub. Or two."*

"Okay, puffball." Alex smiled at her furry Familiar. "Belly scratches at bedtime." She sighed. "Which will be awhile yet, though."

～

AFTER A QUICK SHOWER and a change of clothes, Alex marched to the old stables with a determined gait, thoughts tumbling around in her mind. *Got to get this show on the road; get Aunt Maia's spirit back, get rid of the undead, and get the meddling gods out of Crossroads business. Then, I can get the heck out of dodge. Yeah, right.* She admitted her herself that the last item on her 'to do' list was becoming less and less likely. She was no longer sure how she felt about that.

As Alex reached for the huge iron handle on the stable door, a tentacle slithered around her and grasped it, effortlessly pulling the door sideways along the rusty track to open it.

"Thanks, Billy."

"No sweat, Alex."

The buzz of conversation within died down as Alex and Billy entered the vast arena. Alex wasn't sure if the lull in conversation resulted from her entrance or from the sight of the sixty-foot squid tentacling in behind her. *Probably both*, she mused.

Billy settled along the back wall, taking up its entire length. Alex strode to the middle of the area, then studied the group of supernaturals seated on the risers lining the walls. She did a double take when she saw the trio of goddesses elegantly holding court in an arrangement of sturdy oak chairs brought in from the stable's office. Hecate, Demeter, and Persephone acknowledged her gaze with regal nods.

Alex waved awkwardly at the gathered supernaturals. "Um, hi, everyone. Thanks for coming. As you know, the ongoing situation at the Crossroads spilled over into Sylvan City today, when those undead creatures—whole ones this time—attacked the funeral home. We think they are traveling here from the Underworld, using the In-Between as a gateway to reach Earth, but don't yet have confirmation of this. We've been investigating this issue for a while, but with little success."

Alex thought sadly of her aunt, currently fighting for her spirit against divine odds, and of the supernaturals who had given their lives in defense of the city during the battle at the funeral home. "We can't have gods interfering with the Crossroads or groups of Underworld undead attacking our city and hurting our friends and family. We need to come up with a plan to stop this shi—er, crap show."

She cringed at her own inadequate words. *Great pep talk, Alex. Now what?* She breathed a silent sigh of relief when Conor entered the arena and strode toward her.

Once he reached Alex, Conor spared her a small smile, then he faced the gathered crowd. His voice rose, firm and commanding, as he issued a call to action. "This Crossroads is being targeted. The group threatening it includes several gods, including the Oneiroi, the triplet gods whose powers include inducing sleep and nightmares. The undead creatures they are helping to use the Crossroads to access Earth won't stop at attacking Sylvan City. If this Crossroads falls, or any other, these undead will have unfettered access to this world and will eventually overrun it, threatening both supernatural and human communities. We cannot let that happen. This must stop. Here. Now." His challenging gaze swept the arena, causing everyone to sit up just a little straighter. "Who is with us?"

The silence pulsed for a moment before everyone started

talking at once. Arguments broke out here and there, and loud voices filled the arena.

"Enough!" The goddess Hecate stood, tall and regal. Her gown glittered in the arena lights as she swept forward to stand beside Alex and Conor. "You have all benefited from this Crossroads over the years. Many of you traveled here from less hospitable places. You came for the safety a Crossroads community offers. You came to build homes, raise families, work, live and play with others of your kind."

The crowd slouched into their seats, eyeing the goddess with awe and not a little sheepishness for their earlier outburst.

Voice ringing with divine authority, Hecate continued her lecture. "I have dedicated my immortal life to building and maintaining Crossroads the world over."

The angry goddess pointed a commanding finger toward Demeter and Persephone. "Millenia ago, we three goddesses formed a triune and worked powerful divine magic to harness the energy of the ley lines. Our goal, originally, was to ensure no divine being could ever be held in the Underworld, or anywhere else, without their consent."

Hecate met Demeter's gaze with compassion, observing as Demeter's hand gently stroked Persephone's bowed head. Understanding flowed between them. Together, they had rescued Persephone from her supposed internment in the Underworld after her abduction by Hades. Neither had been aware of Persephone's collusion with Hades. Once Persephone was rescued and returned to her mother, the three goddesses had formed a triune, their powers multiplied exponentially by the union. Together, they built the Crossroads to ensure such a thing never happened again. Not to Persephone or to any other god.

Hecate returned her focus to the audience. "Our magic built the In-Between. We used this magical space between the realms to connect ley lines the world over, then formed a gateway, a Crossroads at each ley intersection. Our creation ensured the gods always had a way out, an escape route between the Underworld and this world, from one part of this world to another, and even between other realms. No longer could divine might conquer and subjugate weaker divine beings."

The goddess's gaze raked the daunted supernaturals. "As you all know, over the centuries, the mission of the Crossroads has expanded to include assisting supernaturals, ghosts and other special beings travel the ley, as well. That's you. All of you."

Demeter joined Hecate in the center of the arena. The two goddesses joined hands as silent communication flowed between them. Demeter nodded once, then faced the gathered supernaturals. When she spoke, her voice was husky with confusion, sorrow, and a bright spark of anger. "There have been attacks and battles over the centuries, but we have always quickly neutralized the threats. Until now. This is the first time gods have mounted an attack on the Crossroads. They benefit from them, still; why would they risk the very ley network that keeps them safe?" Demeter's question dropped into the gathering like a stone.

Into the heavy silence, a silvery voice spoke. "I think I know the answer to that, as do you both, even though you hesitate to admit it." Persephone rose and joined the other two goddesses. She met their gaze with sad knowledge. "There is only one goddess with both the power and the desire to conquer the ley lines. She is also the only goddess who can control and direct the Oneiroi to aid in her mad quest."

The voices of the three goddesses entwined in a single strand, as together they uttered a name, like a curse. "Nyx."

Members of the audience cried out in fear and dismay. The ground rumbled as Billy growled his displeasure.

Perplexed, Alex queried the goddesses. "Okay, but why? Why would Nyx want control of the ley lines and the Crossroads that connect them? She's a goddess. She can use them any time she wants, without having to control them."

Persephone gave Alex a small smile and shook her head in denial. "That's the thing, Keeper. Nyx cannot travel the ley lines or enter a Crossroads. Since time immemorial, the gods have confined her to the edges of the Underworld. Her divine form is bound there with deep magic. Nyx is one of the primordial gods. All Primordials are too dangerous to be allowed direct access to Earth. But Nyx, she is the most dangerous of them all. Her power rivals the strongest of the Titans, and surpasses that of the Olympian gods, even that of Zeus. Chaos, the original Primordial god, is her father, and she is heritor to all his chaotic powers. The Oneiroi, whose power is that of the terrors and darkness of nightmares, are her grandchildren. Nyx has ever sought to spread these ills, and more, both in the lands of the gods and even to the realms beyond."

The goddess sighed deeply, pausing to commune silently with her sister goddesses. Each nodded once, in agreement, then Persephone spoke into the expectant silence. "The truth is, Earth has always held a special interest for Nyx. Tales of her jealous desire to wreak havoc upon the human population have been told for millennia. She feels humans, with their weak wills and propensity for their own brand of evil, are uniquely suited to magnify chaos. If she gains access to this realm, she will bring Hell to Earth and rule here for eternity." The goddess's shoulders rose and fell in a fatalistic shrug. "Or at least until there's nothing left to rule."

Hecate bowed her head in acknowledgement of the truth of Persephone's words. "It is true. Nyx brings the danger we currently face. Since we confine her to the dark hills on the edge of the Underworld, she must be directing the Oneiroi to do her bidding. But there has to be be a reason for this attack. She is using her most powerful Oneiroi grandson, Morpheus, to bring sleep even to the gods, so she can bring her nefarious plans to fruition. We must discover her purpose and stop her, or chaos and destruction will cover the earth as never before."

Conor interjected. "But what about the undead that are breaching the Underworld and using this Crossroads to access the land of the living? How—why is she doing this? It should be impossible. Once a human spirit crosses the River Styx, there is no way back, with or without a body."

"That is an excellent question, Barghest." Hecate nodded in approval. "I have a few theories, but we'll need to ask hard questions of our prisoners to confirm them."

An evil smile twisted the goddess's lips. She gestured to the arena's door, where the Indigo Fae warriors were herding in the few remaining undead who had not been ashed in the battle at the funeral home. Blue bands of magic shackled each undead at wrist and ankle, forcing them to shuffle slowly and in unison as they entered the arena. At a command from Tyre, the captive group fell unwillingly to their knees. The blue bands of magic forced them onto the dirt floor of the arena.

Hecate prowled toward the small band of kneeling undead. Several shrank back in fear, while others snarled in anger. Circling the ragged group, the goddess examined them critically from head to toe.

Once done with her intimidating perusal, Hecate wrinkled her nose and stepped away from the prisoners. She issued a cryptic verdict. "Their bodies stink of death, but there is a spirit residing within. Where the spirit resides, there is life. Yet the spirit and the flesh of these creatures do not belong together. The bodies you see before you do not appear as they did in life."

Alex pursed her lips and studied the creatures through narrowed eyes. "That's easy for you to say. But what does it mean? What are these things? Or do you even know?" She glanced at Hecate and added helpfully, "Oh, and they turn to ash when you kill them, if that helps explain things."

The goddess raised her brows and smiled enigmatically.

Conor and Vinnie approached the prisoners, sniffing and staring, before turning to Hecate with identical looks of dawning comprehension.

Vinnie said, "These things are Regenerants, but unlike any I've encountered before."

Conor nodded in agreement.

Confused, Alex asked, "What's a Regenerant?"

The two friends exchanged a long look, then together aimed

heavy gazes toward Hecate. With a brief nod, she bade them answer Alex's question.

Conor cleared his throat and gave Alex an inscrutable look. "A Regenerant is a creation of dark magic. They are created by taking a recently dead human body and binding the spirit to it so it can't leave." He grimaced in disgust. "Typically, the spirit used is that belonging to the body itself. However, in theory, any human spirit can be bound to the dead body. The bound spirit prevents the body from—decaying. It also animates the body, so it can return to a sort of living—without actually being alive."

Vinnie took up the explanation. "Necromancers, mages whose magic centers on the dead, are the only ones who can perform this type of dark magic. Their powers over the dead infuse the spark needed to bind spirit to flesh in order to create and regenerate the undead creature." With a weary shrug, he added, "We are fortunate that necromancers are historically rare and that most have not been strong enough to perform regeneration magic. Many have tried, and died for their efforts. The Fates dislike being denied their control over the lives—and deaths—of men."

Alex puzzled through what she'd just been told. "So, it takes a powerful mage, whose powers involve necromancy, to create these Regenerants. But I'm assuming that mages are human, and you said the dead bodies they use are human. Since both the mage and the dead bodies they regenerate are human, they're both limited to Earth, right?"

Frowning in confusion, Alex studied the bound undead huddling together under the watchful gaze of the Indigo Fae. "These Regenerants are coming through the In-Between, then using the Crossroads to travel to Earth, which seems to indicate they originated in the Underworld. Correct me if I'm wrong, but dead human bodies don't leave Earth when someone dies. They stay here and are, uh, returned to the earth. Dust to dust and all that. Only the spirit travels to the Underworld, right? So, how can these Regenerants be coming *from* the Underworld?"

Conor's carefully blank gaze gave Alex no answers.

Vinnie studied the cigarette he rolled in his fingers, refusing to meet Alex's eyes.

It was Hecate who replied. "That's a good question, Alex." She strode with purpose toward the Regenerants, gesturing Alex to join her. "It's time to see what answers we can get from these necromantic nightmares."

The goddess studied the group of Regenerants with a dispassionate air. One of them fought against the blue bands of magic holding the group in place and stood. He gestured roughly at the others to remain on the ground. The binding magic at his wrists and ankles prevented him from reaching Hecate or Alex, but Alex stopped well short of the group, anyway.

The Regenerant straightened and fixed a baleful glare on Hecate, who had stepped right up to him. The goddess's hard gaze was no less forceful for having to look up to meet the undead creature's eyes. "What is your name, Regenerant?"

The heavy-set figure towered over the goddess. He sneered down at her and snarled his reply. "My name is Carl. But that's the only information I'm giving you, lady, so piss off." Carl's lips curled in disdain, then opened to add to his harsh words.

Before he uttered another word, Hecate's hand flashed out and touched his chest lightly. Carl's eyes widened in terror, and he choked out a gargled scream. Within seconds, his body disintegrated into ash, the dirty gray flakes drifting lazily to the dirt floor of the arena.

Alex and the rest of those in the arena stared at the goddess in dismay.

Hecate dusted her hands free of ash, smiling at Alex's horrified gaze. It was not a pleasant smile. "He would never cooperate. Now I've given the others an incentive to do so."

Vinnie stepped up beside the goddess, carelessly kicking at the dirt to disburse the small pile of ashes—all that remained of Carl. He studied the Regenerants impassively. "She will kill every one of you to get the answers we require. Is there anyone here who'd like to see another day on Earth?"

Most of the Regenerants shrank back from Vinnie's harsh words, eyes darting amongst their small group in terror. Then the smallest among them slowly climbed to his feet. Hampered by the blue bands of magic binding his limbs, he shuffled forward, then drew to a stop in front of the angry goddess.

The Regenerant bowed his head respectfully. "Goddess Hecate, creator of the Crossroads, I'm willing to answer your questions. I warn you, however, that it is likely none of us have all the answers you seek. I will do my best, however, and ask that you consider a reprieve for me in return. I can help you."

Slightly mollified by the respect shown her by the Regenerant, but still wary, the goddess nodded her head once in acknowledgement of his words. "What is your name, Regenerant, and where do you come from?"

"My name is Leonard Allard, my lady. I lived—and died in the late 19th century, in Lyon, France. I spent the last months of my life in jail before being hung for my...sins. When I died, they buried my body in a pauper's grave. To my knowledge, my bones remain there still."

"What dark magic created you? How did you pass through the veil from the Underworld to Earth?" Hecate frowned in confusion. "Why does your energy feel so wrong?"

Leonard bobbed his head and answered readily. "There is a powerful, necromantic mage in the Underworld. He is working in concert with a group of gods to regenerate those who agree to serve them—"

Larry's panicked voice spearing into her mind broke Alex's concentration on the words of the Regenerant. *"Alex, they're coming! A bunch of Regenerants just breached the Crossroads, and they're heading for the arena! Grenoble and I ashed a few, but these suckers are fast, and there's a lot of them! We're on our way. Warn everyone!"*

Alex gasped and lurched forward, interrupting the flow of the Regenerant's speech.

"Everyone, Larry just told me that more Regenerants, a lot

more, have breached the Crossroads and are heading this way! We will need to fight them!"

Alex's words triggered a flurry of activity as everyone scrambled off the risers and readied their weapons. Some members of the posse herded the old and young into the stalls at the back of the arena, while others directed those able to fight into a loose formation before the stable doors.

Tyre approached Alex as she stood next to Hecate and spoke in a low voice. "What would you have us do with these Regenerants, Keeper?"

Before Alex could reply, Hecate responded. "Ash them. All except this one, who has been giving us some answers. Take him to the dungeon and guard him well."

The Indigo Fae nodded respectfully and gestured to his troops, instructing them to carry out the goddess' wishes.

Alex's mind rebelled at Hecate's words, and she turned her back from the carnage. But she admitted it was the right decision. They couldn't risk the attacking Regenerants freeing their compatriots, who, she was sure, would be only too happy to join forces and fight beside them.

A random thought struck Alex as she unsheathed her sword and called for her Keeper staff. "We have a dungeon?" she asked of no one in particular.

Shouts echoed and stampeding feet pounded the ground as the Regenerants approached the stables at speed. Some of the posse spilled out of the stable doors to meet the undead attackers.

A white blur streaked through the door, skidding to a stop in front of Alex. *"Grenoble joined the fight out front. Take my power to add to yours. You'll need it."*

"But we've only practiced that. I'm not sure I can." Alex cried, overcome with a sense of inadequacy.

Larry placed his front paws on Alex's leg, then met her eyes with urgency. *"You better get over your nerves and just do it, Alex. There are a lot of them, and they have serious weapons. I could swear I saw a freakin' rocket launcher. Or two. Just touch my fur and pull the magic you need."*

Quickly, Alex placed her hand on Larry's fluffy head and called to his magic. "Will this hurt you? Can I accidentally pull too much? I don't want to hurt you."

"I may be stuck in a stupid poodle suit, but I have much more power than you can use. Take as much as you need. You can't hurt me." Larry cast a worried glance over his shoulder. *"But a rocket launcher sure as hell can, so hurry up."*

The swirling gold of Larry's magic swirled under Alex's hand as she touched his fur. She latched onto his magic with her own and pulled hard. A torrent of golden power poured into her, filling her senses until she cried out in pain and released the link. When she opened her eyes, the world around her looked different. All her senses sharpened and became laser focused on the coming battle. She moved forward to join the fight and gasped at her increased speed. *Cool,* she thought, as she swung her sword at the first Regenerant through the door, lopping his head off with little effort. Another attacker shoved through the ashes of her first kill, his empty gaze boring into hers as he pointed a deadly-looking gun at her and pulled the trigger.

Alex heard the crack of the gunshot and moved to avoid the bullet, knowing it was futile and preparing for pain. Surprise filled her when she realized her enhanced speed had propelled her out of the bullet's trajectory with seconds to spare.

Better not give him another shot, Alex thought grimly. She pointed her staff at the attacker and quickly pushed her red-hot magic through it. A stream of destructive red-blue energy arced from her staff and reached the man's chest just as his gun targeted her new position. The second gunshot echoed in her ears as the man holding the gun disappeared in a haze of ash. Amazingly, the shot went wide as the gun fell from a now non-existent hand.

After what seemed like hours, but was likely only minutes, the battle was over, and silence descended on the stables. The posse stood, exhausted, amongst ash-filled air.

After the battle-rage diminished, Alex tried to sort out the sequence of events after the second shot had missed her. She remembered only that a storm of red-gold magic had filled her, spurring her into the depths of the fight as she slashed and stabbed with her sword and streamed arcs of destruction through her staff. She even remembered biting the attackers a few times until the taste of ash forced her to reconsider that strategy. Alex shook her head to clear it and spit out a mouthful of ash. *Yuck, Larry's right. They taste awful*, she admitted to herself.

Vinnie strode through the stable door, wiping blood off his hands with a once-pristine linen handkerchief. "We got the last of them. A couple tried to make it back to the Crossroads, but we ashed 'em. I dunno know if their journey to Earth is one-way, or if they can travel back to the Underworld, but we can't take any chances. We can't have 'em reporting back to whoever is sending 'em here."

He took in Alex's ash-streaked face and apologized. "Sorry, doll. Yes, this is more than you signed up for. But it is what it is. We'll deal with it, then things will improve."

Firm orders issued from the vampire, directing the posse's efforts at after battle clean-up. Posse members and townspeople scurried to obey. Smiling benignly, like the old family friend-turned uncle he was, Vinnie gave Alex her own marching orders. "Alex, honey, why don't you and Conor head down to the dungeon to question the remaining Regenerant. We need his answers."

"Uh, sure, Uncle Vinnie, but—" Alex began, but her words cut off as a giant squid hove into view, blocking her uncle from sight.

"All gone," Billy growled, his tentacles waving in the air in a vain attempt to disburse the floating gray ash. "But we need to figure out how to stop these yahoos from coming through the Crossroads. We can't keep this up."

"You're right, Billy, we can't." Alex agreed. "I think we need to bring the battle to them. But first, we need more information, so

I'm going to have a chat with the Regenerant in the dungeon." She set off with purpose toward the back of the arena, but then stopped and faced Billy again. "Uh, which way is the dungeon?"

Before Billy answered, Conor appeared beside him, pushing one of Billy's still-waving tentacles out of his face with his free hand. His other hand had a firm grip on the arm of a tall Regenerant who was missing an ear, but otherwise appeared uninjured. A large handlebar mustache filled the lower half of his face but didn't hide his cruel smirk. The undead man regarded them indifferently with large gray eyes set above a face streaked with blood.

"So, we've captured another one alive?" Studying the Regenerant with repelled interest, Alex amended her statement. "Well, as alive as these things get."

Conor gave the man he held a rough shake. "This one fought in today's attack. I caught him trying to slip away toward the end of the battle. He may have information on our enemies that the one in the dungeon doesn't." Conor fixed the man with a challenging glare. "I thought we might offer him the chance to cooperate."

"Sounds like a plan." Alex nodded in agreement, then asked again. "Which way to the dungeon?"

22

QUESTIONS & ANSWERS

Alex muttered as she navigated the steep steps that wound down into the earth under the stables. "I never would have thought to look in the restroom for the entrance to the dungeon."

Ahead of her, Conor chuckled at her comment, grunting as he hustled the reluctant Regenerant before him down the worn stone steps. Alex could hear Larry's claws skittering down the stairs behind her. She took comfort in knowing her Familiar had her back as she descended into the darkness.

Conor spoke over his shoulder, answering her unasked questions. "The dungeons have been here since the first stables were built on this site, about three hundred years ago. Back then, ruthless colonial explorers, unhappy indigenous people and a bunch of fanatical Spanish priests building Missions were the only humans living in the area. Between them, they caused more than a little trouble for the Crossroads Keeper at the time. Her father was a Spanish nobleman and explorer, and her mother was a from a local indigenous tribe. She learned about dungeons from her father, who told her they were all the rage in Spain, so she had one built."

The history lesson filled the time as they descended the steep stairs and finished when they reached a low-ceilinged room at the bottom of the long, winding stairway.

Alex appreciated Conor's narrative as it took her mind off the careful trip down the worn steps, but now claustrophobia crept in as she glanced around at the rough stone walls of the dungeon. Ancient wooden doors with huge iron hinges and rusty locks interrupted the stone walls every eight feet. Alex tried counting the number of doors, but the narrow corridors disappeared into darkness. The flames from the torches set in ornate metal brackets on the walls were not strong enough to light more than the foyer, nor to reveal more than few doors in either direction.

She considered the prisoners who had occupied this shadowy space over the centuries, and a shiver raced through her, raising the hair on her arms. What crimes had they committed? Had any prisoners left the dungeon alive? *Okay, Alex, she berated herself, now is not the time. We've got enough to deal with.*

The Regenerant captive, still held firmly in Conor's iron grip, struggled briefly as he realized he was moments from being incarcerated in a small, dark cell.

"Knock it off, asshole." Conor jerked the prisoner to a halt. "You're not going anywhere. We need answers from you." He issued another terse command. "Larry, guard the stairs. Alex, follow me."

Conor's instructions interrupted Alex's morbid thoughts. She joined Conor in front of the first cell door, before glancing back at Larry, who gave her a confident grin.

"I've got this. No one will get down these stairs while I'm on guard duty. Be careful. Call out if you need me." Larry stationed himself facing the stairs, the golden glow of his magic outlining his fur in the shadows.

Conor pulled a heavy iron skeleton key from his pocket, using it to unlock the nearest cell door. He hauled the Regenerant into the cell. "We'll start with this guy. He was most recently in the Underworld, so he may have knowledge that our earlier captive does not."

Alex entered the open cell door behind Conor and the Regenerant. The dank, musty smell within stung her nose. The disuse of decades grimed the floors and walls and hung in dusty cobwebs from the low ceiling.

At a murmured word from Conor, a torch set within a metal grate on the wall came to life, its flickering flame illuminating the cramped cell. A low, stone, bed-sized platform occupied one wall, while a rough wooden table and two rickety chairs filled the center of the cell. Dust motes glinted in the torchlight.

Conor pushed the Regenerant into the closest chair, binding him to it with bands of glittering black rope he conjured out of thin air.

Intrigued, Alex exclaimed, "Wow, that's cool. Can you teach me how to do that?"

An affectionate half-smile touched the corners of Conor's lips. "Of course, I can. Keepers have the magic to bind things, sweets. We'll work on that another time, though."

"Yep, I get the message. Now's not the time. We have important interrogation stuff to do. Uh, will this get bloody? Should I stand out of the way?" Alex debated with herself, wondering if she really cared if it did. *Nope*, she thought, *don't care*. These creatures were attacking 'her' Crossroads and killing people in 'her' city. She was in, whatever it took.

The Regenerant eyed them sullenly. "I ain't gonna answer any of your questions, so we might as well get to the bloody part." A sinister smile curved his lips as an excited gleam flared in his dark eyes. "I like blood," he purred.

"Oh, great. A psychopath." Alex studied the Regenerant with a moue of disgust.

Conor seemed unconcerned by the man's words. "What's your name, Regenerant?"

The undead creature considered Conor through narrowed eyes, then shrugged. "No harm in telling you the name of the man who is going to kill you both. It's Herman Mudgett, but I prefer H. H. Holmes. It's what the press called me in my heyday."

"And when, exactly, was your heyday?" Conor asked the question casually, as if unconcerned with the man's answer. But Alex saw the coiled tension in his posture.

He suspects something, Alex realized, her stomach clenching in anxiety. *And I won't like it if he's correct.*

"Late 1800s," Herman replied, "Chicago. Specifically, the Murder House."

Conor blinked once, a pained expression flickering across his face so fast Alex almost missed it.

"So, in your previous life, you were a mass murderer, correct?"

"Well, that's what the authorities said. But I'm ... I was a man of medicine. I needed bodies for my studies, as all ambitious medical students of the times did." The Regenerant studied Alex with an appraising air. "I don't usually go in for female cadavers, but I'll make an exception for you."

A sharp crack reverberated in the small space as Conor's fist met Herman's smirking mouth. "Do not talk to her. Do not even look at her. I promise you I can cause you so much pain you will beg for your second death. Do you understand me?"

The Regenerant licked blood off his lip and eyed Conor with interest and a flicker of fear. "And you call *me* a psychopath?"

Conor sat in the chair opposite the undead man and regarded him with disdain. "Enough with the small talk. How did you come to be? Who made you, or rather, re-made you? Who sent you, and what is their purpose?"

"That's a lot of questions, Barghest. What's in it for me if I answer them?" A sly grin slid across Herman's face. "Yes, I know what you are, Guardian." He jerked his chin at Alex. "And I know who she is. Looks like I got all the answers, don't it?"

The undead strained against the black bands of magic that fastened him to the chair as he leaned toward Conor. "I ask again, Barghest. What's in it for me?"

Stark menace laced Conor's reply. His whispered words filled the cell with shadows. "Answer me, and you get to die quickly and without pain. Don't, and you die slowly, begging to be reduced to ash as I chop off a bit of you at a time. Your choice, Regenerant."

Deadly silence ensued as a battle of wills played out across the narrow table. Conor's magical energy crackled and snapped in the small space, and an inhuman, rumbling growl echoed from the stone walls.

Finally, the Regenerant blew out an angry huff of defeat. "Alright. You win—this time. Obviously, I don't like either choice, so I'm gonna give you *some* answers, but not all." With a grunt, he added, "I don't even know them all, but I'll tell you enough to earn a quick death. Agreed, Barghest?"

"Agreed."

"There's a powerful necromancer in the Underworld. He showed up a couple decades ago and quickly made a name for himself, 'cause he can control the spirits of the dead. He can even make 'em serve him or fight for him. They call him The Professor, but his real name is Talon. A while ago, he came to the attention of a certain goddess, who has been nursing a grudge for a long, long time. The two of 'em teamed up and are working some very dark magic." Herman smiled malevolently. "My kind of magic."

"What else?" Conor pressed for more. "How do they create the Regenerants? For what purpose?"

"I'm not gonna say much else, 'cause I either don't know the answers, or it's worth more than my death to tell you. Don't forget, when you kill me, my spirit will return to the Underworld, where Talon and Ny—the goddess he works with, have power." Herman shuddered. "Whatever you do to me is nothing compared to what they can do if I tell you much more. They have a spy here on Earth who'd tell them of my betrayal."

Worry knotted Alex's stomach. Spy? If this man thought word of his confession would reach the Underworld, the spy would have to be close to the action. Someone in Sylvan City ... or even someone in the posse. The bitter taste of betrayal filled Alex's heart with despair.

Conor's eyes flicked to hers, and she saw in his gaze the same concerns.

Conor tried for answers one last time. "What else can you tell us, without getting yourself into trouble in the Underworld?"

Herman smacked his lips, considering. Then he gave Alex a quick, knowing glance. "Not sure if this'll get me in trouble or not, but it's worth sharing anyways, just to see the look on your faces. Word is the necromancer has connections to this Crossroads. Family ones. He thinks he can use those connections for his purposes. That's why him and the goddess chose this Crossroads for their plans."

A shaft of painful knowledge illuminated Alex's mind. She gasped as emotional pain overwhelmed her. The awful clarity the murderer's words brought doubled her over in grief as tears streamed down her face. She barely noticed when the dirty gray ash of the dead Regenerant settled on the dirt floor at her feet.

23

PAINFUL TRUTHS

"**A**lex, are you okay?" A gentle hand touched her shoulder.

Summoning all her willpower, Alex straightened and swiped at the tears still tracking down her face. A pristine white handkerchief appeared in front of her, which she accepted to attempt a cleanup.

After wiping off the last of her tears and blowing her nose with Conor's now-no-longer pristine handkerchief, Alex placed it in her pocket. She'd have to launder it before returning it to him. *If he'd even take it back,* she mused distractedly. She wrapped her arms around her body, as if to ward off the emotional effects of the words she had to speak.

"The necromancer is my father ... right? His name is the same. Talon. My father was a professor at Yale, which is where my mother, the wannabe Keeper, met him. I know how power hungry she is. She wouldn't have married a mere human, would she?" Alex answered her own question. "Nope. Only a mage for my mother—right? That would explain the 'family connections' crap that Herman mentioned."

Conor hesitated before replying. "Well, we can't be sure if what he told us is true—"

"Oh, but we really can." Bitterness laced her words. "We know my mother thought—and likely still thinks—that she should be the rightful Keeper of this Crossroads. We know she tried several times to steal the Keeper position from my aunt, Maia, starting when she was a mere child."

"Alex, honey." Conor reached out to comfort her.

Alex stepped out of his reach, shaking her head. "No. We don't have time for sentimentality. I always knew my mother was a cold-hearted bitch. I just didn't think she was evil. She must have realized my father was a powerful necromancer when she met him. I'll bet she thought she could use his magic to overpower my aunt and make the Keeper role hers."

Her voice husky with pain, Alex ground out the last part of her revelation. "Instead, their attempt to take the Crossroads killed him. All she ever told me was that my father died when I was a toddler, while away on a business trip. I always thought she meant he had a car accident or something. Now I have the truth. She targeted him, married him, and convinced him to help her conquer the Crossroads. She brought him here to help her take the Keeper role, by force, and he died in the attempt, didn't he?"

Alex approached Conor and beat her hands against his chest as she wailed. "Didn't he? You would know. You were the Cross-roads Guardian back then, weren't you? Tell me the truth! Have you known all this time about my father? You bastard! Why didn't you tell me?"

Drawing her close, Conor held her, softly stroking her hair as she wept. Finally, she drew back, gingerly wiping her face with Conor's now-filthy handkerchief.

Conor sat wearily at the table, gesturing for her to take the seat opposite. Alex hesitated, doubtfully eyeing the thick gray ash covering the seat. She shrugged and used the last dry spot on the abused handkerchief to wipe the ashy remains Regenerant onto the floor, then sat.

"Well?" Alex demanded answers from Conor. She needed to know the truth about her father. Morosely, she mused. *After all, I've already got one evil parent. Why not have two? That makes a pair.* She shook her head to clear it, before fixing Conor with a narrow-eyed glare. "Answer me, dammit."

"You sure you want the truth?"

"Yep. Now. Talk."

With a sigh of defeat, Conor nodded once. When he spoke, his voice was emotionless and even. "Alright, here's the truth. You're right. About almost everything. Yes, I knew your father was a mage with strong necromantic powers. When your mother married him, I realized she planned to use his powers to further her ambitions. I ... we kept an eye on her from afar, in case ... well, just in case."

Conor paused, eyeing Alex warily.

"And?" Alex pushed for more. "What happened when they attacked? From what you've just told me, you knew they would. Eventually."

Conor's nostrils flared as he drew in a deep breath, then let it out in a whoosh. He met Alex's enquiring gaze, his eyes dark with remembrance.

"I was guarding the Crossroads when he and his team of undead attacked. They were not the kind we are seeing now, but regular ones, created on Earth, using the body's own spirit. Your aunt was there, too. We fought hard. They almost overpowered us, but we were lucky that night. Vinnie and some of his men were close by, and they came to help us defend the Crossroads."

Voice rough with pain, Conor told her the rest of the tale. "I'm sorry, Alex, but your father died in the battle, as did all his Regenerants. And no, before you ask, it wasn't me that ended him."

"Oh. Okay. How did my mother get away?" Alex felt detached from Conor's words. Her emotions had shut down. It was as if he was talking about someone else's mother and father. Someone else's sad tale of betrayal and death.

Conor's sigh echoed in the small cell. "Your mother insisted she knew nothing about his plans. She wasn't present during the attack ... or not that we could prove. The story she stuck to was that she was just visiting the Crossroads to introduce her new husband and child to her sister and show them around her hometown. She maintained your father must have targeted and married her for her connection to the Crossroads and insisted she had no idea he was planning an attack."

"Yeah, right. One thing my mother isn't is clueless. She knew. She planned it. I'm sure."

"I agree. So did everyone else, at the time." Conor shook his head slowly. "Unfortunately, we had no proof that she was a co-conspirator in the attack. And your father was dead, so he couldn't speak for himself. We had to let her go, even though we believed she was complicit in the attack, and we fully expected her to try again. So, the Council Court made her agree to certain restrictions in return for closing the investigation without charges."

A pensive, sad expression settled on Conor's face. Finally, he spoke the words that Alex had already suspected he'd utter. "Your mother agreed to give full custody of you to your aunt, with only one supervised visit a month." A crooked smile tilted his lips. "Didn't you ever wonder why either Vinnie or I accompanied you during every one of your mom's visits? Or why it was always Vinnie's restaurant where you both ate?"

Alex nodded mutely, then changed the motion to a head shake. "No, I never wondered, but now it makes sense." She sighed wearily. "Is there anything else I need to know? Now's the time to tell me. It won't go well for you if I find you've held anything back."

Conor gave Alex a searching look, then spoke quickly, as if to get the rest of his words out as fast as possible. "Your mother signed an oath, committing to stay at least a thousand miles away from this Crossroads and to never visit or attempt to use any Crossroads, ever. The Council Court was afraid of the damage she could wreak at this, or any, Crossroads, if she thought she had another chance of success at gaining a Keeper role."

After a beat, he asked softly, "Do you, um, remember anything about when your mother kidnapped you from the estate, when you were twelve?"

Alex met Conor's compassionate gaze. A mix of anger, sorrow, and worry washed over her. "I don't remember much. My mother just showed up at the estate, took me to lunch—somewhere besides Vinnie's restaurant. She explained that my Aunt Maia had died during her trip to France and told me I needed to pack up and go back to live with her in Connecticut. She wasn't any more thrilled with the situation than I was. At least, I thought she wasn't."

She searched Conor's face for an answer. "Why do you want to know what I remember? Don't tell me there's more involved in that whole mess."

Eyes closed, face weary, Conor took a moment before replying. "Maybe that's a story for another time."

A dark memory stirred in the back of Alex's mind. It was, mercifully, still shrouded in fog, but she felt its malevolence and shied away from probing further. "Well, fuck. It's bad, isn't it? No, don't answer me. I've had about all I can take tonight learning about my parents' propensity for monumentally unacceptable behavior."

After an awkward pause, Alex asked in a quiet voice, "Do you think my mother has anything to do with this situation?"

Conor slowly shook his head. "No, I don't. But I do think she may try to take advantage of the chaos this situation has created. We should keep an eye out for her."

"Great, so that'll be one more family member trying to kill me." Alex grimaced and crossed her arms for comfort. "No wonder I have issues."

"I'll protect you." Conor stated it as fact, with no bravado, but with a quiet confidence.

"Let's both try to fix our current situation—and stay alive, okay?" Alex's comment came out harsher than she intended, but she let it stand. "Don't we have another Regenerant to question?"

She followed Conor out of the cell and toward a second cell across the corridor from the first.

Hopefully, this interrogation ended better than the first.

24

AN UNLIKELY ALLY

The heavy cell door whined in protest as Conor swung it open. Conor entered the dimly lit cell first, with Alex close behind.

Alex realized the cell's setup was identical to the one across the hall. A memory of floating ash and final death flashed into her mind. She closed her eyes and swallowed back a wave of nausea.

Conor closed the cell door behind them with a bang, jerking Alex back to the present. *Different cell*, Alex reminded herself, *different prisoner.*

The cell's occupant scrambled to his feet. The torch flared at Conor's touch, allowing Alex to study the Regenerant standing before her. Under her impassive gaze, the man straightened, standing as tall as his short stature allowed. His wiry arm shot out and up, startling her, before she realized he was saluting. The click of his booted heels echoed off the stone walls.

"Gendarme Allard of the Gendarmerie Nationale, Lyon Detachement. At your service, monsieur and mademoiselle." The man's English was near perfect, but the lilt of France laced his speech, hinting at his native tongue.

Alex met Conor's eyes and noted they mirrored her confusion.

Conor quickly regained his equilibrium and returned the

Gendarme's salute. "I'm Conor Striker, Barghest and Guardian of the San Antonio Crossroads. This is Alexandria, Priestess of Hecate and Keeper of the San Antonio Crossroads."

The Frenchman nodded, his reply polite. "It is a pleasure to make your acquaintance, even in such unfortunate circumstances."

"Gendarme?" Alex questioned, before providing the answer herself. "Oh, you're—you were, a police officer!"

The little man smiled slightly. "Yes, mademoiselle, similar to your policemen, although the Gendarmerie Nationale is actually part of the military. I transferred there after my service in the army."

The incongruity of formal introductions occurring while they stood in a musty cell at the tail end of an eventful night struck Alex. A slightly hysterical giggle escaped. She accompanied it with a small finger wave at their prisoner before gaining control of her emotions.

The gentle touch of Conor's hand on her back helped center Alex and reminded her of the purpose of their visit. They needed to interrogate an undead creature brought to 'life' by her father's black magic—and to get answers from him by whatever means necessary.

Conor pointed at the sleeping ledge against the far wall. "I'm sure you're exhausted, Alex. But we need some answers. Why don't you rest while the Gendarme and I talk?"

Alex sank gratefully onto the cold ledge but remained upright. She was so tired; she knew she'd fall asleep if she lay down, despite the chill emanating from the rough stone surface and the undead French police officer standing just a few feet away.

Conor took charge of the interrogation. He waved the prisoner into a seat at the table, before taking a seat across from him.

He jumped right into the interrogation, repeating the same questions he'd asked their first prisoner. "How did you come to be? Who made you, or rather, re-made you? Who sent you, and what is their purpose?"

The gendarme straightened, then placed his hands flat on the table, as if preparing to give a speech. "I'll answer all your questions to the best of my ability, sir. Where would you like me to start?"

The honesty and lack of hostility in the man's words struck Alex in stark contrast to their earlier interrogation. *Hopefully, we get some answers, and this meeting goes better than the first one did,* she reflected wryly. She was totally tired of the sight, smell, and taste of ash.

Alex interjected. "Why are you so willing to help us? You were trying to murder us a couple of hours ago."

The dapper Frenchman turned in his chair so he could face Alex. Both pain and pride filled his gaze, while his lips curved in a weary smile.

"I wasn't actually trying to murder anyone, mademoiselle. Even in life, I murdered no one." The gendarme hesitated, a shadow of sadness darkening his expression. "Killed, yes, murdered, no."

"Call me Alex, please. And that's a distinction without a difference, isn't it? Your victims are just as dead, either way."

"As you wish, madem ... Alex. And please, call me Leonard. In answer to your question, ah, but there is a difference. If someone were trying to kill you and you killed them in self-defense, that would not be murder, oui? Of course, they hung me for the deaths, so I suppose the point is moot." Leonard pursed his lips and gave a Gallic shrug.

Conor's hand slapped down on the table, the crack reverberating from the stone walls of the small cell. "Explain. Succinctly."

The Regenerant sobered quickly. He nodded once, before taking a deep breath and closing his eyes, as if he needed to sort his thoughts into bite-sized pieces behind closed lids. After a moment, he opened his eyes, met Conor's enquiring gaze, and began his report.

"In order to explain why I'm here, and willing to aid you in your quest, first, you must understand a little of my history. In 1893,

I achieved my dream. After a decade of service in the army, I transferred to the Gendarmerie Nationale at the rank of Gendarme. Being of Jewish descent, in a land and time rife with antisemitism, a career in the military or law enforcement wasn't an easy path. But I did it, and for a time, my career prospered."

Remembered sorrow and horror washed across gendarme's face. "Five years into my law enforcement career, I was investigating a series of gruesome murders. Barmaids and innkeepers across the city found stabbed to death, their bodies cut up and submerged in beer barrels in the inns' cellars. We realized the murders were linked, and we suspected the culprits killed the poor souls to prevent them from exposing a large smuggling ring we'd been after for several years. We suspected there were both military members and government officials involved in the smuggling ring, as they were always one step ahead of us. There was a lot of pressure to solve the case, as it was affecting trade, which is never a good thing in a merchant town. My partner and I eventually narrowed our search and confronted the man we suspected of the murders."

The little Frenchman sighed in despair. "By the end of that dark night, my life was over, and my soul forfeit, even though I still breathed. My partner and I cornered the villain in a lane behind the inn we suspected would be the next target. The man lunged at me with a knife, so I shot him. My bullet hit its target, but my celebrations, and nearly my life, were cut short when my partner attacked me from behind. He attempted to slit my throat. I realized in that instant the criminal enterprise involved him and he had always planned to kill me if I got too close to answers. My years in the army had given me some fighting skills. I turned the tables, and instead of being the one who died that night, it was my partner who lost his life, by my hand."

Grief-stricken, the gendarme rubbed his hands over his face, attempting to wash away the memories. "With the benefit of hindsight, it would have been better had I been killed that night. But I wasn't. Instead, I reported the attack and gave my statement to the

Lieutenant. He did not believe me. Nor did the Captain, or the Major, or any of the town officials to whom I pled my case. They arrested and tried me for the murders of my partner, my attacker, and those of the victims whose murders we had been investigating. I was convicted and hanged in relatively short order."

Alex gasped, appalled at the unjustness of the man's treatment. "That's not right! How could that happen?" She shook her head as she realized with a pang that miscarriages of justice still occurred with unrelenting frequency, even more than a century later.

The Regenerant nodded to acknowledge Alex's words. "I never knew if my religion led to my conviction or merely the complicity of a corrupt police and judiciary. After my death, when I found myself in the Underworld with nothing but time on my hands, I dwelled mightily on the events leading to my murder—for that is what it was. It took almost a century before I stopped concerning myself with the matter."

"Recently, however, my mind turned to other things. When I heard rumors of a criminal enterprise gathering forces in the Underworld, with plans to attack Earth, I could not prevent myself from investigating." With a reluctant, self-deprecating grin, the Frenchman shrugged and finished his tale. "Once a policeman, always a policeman. Isn't that what your modern policemen say?"

"We call them police officers now. It's sexist to imply only men are members of the force." Alex murmured absently.

"My apologies, Alex." A slight blush colored the gendarme's cheeks. "I'm sure women make exemplary police officers, now they are allowed on the force."

An uncomfortable silence stretched as Alex and Conor sought the truth in each other's eyes. Was the polite police officer an unlikely ally, or accomplished liar?

"I believe him," Alex stated.

"So do I," Conor agreed. "As a Barghest, I can usually smell lies, especially on humans ... dead or alive. Leonard here is telling the truth."

"So, Gendarme Allard—"

"Leonard, please." The Frenchman waved his hand in dismissal of his former rank. "I haven't rightly held that title in a century, although I slip up and use it now and then, especially when I think it might facilitate a conversation instead of an interrogation." He gave them both a sheepish, crooked grin.

Conor burst out laughing, and Alex found herself joining him. Leonard chuckled merrily with them. After they had laughed some of the stress away, a somber atmosphere filled the cell.

Questions still needed to be asked and answered. Conor met the Regenerant's direct gaze. "So, what can you tell us, Leonard? What the hell is going on?"

"Well, I don't know everything, as I didn't want to show my hand by being too inquisitive, but I have enough information to help you, so here is my report."

Leonard sat upright in his seat, as if reporting to a senior officer. "Several months ago, I heard a rumor that a powerful mage sought volunteer spirits for a major project involving high-level magic. Word was that volunteers might gain their original body— and their human life—back, and perhaps even be able to return to Earth. The mage made no promises, and he stressed the danger of the endeavor, but there were many dark souls willing to accept the risk for a chance, however small, to return to their former lives. Many volunteers died a final death in the process, their souls burned out of existence. Still more volunteers came. For a chance at life.

"The mage had specific requirements for recruits: applicants must have had a criminal background in life, preferably with murder blackening their soul. My thoughts instantly turned to the reason for this requirement. Why would a mage seek to form a team of hardened criminals, then give them back their lives and send them to Earth? Certainly, his intentions were dark."

Leonard shrugged. "So, I volunteered." He gazed at the cell's low ceiling, as if seeking answers to his actions in the grime-covered stone. "My plan was to learn as much as possible and do what I could to block the mage's efforts."

His gaze intent, Conor sat forward and asked, "What did you learn?"

"I discovered the 'price' of participation was unquestioning service to the mage and to his cohorts on Earth, if we could break through the Crossroads and access this realm. I was told there were gods involved in the effort, but I never met them and don't know who they are."

"We already suspect who they are. Or at least, who the major players are," Alex said. "But why? That's what I don't understand. Why do these yahoos want to create an army of Underworld Regenerants, and why send them to Earth?"

"I can answer only part of that. How the gods are involved, I don't know. As far as the mage, my guess is that, when he perfects the regeneration process, he plans to take advantage of it himself and join his undead army to create havoc here on Earth. Here is the rest of what I've discovered."

Leonard ticked the additional discoveries off on his fingers as he listed them. "First, there is already an organized criminal network here, which is ready to receive these Regenerants and put them to work once they reach Earth. Second, the mage involved—his name is Talon—has some connection to this Crossroads, which is why he is targeting it for his incursions. I once overhead him say he plans to rule from Sylvan City once he conquers this Crossroads."

The Regenerant stretched his arms out, peering at his hands in wonder, before speaking again. "And last, I was in the most recent group he regenerated. Don't ask me how he does it because I don't know. He somehow puts our spirits to sleep before the process starts. When we wake up, our spirit is back in what looks like our original bodies, but can't be, as they were long ago dust."

With a grimace of disgust, Leonard looked away from his hands. He put them under the table, out of his sight. "The body my spirit is occupying is not my own, although it exactly mirrors my appearance in life. I know this body was recently dead. Talon bound my spirit inside it after death. I do not understand what dark magic did this, but it is against nature. You must stop this mage, or he will create enough Regenerants to conquer this Crossroads. They won't stop there, though. This dark mage's undead army will spread destruction across the earth—of that, I'm sure."

A grim silence settled on the trio as each considered the danger before them.

Alex slapped her hands on her thighs and shot to her feet. "Well, that explains a whole hell of a lot. But it doesn't tell us how to stop them. And by them, I mean him. Talon. My father, the evil, dark necromantic mage." She snorted in disgust, before subsiding into a dark silence.

Leonard's face was a study in shock. "Talon is your father? Oh, my dear, I'm so sorry. So *that's* his connection to this Crossroads!"

"Yuppers. The connection is me. I'm his dear daughter. I sure hope he doesn't think I'm going to help him take over the world because *that's* sure as fuck not happening. I'm going to stop him, even if I have to go straight to Hell itself and wring his scrawny neck."

Conor flicked a wary side eye at Alex, then met the Regenerant's surprised eyes. "Leonard, thank you for your information. We appreciate your honesty. I'm sorry, but I'm afraid we have to keep you locked up for the time being. I don't know if Talon has any way to control your body against your wishes, and I can't take the chance."

Leonard stood and snapped a smart salute. "I completely understand. I'd do the same if I were you, sir. I stand ready to assist, as and when you deem it fit."

Alex admitted Conor was right. They had to leave the helpful gendarme locked in the dungeon, for now. She offered some hospitality. "Is there anything we can get you? Do you need food? Water? I can ask my aunt to have someone bring down a pillow and some blankets."

"Thank you for your kindness, Alex. I don't feel hungry or thirsty. I suppose, as my body is technically dead, I have no need of food or water. A pillow and blanket would be much appreciated, though."

As Conor and Alex exited the cell, Leonard gave them one last piece of information. "Oh, and one last thing. It's important. You have a traitor in your midst. I don't know who it is, but it's someone close to you. Talon gets regular reports of happenings at the Crossroads and in Sylvan City. That's why he sent forces to attack the funeral and why he sent another team to finish you off tonight in the stables."

This last revelation shook Alex to the core.

Conor turned the key in the rusty lock, then leaned his head against the ancient, warped wood of the cell door.

They both uttered a curse simultaneously. "Fuck."

25

IT'S ALL MY FAULT

W hen Alex and Conor returned to the surface and entered the arena, they saw the crowd had lightened. Only the members of the posse remained, but the volume in the arena was still deafening.

Alex sighed, then shouted above the cacophony of voices. "Alright, everyone, listen up! I've got a plan, and it isn't optional! I'm going to the goddess Hecate to ask her to get me through the In-Between into the Underworld. Once there, I'm going to find my father and put a stop to his world domination plans."

Her determined gaze surveyed the alternatively angry and anxious faces of the supernaturals gathered around the walls of the arena. "And yes, folks, I'm going alone. This started with my family, and it's going to end with my family." Alex muttered a last comment under her breath, knowing the most likely outcome of her task. "Even if it means my permanent end."

Vinnie and Conor both stood, stiff-backed, opposite Alex. They bore identical expressions of resolve and anger. Vinnie's men, including the oh-so-distracting blue-eyed Abel, stood to attention behind him, intent on backing up his bullish position.

Vinnie spoke first, his tone an odd mix of soothing and steely. "Alex. Mia cara. You cannot go into the Underworld and attempt this task alone. You have no idea what dangers await you there. Your success or failure means the difference between life or death for the supernaturals at this Crossroads—and all the others. Don't you think your stubborn determination to fix this yourself is a little selfish? When ... if you fail—"

Before Alex could voice her angry response, Conor placed a restraining arm on Vinnie's shoulder. "Vinnie, let me deal with this." He glanced out the stable door at the lightening sky. "Besides, you need to get back home. Dawn is almost upon us."

Vinnie capitulated with a disgruntled snort. He threw a final frustrated glare in Alex's direction, before gesturing abruptly to his men and stalking out of the stable doors, his men following in his wake like dangerous ducklings.

Alex relaxed a hair but knew she still had to deal with Conor's objections—and that was after she finished dealing with the rest of the posse, all of whom continued to regard her doubtfully from their positions on the risers around the perimeter of the arena.

Conor solved the problem of the posse by thanking everyone for their support and asking them to go home and get some rest so they would be fresh for whatever danger the new day brought.

Grumbling and giving Alex serious side-eye, everyone eventually shuffled out of the stable doors with Billy bringing up the rear.

Before heaving his massive form through the door, Billy counseled Alex, worry filling his rumbling words. "Listen, kid, you can't do this yourself. You don't have to. That's what the posse is for—to help the Keeper defend the Crossroads and its supernatural community. You have friends and family now. Let us help you."

Alex shook her head in denial. She scuffed her feet in the ash-covered dirt of the arena as she watched Billy's last tentacle leave the building. She huffed a sigh and braced herself for Conor's attempts to persuade her to endanger himself and the posse in what was essentially her family's hot mess.

When she looked up from where her feet traced circles in the dirty ash, Alex saw Conor regarding her thoughtfully, disappointment filling his narrow-eyed gaze. She felt a stab of guilt for her determination to handle things herself.

"What?! Why are you looking at me like that? You won't change my mind, you know! My family. My mess to clean up."

"I know. I won't try." Conor blew out an exasperated breath, tension showing in his white-knuckled fists and tightly crossed arms. "I'm just going to tell you that you are *not* going to the Underworld by yourself. *We* will all go in as a team, but not without more information and a solid plan. We must succeed. This isn't about you, Alex, or the guilt you feel because your father is involved in this. You need to suck that up, along with your damnable desire for complete independence, and learn to rely on your friends ... and your family." Softening his gaze and his voice, Conor pleaded. "Do you understand me?"

Alex wrapped her arms around her body to protect herself from Conor's anger and disappointment. "My mother always told me you come into this world alone, and you leave it the same way. God knows she wasn't right about many things, but I think ... no, I believe she's right about that. I can't be responsible for anyone else losing their lives for me—or for anything my evil family has wrought." Her sad, but resolute gaze begged Conor to understand. "I just can't let anyone in again. My heart can't handle the pain of any more loss. I'll fix this mess by myself."

Conor's angry laugh pierced Alex's heart, and his harsh words broke what was left of it to pieces. "You stubborn woman! This isn't about you, or your pride or your need for independence ... or even familial vengeance. It's about the very survival of this Cross-roads and those reliant on it, and all the other Crossroads that will be vulnerable if our enemies breach this one. We don't have time to cater to your feelings on this matter." He paused, drew a steadying breath, and moderated his tone. "I'm the Crossroads Guardian. Your Guardian. It's my job to keep this place—and you, safe. I won't abandon my duty, not even to spare your feelings."

A mix of anger, pain and despair boiled in her gut but Alex bit back an angry response. She thought about stamping her foot in anger, but admitted to herself that would just confirm Conor's opinion of her as a petulant child. He was right; she couldn't battle her father and his evil cohorts by herself. However, that didn't make his dismissive words hurt any less. Instead, she gave him a sharp nod, then spun toward the stable exit, planning to head back to her room to prepare for her journey to the Underworld. After she had a private ugly cry.

Conor's arm around her waist stopped Alex in her tracks.

"I'm sorry, sweets. I really am. I had to get through to you that the importance of protecting this Crossroads outweighs everything else, even my feelings for you."

Any other time, Alex would have been overjoyed to hear Conor confirm his attraction to her. But now it just crushed her already wounded heart. "Let me go. Please."

"Where are you going?"

"I was going back to my room, but I think I'll go see my aunt, instead. They brought her back to the Crossroads, right?"

Conor released Alex and stepped back. He rubbed his hands over his face wearily before replying. "Yes. She is resting on the altar in the temple. We thought being at the Crossroads might help her. She is under heavy guard, and the healer is with her."

"Thank you. I'm going to visit her now." There was nothing else to say, so Alex turned away, her heart strangely empty of emotions, then trudged from the arena out into the early dawn light. The soft nudge of a cold, wet nose told her that Larry had been waiting for her outside the stables.

Larry fell in beside her as she made her way down the path leading to the Crossroads. The stark red light of dawn touched the path, causing sharp shadows to stretch out before them.

Alex could feel Larry's disquiet and see it in his stiff-legged trot. His serious side-eyed glances finally caused her temper to flare. "And just don't *you* start. I've had about enough of everyone telling me what to do."

"*Wouldn't dream of telling you what to do,*" Larry responded. "*However ....*"

"Here goes. Now you're going to tell me what to do." Alex snorted in annoyance. "Go on, you furry pain in my ass, get it over with."

Larry increased the wattage of his side-eye. *"As I was saying before I was so rudely interrupted, your plan for going to the Underworld alone isn't the smartest. It really isn't all about you and your need for control and independence, you know. You need help, and you're going to get it, whether you like it or not."*

A violent sneeze, followed by a low growl, emphasized Larry's next words. *"And it's not your fault that your father's an evil-minded, criminal dick."* He paused and shot her an apologetic look. *"And your mother's no prize, either."*

With a reluctant laugh, Alex admitted Larry was right. "I know. You're right. I can't go in alone. I realize it's not just about me and my desire to right the wrongs of my family." She hesitated, then finished her confession. "And run for the hills once we sort things out." A deep sigh welled up from the depths of her soul. "I just don't know how to let people in anymore, you know?"

They reached the end of the path, the Crossroads now revealed before them. Alex stared in awe at the temple as the morning sun highlighted the stark white carvings on the columns and threw sharp shadows over the temple entrance.

Her heart squeezed in pain, and her determined stride ground to a halt. Alex envisioned her aunt within the temple, her ghostly spirit fading as she fought with a god for her right to remain on Earth.

Larry's voice in her head startled Alex out of her reverie. *"I got news for you, girl, you already have."*

"I have what," Alex asked absently, as she resumed her journey. She crossed the cobbled courtyard, shading her eyes with her hand as she approached the temple. The building's white stone glowed in the bright morning sunlight.

"You've already opened your heart to your aunt, to Conor, to your Uncle Vinnie ... to me." Larry grinned, his pink tongue hanging out of the side of his mouth as he gazed at her knowingly. *"It's too late,*

kid. You already care, not just about your heart-family, but about the Crossroads and the supernatural community dependent on it. You need to stop letting your hard head interfere with your soft heart."

Alex knew deep down that Larry was right, but she wasn't quite ready to admit it, not even to herself—and certainly not to the furry smart-ass grinning up at her.

"Oh, shut up."

"Whatever you say, oh caring one."

Chagrined when she couldn't think of a response, Alex shot a glare at Larry. Instead, she stuck out her tongue. Maybe it was childish, but it made her feel better anyway.

Larry grinned in amusement, before wheeling around and trotting back down the path. *"Call out if you need me. I'm off to visit the kitchen. The chef should be up by now, and I might just beat Grenoble to the morning table scraps."*

Alex watched Larry's white form disappear down the path. She could swear he had called his power, as his small body glowed with a golden haze. *Probably a good idea,* she mused, as she climbed the stone steps and passed between the massive carved stone columns standing tall in front of the temple entrance. Who knew what dangers were lurking about the estate, especially now they were aware there was a traitor in their midst.

After a deep, cleansing breath, she pushed open the tall, iron-studded doors leading into the temple and entered the sacred space.

∼

A LOW MURMUR broke the hushed quiet of the temple. Movement to Alex's left caused her to whip around, her hand on her sword.

"Greetings, Keeper." The flickering torchlight revealed the slender form of the Fae healer. Alex relaxed, hoping the woman hadn't seen her defensive actions.

"Oh, hello. Sorry, I've forgotten your name. How is my aunt?" Alex cringed inwardly at her abrupt words. *Oh well,* she mused, *people will just have to deal with me the way I am—and that is angry, discouraged, and grief-stricken right now.*

The healer moved aside and gestured to the altar. "There is no change. She is no better ... but no worse. Your aunt is a fighter."

Alex approached the altar. At each corner of the waist-high stone slab, iron candelabras stood sentinel, each one filled with a dozen candles. She gazed sadly at the translucent spirit sunk into the blanket-covered pallet covering the altar's surface. Her aunt's spirit flickered and pulsed, her soul locked in a deadly battle with the malevolent gray mist sent by the Oneiroi.

A sob escaped Alex as she sunk down on the pallet beside her aunt's tortured form. She reached out, her hand hovering over the white coldness of her aunt's cheek. "Aunt Maia, I'm so sorry this is happening to you. Please, keep fighting. We are coming for you. I ... we are going to travel to the Underworld and end this, once and for all. You have my word. Please, keep fighting."

Alex could swear her aunt turned her head into Alex's hand, where it hovered above her cheek. Her aunt was strong. She was fighting a god's diabolical darkness that pulled her spirit, inexorably, into an Underworld nightmare from which she'd never return.

It was Alex's turn to fight. Time for an early morning fireside chat with the goddess Hecate and her divine cohorts.

26

CHOOSING SIDES

Alex strode out of the temple, nodding curtly at the guards stationed at the entrance. She vaguely recognized them as posse members, but she couldn't remember their names.

Both guards gave her a respectful nod and acknowledged her presence. "Keeper."

Realizing she had been so preoccupied as she approached the temple that she had walked right by them, Alex felt obligated to greet them now. "Uh, hello guys. Thanks for guarding my aunt. I'm just going to touch this column over here by the steps because I need to visit the goddess in the In-Between. Don't freak out when I disappear."

The guard on the left chuckled and spoke in a curiously sing song voice. "We are familiar with the In-Between, Keeper. They chose us for this guard post because we both can travel the ley lines. We can back up the guards stationed in the In-Between if needed."

Alex regarded the man as he spoke. He was very tall, with a silvery glow to his skin, elegant cheekbones, and striking gray eyes. Fae, she suspected. "Okay, thanks, guys. Please don't leave my aunt unguarded, though."

"Do not fear, Keeper. We are only the guards you can see. Over a dozen others are posted around the Crossroads and temple at all times."

The Fae's words made the hair on the back of Alex's neck stand up. She hadn't realized unseen supernatural guards surrounded her as she approached the Crossroads. With a small sigh, Alex reflected glumly on her lack of magical awareness. *Some kind of Keeper I am, if I can't even sense other supernaturals when they're all around me, let alone tell friends from enemies.*

Shrugging off her gloomy thoughts, Alex placed her hand on the carved stone column and closed her eyes, whispering her desire to the cold stone. "Goddess Hecate, hear my request. I need to speak with you in person."

THE NOW-FAMILIAR PULL of the In-Between wrapped around Alex. She opened her eyes once the feeling subsided. Smoke wafted from the fire blazing in the hearth. Alex eyed the trio of goddesses sprawled on the comfortable couches around it.

Hecate gestured her to approach, pointing at the one unoccupied seat. "Sit, Keeper, we have much to discuss."

Movement in the shadows caught Alex's attention. She realized there were half a dozen posse members stationed around the chamber's stone walls. A shiver of apprehension rippled through her as she sat. *What if one of these guards was the traitor?*

Alex started when she sensed Hecate's voice in her head. *"None of those present in this chamber tonight have betrayed us, Keeper. I have examined their souls, and they are pure."*

Tempted to ask why the goddess hadn't examined the souls of the rest of the posse to expose the traitor, Alex merely nodded and pursed her lips.

The regal goddess's sharp eyes considered Alex. She issued a stern warning. "Careful, Keeper. I can read your thoughts as clearly as if you spoke them aloud."

Alex shifted uncomfortably and looked away from Hecate's penetrating gaze. "Apologies, Goddess. I'm merely upset with everything that has happened today—yesterday, now. We're operating at a disadvantage here and have been since the beginning of this mess."

Hecate bowed her head in agreement. "You are correct, Keeper, we have been. I make no excuses, as there are none. For the longest time, I denied, even to myself, that certain gods might be behind the current threat to the Crossroads. For millennia, the gods have remained neutral. The benefits of the connected ley lines have kept them from interfering with the Crossroads." The goddess shook her head sadly. "It appears a perfect storm has arisen. A dangerous goddess, long denied access to the Crossroads, has joined forces with a powerful mage who has the skills to help her gain such access. And this goddess has recruited her grandsons, the Oneiroi, to her cause."

"Nyx." Alex spat out the single word, and it darkened the atmosphere of the chamber. Her gaze taking in all three goddesses, Alex asked, "Have you been able to find out any more about her plans, and who else she's working with?"

Demeter took up the tale. "Persephone has many friends in the Underworld, since she spends so much of her time there. She has tapped her sources and discovered some unsettling news." Demeter gave her daughter an encouraging smile. "Tell them, dear."

Persephone wrung her hands together, then clasped them tightly before speaking, her voice a low, painful whisper that Alex had to strain to hear. "I think Hades, my—er, husband is involved." A lone tear escaped her huge brown eyes and tracked down her cheek. "I have discovered he has granted Nyx passage from the outer mountains of the Underworld and is allowing her to reside in his castle. One of her grandsons, Morpheus, is also there, along with a score of demons loyal to her and the mage, Talon."

The goddess closed her eyes, her face drawn with pain. "It

seems Talon is working his black magic in the dungeons of my husband's castle."

Alex leaned forward, fascinated and appalled. "Is he holding part of my aunt's spirit there? Is that where they are making the Regenerants? How are they getting the dead human bodies there? I thought only gods and some supernaturals can physically travel to the Underworld. Humans only travel there in spirit form. Right?"

Persephone dissolved in tears, her shoulders shaking as she wept.

Alex realized they'd likely get no more out of the bereft goddess for the time being. Despite her tears, Persephone's face remained beautiful, her eyes clear. *Of course* goddesses don't have ugly cries, she mused, a tinge of jealousy edging her thoughts. She remembered her own delayed ugly cry and sighed. Time for that later.

Demeter stroked her sobbing daughter's hair, her mouth a thin line of suppressed anger. She sighed. "Yes, Keeper, to all of your questions. Morpheus is pulling your aunt's spirit into the Underworld. It appears these unnatural Regenerants are being created inside the castle. And, lastly, yes, only gods and some supernaturals should be able to travel to the Underworld in their physical forms."

Alex reiterated her previous question. "How are they getting the human bodies—"

Demeter frowned in annoyance and interrupted. "Keep your hair on, Keeper. We don't quite know the answer to that question. Yet."

Persephone gathered herself enough to rejoin the conversation. She wiped her face on her robe, giving her mother a reproachful glance before turning to meet Alex's eyes. The goddess' gaze contained a deep well of pain and betrayal. "Yes, Keeper, we know, or at least suspect, how they are transporting the human bodies to and from the Underworld." On a breath, she uttered a single name. "Charon." Persephone again buried her head in her robe, weeping softly.

Alex tried not to roll her eyes, wondering to herself what the hell Hades saw in the timid goddess that made it worth his part in her kidnapping all those millennia ago.

Demeter and Hecate exchanged a long, weighted look. Demeter nodded, before turning her attention to her sobbing daughter and leaving Hecate to fill in the details.

The goddess sighed deeply, a note of irritation coloring her voice as she explained. "As you may or may not know, Alex, Charon is the god who oversees the River Styx, over which all beings must pass to enter the Underworld. His boat plies the waters, bringing gods and supernaturals back and forth. For humans, the journey is in spirit from only, and the trip one-way— from Earth to the Underworld."

Hecate gave Persephone a fleeting glance. "The plot must involve Charon. It is the only explanation. As Underworld ferry-man, he is the only one who can feasibly transport physical human bodies to the Underworld—and then return them as Regenerants back to Earth."

Demeter interjected. "Persephone is having some trouble believing Charon is involved. She regards him as a bit of a hero, as he is the one who revealed her location to Hecate after her abduction by Hades. Without him, it would have been much longer before we found her."

An unknown voice entered Alex's head. Demeter's intense gaze told her the words belonged to the goddess. *"My daughter has a bit of a crush on Charon, in case you couldn't tell. For some reason, she still harbors feelings for that degenerate husband of hers, Hades, as well."*

Alex replied silently, and without thought. *"No shit. What a hot mess. Oops, sorry. Didn't mean any disrespect, Goddess."*

Demeter hid her smile and returned to comforting her broken-hearted daughter. *"No offense taken, Keeper. I've been dealing with my daughter's crush on Charon and messy involvement with Hades for millennia. It does rather get old."*

Alex snickered softly at the goddess's long-suffering reply. She gathered her thoughts and processed them before speaking aloud. "So, there's a cohort of gods working together with my fath—this mage to create these Regenerants. They are using existing spirits already in the Underworld and inserting them in random dead bodies that Charon is ferrying across the Styx. Somehow, when the bodies are regenerated, they take on the appearance of the spirit that is bonded to them."

A trio of divine heads nodded in agreement. "That's an excellent summary, Keeper."

Hecate's praise colored Alex's cheeks. Then she remembered the reason she traveled to the In-Between. Time to give the goddesses an update.

"I've got a bit of information to share with you from our interrogation of the captured Regenerants. It seems they only take volunteer spirits, and they must have a pretty black criminal background to get accepted into the Regenerant program. We've been told the Regenerants are being sent here to join a worldwide criminal organization that already exists—what for and who runs it, that we don't know. And there's a spy—"

A familiar form stepped out of the shadows. Alex realized Conor had joined them. His presence both warmed and annoyed her.

"Greetings, goddesses. Alex." Conor strode to the hearth and braced his shoulder wearily against the mantle. "I can fill in some of the blanks."

Conor held their rapt attention as he shared his knowledge, gained from a betrayal that cut deep. "I found our traitor. Once I discovered we had one, I realized there were only a few supernaturals who could lie to a Barghest and get away with it."

Conor rubbed tired hands over his face, before stringing them through his hair. His frown and the grim set of his mouth revealed new lines of sadness. "The spy is Chris Fernwood, the Dark Fae. When I confronted him, he tried to deny it, but a little 'persuasion' convinced him to admit his betrayal. I won't go into the reasons he used to justify his actions, but they are many." Conor shrugged in weary resignation. "Some may be accurate. Dark Fae are regarded with suspicion and scorn by the rest of the supernatural community."

Dismayed, Alex objected. "But that doesn't justify betraying the whole community!"

"No, it doesn't." Conor shook his head slowly and heaved a sigh. "There's something else. Chris believes Nyx and her cohorts have imprisoned his dead wife's spirit and that she is being tortured. He claims he sees the torture and her pleas for help every night in his dreams. He says he was told by her captors that the price of her release is his betrayal, and that's why he's been spying for them." Conor hesitated, his gaze caught by the flames in the fireplace. "And there's more ...."

"Get on with it, Barghest," Hecate snapped.

Alex realized everyone was tired, heart-sore, and anxious to hear the worst, just to get it over with so they could figure out how to win this unwanted war.

Conor's face bore no expression as he dropped his final bomb-shell into the strained atmosphere. "According to Chris, Nyx has been using her grandsons as intermediaries for decades. With their powers over sleep, dreams, and nightmares, they have coerced, bullied, bribed and done whatever it takes to develop a criminal network here on Earth. It appears they told him this to convince him their power extends into the earthly realm. Not only could they torture his wife in the Underworld, but they could get to him on Earth, anytime they wanted."

With a shake of his head, Conor finished his report. "Unfortunately, I believe him ... about most of it. But not about his wife's torture. I'm sure they don't have her, and I'll explain why later. However, they convinced Chris of his wife's imprisonment, and secured his cooperation when Morpheus infiltrated his dreams and played with his mind."

Alex gasped, "So, it's not really all his fault—"

"Oh, it's his fault." Conor's intense gaze met Alex's. "He should have come to me, to Hecate, to anyone in Sylvan City, told them what was supposedly happening to his wife, and asked for help. We would have helped him—and likely discovered this plot long before now. Instead, he betrayed the Crossroads and the very community that gave him refuge."

Hecate spoke softly, as if to herself. "So, why is Nyx involving herself in this sordid affair? Why is Nyx busy creating a criminal organization on Earth, when she is barred from ever setting foot in this realm? What is her end game?"

Conor answered Hecate's query. "Nyx is playing a long game. I'm not sure what her plans were for this organization when she created it. Until now, she's had no way to directly access it. She's been biding her time and amusing herself by sowing chaos on Earth, even if from afar. But things changed several months ago."

His compassionate amber eyes trained on Alex, Conor spoke softly, but inexorably. "Talon's appearance in the Underworld, along with his skills, gave Nyx the last piece to her plan. She now had a way to create undead criminal creatures loyal only to her that she could use to conquer a Crossroads. These Regenerants have been not only a means to an end—but a test. Once Talon perfected the art of bonding spirits to these bodies and figured out how to get them in one piece to Earth, she would have him do the same for her. That would give her access to a physical body with which she could escape the Underworld and travel to Earth, bringing her own brand of divine chaos with her."

The silence in the chamber was complete as everyone absorbed the ominous impact of Conor's words.

Hecate was the first to recover. "It is worse than we suspected." Her gaze swept across the other goddesses. "I—we should have seen this coming. After millennia of peace, we grew complacent. We must stop her, or it won't be only this Crossroads that falls to her and her conspirators, but all of them, followed by the whole of the earth—as well as the realms beyond."

Hecate gave Alex and Conor a weary smile. "Keeper, you look exhausted. You as well, Barghest. We three goddesses will use this day to continue the investigation and gather our allies amongst the gods. Go now, and rest. Please gather the posse this evening at sunset, so we can plan our attack."

ALEX AND CONOR suddenly found themselves outside the entrance to the temple, blinking in the bright light of mid-morning.

Conor took Alex's hand and drew her toward the path leading to the house. Alex didn't resist, too exhausted to do anything but trudge alongside him.

"We will do as the goddess commands and rest. But first, let's grab something to eat. I'm starving."

Her stomach growled in response to Conor's words, so Alex merely nodded in acquiescence.

As they entered the main house and headed toward the kitchen, Conor finally spoke. "We will question Chris this evening at the meeting. He is currently cooling his heels in the dungeon." With a grim smile, he added, "The Fae might be more forthcoming after a day in darkness."

After a disconsolate lunch, Alex returned to the carriage house and fell into a deep, dreamless sleep, Conor on the bed beside her.

AS THE LATE afternoon sun shone through the curtains, Alex woke. She rolled over to find Larry curled into her side, snoring in unison with Conor.

A quick shower and change of clothes refreshed Alex. As darkness covered the sky, the trio headed to the stables for the battle meeting and to resume questioning the Dark Fae.

Chris' betrayal had hit Alex hard. Her heart contracted with pain as she remembered with sadness her earlier commitment to let people into her heart. She had realized then that caring could bring heartache and even betrayal, as it had in her past, but she had decided that the benefits of happiness and community a heart-family would bring were worth it. Upon entering the dimly lit cell, Alex gazed sadly at the defiant Dark Fae who had betrayed them all and wondered again if she had made the right choice.

"Oh, Chris," Alex whispered, "why?"

"I had no choice." Chris' words were full of pain.

Conor gripped the Fae's arm in an iron hold and dragged him out of the cell. "Sure, you did, traitor. But let's get you upstairs, so you can explain to everyone why you betrayed them."

After a disconsolate trip up the steep, winding stairs from the dungeon, they reached the arena. Conor released his tight grip on Chris' arm, and the defeated Fae dropped on his knees in the arena's dirt. The gathered posse and goddesses stared stonily at their betrayer.

Hecate's voice cut across the loaded silence. "Explain, Fae. Why did you betray the very community that offered you sanctuary? And what else can you tell us about our enemies' plans?"

Chris cringed at the anger in the goddess's words, but he gathered himself and rose to his feet. Defiantly, he set his shoulders and spoke in a firm voice. "My precious Phea, my wife, died a decade ago, not long after our marriage. I mourned but took comfort knowing she was happy in the Shadowlands—"

Conor shook the Fae roughly, his face filled with disgust. "What does this story have to do with anything? Get to the point. Do you have anything more of substance to tell us? We really don't want to hear why you betrayed your friends and family."

The Dark Fae pulled out of Conor's grip and dropped to his knees again. Head hung low, tears dripped down his face, before splatting onto the dirt floor. "You don't understand! I truly had no choice!"

Alex rolled her eyes and huffed in frustration. "Okay, Chris, since you seem to believe it matters so much, tell us why you did it."

Sniffing mightily, Chris wiped his tear-streaked face on a dirty sleeve. He gazed at Alex with defeat etched on his weary features. "Several months ago, the dreams started. In them, I saw the spirit of Phea, my late wife, being tortured. And worse. Every night, she screamed pain and fear as her abusers hurt her. She cried out for me to save her spirit. She said they'd only let her go if I agreed to help them."

"Who was hurting her?" Conor prodded the broken Fae. "And what did they want?"

"I'm not sure who they were ... are. It's hard to see them through the gray mist that shrouds each dream. They asked me to spy on you, to report on everything happening at the Crossroads. They said they'd stop hurting her as soon as I agreed, and they'd free her after I completed the tasks they set me." Chris gazed imploringly at Alex, and whined, "I had no choice! Phea was ... is the love of my life!"

Alex rolled her eyes and caught Conor doing the same.

Conor's chest rumbled as he growled deeply. With effort, he regained his impressive control and continued the questioning. "You are Fae. Your kind can travel freely to the Underworld, even if most choose not to. Why did you not go and free her yourself, instead of agreeing to betray your friends? Why did you not ask us for help?"

Chris uttered a sharp, bitter bark of laughter. "I'm not fully Fae, Barghest. I have no ability to enter the Underworld. My father was human." He sneered in disgust. "My mother had a 'thing' for humans. She got pregnant and bore me, a half-breed. My mother's family was powerful. They covered up the circumstances of my birth by quickly marrying my mother off to an elder childless widower. He was happy to have a new wife who brought a child into the marriage." He curled his lip. "The fool knew enough not to ask too many questions."

A twinge of pity for the heartbroken Fae entered Alex's thoughts, then she remembered the harm his betrayal had wrought, and her sympathy dried up.

Hecate, who had been stonily observing the Fae's confession, interrupted Alex's jumbled thoughts with a bald statement. "Fae, they have fooled you. Your betrayal is based on a lie."

Chris jumped back to his feet, anger in every line of his tense body. "I am not lying, Hecate!"

"I didn't say you were, fool. Only that someone has been lying to you. Those dreams you had, which you assumed revealed truth, were not real. The gray mist you saw tells us that if nothing else." Hecate gave an ungoddess-like snort and slammed her hand on the arm of her chair. "Morpheus and his demented brothers, the gods of sleep, dreams, and nightmares, delved into your psyche and used your worst fears to create this fiction, which they used to bend you to their will. If only you had come to us, we would have saved you untold pain and this community many innocent deaths."

"You don't know that for sure," Chris replied, a scowl marring his handsome face.

A silvery voice softly interjected. "But I *do* know it for sure." Persephone eyed the dejected Dark Fae with sympathy, then she broke his world apart with her next words. "I know your dreams are not true because I know where your wife is and has been since she left you a decade ago."

"She didn't leave me! She died."

"No, Fae, she left you." Persephone hesitated, before rushing out the next words, as if by speaking quickly she could lessen the pain of her revelation. "Phea didn't want you searching for her after she left, so, during your annual trip to visit your holdings in the north, she glamoured herself to appear dead and obscured your memory to make you believe her body burned on a funeral pyre after her death. This is the story she planted in your mind, and the one which you relayed to both your families upon your return to Sylvan City, alone."

The goddess shrugged helplessly. "Phea didn't die, Chris. She left you during that trip, traveling far from Sylvan City." She eyed Chris and pursed her lips, as if debating whether to continue her tale.

"Tell me the rest. There's more, I can tell from your face. I need ... deserve to know the truth." Chris spoke through stiff lips, pain tightening his voice.

"You are right, Fae. The rest needs to be said." Persephone heaved a sigh, then reluctantly resumed her tale. "Several years after she left you, her travels took her to the Elysian Fields and there she met her lover, Pan. She lives there, still, with Pan and his satyr brethren, as their shared lover. I've seen her many times in my travels through the Fields." Persephone blushed a pretty shade of pink and her eyes narrowed with a touch of jealousy. "Her story is a bit of a legend in divine circles. She has those satyrs wound around her little finger."

The impact of Persephone's words hit Chris with the force of stones, reducing him to a puddle of grief, anger, and remorse. He crumpled to the floor and wept, whispering a repeated litany, "How can this be true? I don't believe it! Sorry, so sorry. I'm so sorry ...."

After that, it was impossible to get any sense out of the broken Fae. Conor sighed in disgust and shoved him toward the door to the dungeon.

27

A HELL OF A TIME

S houlders slumped in exhaustion, Alex watched, bleary-eyed, as the posse's meeting progressed. When Conor returned from escorting Chris back to the dungeon, he took charge of the battle planning discussion—and there was A LOT of discussion. No one took Alex's desire to travel to the Underworld by herself seriously. Alex assumed everyone figured it was the new Keeper's prerogative to engage in 'crazy talk,' but that it was a given she'd need help in the upcoming battle ... and the posse would provide it.

When Alex protested weakly that she would go into the Underworld alone, Greta snorted and told her she was a fool about many things, but certainly about thinking the posse would let the fate of the Crossroads rest upon one person. Alex correctly interpreted Greta's subtext to imply that she could not be further unsuited for a leadership position such as Keeper, whether assisted by the posse or not.

Alex tried to marshal arguments to refute Greta's opinion but realized she had none. She watched silently as everyone discussed plans and strategies that would aid them in the upcoming incursion into the Underworld.

There were many volunteers, but Conor carefully chose a small team that would offer both strength and flexibility.

Once the rest of the posse left to go about the tasks Conor assigned them, only the Underworld attack team remained.

The team continued to strategize, while Alex remained silent. She hadn't the first clue about battles, evil mages, or fighting gods in the Underworld. Never had she felt more alone and unprepared than she did as she had listened to her team discuss their plan of attack and their hopes for a victory.

THE GOLDEN LIGHT of sunset limned the brick path as everyone left the stables. Alex blinked in the sunshine after the dim light in the arena. The team quickly disbursed to prepare for the upcoming trip to the Underworld. They would depart the following evening.

"You were quiet in there." Conor queried Alex as they slowly ambled down the path leading back to the house. "You do understand that we all just want to help you protect the Crossroads and save Maia's spirit, don't you?"

Alex paused before answering, discarding her first impulse, which was a defensive denial of the need for help. From Conor or anyone else. "Yes, I was quiet. I realized that plans for the attack were better left to those with experience. You know I don't have much ... hell, any experience in defending this Crossroads or in fighting evil mages or destructive gods."

Tears threatened, but Alex refused to let them fall. Instead, she heaved a frustrated sigh. "I *know* I need help with this, Conor. I'm just not used to doing anything as part of a team. One thing my mother's coldness and distance did for me was to teach me to be independent and to take care of things myself."

"And you think that's a good thing, why?"

"What do you mean? Of course, being independent is a good thing!"

Conor frowned at Alex, his narrow-eyed gaze sparking with

anger. "Part of being an independent adult involves realizing when you need help. Otherwise, how do you maintain your independence? No one can do *everything* themselves, or at least not well, can they? Eventually, a wholly independent person, one who resists requesting help and refuses to form alliances, will fail. This is especially true in the supernatural world, where a quest for total independence usually results in harm, or even death." He threw up his hands and huffed in exasperation. "Can't you see that?"

Alex's mind rebelled at Conor's words, even while her heart admitted the truth of them. "I've suffered a lot of loss in my life. People I thought I could rely on like my aunt and my stepfather ... and even my ex-fiancé. My mother's example of not letting anyone get close enough to hurt you, of relying on only yourself, seemed like the best choice. At the time. As far as the dangers of self-reliance in the supernatural world, nope, that's all news to me, although I'm starting to understand. I think."

As the threatened tears fell, Alex covertly wiped her eyes. Conor already thought she was behaving like a child. She'd be damned if she let him see her cry. "I understand I need help, and that independence isn't all it's cracked up to be—especially in the supernatural world, when you're in charge of protecting a Crossroads and all those who rely on it." Her last words tumbled out unbidden. "But it's just a lot, you know?"

Conor's arm wrapped around Alex's shoulders. He pulled them both to a stop beside an extravagantly flowering bush, its sweet perfume scenting the air. "Yes, sweets, I know it's a lot. It would be for anyone, but especially someone as brave and self-sufficient as you."

"I'm not brave," Alex said, "and we've already discussed the fact that self-sufficiency isn't in the cards for a Crossroads Keeper."

"Yes, you are brave. Here you are, only a couple of weeks into a whole new life, where your beliefs are being challenged each day and your world reshaped out of all recognition. I think you are coping quite well, considering."

To keep further tears at bay, Alex studied the giant yellow

flowers on the bush at the edge of the path and breathed in their heady fragrance.

Conor's finger under her chin tilted her head up to meet his warm gaze. "Self-sufficiency is fine, sweets, in its proper place, but you certainly can't do *this* yourself ...."

Warm lips sensuously caressed Alex's neck, then worked their way up to her jaw, then her lips, which responded to Conor's kiss, seemingly of their own volition. Conor deepened the kiss, and Alex's world fell away. Conor's arms around her, his lips on hers, his hand tangling in her hair. Her arms wrapped around his lean shoulders felt as good as she suspected they would.

A low snicker, followed by a coughing bark, brought Alex back to her senses. Over Conor's shoulder, she spied a smirking Larry and a grinning Grenoble, both eyeing them from the far end of the path. She quickly drew her arms back and almost jumped out of Conor's embrace. A blush tinted her cheeks as she smoothed back her hair.

"Um, nope, you're right. I certainly can't do that by myself."

Conor grinned lazily and took her arm, turning them again toward the path to the house. He glared at the intrusive pair ahead. "If you two perverts value your lives, I'd make yourselves scarce right now."

Alex giggled at the look of horror that crossed both Larry and Grenoble's faces seconds before they took off down the path, away from the angry Barghest, as fast as their short poodle and goblin legs could carry them.

28

HEAD AND HEART

Alex and Conor shared a quiet dinner in the kitchen with only the chef for company. Henri placed platters of food on the table, nodded absently, then returned to his preparations for the morning, which appeared to involve rubbing cleaning cloths on every available surface while muttering imprecations in French at the recalcitrant appliances and countertops that dared get themselves dirty during the day's cooking activities.

Pushing away her half-eaten meal, Alex sighed gustily. "I'm sorry. I know I'm not great company right now. I've got a lot of stuff to process, and I'd like to get an early night. I'm going to visit my aunt first, then heading to bed, unless there's anything else we need to talk about?" Alex fervently hoped Conor would let her go without further discussion, as her mind was in turmoil, both from the battle ahead and from Conor's kiss, and she really needed time to process things.

Conor finished the last of the food on his plate, before standing up and taking Alex's hand. "I'll accompany you to the temple, then I'm going to head out to see Vinnie, as darkness isn't far off, so he'll rise soon. I need to bring him up to date on the posse's plans. When you're finished at the Crossroads, please have Larry or one of the guards walk you back to your rooms."

The strength and warmth of Conor's hand wrapped around her own caused conflicting feelings for Alex. Her head told her to pull free, to keep her promises to herself regarding maintaining her independence and avoiding emotional entanglements, romantic or otherwise. Her heart told her it was too late, as these promises had already been irretrievably broken. She wondered if her heart's truth made her happy or sad. *Maybe a little of both,* she mused.

"Okay, let's go." Alex kept her hand in Conor's and used their joined hands to pull him toward the back door. "When I'm done at the temple, I'll summon Larry and have him walk me back to the room. I'm sure his little green pal with accompany us, as well. Tell Vinnie I said hi."

As they ambled down the path toward the Crossroads, still holding hands, Alex felt Conor's gaze. She glanced up and realized he was eyeing her with a worried frown. "What? I'm fine!"

"Hmmmm. Sure, you are. Who are you, and what have you done with Alex?"

Alex giggled. "Very funny, Barghest. I'm sure your super-sensitive nose knows it's the real me you're leading down the garden path." Internally mortified, Alex questioned herself. *What the hell am I doing, flirting with Conor!* Good goddess, her mouth had NO common sense ... and her heart appeared questionable on that issue, too.

CONOR LEFT Alex at the bottom of the temple steps with a quick kiss before he disappeared down the path leading back to the house.

Alex remembered the guard's words during her last visit and wondered how many supernaturals stationed around the temple had observed their kiss. Then she waited until her blush had receded before mounting the steps to the temple and greeting the grinning guards at the entrance. *Damn it, there's NO privacy around here*, Alex grumbled to herself as she entered the sacred space.

Sorrow and worry clutched at Alex's heart when she saw her aunt's fading spirit sunk into the pallet laid on the altar. The ghost's ever-more-translucent form did little to hide the pattern on the blanket laid under her. A storm of gray mist swirled sluggishly in her chest, flowing in angry-looking waves, like a hurricane seen from above. It was obvious Maia's spirit was losing her battle against the gods.

A loud clatter echoed in the still air as something heavy hit the marble floor, startling Alex. Her Keeper staff lay on the floor at her feet, still wobbling from its journey, the crystal set in the top of the magical tool glowing gently.

Momentarily frozen with confusion, Alex considered. She knew she hadn't called her staff, but perhaps it sensed her need. A blue flame of divine magic slid up her arm as she grasped the heavy wood of the staff. Her magic immediately responded, its red flame joining in a twisting dance with the staff's blue one.

The triple goddess pendant around Alex's neck warmed. The pendant's moonstone glowed, casting a luminescent blue light over her aunt's translucent form. Acting on instinct, she grasped the glowing pendant in one hand, then placed the flaming staff on Maia's chest, aiming its crescent moon tips at the gray storm cloud swirling within the translucent figure.

A black, roiling mist filled the air. Lightning bolts of red and blue energy crackled, the air vibrating with the ferocity of the sudden magical storm. Alex heard her aunt's desperate plea pierce the electric grayness. "Leave this place, niece. The Crossroads needs you. Let me fight my battle, while you plan yours. You have given me enough power to hold on … for a while longer. I love you."

An endless moment later, Alex found herself sprawled on the floor beside the altar. One hand rested on the smooth stone of the altar's base, while the other maintained a fierce grip on her staff. The crystal nestled between the tips of the crescent moon was dark, and the staff was completely drained of magic. The crescent moon pendant lay cool against her skin, it's moonstone quiescent. *Well, at least I got her some magic to help in her fight*, reflected Alex, as she slipped beneath heavy waves of unconsciousness.

A rough, wet tongue licked Alex's face. As she returned to consciousness, she pursed her lips to prevent the tongue from making a foray into her mouth. She reached out to push the licker away. "Larry, stop. I'm awake now, thanks."

"What is it with you and fainting? I thought women only fainted a lot back when they had to wear those stupidly tight corsets a couple centuries ago." Larry sat on his haunches and peered at Alex, concern darkening his chocolate brown eyes. *"Seems I was wrong. Sorry, you only got me to rouse you this time. Your hunky Barghest is off-premises right now."*

Alex shook her head and sat up, gathering her thoughts. "My aunt. Does she look more solid?" She got to her feet to see for herself.

"Whatever the hell you did, I'm damned sure it's not in the Cross-roads Keeper handbook, and it's probably illegal in all the realms, but yes, your aunt's spirit has stabilized, at least for now." Larry snorted and placed his paws on her leg. *"But don't do it again, okay? I felt that burst of magic all the way over by the fountain pond. You could have killed yourself ...and me."*

"Oh, Larry, I'm so sorry! I didn't know what I was doing. My staff just appeared, all charged up and ready to go. When I picked it up, my magic met it, and both were raring to go. So, I just touched her with the tips of the staff—"

Larry gave her a curled-lip glare. *"If the staff told you to jump off a bridge, would you do it? Don't answer that. You probably would. Listen, the staff and its magic, as well as your own, are YOURS to control. They need to do what YOU want, not what they want—which is all magic, all the time, no matter the consequences. Got it?"*

"Got it." Alex wondered dismally if she'd ever truly get it. She'd better woman up and get this Keeper magic thing figured out by tomorrow night when she and the posse were due to leave for the

Underworld. No wonder no one had included her in the battle planning.

Alex realized that, unless she got her shit together, she'd be a liability, not an asset, during the upcoming battle. Her head and heart needed to be on the same page, and her magic needed to be firmly under her command.

⁓

As ALEX OPENED the door to her room, she heard a deep snore coming from within. Conor was back. A deep, glad warmth filled her heart, and this time, her head was in full agreement. This particular battle was over, she realized. She cared deeply for Conor and knew she'd let the relationship deepen when they returned from the Underworld battle. If they returned. Sigh.

Larry hopped up on the bed, turned around once, and plopped down in sleep position. *"Don't go getting all sexy with the Barghest tonight. I'm not into voyeurism, so when you two finally decide to get it on, please give me a warning so I can make myself scarce. Plus, we all need our sleep tonight. Battle tomorrow, remember? Smoochies after we come back."*

Alex threw her slipper at the grinning face peering at her from the foot of the bed. "My relationship with Conor is off-limits for discussion, you perv. Go to sleep."

In the bathroom, with the door firmly closed against the men in her life, Alex brushed her teeth and prepared for bed. She admitted silently that Larry's words about her burgeoning relationship with Conor echoed her own thoughts. Wait. *Can that furry little weasel read my mind? Ughh!*

After much tossing and turning, with her mind doing the same, Alex realized it really *was* that simple. Her head and heart *did* need to agree. It was no longer possible to deny her growing feelings for Conor, or for the rest of her heart-family. It was no longer possible to disconnect her feelings or assert her emotional independence from those around her, even if she wanted to.

Plans to return to her old 'normal,' receded. The new normal was so much more. Yes, it demanded more of her—more pain, more joy, more commitment than she even realized she had to give. But it was worth it. It would be worth it if they could win the upcoming battle for her Crossroads, for her town, for her people.

Her Crossroads. Her people. Her thoughts repeated these words as her mind and body fell into sleep. For the first time in two weeks, she slept deeply and without dark dreams.

29

APOLOGY IN ACTION

"And so, I'd like to apologize to everyone for not having my head in the game and for thinking I could do this by myself. I may be the Crossroads Keeper, but I'm only one person ... uh, supernatural. I can't protect this Crossroads from this current threat, or any others, without the help and support of those of you here this afternoon." As she gave her apology, Alex ensured she made eye contact with every one of the posse members present for the meeting, including Larry, Grenoble, and even Conor.

Most heads nodded in acceptance of her apology. Greta, being Greta, merely snorted and shook her head in exasperation before sniping a response. "Okay, alright, so you're sorry. And you admit you need us to help you protect the Crossroads. Duh. Can we get on with the meeting now?"

Several of the ghosts from her aunt's weekly poker game were present, their translucent bodies hovering over the wooden bench. They muttered amongst themselves before one rose to her feet, her regal gaze fixed firmly on Alex.

"Keeper, your apologies for your lack of effort and general incompetence are noted. Perhaps now you can redeem yourself by leading the posse to victory in the upcoming battle." Queen Elizabeth sniffed, peering down her long nose with a skeptical glare, making it clear Alex was living down to her low expectations of Alex's capabilities.

"Thank you, Quee—Liz. I really appreciate your supreme confidence in me and my team. We will do our absolute best to bring this battle to a successful conclusion, thus ensuring a continued safe-haven for you and your ghostly colleagues, as well as the other residents of the Crossroads and those of Sylvan City." *So there, queen ghost lady, I can do bitchy, too. Oops, there you go again, girl, engaging mouth before brain.* Alex took a deep breath, then threw a slightly apologetic glance at the regal and now quite angry-looking leader of the ghost squad. Probably not a good idea to piss off a queen, even if said queen hadn't sat on her throne for neigh on 500 years. *She sure still acted like she did, though,* Alex reflected with a heavy sigh.

Soft snickering reached Alex, coming from the trio of goddesses lounging on wooden office chairs to one side of the viewing stands. Great, now even the goddesses were laughing at her. If she could have sunk into the floor, maybe even all the way down to a nice, quiet cell in the dungeon, she would have done it right then.

Conor stepped forward, took Alex's hand in a subtle show of support, then faced the audience. "Thank you, Keeper. We accept your apology and understand that taking on your responsibilities to this Crossroads and community wasn't something you could prepare for in advance. Your mother's actions in removing you from your home as a child denied you the right to grow up with, and into, your heritage. That is not your fault. We all know you are doing your best to learn and undertake your duties now that you are here, where you belong."

Conor's words both warmed and chilled Alex. *'Back where you belong.'* Did she belong? Truly? Last night, she was sure of it, but now, in the light of day, challenges and doubts gnawed at both her confidence and her commitment.

With a businesslike air, Conor queried the posse. "Can those tasked with preparations for tonight's journey please give your reports?"

As various members of the posse provided details of their efforts, Alex felt the heavy pressure of her earlier thoughts recede. Larry's warm body pressed against her legs, and she wondered idly if her Familiar was able to reduce her stress magically. *Heck, normal dogs could do that, even without magic,* she mused.

Soppy thoughts about how great it was to have the loyalty of a dog, especially a magical one, made Alex's lips curve.

Larry's sarcastic voice intruded. *"Okay, now that you have apologized to the posse—good, and insulted the freaking Queen of England—bad, can you stop with the negative thoughts and get on with things?"*

"Yes, oh caring and sensitive one." Alex mind-snarked back. *"I'm now over my crisis of confidence. I ... we need to do this thing."*

Larry responded, his tone serious. *"Yes, we do."*

"WE HAVE several hours until darkness falls and our journey can begin. In the meantime, it behooves us to discover if the traitor, Chris, has any further information that might help in the coming battle. Alex and I will question him one last time." Conor cast an intent gaze around the arena. "Members of the attack team, if you have any final preparations to make, or goodbyes to say, now is the time. Please return by sunset. Everyone else, thank you for coming. We'll see you on the other side."

As they descended the worn stone steps leading underground to the dungeon, Alex considered the tons of earth over their heads and thought it a suitable metaphor for the weight of responsibility she and the posse bore for the success of their venture into the Underworld. First, they had to get there, then they had to undertake a dangerous journey to reach Hades' castle, inside which lurked the Regenerant creation lab overseen by her father and Nyx. Once they reached the castle, the posse had to break in, destroy the lab, capture or kill those involved, convince Nyx,

Talon, and her co-conspirators to end their bid for access to Earth, and rescue her aunt's spirit. That's all. No problem, right? *Yeah, right*, Alex reflected dismally, *no problem.*

"We will do this, and be successful, because we have to be. There is no other option." Conor's firm voice cut through Alex's dark musings.

"Are you reading my mind? Can you do that? My God—you can, can't you?" Alex recalled with dismay the many times her mind had wandered to thoughts of Conor's kisses. And her happy anticipation of more.

Larry and Conor both burst into merry laughter. Larry laughed so hard he lost his footing and tumbled into Alex's legs, almost sending her headfirst down the last of the steep steps. Luckily, Conor was in the lead, and Alex halted her fall by placing her hands on Conor's sturdy ... *strong, sexy,* back. Damn, she couldn't keep her mouth from getting her in trouble. How in the hell was she going to police her thoughts?

Conor reached the firm footing of the dirt floor of the dungeon antechamber first. He quickly grabbed Alex around the waist and lifted her down the last few steps before placing her gently on the ground next to him.

Larry tumbled down the last few steps and landed on his side, a puff of dust from the dirt floor billowing around him. He sat up and shook off the dirt, his laughter subsiding into a big doggie grin.

With matching evil grins, Conor and Larry glanced at each other, before turning their amused gazes to Alex, letting her know they had no plans to ignore her earlier question about mind reading.

Face flaming, Alex decided she couldn't be any more embarrassed, so she might as well get a straight answer. She glared at Conor and asked, "Well, can you? Read my mind, that is."

Lips pursed, Conor weighed his answer carefully before replying. "No, I can't exactly read your mind, sweets. I get general impressions of your feelings because we are psychically connected through our mutual bonding to the Crossroads." His eyes twinkled down at her. "But don't forget—Barghest here, remember? What I can't read from your mind, I can get from my other senses, including my very acute sense of smell."

Larry mind-snarked to Alex. *"So, every time you have a sexy thought about Mr. Man here, and get all hot and bothered by it, he can smell your attraction, you dingleberry."* Her Familiar gave her a quick wink before turning his smirking muzzle back to Conor.

Alex saw Conor smother a smile. Larry had obviously shared his comment with him. *Well, I'm already way underground in the dungeon,* she brooded glumly, *so it's redundant to hope the ground will open and swallow me. It already has.*

Realizing further verbal sparring with Conor was a lost cause, Alex subsided. Yes, he made her pulse race, dammit, and yes, he knew it. Sigh.

Alex transferred her attention to Larry. "Well, can *you* read my mind, since you're my magical Familiar?"

Larry fixed Alex with an inscrutable stare. *"Wouldn't you like to know?"*

"Yes. Yes, I would. So, tell me, you furry little terror." Alex crossed her arms and tapped her foot, waiting for an answer.

"Can I plead the Fifth?"

Alex closed her eyes and counted to ten, then did it again. She loved Larry like family. He *was* family. And nobody could try your patience like family. "No. This isn't a court of law. It's a dungeon, so unless you want to cool your paws in one of these cells, I'd suggest you answer me. Honestly."

"Would I lie?"

"Yes, if you thought you'd get away with it. So, an honest answer, please. Can you read my mind?"

"Not exactly. And that's the best I can give you—really!" Larry growled softly and met Alex's eyes. *"I'm your Familiar, so we are magically and psychically linked. Just as I can mind-speak with you, I can also get a sense of what you're thinking, but not exact thoughts. There. Does that answer your question?"*

"Mostly." Alex doubted she'd gotten 'the whole truth and nothing but the truth' from her furry Familiar, but realized they'd have to continue this conversation later. After all, they had a prisoner to question and an Underworld battle to win.

WHEN THEY OPENED the door to his cell, the trio found Chris curled up on the sleeping platform, muttering and whimpering, trapped in a nightmare.

Conor shook the Dark Fae roughly and shouted in his ear. "Hey, traitor, time to wake up and answer some more questions."

Chris shot up from his prone position and quickly backed into the corner of the platform. His eyes rolled wildly as his body pressed to the rough stone wall behind him. He begged for help with whispered pleas. "They have her. They're torturing her. I'm sure of it. You must help her. I don't care what that goddess says about my wife living happily with a bunch of horny satyrs. She would never have lied to me or left me."

Conor huffed in irritation, then rolled his neck in an obvious bid for patience. "They DO NOT have your wife, Chris. She's living it up in the Elysian fields with her goaty lovers, you fool. Your dreams are lies, as previously explained to you—by a goddess, no less."

"I don't believe you. Or her."

Alex eyed Conor warily. His thunderous expression and low, rumbling growl made the hairs on the back of her neck stand up. If Conor was scaring her, she realized how much worse it must be for the terrified traitor. Just as Alex was about to intervene, Larry hopped up on the stone sleeping platform, careful to stay out of reach of the moaning man huddled in the far corner.

"*Maybe I can help.*" Larry interceded. "*If I join my magic with Alex's Keeper magic, I should be able to contact those on other planes of existence.*" Larry threw Alex an apologetic look. "*I have done it before, with other magical partners. But never with you, Alex. I'm not sure if your power is ready to be used in such a way."*

Alex ruthlessly suppressed a stab of anxiety. If she didn't believe in herself, how could she expect others to do so? "I'm game. Let's do this thing. Uh, what do I need to do?"

"Call your magic and touch my body. I'll do the rest. Don't panic if you're carried into the magical conversation." Larry studied Chris with barely concealed disgust. *"I'm going to need you to reach out and touch me, as well. If this works, we should connect with Phea, wherever she is. Kind of like a magical FaceTime call. You'll be able to see and hear her, and vice versa. You'll be able to talk to each other, as well."* Larry curled his lip at the disconsolate Fae. *"Just don't try anything smart while you're touching me, you miserable excuse for a supernatural."*

Conor frowned down at the Fae's crumpled form, his face dark with anger and frustration. "Will that convince you these night-mares of yours are filled with lies? Will talking directly to your wife and asking her for the truth do it for you?"

Chris sighed, peeled himself out of the corner, then sat cross-legged on the stone sleeping platform. He rubbed his puffy red eyes and sniffed. "So, my choice is to believe I'm being lied to about the torture of my dead wife in my dreams or to discover that my wife lied to me about her death and is living it up in another realm. Both choices suck."

Growing tired of the Fae's pity party, Alex challenged the Fae. "Look, if your wife was that unhappy with you, how did you not have an inkling? You must have suspected she wasn't happy. I think you *do* know the truth. You just don't want to admit it." She snorted in disgust. "You'd rather believe in a wife that's dead and buried who suddenly, after years of being dead, shows up in the Under-world being tortured than in a wife who was merely unhappy, left you, and is now living happily somewhere other than with you?"

A ghost of a smile crossed Chris' face. "Since you put it like that, Keeper, yes, you are right. I realized Phea was unhappy, but I was striving to change that. Our marriage was not exactly an arranged one. However, it *was* strongly encouraged by both our families. Our families' business interests were ... and still are, interconnected. We grew up living next door to each other, so we've known each other most of our lives."

"*So, lemme get this straight.*" Larry's mind-spoken voice dripped with sarcasm. "*You just 'fell' into a not-quite-arranged marriage with a not-quite-willing Light Fae. That about right?*"

A zing of shock raced through Alex. While she didn't know as much as she should about the supernatural, her intuition told her that Light Fae and Dark Fae didn't sound like a good marriage match. "Correct me if I'm wrong, but is it usual for supernaturals to marry outside of their ... uh ... species, subspecies ... whatever?"

Conor snickered. "Until recently, it was uncommon for Dark and Light Fae to marry. However, things have changed over the last century or so, especially for the few Fae not at either Court, but living in this realm. Classic Fae, of either type, are not common in Crossroads communities, so they often broaden their marriage horizons, out of necessity." Conor's gaze raked the disconsolate Dark Fae. "It doesn't always go well, as is clear in this case."

"*Let's get this show on the road.*" Larry edged close enough to Chris for him to reach out and touch, but not too close. The golden glow of his magic already hovered over his fur, adding a surreal light effect to the dimly lit cell. "*Okay, everyone, touch me somewhere on my body. Gently, now. Alex, you may experience a magical tug as I connect with your magic.*"

When her hand settled on Larry's fur, hard pull on her magic made Alex's head spin. She suppressed the urge to fight the energy draw and closed her eyes. A sun-filled green field filled her mind's eye. The slight breeze ruffling the tall grass carried a tinkling laugh on its current. A slim woman with long golden hair strolled into view, surrounded by a herd of satyrs.

The woman's deep blue, extravagantly lashed, eyes focused on the trio intruding on her serenity. She motioned to her satyr companions to stay back and approached Alex. "Keeper, to what do I owe the pleasure?"

"Uh, hi. You're Phea, right? I'm Alex, the Keeper of the San Antonio Crossroads." Alex stammered her response.

The woman frowned in confusion as she glanced to Alex's left, then her right. "Yes, I'm Phea. I see you have company, Keeper." The beautiful Fae nodded a polite greeting. "Barghest, Familiar, good day. Chris, what are you doing here?"

"So, it's true? You glamoured me to think you were dead, then left me for these horny goat-men?" Chris' voice was hard, his face filled with dismay and disgust.

The stamping of many cloven hooves drew Alex's eye to the herd of satyrs now angrily pacing on the far side of the field.

Phea held her hand up and spoke over her shoulder. "No need to get yourselves in a tizzy, gents. I can handle this."

The Light Fae fixed Chris with a steady look. "I told you before we married it was not my desire to do so. I obeyed the wishes of my father in the pairing. He told me I'd come to love you. You told me you had enough love for both of us. I was young and foolish. I believed both of you. For ages, I tried to make it work." Phea sighed in frustration. "I told you I was unhappy many times, but did you listen? No. You always said things would get better. Both you and my father spoke about how much better both businesses were doing since you'd joined forces. What was I supposed to do? If I left you, the family alliance would have broken. Both businesses would have suffered. Our families would have suffered. Instead, with me 'dead,' you'd all be able to go on as always. You would no longer need me to glue the alliance together. Or be the cause of it breaking apart."

With a shrug of her shoulders, Phea finished her tale. "So, I arranged my death. Then, I traveled far away from the Crossroads. I met Pan and his brothers here in the Fields several years after my supposed death. We all fell in love. I'm incredibly happy here."

During Phea's explanation, the herd of satyrs had shuffled closer and were now standing directly behind her. The white fur on their goat-like legs caught the light, glinting in the sun's rays. The Light Fae's white-blond hair matched that of her lovers' fur. It flowed silkily through their fingers as they caressed it while murmuring soft words of support into her ear.

"Okay, time to go now, before this gets any more awkward." Larry's voice cut through Alex's mind, and her eyes popped open, revealing the rough stone walls of the prison cell.

"Now do you believe that the nightmares of your wife's torture in the Underworld are the lie and that Persephone spoke the truth about your wife's whereabouts?" Conor's voice was rough with anger.

Chris nodded and wiped his streaming eyes. "Yes, Barghest, I now believe the goddess, and you. How can I not? That was my wife, or rather my ex-wife now, I guess. She's happy, and that's all I ever wanted for her." A bitter anger kindled in the Fae's eyes. "How can I help you put an end to this horror? I'll help if I can. It won't make up for what I did …."

Conor's eyes narrowed at the Fae's words, and he barked a question. "You said they have a wish. What is their wish? What are they trying to accomplish?"

Scratching his head in thought, Chris considered his answer. "I only know what I sensed, or read between the lines of their questions, and the information they sought on the happenings at the Crossroads. They told me they were building an army to send to Earth on behalf of the goddess in charge and that, if I helped them by providing information on the Crossroads, they would release Phea and allow us to return to the Fae realm together. They said they have no quarrel with the Fae realm and only want to travel through the Crossroads. Their goal is to make the earth realm their own. I believed them."

Suddenly, the Fae's gaze hardened, and a gray mist floated eerily behind his dark eyes. "I still don't think they have any ill intentions toward the Crossroads or the supernatural community it protects. Their plans for the human realm are not our concern."

Conor gazed at his former friend with sadness. "Your mind is warped by the evil filling it every night. It must be so, as your words do not reflect the Chris I know—or thought I knew. So, your betrayal doesn't bother you? You really are willing to sacrifice everything and everyone on Earth for your deluded dream of a second happily-ever-after with your wife? What about the inconvenient fact that, based on your knowledge at the time, you thought your wife was dead?"

Chris hung his head. "They told me they had a way of returning her to life, like they are doing for their army." A spark of defiance filled the Fae's face. His eyes were now completely gray, filled with a thick, swirling fog. He met Conor's eyes with angry determination. "I've spent years being sneered at by the supernatural community for my Dark Fae heritage. Why should I defend a Crossroads community that despises me? My human father is long dead, so my loyalty to the earth realm and its human residents is nonexistent."

Conor met his friend's gaze with a look of weary finality. "That's not you talking, Chris. You've always been a helper— always been someone others could rely on. Those damned Oneiroi have infected your mind and soul and warped them out of all recognition."

"That's not true! I've always felt this way. I think. It just took the dreams over the last several months for me to realize it."

Conor shook his head, dismissing the Fae's heated denial. "Whatever. Let's get on with things. Do have any more information about how they are creating these Regenerants, or anything else that might help us defeat this threat?"

"No, I don't. They didn't tell me much at all. Just what I already told you."

Alex cut in, her voice harsh. "What did you tell them about the Crossroads?"

Chris cringed at her tone. "N ... nothing much. They asked about the new Keeper, so I told them about you. They asked about your aunt's funeral, so I told them when and where it would take place. That's it. I swear!"

"Chris, I trusted you. We all did." Grief etched deep grooves on Conor's face as he passed judgement. "You violated that trust and betrayed us to our enemies. The evil that has infiltrated your dreams has warped your very soul. You would sacrifice the community you used to love for newly perceived grievances and false hope and willingly condemn the earth realm to a living nightmare of divine chaos." Conor sealed the Fae's fate in a low, pain-filled voice. "I can't let you go, Chris. You understand that, don't you?"

Chris nodded once, his face set in resignation. "I understand, Barghest. Make it fast, please."

As Conor reluctantly reached toward his former friend to end his life, Alex pushed him aside and called her staff. The moment she felt the smack of the wood in her hand, she pointed the curved tips at the Fae and loosed her magic. The staff gobbled up her stream of raw red power, wrapped it in Hecate's divine blue, and arced them both toward the traitorous Fae.

It was fast. The Fae's dead body lay smoking on the dirt floor of the cell while Alex threw up in the far corner. As she retched, the warmth of Larry's furry body, where he pressed himself against her leg, offered comfort. A gentle hand pulled her hair back out of the way, and another massaged her neck as she finished purging her stomach.

"You didn't have to do that. That's what I'm here for. It's my job to protect the Crossroads." Conor's words held both sadness and a slight reproach.

"It's my job, too, remember? Plus, it would have hurt you to kill your friend, so I took care of it." Alex wiped her mouth with the white linen handkerchief Conor held out to her. "This Crossroads Keeper thing really sucks sometimes, you know?"

Conor's smile was bittersweet. "I know. It's a lot, right?"

She took Conor's extended hand and stood before replying. "Yes, it is a lot. For both of us."

~

ALEX TOOK the heavy iron key from Conor and opened the door to the cell belonging to the French gendarme.

Leonard had heard them coming. He was standing at attention next to the small wooden table resting in the middle of the dim, dank room. His wrinkled clothes hung on his slight frame, and a light beard peppered his weary face.

Wise, sad, tired eyes gazed at Alex with compassion. "I'm so sorry, Keeper Alex. That Fae betrayed both you and the Crossroads in such a terrible way. I'm grieved that you must now bear the burden of taking another's life—no matter how necessary it was."

Tears filled Alex's eyes at the man's sympathy, but she quickly blinked them away, using icy words to turn aside the Regenerant's kindness. "I did what I had to do just now, Officer Allard. It was no big deal. I've killed before. At the funeral battle, I ashed half a dozen Regenerants."

The gendarme's kind, knowing gaze did not waver. "But those men were already dead, so it's not quite the same, is it, my dear? For Regenerants to even have the opportunity for a second death is a gift all its own, wouldn't you agree?"

Alex's shoulders drooped as a wave of exhaustion crashed over her. She plopped down in a rickety wooden chair near the table and nodded sadly. "You're right, Leonard, as seems usual with you. I'd rather not talk about this anymore, though." She gestured to Conor. "He has a few more questions for you."

The Frenchman nodded sharply and clicked his heels before meeting Conor's enquiring gaze directly. "Sir! How can I be of assistance?"

"At ease, Officer." Conor waved the man into the chair opposite Alex before taking a seat on the stone sleeping platform. Leaning forward, Conor began the interrogation. "Since we last met, have you remembered anything else that might help us? Have you slept? If so, have the Oneiroi infiltrated your dreams?"

Lips pursed, Leonard raised his gaze to the cobwebs draping the low stone ceiling of the cell, studying them as if he'd find dusty answers there. "I told you all I knew last we met. Yes, I have slept since then. Yes, the Oneiroi have since visited me with nightmares and attempted to influence my thoughts and actions. However, I'm able to fight them off and force myself awake." The Regenerant theorized. "I'm not sure why I'm now able to resist their influence, but proximity to the Crossroads may be a factor." He rubbed the dark stubble on his chin. "Perhaps my return to Earth has restarted this human body, as evidenced by my need to shave. It also appears that residing in a living physical form provides my spirit a measure of independence."

With a Gallic shrug, Leonard threw his hands up. "Your guess is as good as mine. All I know is that my mind is my own, as are my actions. I don't expect you to believe me—or free me—yet. I do hope I'll eventually prove my loyalty and win a reprieve that will enable me to serve you and the Crossroads in whatever way you both see fit."

Alex exchanged a loaded look with Conor, who gave her a brief nod. She turned to the Frenchman and replied, "Thank you for your honesty, Leonard. Now is not the time for us to be making plans for your future, but I will tell you that, once this is over, we'll give you a fair shot to prove your loyalty and earn at least some sort of reprieve."

"That is all I ask, Keeper Alex. Thank you." Leonard placed his large hand gently over Alex's, where it rested on the table. "I wish you success in the coming battle. This evil must be rooted out and destroyed before it intrudes any further into this realm."

Alex resisted a shiver at the cool, dry touch of the Regenerant. "You're welcome. We'll see you on the other side of this thing. Hopefully."

30

TIME TO END THIS

A s twilight gave way to night, members of the attack team trickled into the old stables. Greetings were subdued; everyone wrapped in their own thoughts.

The goddesses lounged in chairs to one side of the staging area, observing the activity with blank faces. It appeared their thoughts were also on the coming battle.

Vinnie was the last to arrive. Once full darkness took hold, he strode in with several of his blood harem, each dressed completely in black and outfitted for battle. Vinnie glanced at Conor. "Everyone here? Time to get this show on the road."

Conor gestured at the men surrounding Vinnie. "Unless I'm mistaken, these guys are still mostly human. It might not be a good idea to take them to the Underworld ...."

The tallest man stepped forward, determination hardening his handsome face, his brilliant blue eyes laser-focused on Conor. Alex remembered him with a start: Abel, the head of Vinnie's blood harem, and likely former criminal associate during her uncle's time as a mob boss in New York.

"We are going with you, Barghest. Those of us here are Vinnie's longest-serving blood harem members. We are now more supernatural than human. We will not let our master go into battle without reinforcements." Abel shrugged. "If the Underworld kills us, Vinnie can turn us, if given the opportunity. If not, it will have been an honor to serve him."

Greta's strident voice cut across the arena. "Nice, noble sentiments, blood human. But we can't carry deadwood on this trip." The river troll cackled at her own play on words. "If you all feel the need to come along as the vampire's reinforcements, what does that make the rest of us? Chopped liver? *We* are Vinnie's reinforcements, as he is ours." With a dismissive wave, Greta instructed Abel and his cohorts to leave. "Go back to your den, you lot."

A stern voice ended the argument. Like the former head of a large crime family that he was, Vinnie issued a terse command. "Enough! Abel made his case to me last night. If he and the others want to risk their lives to help protect both me and this Crossroads, we will let them."

Greta subsided with a grumble. "On your head be it, vampire. They need to keep up and carry their weight, or they'll get left in the Underworld to die."

Oh boy, mused Alex glumly, *we haven't even left for the journey, and we already have dissension in the ranks.*

Conor took charge. "Thanks for your input, Greta. However, any member of the Crossroads community who wishes to offer their lives to support this mission is welcome." He addressed the assembled team. "Is everyone ready? Remember, radio silence until we reach the River Styx. Take out any hostiles we encounter on the way quickly and quietly. Once at the river, Persephone will approach Charon to see if she can garner his cooperation. She has a history with him, so we're hoping she can convince him to cooperate. If not, we make him do so."

Alex gave a start and glanced over at Persephone. She must have missed the part about the goddess accompanying the attack team to the Underworld. Her look revealed the goddess attired in a short toga and armed to the teeth, a fierce and determined expression marring her pretty face. *Huh, how did I miss that? The kitten has claws and wants to fight,* she mused.

Alex's attention returned to the gathering, and she realized everyone was preparing to move out. She hurried forward, hand on sword hilt and staff in hand, and joined Conor at the head of the procession.

As they passed the temple, a sharp bark alerted Alex to Larry's presence. A low grumble assured her Grenoble wasn't far away from her Familiar's side. She knew the goddesses had tasked them with helping guard her aunt while the attack team traveled to the Underworld.

Larry had explained to Alex he could not accompany the team to the Underworld, as he might be considered ready for his next Familiar gig and reassigned, leaving Alex without a Familiar. Alex would not take that chance. Aside from their magical connection, she loved the furry tyrant and didn't want to take the risk of losing him. Nope. No way. Grenoble, good friend to Larry that he was, had agreed to stay behind with him and the other guards to help protect her aunt's spirit.

A sharp magical tingle informed Alex the entrance to the Crossroads ley line station was at hand. The team planned to travel to the entrance to the Underworld in small groups. Once everyone made it there, they would move out. They hoped to travel in stealth and reach the River Styx without setting off alerts or engaging in any skirmishes. Persephone had informed them the journey to the river should take about two hours on foot. Hellhorse and carriage, the normal method of transportation in the Underworld, were out of the question. The clatter of the horse's metal hooves and the glow of their fiery eyes would draw the attention of the formidable demons protecting Hades' realm.

～

ALEX FOUGHT against the nausea that ley line travel still induced as she waited for the rest of the attack team to make it to the rendezvous spot on the edge of the Underworld. She wrinkled her nose at the smokey haze permeating the air and peered over the small earth berm protecting them from view.

The huge, fiery Underworld gates she saw filled her with apprehension. Large, heavily armed demons with blue-black fur patrolled the wide road leading to the gates. Low slung guard huts on either side of the road spewed guttural laughter as the off-duty guards inside engaged in revelry. *There are so many of them,* Alex despaired. How the hell were they going to slip unnoticed into the Underworld? Was the battle over before it even started? She blew out a soft sigh.

Conor's hand slipped into Alex's and squeezed it gently. "No worries, sweets. Barghest here, remember? Our kind originated as Hades' elite strain of Hellhounds—until he had to give us to Hecate as reparation for the whole Persephone fiasco." Conor winked, then shared startling news. "I still have family here and visit occasionally. My cousin, Rafe, is going to meet us here shortly and lead us into the Underworld on one of the many alternate routes available."

Alex peered again at the enormous gates glowing red with the fires of Hell, guarded by an army of terrifying demons. "But, why—"

"Ah, yes. The massive gates. Well, Hades has a bit of an ego, along with a large streak of insecurity. He had the gates built just before he staged Persephone's kidnapping. He wanted to impress her with the size of his gates when they arrived in the Underworld."

Alex snorted. "So, the huge gates are his way of compensating for his small brain and even smaller—"

A cool, amused voice interrupted Alex. Persephone murmured, "I assure you, Keeper, while Hades may not be the smartest god in all the realms, I have no complaints about the size of his ... ah ... gates."

Alex, her face almost as red as the hellfire engulfing the gates, prepared to apologize to the smugly grinning goddess. To her immense relief, the last of their team arrived, distracting everyone, and negating the need for Alex to make an extremely uncomfortable apology.

A low chuffing sound came from a grove of twisted black trees behind them. The team's hands went to their weapons, expecting an attack. The chuffing sounded again. Then a huge black dog detached himself from the shadow of the trees and loped toward their group.

Conor whispered urgently. "Stand down, everyone. That's my cousin, Rafe. He's going to guide us along an alternate route into the Underworld."

Alex watched as, between one step and another, the enormous black dog transformed into a tall, leanly muscled man. A very naked, very handsome man, she observed with some admiration.

A large hand covered her eyes, and a wry voice interrupted her thoughts. "No ogling the handsome Hellhound, sweets." Conor snickered. "You can ogle me all you want when we return home."

When Conor removed his hand, Alex noted with some disappointment that the Hellhound had wrapped a short fabric skirt around his waist. As her gaze raised from his waist to his face, she found the man's dark eyes observing her with amusement and some heat. "Hello, Keeper. Welcome to the Underworld, where the Hellhounds are real, and more than the hellfire is hot."

"Knock it off, Rafe." Conor warned the Hellhound with a feral smile. "Or I'll tell your very scary wife that you've been flirting. Again."

The sexy grin slid right off Rafe's face, and he became all business. He explained the route they would take to avoid the ostentatious Underworld gates, whose glow lit the night sky behind them.

"Scary wife, huh? What kind of demon is she?" Alex whispered to Conor.

"Oh, she's scary, all right. She's a Hellhound, too, though not a demon. The females of our species are much larger than the males when in Hellhound form. Celi would cook Rafe's balls for dinner if he cheated on her, and he knows it. He couldn't resist teasing me because he knows that I ... uh ... really like ... you."

Rafe's urgent whisper prevented Alex from responding to Conor's revelation. "Time to head out, everyone. The guards will make their rounds shortly, and they do occasionally patrol out this far."

Alex watched as Rafe smoothly transformed back into his Hellhound form, leaving the scrap of cloth he had wrapped around his waist in human form lying forlornly on the ground as he loped into the shadows. She wondered where he'd gotten the fabric and idly considered grabbing it as she passed so she could give it to him for later use when he transformed back to his human form. Then reconsidered. *No fabric, no covering of the spectacular view*, she mused with a silent snicker.

THE TREK through the Underworld to the River Styx was long and tiring, but mostly uneventful. Rafe's expert knowledge of the terrain and sixth sense for danger kept the team safe and unobserved.

They had startled a mother guarding her nest of baby demon-vipers. Fortunately, the creatures died quickly. Alex cringed at the killing of the babies. Rafe's amber eyes watched her reaction, his pink tongue, now flecked with demon-viper blood, hanging from between sharp canines set into his long muzzle. His deep voice echoed in her mind as he explained that demon-vipers were a scourge in the Underworld. Their venom paralyzed most demons. Once immobile, the vipers would eat the demon alive. Slowly.

Alex worked on recovering from visions of a bunch of baby demon-vipers eating a huge, paralyzed demon piece by piece. Conor's hand on her arm made her jump.

"Sorry, but we're almost at the River Styx. The team will take cover in this ravine while Persephone attempts to win Charon's cooperation."

Conor sighed, and Alex commiserated with him. During the battle planning, he argued against giving Charon a head's up about the assault, but Persephone had insisted. She thought the team would have a better chance of success with Charon's cooperation than without it. She had explained that, while it was possible they could coerce the powerful ferryman into transporting the team onto the river and toward the heart of the Underworld, there was no telling if any of them would make it across alive.

There were tales of whole boats full of passengers going missing between one shore of the dark river and the other. No one dared ask Charon what happened to those passengers. The dangers of the River Styx were well known, along with the fact that she demanded the occasional sacrifice from the dark ferryman who plied her waters.

AFTER A TENSE HALF hour of waiting, with the team huddled together in the tight space of the ravine, a soft whistle from the shore alerted the team that Persephone had secured Charon's cooperation.

As they climbed the narrow path leading out of the ravine, Alex murmured a query. "Are we sure that's Persephone's whistle? And can we trust her word about Charon? According to Demeter, she's got a bit of a crush on him."

Conor gave her a mysterious smile before disappearing over the lip of the ravine. His face appeared over the edge, and he held out his hand to guide her up onto the rocky shoreline, where Alex came face-to-face with an angry goddess.

"Why don't you ask her," Conor said, "and the man himself?" He stepped aside to reveal a tall, lean man draped in a stylish black cloak. Charon's chiseled cheeks and olive skin set off his deep black eyes, which gazed reprovingly at Alex. Charon held a twisted and blackened shepherd's crook in one strong hand while the other hovered at Persephone's elbow, offering her support should she need it on the rock-strewn shore of the fast-flowing River Styx.

"I can be trusted, Keeper." Charon's rich, deep voice resonated in the night air. "I'd never do anything to harm Persephone." A smile touched his lips. "And, yes, you might say we have a crush on each other. I'm aware of her feelings for me, and return them unreservedly, although we both understand we can never act on them, as we are of different worlds, and each have our own responsibilities." Charon narrowed his eyes. "Besides, Hades is not a god I'd challenge for the affections of his bride." A dark, angry shadow passed across the man's face. "I'd win, of course, but the Underworld, and perhaps even the whole of Earth, would lie in ruins."

Alex shivered. She believed him ... about everything. "But if you value Persephone and don't want the Underworld or Earth to be destroyed, why have you been helping Nyx and my fath—the necromantic mage, Talon?" She cleared her throat and looked to Conor for support before returning her questioning gaze to the handsome ferryman. "We know you have been transporting the physical remains of dead human bodies across the river and bringing the unnatural creations made by the mage back to this side of the river, giving them access to the Crossroads ley lines that allow them to reach Earth. You must have known their intentions were dark."

Charon had bowed his head as Alex spoke.

Persephone gently stroked the ferryman's shoulder, then slipped her hand into his. "Nyx and Talon showed up at Hades' castle several months ago. They convinced him they had a plan that would bring the Crossroads under Hades' control. He has always resented Hecate for creating the Crossroads, and for demanding his prized Hellhounds to guard them. He was, and still is, loath to give up his control over the many supernaturals in this realm who in the past had to rely on his good graces to leave it. Since the creation of the Crossroads, the Underworld can hold neither gods nor supernaturals against their will."

The ferryman's haunted eyes met Alex's. "Nyx's lies and flattery fooled Hades. She promised him control of the Crossroads, so he allowed her to make the castle headquarters for her nefarious plans. Nyx forced my cooperation by threatening Persephone's life and the lives of the other two goddesses who form the triune that created the Crossroads."

Persephone explained. "Charon knew that if he didn't cooperate, the Crossroads would fall sooner rather than later. The death of Hecate, Demeter, and myself would see to that."

Confused, Alex asked Charon why he had held back his knowledge. "But if you knew that helping Nyx and Talon would lead to the fall of the Crossroads, why worry about it falling at all? Couldn't you have warned Persephone of the danger and let the triune sort it out?"

Charon fixed his gaze on the pitch-black river flowing past them, its swirls and eddies seemingly with a life of their own. "I'm bound to this river, Keeper, and cannot leave it unattended without dire consequences for all the realms. I had no way to contact Persephone directly unless she passed this way on her travels. I have been doing what I can to sabotage Nyx and Talon's plans while hoping to get word to her about the danger to the Crossroads and all who rely on them."

Alex squirmed under the ferryman's powerful gaze. She instinctively knew the ferryman saw her very soul. A piece of the puzzle clicked into place. "So, *you* were the reason the first several attempts at getting the Regenerants to Earth resulted in their final deaths, their body parts split between this realm and the next?"

Charon's lips curved in a dark smile. "Yes. I have attempted to delay Nyx and Talon's plans as much as possible without rousing suspicion." The ferryman gestured at Rafe, who nodded in response. "Word from the In-Between recently reached me through this Hellhound, who told me your Crossroads had a new Keeper and that you were aware of the danger. I knew then that Persephone would come to me for help in ending Nyx's attempt to bring chaos to the Crossroads and the realms beyond."

Charon nodded once before turning away. He strode toward the large wooden boat bobbing at the end of a rough wooden pier that jutted into the dark waters of the Styx. "Come, let me get you all across this river and on your way."

As the team approached the boat, Charon held out his hand. Conor produced and handed over a leather bag that chinked as it hit the Charon's palm. Alex knew it was full of coins. Two for every member of the attack team.

The ferryman had received his due; their journey across the River Styx was paid in full.

31

INTO THE MOUTH OF HELL

After an uneventful journey across the murky river, the boat gently bumped up against the rough wooden dock on the far side. Charon hopped nimbly out and tied the craft to the large wooden poles rising from the black water.

"Move quickly now." Charon counseled the team in a whisper. "There are more guards on this side of the river." He pointed past the steep riverbank. "Hades' castle stands on a plateau at the top of that mountain."

The team disembarked at a rapid rate, using the concealing darkness of night in the Underworld to melt into the shadows. Rafe lead the team up a steep path cut into the side of the mountain. They kept to the inadequate cover of a deep drainage ditch that paralleled the narrow road.

Several times, the heavy tramp of boots belonging to demon guards sounded along the road above them, causing the team to duck deeper into the ditch and freeze until the sound of footsteps faded away. Alex puffed as she and the team trotted to keep up with the fast pace set by Rafe. Still in his Hellhound form, Rafe's huge paws moved with assurance and speed as he led the team into the foothills of Hades' mountain lair.

Alex shivered in the humid night air. The oppressive

atmosphere emanating from the unseen castle perched high above raised goosebumps on her sweating skin.

Rafe finally drew to a stop at the mouth of a narrow gully that diverged from the drainage ditch through which they had been traveling and whispered over his shoulder at the team. *"Now we follow this path to reach the shortcut through the troll tunnels. The tunnels are dangerous, but they are the only way into the castle without using one of the well-guarded gates."*

Alex swallowed reflexively, fear drying her throat. "Uh, troll tunnels?"

Conor shot her a reproachful look. "Weren't you paying attention during the planning meetings when Greta told us about the ancient troll tunnels? We realized they provided the only way to infiltrate the castle without a head-on fight—and heavy casualties."

"Won't the trolls mind us using their tunnels, though?" Alex envisioned angry green creatures with huge, spiked clubs chasing them through cramped underground corridors.

A gruff snicker from Greta interrupted Alex's fevered imaginings. "You really weren't paying attention during the planning meetings, were you, Keeper? Trolls are long gone from the Underworld. They migrated to Earth at the end of the last ice age. My people, the river trolls, are only one small branch of their many descendants. I grew up hearing stories about the ancient tunnels burrowed through this land and how my ancestors used them to run rings around the newcomer, Hades, and his not-so-merry band of misfits when he moved to the Underworld after the gods on Olympus kicked his ass to the curb." Greta sobered. "Let's hope tales of the tunnels weren't merely fairytales told to troll children at bedtime, or we're screwed."

Rafe's smooth voice spoke into Alex's mind. *"The tunnels aren't just fairy stories. We Hellhounds have used them as dens for millennia."* He snorted in disgust. *"Hades and his demons don't pay any attention to us. We're only packs of wild dogs to them. The truth of the tunnels hides in the mists of memory and our pack matriarchs guard it jealously."*

The team's nodding heads told Alex that Rafe had shared his story with everyone. Her mind caught up with his words and her mental ears perked up. His explanation sounded like actual history, the focus of her graduate degree. "So, Hellhounds have a matriarchal society?" Alex queried Rafe as they left the ditch and road behind and followed a thin path into the rocky foothills.

Conor chuckled, and Rafe ducked his shaggy head in confirmation before replying. *"Of course. It's the best way."*

Alex couldn't really argue that, despite thinking gender equality might work just as well, if not better. *Millenia of patriarchy-based societies on Earth sure as hell hadn't worked out so well,* she mused. *Who am I to argue with Hellhound gender roles?*

A small clearing in the twisted trees and tall brush that draped the foothills appeared ahead. Rafe stopped the team in the shadow of trees outside the clearing. His eyes flashed a warning. *"Stay here and don't move, no matter what happens next."*

He gave a low woof, which was met by a low woof from the far side of the clearing.

"Stay here and don't interfere. I need to negotiate our passage into the tunnels with the matriarchs of this territory." Rafe loped into the clearing. Several massive black dogs twice Rafe's size moved to meet him, their eyes glowing fiercely in the night as they gazed at the smaller Hellhound. Rafe's inky black fur morphed into smooth human skin as he shifted into human form. They exchanged a complicated ritual of greeting. Rafe and the Hellhounds sat across from each other, unmoving.

"Rafe is mind-speaking with them." Conor whispered in Alex's ear. "They would have taken it as a challenge if he stayed in his Hellhound form when they met, so that's why he shifted."

After what seemed like hours, but was likely only minutes, Rafe bowed his head to the Hellhounds seated opposite him. As one, the massive creatures stood, then turned their heads, their glowing gazes piercing the shadows hiding the team. Alex realized there was no hiding from Hellhounds, in this realm or any other. Not only did they have an extraordinary sense of smell, but they clearly had perfect night vision.

A tense moment passed before the matriarchs melted back into the woods at the far side of the clearing. Rafe chuffed a sigh before rising and gesturing the team forward.

No fabric blocked Alex's view of Rafe's naked human form, but she was too worried to appreciate the view. Anxious, Alex asked him, "I'm assuming they agreed to let us use their tunnels?"

Rafe nodded once, his reply a careful murmur. "You may not see the Hellhounds who make these tunnels their home, but they are still watching and listening. Yes, the matriarchs of this pack have granted us passage through these tunnels ... for a price."

Conor's brows lowered in concern. "What is their price? And can we pay it?"

"My wife is going to kill me, but yes, we will pay their price." Rafe sighed with feeling. "Their pack's last several litters produced too many females. The pack matriarchs see this as a potential problem, as dominance fights amongst females once they reach adolescence are vicious and can even be deadly. They wish my pack to take in three young female Hellhounds and raise them as our own." Rafe huffed out a worried breath. "Our pack has a fair number of young females of our own, so adding more is going to set off more than a few bloody battles for pack position once they all hit puberty."

Conor's thanks were grateful. "Thank you, cousin. We appreciate your sacrifice."

Alex couldn't help herself. "But why are you willing to do this? I know, Conor's your family and all, but this isn't your battle."

"Of course, it is, Keeper." Rafe's words were patient as he explained. "If Nyx and her cohorts breach the Crossroads and proceed with their plans to ravage Earth, do you think the gods will allow it to continue without waging a war that will devastate all the realms? There would be no safe place for anyone, including us."

"Oh." Alex hadn't really considered the devastating extent of the consequences if Nyx and Talon were successful. She had been too busy concentrating on the immediate danger to her Crossroads. "I understand now. I apologize for my ignorance. But still, thank you."

"You are very welcome, Alex. Please make sure you win this battle, for your defeat would give divine chaos free rein to ravage all the realms." Rafe's serious gaze pinned Alex in place for a moment before he shifted effortlessly into his Hellhound form and loped into the trees on the far side of the clearing. His amber gaze invited the team to follow.

As the team picked their way through the increasingly rocky, steep terrain, the boulders grew larger and the paths between them narrower. Soon, they came to a smooth, blank wall. The rocky walls on either side crowded close.

Rafe paused beside the wall, shifting back into human form, and stooping to pick up a compact bundle of clothing half hidden in the grass.

Alex watched with a trace of disappointment as Rafe quickly donned black trousers and t-shirt and laced a pair of sturdy boots. "Did you leave those here earlier?"

Rafe chuckled as he tied his last bootlace. "No, this area is in another pack's domain. I've never been here before. When I spoke with the pack matriarchs earlier, I requested one additional boon, in exchange for agreeing to take on several of their young female Hellhounds. Clothing."

With a merry twinkle, Rafe explained. "The matriarchs were happy to supply the clothes. These mountain Hellhounds are a bit prudish. They don't want their young females, who can't shift or mind-speak until they reach puberty, eyeing my magnificent human form the entire way back to my pack's domain."

Glad the dark night hid her rosy cheeks, Alex envisioned Rafe traveling the Underworld in human form. Naked human form.

Conor's voice, soft in warning, slipped into her mind, chiding her. *"Focus, Alex. I told you that Rafe's off-limits."* He chuckled slyly. *"But I'm not. Maybe I should shift more often. And forget my clothes."*

Alex's blush deepened as her thoughts happily shifted to a vision of a naked Connor. She groaned in embarrassment, knowing his sensitive Barghest nose would smell her arousal. Now was *so* not the time.

Rafe's businesslike voice interrupted her thoughts as he addressed the team. Alex resolved to concentrate on the mission instead of daydreaming about hunky Hellhounds and bare-naked Barghests.

"We have reached the entrance to the troll tunnels. Please have your weapons ready, but don't draw them unless I tell you to. After my successful negotiations with their matriarchs, the Hellhounds within the near tunnels present no threat." Grim determination hardened Rafe's eyes. "But the same doesn't apply to the troll's abandoned pets in the deeper tunnels."

"Um, pets? What kind of pets," Alex asked. A tremor she couldn't disguise made her voice quaver. "And just exactly how have they survived in these tunnels for tens of thousands of years since the trolls left?"

Greta's mocking laugh filled the night air. "The creatures now living in these tunnels are descendants of the monstrous Underworld pets that generations of my troll ancestors threatened children with if they misbehaved. I assure you, Alex, these abandoned pets are *more* than capable of fending for themselves." The river troll shook her head, knuckles showing white from a steely grip on the hilt of her sword. "Let's go. No time like the present."

Conor held up a hand to halt forward movement. "Wait! Rafe, you warned me earlier of dangerous creatures in the tunnels but didn't give any details. Greta seems to understand the threat these abandoned pets pose, but it wasn't specifically addressed in our battle planning. Perhaps now is the time. What are these dangerous creatures we face inside the deepest tunnels?"

"Cats." Rafe uttered the single word succinctly.

"Cats?" Alex's jaw dropped in disbelief.

Rafe's face held a thin smile, but darker emotions lurked in his eyes as he explained. "Yes, cats. But not the small, fluffy ones your kin keep as pets on Earth, Keeper. These cats are bigger, even bigger than your earthly leopards and lions. The Underworld gave many monstrous creatures to the earth realm in times past." Rafe gave a low laugh at the looks of dismay on the team members' faces. "When the trolls abandoned this realm for Earth those many millennia ago, they took their favorite saber-toothed kittens with them. They abandoned the adult cats here in the Underworld. And boy, were they pissed at getting left behind." He shrugged. "Their progeny still hasn't gotten over that long ago betrayal."

Alex listened with growing dismay to Rafe's words as she eyed the smooth stone wall ahead of them. "Two questions, Rafe. First, where is the entrance to the tunnel? All I see is a solid stone wall. Second, if there are giant, angry saber-toothed tigers in these tunnels, how do Hellhound packs use them for dens?"

"The tunnel entrance is straight ahead. Once our negations were complete, the pack matriarchs gave me a key. It will pierce this illusion and allow us access to the tunnel." Rafe made a sad chuffing sound. "As to your second question, Hellhounds have always had to fight for their dens, and many have died claiming them. Once we clear a tunnel of cats—which can take decades, we seal and guard it well."

A cylindrical green stone appeared in Rafe's hand. He placed its tip on the smooth surface of the wall. "The tunnels in this mountain are endless. Most Hellhounds avoid this area, but as our population grows, newly formed packs must clear and claim even undesirable tunnels such as those weaving through the bowels of Hades' mountain. The pack claiming this tunnel has cleared and claimed the first part of this labyrinth, but we must proceed past that, into uncleared tunnels, to reach the castle."

∽

ALEX RAISED her wand as the still-smoking body of the giant cat fell to the dirt floor of the tunnel with a rumbling crash. *Damn,* she thought with exhaustion, *these things are freaking huge.* The team had discovered that, if the killing blow wasn't struck exactly right, a massive dead cat carcass would block a narrow tunnel. Fortunately, this one had fallen in a wider section, meaning no one had to drag the smoking corpse out of the way, or climb over it, or tunnel under it—all things she and the team had done over the past several hours to continue their journey into the heart of Hades' mountain.

As she wiped sweat off her forehead, Alex wondered how she and the team were going to have the energy to fight the main battle once they reached the castle. She was well beyond her second wind and didn't think she had a third in her. Trying not to whine, Alex asked, "Are we getting close—"

"Shhhhh. We are now directly adjacent to the castle's dungeon. I can hear faint movement on the other side." Rafe pointed at the smooth stone wall of the tunnel and whispered. "Now, we need to find one of the cat flaps."

"Cat flaps?"

"You know, pet doors. How do you think the trolls' cats got in and out of these deeper tunnels," Rafe exclaimed. "You think the trolls felt like getting up to open the door whenever the damn things wanted in—or out?" A cunning smile replaced his frown. "The intransigence of the typical feline really helps us now, though. When Hades claimed this mountain as his domain, and built his castle on the peak, his workers carved dungeons out of a natural cave system that existed long before the castle was built. The troll tunnels we are in now intersect with this cave system. I'm told there are still several ancient cat flaps that open into undeveloped parts of the caves. They are located near the dungeons."

After several anxious minutes of searching along the walls of the tunnel, a muted shout went up. "Found one!"

Everyone hurried toward the voice. The team gazed in disappointment at the rough, square opening cut into the solid stone of the tunnel. A clumsily built brick wall blocked the rather small pet door.

Alex eyed the opening doubtfully. It appeared barely large enough for a golden retriever to fit through. "Are you sure this cat flap is big enough for us? And how in the flames of Hell did saber-toothed tigers fit through these things?"

Conor snickered. "You're not a cat person, are you? Cats can fit through the smallest openings. In fact, the smaller the better."

"If you say so."

Vincent's blood harem came in handy, as they had brought tools and could work in complete silence. Within minutes, carefully removed bricks revealed a small, dark cave on the other side of the ancient cat flap.

Conor pointed to a spot on the far side of the cave. "See that? The ground becomes level, and the walls show chisel marks. That must be the beginning of the dungeons."

The team members individually squeezed through the opening until they were all crowded into the small cave leading to the dungeons.

Rafe instructed the team to remain in the cave. "Stay here, everyone. Conor and I will do a reconnaissance and report back. We smell familiar to demons—like dogs, so it shouldn't alert them to our intrusion."

Crowded into the small space, the team shifted restlessly while waiting for Conor and Rafe to return from their reconnaissance. A soft footfall at the entrance to the dungeons brought everyone to high alert, weapons at the ready.

"It's just us, guys." Conor warned the team as he and Rafe appeared around the corner of the cave. "The corridor ahead leads to an unused portion of the dungeons. There's a heavy metal gate about halfway down, with a guard station in an alcove further down the hallway on the other side of it." Conor's voice held disappointment and frustration. "Looks like the demons guarding this place aren't as lax in their duties as we'd like them to be."

Greta pulled her sword from its scabbard. "Well, what are we waiting for? Let's go knock some heads together."

"Not so fast, everyone." Alex surprised even herself by speaking up. "We can't go rushing up to the metal gate expecting the guards on the other side to sit around on their asses while we try to knock it down. We need a plan."

At Conor's approving glance, Alex's face heated in embarrassed pleasure.

"Alex is right. We can't just charge down there and expect to remove the gate in time to stop the guards on the other side from raising the alarm."

After much whispered argument, the group decided that Vinnie and his blood harem would attempt to breach the gate. Vinnie swore his vampire skills at compulsion would enable him to compel the demon guards to open the gate and cooperate with the attack team. Greta led the argument against this plan, but eventually, a team vote overrode her objections.

Vinnie and his blood harem disappeared around the corner and silently slipped down the hallway. Silence ensued as minutes trickled by, everyone hoping for the best but with hands on their weapons, preparing for the worst. Conor's hand rest on Alex's shoulder, offering what comfort he could as they waited.

Just as the team wondered if the guards had caught Vinnie and his blood harem, Abel, the harem's leader, stuck his head into the hallway. "All clear. Vinnie put all but one guard to sleep and compelled the remaining guard to open the gate." Abel smiled. "They're all sleeping peacefully now, locked in the cells. They won't wake for a day or two."

Conor motioned the team forward as the battle began with silence and sleep.

～

THE TEAM cautiously navigated the cell-lined passageways, moving ever deeper into the dungeon complex. So far, the cells they passed were cobweb draped and empty. In this unused part of the dungeon, they encountered several smaller groups of bored guards, all of whom Vinnie quickly compelled to sleep. Abel and his cohorts silently moved the guards to the stone floors of nearby cells, locking them inside.

A familiar presence in her mind startled Alex. "Maia's spirit is being held in a cell up ahead," she whispered, her words vibrating with excitement at the thought of rescuing her aunt.

Conor's firm hand drew her to a halt as she tried to increase her pace. "The cells up ahead are occupied by others, as well as your aunt. While some prisoners may be sympathetic to our cause, there are likely those who would attempt to curry favor with their captors by raising the alarm. Occupied cells also mean a stronger guard presence. We need to advance slowly."

A deep breath helped Alex contain her impatience. She nodded once to show she understood the need for caution. Progress after that was painstakingly slow. Vinnie slipped into the shadows and crept along the corridor, compelling both prisoners and guards to sleep.

About halfway down the passage, a whispered word, followed by a low exclamation, filtered down the hallway. Alex barely heard Vinnie's low whisper. "The way is clear. Alex, come to me, I've found your aunt."

Alex sped toward her aunt's cell, while Vinnie instructed the team members to move ahead. "Everyone, please proceed with caution to the next intersection and stand guard."

Her uncle's dark eyes shone with compassion as he motioned Alex into the cell. "She's in here, niece. Her spirit is fighting hard, but it looks like she's more present in this realm now than on Earth."

Alex gasped in horror when she saw the ghostly figure of her aunt bound to a low wooden cot inside the dirty stone cell. Ropes of writhing gray mist bound her struggling form tightly to the cot's frame. Her translucent mouth moved in a constant indistinct murmur and her eyes moved rapidly behind closed lids.

"That fucking bastard Morpheus." Alex swore softly as she leaned down to lay a comforting hand on her aunt's shoulder. "He's got her trapped in a nightmare and is using it to pull her spirit the rest of the way into the Underworld."

Conor spoke from outside the cell, his voice low but urgent. "Don't touch her, Alex! Morpheus may sense if another interferes with his nightmare magic."

"Well, I'm not going to leave her here like this! One reason we came to this godforsaken place is to free her spirit, and dammit, I'm going to do that if it's the last thing I do."

An unfamiliar voice replied, "And it would be the last thing you do, Keeper."

Alex swung around to see a tall man leaning against the open cell door, blocking her exit. His tattered cloak did little to conceal his toned, muscular physique, but the hood drawn low over his head obscured most of his face from view. "Hello, dear. Nice to meet you outside of your nightmares."

"I sure as hell can't say the same, Morpheus, you asshole." As Alex spewed verbal venom at the god of her nightmares standing before her, she surreptitiously peered around his tall form. A wave of disappointment filled her as she saw Conor and Vinnie prone on the stone floor of the hallway, both struggling as they slept, trapped deep in divine nightmares cast by the powerful god standing before her. She assumed the rest of the team were similarly indisposed but hoped desperately she was wrong.

"Step away from your aunt, please." Morpheus gave Alex a thin smile. "It wouldn't do for you to wind up trapped in her nightmare, now, would it? I am quite sure you'd be much unhappier with one all of your own."

～

ALEX REMAINED STILL, gripping her staff behind her back, hoping for a chance to use it either to release her aunt's spirit from its nightmare bindings or to disable the smirking god before her.

Preferably both. She'd absolutely love to knock that grin right off his face.

"I said, step away from your aunt, Keeper. I won't give you another chance to comply without unpleasant consequences." Morpheus chuckled softly. "Or rather, even more unpleasant consequences than those I already have planned for you."

Desperately, Alex considered her options. She was almost positive she could free her aunt's spirit, but that would likely result in her own immediate death or, at best, an extended nightmare from which she'd never return.

Movement in the hallway behind Morpheus' shoulder distracted Alex. She saw the familiar short figure of Greta moving silently toward the god, a sword in one hand and a softly glowing crystal in the other. The river troll caught Alex's eye and shook her head sharply, reminding her not to draw the god's attention to Greta's stealthy approach.

Alex quickly returned her gaze to the nightmare god and began talking smack to distract him. "So, you and your brothers decided it's a smart idea to help your grandmother, Nyx, with her evil plot, huh? What's in it for you? Or are you all just a bunch of grandma's boys who do whatever she tells you?" She closed her mouth with a snap. *Can't keep my smart mouth closed for anything,* she mused grimly.

Morpheus straightened from his casual pose against the cell doorway, his angry gaze pinning her in place. *Good,* Alex thought, *he's focused on me. Hopefully, Greta can get a jump on him before he fries me to a crisp.*

"Listen, you pitiful excuse for a Keeper, I can destroy you—"

Morpheus's threatening words cut off as he stumbled into the cell, followed closely by Greta, who had her sword buried in his back. As the god fell to his knees, he reached back and grabbed Greta's sword arm, wrenching it away from his body. Greta cried out in pain as her shoulder left its socket. The injured god dragged Greta down to the rough stones of the cell as he fell, his roar of rage turning into a cry of pain as Greta pressed the glowing crystal into the skin at his neck.

The cell filled with a light brighter than day as brilliant green and blue shafts of luminescent magic patterned the walls. Alex closed her eyes against the pain of the magical light show, but quickly forced them open so she could take at least one action while Greta's attack distracted Morpheus.

"Hecate, please hear me and lend me your strength." Alex whispered a fevered entreaty to the goddess as she called up her magic and activated her staff. Quickly, she touched the now-glowing staff to the writhing gray bindings securing her aunt's spirit to the cot. She poured all her magic and determination into her plea. "Please, Goddess, free these bindings and call Maia's spirit to her rightful place at the Crossroads. Call my aunt home."

The triple goddess pendant around Alex's neck warmed. A luminescent blue light shimmered from the gemstone set between the crescent moons, casting a faint glow on the cot containing Maia's struggling spirit. Alex interpreted the pendant's warmth and light as Hecate's blessing on her endeavors.

Sounds of a desperate struggle continued behind Alex, and grunts of pain echoed in the air. Alex shook her head to clear her mind. Unable to worry about what was happening behind her, she hoped Greta's distraction gained her enough time to free Maia before the god of nightmares gained the upper hand against the badly injured river troll. She pushed even more of her own magic into the staff. Pain shot down her arm as a massive surge of Hecate's divine power joined her own. Blue-red flames poured from the staff, sizzling as they wrapped around the nightmare bindings. The writhing gray ropes fought back, swirling ever faster and constricting even tighter around her aunt.

Alex realized she wouldn't be able to keep up the magical battle to free her aunt much longer. She screamed in fury as she poured one final push of magic through her staff.

A loud boom echoed off the cell's stone walls. The bindings around Maia cracked and fell to the dirt floor of the cell. Alex watched her aunt's struggling translucent form still, her nightmare broken. Maia's eyes opened, and a soft smile curved her lips. "Thank you, niece. Hecate is calling me home to the Crossroads. Please, dear, win this battle..."

Alex watched with mingled joy and pain as the last of her aunt's spirit faded into nothingness. She'd won this skirmish. Her aunt's spirit was free and back where it belonged—at her beloved Crossroads. But she knew the battle was far from over.

Wet gasping behind her struck terror in Alex's heart. She spun around and gaped in horror at the scene before her. Greta's twisted form lay on the rough stone floor, blood trickling from her lips. She had felled the god, who now lay unconscious. But his slow breaths suggested Greta's victory wasn't a permanent one.

Alex dropped to her knees by Greta's torn body. Gently, she placed a hand on the river troll's shoulder. "Oh, Greta, I'm so sorry. Is there anything I can do?"

Pain-filled eyes focused on Alex. Blood dribbled from Greta's mouth as she whispered a last command. "You better kill these fuckers. Win this war, Keeper, or we're all lost."

Greta died on a sigh. Alex heaved a sob, tears trickling down her face as she gently closed the gruff river troll's eyes. "I promise, Greta. I promise I will."

A SARDONIC CHUCKLE behind Alex ended her grief-filled reverie. She was so angry at the god behind her. So angry. She spun around and shouted. "Morpheus, you son of a bitch! I'm going to kill you if it's the last thing I do."

"I'll have to take a rain check on the killing, Keeper. Just so we're clear, when we meet again, it'll be me killing you, not the other way around."

Alex met the god's eyes and saw the promise of death in them. Her glare gave the god the same promise. "We'll have to see about that, won't we, asshole?"

Morpheus gave a thin smile and gestured to the guards now waiting outside the cell. "Now, now. Language, dear. While I'd love to stay and chat further, I've got places to be and things to do."

As his body shimmered into gray smoke, Morpheus's parting words pierced Alex's heart. "I'm off to collect your aunt's spirit. All of it this time."

Alex closed her eyes and issued a quick warning to Hecate. "Goddess, Morpheus is on his way. He's pissed and wants my aunt's spirit back—"

Before she finished her entreaty, a rough hand grabbed Alex's arm and pulled her to her feet. Behind the huge demon gripping her arm tightly, Alex saw a host of other guards leading her now awake, but groggy, team down the narrow corridor. After a last sorrowful glance at Greta's crumpled form, Alex turned a glare on the demon guard who held her captive. "Okay, loser, take me to your leader. Now."

32

UNHAPPY FAMILIES

Aᴀ fter many twists and turns, and traipsing up untold amounts of stairs, Alex saw the rough gray stone of the dungeon give way to textured stucco walls. Sparkling marble tiles replaced bare flagstones. Persian rugs stretched across the smooth expanse of polished floors.

The guards leading Alex and her team halted outside a massive set of carved wooden doors that extended halfway to the ceiling. Alex heard Persephone speaking to a guard stationed at the doors. "So, my husband is in the throne room? Let's get on with things." With an imperious gesture, the goddess motioned to the entry. "Open the doors immediately, guard, and let us through."

Alex hid a smile at a flustered look on the guard's face. He gripped the brass handle on the massive door, but paused in indecision, as if unsure of Persephone's right to command him. His eyes slid away from her penetrating gaze, and he pulled on the handle. As enormous doors creaked open, the hulking demon guards holding Alex and her team captive strode forward, dragging everyone into the vast room.

At first, the size of the space and the elegance of its furnishings overwhelmed Alex. A vaulted ceiling soared three stories overhead. Silken flags adorned with unfamiliar coats of arms hung from the ancient rafters. Elaborate tapestries covered most of the room's walls. The gleaming marble floors were mostly bare, except for a long oak refectory table lined with chairs along one wall. A narrow red carpet led across acres of floor space before ending at a raised dais, upon which sat several large, ornate thrones. Regenerant guards lined the sides and back of the platform.

Alex studied the figures lounging on the thrones as the guards led the team forward, before pushing them to their knees in front of the dais. A short, squat woman with blunt features sat on the largest throne, her mouth pursed in a moue of distaste as she studied Alex and her bedraggled team, now kneeling on the cold marble tiles.

A dark-eyed, muscular man with a weathered face framed by long black hair perched on the edge of the smallest throne to her left, his demeanor distinctly uncomfortable.

An oddly familiar face occupied the last throne. Alex eyed her father as he stared back at her, his emerald green eyes the mirror of her own.

"Hi, Dad. Long time no see."

A wintry smile spread across Talon's thin face. Alex's heart contracted as she watched her father's lips twist into a sneer. The face that had smiled at her from a framed photo by her bedside as a child might look like the man now glaring down at her, but Alex knew that no mercy would be forthcoming from the haughty man occupying the throne above her. She realized with a stab of pain that she'd still hoped her father was being coerced into his dark actions by the goddess Nyx. No, this man—her father—was pure evil. Waves of malevolence emanated from him. She watched in growing disgust as her father's dark magic embraced the chaotic magic surrounding the stout goddess to his right. *Talon may be my biological family,* she reasoned, *but he is certainly not my heart-family.*

"Daughter. Welcome to Hell. Join us and live. Fight us and die."

"So dramatic, Talon. And please, call me Alex. My father died decades ago. I haven't seen him since. But if I did, I'd tell him to go fuck himself."

Talon's hand crashed down on the wooden arm of his throne, his face a rictus of rage. "You will not disrespect me, daughter. How dare you speak to me thus?"

"Oh, come on, old man. 'Thus?' You've been reading too much Shakespeare. I'm not into pompous, antiquated speech. Or tragedies." Alex paused, as if reflecting on her answer, before adding a final retort. "Or assholes like you."

Only Nyx's restraining hand on his arm kept her father from launching himself at Alex, his eyes filled with death.

Nyx spoke in a soft, mesmerizing voice. "Now, now, Alex, a child should always respect her parents. Your father gave you life, and he is offering you a chance for immortal life, to rule at his side ... our sides. Don't you want that?"

The goddess's deep, seductive voice snaked its way into Alex's mind, her words seemingly reasonable. Who wouldn't want immortal life? So what if a few people had to die so she could have it? Horrified, Alex shook her head violently to clear it.

Conor shuffled closer to Alex, pressing his shoulder against hers. His presence helped ground her, and sanity returned.

"Fuck you, Nyx." Alex glanced between the goddess and her father with revulsion. "You two deserve each other. You're both steeped in darkness, your souls twisted beyond recognition. Even Hell is too good for you."

A silvery voice interrupted. "She's right, Hades." Persephone stood in front of her husband, head unbowed, her gaze sparking with anger. "What were you thinking, husband, agreeing to give these two miscreants sanctuary and allowing them to use the castle—our castle—to further their evil plans? And what the hell are they doing sitting on your—our thrones?"

"Now, honey—"

"Don't you 'honey' me, you big oaf." Persephone groaned and

threw her hands up in frustration. "I can't leave you for five minutes without you making idiot decisions like this."

"But dear—"

"No. Nope. There's no excuse." Softening her voice, the goddess cajoled the god of the Underworld. "You know I love you, husband, but I cannot support your actions in this matter. You understand well that Hecate built the Crossroads so gods and others could travel unimpeded from one realm to another. And I realize it chaps your butt sometimes that you no longer have full control over who leaves—and who must stay, here in your realm. But there are still rules."

Persephone gave Nyx a disdainful nod. "There are those for whom such travel is forbidden, in order to protect all the realms." She waved a dismissive hand at Talon. "And those for whom the trip to the Underworld is meant to be one way."

Nyx's voice cut across Persephone's scolding. "Your husband knows more than you think, dear. He is on the right side of this battle." A cat's smile curved Nyx's lips. "Which side are you on, Persephone? Choose wisely, whore."

"Now, there's no need to speak to my wife like that—"

"Oh, grow up, Hades." Nyx sniffed in censure. "You know she sleeps around."

Persephone gave her husband an enigmatic look.

Hades nodded once and stood, squaring his shoulders as he towered over the dark goddess squatting on his throne. "Nyx, I hereby rescind your right to use my castle for your nefarious plans. Please collect your grandson, Morpheus, and your tame demons. I want you packed up and out of here within the hour." He gestured at Talon and the line of Regenerant guards standing at attention behind him. "And take your mage lover and his unnatural creations with you." Hades barked an order at the guards surrounding Alex and her team. "Free them. Quickly."

Within seconds, Alex's bindings loosened. She cheered silently as Hades' guards quickly freed the rest of her team.

TALON'S VOICE rang from the walls as he shouted. "No!" He spurred his Regenerants into action. "Rebind the prisoners, my daughter first."

Alex and her team wasted no time, retreating into a tight formation to one side of the dais. Those with magic called or created weapons and prepared for battle.

The room descended into chaos. Nyx, the goddess of Chaos, clapped her hands and chortled in unbridled pleasure. "Oh goodie! A bloody battle. One of my very favorite things!"

As she prepared to fight, Alex noticed Hades and Persephone embrace briefly, the goddess softly stroking her husband's long black hair. She whispered into her husband's ear, and he nodded in understanding and agreement before gently kissing her cheek.

Hades roared an order to his guards. "Demons, fight with my wife's team. Kill the Regenerants but leave Nyx to me."

The battle commenced, but now the odds were even.

A powerful arm snaked around Alex's neck, pulling her back against a hard body. "Hello, dear. So nice we could meet like this." Her father shoved her forward, and she stumbled, almost losing consciousness as his arm tightened around her neck. "Time to go now, daughter. I can see the necromantic power buried deep within you." Talon chuckled in her ear as he pushed her to the edge of the room. "My genes run true, even though it appears your mother did her best to conceal your heritage from you. You'll join me, one way or another, daughter. Together, we'll conquer the realms."

Alex's sluggish mind attempted to comprehend his words as she felt herself being dragged away from the fray. Her mind darkened as consciousness waned. *Wait. My heritage. He can't be talking about my Keeper heritage, as that comes from my mother's side of my family. No. Oh, no.*

The shock of her father's revelation ripped at Alex's soul. Fortunately, the pain sharpened her senses. If he wanted her for her power, it was because it was like his. She was a necromancer. Okay, then. Time to test a power she didn't know about two seconds ago. But first ....

The smack of her Keeper staff in her palm gave Alex the power to resist her father. She straightened and planted her feet, halting their backward progress and startling her father into loosening his hold.

Alex called to her magical power and poured everything she had into the staff. Her raw, red power rushed in, mixing with the bright blue of Hecate's divine power. Both red and blue magics swirled in a deadly dance, sparking and crackling with immense energy. As her father's arm tightened around her neck, she swung the staff hard behind her. A loud crack split the air when the flaming staff connected with Talon's body. The arm around her neck fell away as her father screamed in agony.

Alex twisted around, ready to bring the staff down on her father's head, but there was no need. His body lay prone on the marble floor, surrounded by crackling red and blue lightning. His anguished screams echoed in her ears as she watched the man who gave her life die a final death, his body disintegrating, his spirit folding in on itself until there was nothing left but gray floating ash.

A sense of both an ending and a beginning filled Alex. She did not mourn her father's death, but she knew she'd have to come to terms with her part in it—and with his revelations about the necromantic powers she inherited from him, once she and her team won the battle. And they *would* win. There was no other choice.

Alex considered her next move. It was crunch time, and there was no Billy the Squid to help jump start her new magical powers. She turned her back on what little remained of her father and faced the throne room, shocked to see the battle still raging, both sides evenly matched. Dead bodies littered the floor while attackers fought around and over them. Alex saw that Persephone and Hades had joined forces and were battling Nyx, who, despite her small stature, was holding strong.

Alex realized with dismay that the magic she inherited from her father might be the only thing that could tip the balance in favor of her team.

33

DADDY'S GIRL

A lex closed her eyes and took a deep breath. She reached deep down inside herself and threw open doors she had only vaguely seen before. She acknowledged the role both her mother and her father played in making her who she was. They were her biological family, but she didn't have to love them, or even like them. Before she could rid herself of their power over her, she'd first have to recognize them as just that, blood family only. Her heart-family deserved that much, and so much more.

As she pushed through the wisps of gray fog still clouding the far corners of her mind, she saw it. There. *Oh. My. God.* A massive fire of raw, red power flickered in the depths of her soul. Blue flames of Hecate's divine power—her blue Keeper power, she realized, flickered amongst the red ones. Shock reverberated in her soul as her mind tried to cope with the revelation. If her Keeper power was blue, the red power must be her necromantic power. She wondered briefly why no one had commented on the strange red magic she could raise and use but realized that was an issue for another time.

Alex called to her necromantic power and raised her staff. She screamed in pain and pleasure as a raging red inferno roared from its hiding place deep in her soul and poured into her staff. Red flames flared brightly around the staff, overpowering her blue Keeper magic. She sucked in a ragged breath, then bellowed at the undead. "Regenerants, I order you to stop fighting. Your creator and master, Talon, is dead. As his daughter, I now command you! Stop!"

She watched in awe as the staff's red flames twisted and flared. Small tendrils of power flowed from each tip of the crescent moon and snaked their way through the battle. The red tendrils wound around each Regenerant.

The Regenerants ceased their efforts one by one. As the red power touched them, each undead faced Alex and fell to their knees. As the last Regenerant's knees hit the floor with a muted thud, the group bowed their heads in reverence. "Mistress," they vowed, pledging their allegiance to Talon's daughter, the heritor of his necromantic power.

Alex's team and Hades' demons, who had been fighting side-by-side against the Regenerants, lowered their weapons, still panting from the battle. As one, they eyed the kneeling undead cautiously. Even the gods had stopped fighting and were gaping at the scene in confusion.

Silence reigned in the throne room.

Alex issued curt orders to the undead. "Regenerants, I command you to capture Nyx, then escort her out of the castle and far away from here. Take her back whence she came and guard her well until I instruct otherwise. Can you do that?"

"Yes, mistress." The Regenerants chorused the words, their voices reverent as they gazed in awe at their new leader.

Nyx let out a scream of rage and attempted to run off the podium, but her short legs were no match for the tallest of the Regenerants. The undead quickly surrounded and subdued the goddess of Chaos, binding her with thick black ropes of magical power provided by Hades.

Alex slumped to the floor, exhaustion overtaking her. She was vaguely aware of Conor coming to sit by her side. "So ... I'm a necromancer, as well as a Keeper. That's just great. Not." She leaned her head into Conor's chest as his arm encircled her shoulders. His warmth comforted her as she finally let go of the frenetic energy that had been fueling her until now. She sighed deeply. "I'm so tired. Can we go now?"

Conor's chest vibrated under her head as he chuckled. "Not yet, but soon, sweets."

A stray thought struck Alex, and she sat up, watching intently as the Regenerants led a bound and extremely angry Nyx from the room. "How come the Regenerants can so easily control her when Hades and Persephone had a hard time fighting her divine powers?"

Conor theorized. "I'm pretty sure it's because she's in a Regenerant body, and that limits her power against other Regenerants created with the same magic. Against them, she's only as powerful as her 'human' Regenerant form. Why she could still use her goddess powers against Hades and Persephone, your guess is as good as mine."

"I can answer that, Barghest." A deep voice rumbled from over their heads. Alex peered up at the tall, muscular god towering over them. "Her divine powers still pack a punch against other divine beings, even when contained in her Regenerant form."

Hades gave Alex a respectful nod. "But her Regenerant form has no power against others of her kind. So, who commands the Regenerants controls Nyx." He hesitated before adding, "For now, at least." Hades reached down and grabbed Alex's hand. "Here, let me help you up, Keeper."

SETTLED at the long table along the far wall, the team rested and chatted amongst themselves. Small purple serving demons, their squat bodies enveloped in white aprons, ferried back and forth from the kitchens, bringing fragrant steaming dishes and chilled drinks to the tired victors.

Alex and Conor sat at a smaller table to one side of the dais, across from Persephone and Hades. Alex was almost too tired to eat, but the food smelled delicious. Conor served her a plate filled with sweet and savory treats that smelled divine. Mouth watering, her appetite returned, and she ate heartily as she eavesdropped on the chatter from the team members seated at the larger table at her back.

As she cleaned her plate, a heavy stare settled on Alex. She raised her head and met Hades' anxious gaze. "Is the food to your liking, Keeper? I had the staff prepare Earth-side recipes that Persephone brings me on her visits."

"Uh, yes, the food is wonderful, thank you." A horrible suspicion entered Alex's mind, and she gazed at her plate with round eyes.

A roar of laughter from Hades made her jump. "No, Alex. None of the food on this table has magical qualities that will bind you to the Underworld for six months of the year." Hades gave Persephone a sheepish look, then winked at Alex and admitted the truth. "There's no such food, actually. But please don't tell Demeter that. Persephone likes her freedom, and I enjoy her visits."

Alex and Conor exchanged a chagrined glance, then both resumed eating. *The food really is delicious,* Alex mused. The long night filled with both loss and discovery had left her strangely ravenous.

Persephone coughed lightly to gather everyone's attention. "It's time I made a small confession. Hades reached out to me through an emissary a few days ago. He was having second thoughts about Nyx and Talon's plot but didn't have the resources to overcome them without help." The goddess offered Alex an apologetic smile. "He asked me to accompany your team to the Underworld to help him out of this pickle."

Alex glared at the goddess. "Pickle. That's what you call it." She spoke through stiff lips, her hands fisted around her cutlery, knuckles showing white. "A plot to overthrow Hecate and take control of the Crossroads so a powerful goddess of Chaos can leave her Underworld prison and wreak havoc on Earth. And you call it a pickle."

Conor placed his hand gingerly over Alex's knife hand. "Alex, sweets, put down the knife, please. Perhaps we can discuss this without brandishing weapons."

Persephone and Hades shared a loaded look. The goddess sighed and waved at Hades to continue the conversation with his own apology.

"I realize it was foolish of me to agree to their plan." Hades ducked his head and flattened his hands on the table before heaving a deep sigh. "It's just, so hard sometimes. I may be the god of the Underworld, but that doesn't mean what it used to. Since Hecate created the Crossroads, almost everyone can come and go as they please—except the demons and human spirits, of course—and I can't do anything about it but watch."

"Oh, boo hoo. Poor you." Alex listened in amazement as her mouth moved of its own accord, blurting out her thoughts and giving her no ability to stop it. "Listen, bud, you're still a god. That's pretty cool, right? You've got the demons ... and the human spirits. Plus, you have the love of a good wom—goddess. That's more than many people have, in any realm. So, knock it off with the pity party, and man up. Behave yourself, or I'll come back down here with my team and kick your ass." Alex flicked her gaze to Persephone, who dipped her chin in agreement. "And I'm pretty sure your wife would help me do so." She returned her reproving gaze to the now thoroughly cowed god and finished her diatribe. "Capisce?"

"Capisce."

"Good."

"Great!" Conor chimed in, as he squeezed Alex's knee under the table to prevent another outburst. "It's probably time to go now."

"Yes," Alex said, "let's go home to the Crossroads."

THE TRIP back took half the time and a tenth of the effort as the journey into the Underworld. Alex and her weary team rode in luxury in comfortable Hellhorse carriages down the steep road to the dock on the River Styx, where Charon waited with his boat.

The team bid farewell to Rafe at the docks. Alex thanked him profusely for his help. Rafe gave Alex a hearty hug, smiling cheekily at a glowering Conor before loping away into the foothills to honor his promise and collect the young female Hellhounds from the matriarchs of the mountain tunnels.

Charon guided the watercraft down the swiftly flowing river after informing the team he would drop them downriver at a small dock situated only a short walk from the Crossroads ley line.

Alex complained quietly to Conor. "If there's a dock down near the ley line, why in blazing hell did we have to trek all the way across the Underworld to get to the castle? Why didn't we come upriver on Charon's boat?"

The ferryman answered before Conor could reply. "My home is near the dock opposite the castle. That is where the toll to enter the Underworld is paid, and that is where Persephone knew to find me." With a sly smile, Charon added, "Unlike a popular song in your world, it's actually much easier to leave Hell than to enter it."

After docking at the small wharf, the team trudged wearily past the demons guarding the now-open flaming gates of Hell toward the Crossroads ley line.

It seemed it really was much easier to leave Hell than to enter it.

34

THERE'S A NEW KEEPER IN TOWN

Dawn was not far off as the team emerged from the ley line at the San Antonio Crossroads. *Home*, Alex mused, no longer able to deny her heart's commitment to this place and its people. The returning victors exchanged hearty hugs and high fives with those left to guard the Crossroads. Sadness laced the group's celebratory mood as Greta's sacrifice became known.

Alex saw the triune of goddesses quietly observing the homecoming from the top of the temple steps. She turned toward them, an anxious question in her eyes. Hecate's lips curved in an amused smile. "Your aunt's spirit is safe, Keeper. We sent Morpheus off with his tail between his legs."

A merry twinkle in Hecate's dark eyes told Alex there was more to the story. Her next words assured Alex the story, and her report to the goddess, could wait. "After last night's successful battle, Keeper, you and your team need rest. You and I have much to discuss, but it can wait a day or two."

Alex heaved a sigh of relief, nodding respectfully at the goddess. She turned away from the temple, planning to make the trek to her rooms for a much-needed rest.

A furry white missile approached at speed, hitting Alex midchest. Laughing, she wrapped her arms around Larry's wriggling body as he bathed her face in sloppy kisses. "Alright, okay, furball, stop with the kisses." Alex spoke through pursed lips as she attempted to avoid a doggie tongue in her mouth. "I thought we agreed, no French kisses for a month."

"Promises are made to be broken." Larry's familiar deep voice sounded in Alex's mind and filled her heart to bursting.

"Oh no, they're not, you little terror. The next promise you break means no steak for a month." Alex didn't mean a word of her threat. Over Larry's poufy head, she spied Grenoble sitting on the low stone wall at the edge of the courtyard. The little goblin had a sad cast to his round, green face.

"Hi, Grenoble. You okay?" Alex placed Larry back on his four paws and gazed at the grieving goblin with sympathy.

"Yes, Keeper. I'm fine." Grenoble rumbled a sigh. "Just mourning the loss of Greta. She was a good friend to me."

A shaft of sorrow lanced Alex's heart at the goblin's stark words. Alex fought through the painful memory, knowing Greta's last words would haunt her dreams for a long time.

Alex slowly approached the sad creature, unsure of her reception but feeling an overriding urge to provide some comfort. She gently placed her hand on his small shoulder. "I'm so sorry for your loss, Grenoble. Greta may have been gruff, but she truly had a heart of gold. She was brave to the end. All those in the community she fought to save will honor her sacrifice."

The little goblin gave a mighty sniff and nodded. Larry jumped up on the wall next to Grenoble and pressed his head against his friend's side, offering comfort in the only way he could.

Alex straightened when she felt a familiar presence behind her. She leaned back into Conor's arms as they encircled her from the rear.

"Time for some sleep, sweets. I'll walk you back to your rooms. But first, your Aunt Maia and Uncle Vinnie would each like to have a brief word."

A chill hand on her shoulder alerted Alex to Maia's presence.

She turned and gasped a sob when she saw the solid form of her aunt. "Aunt Maia! I'm so glad you made it back from the Underworld. You look ... great, uh, for being dead and all."

The small group of friends and family gathered around roared with laughter at Alex's awkward words, bringing an embarrassed blush to her cheeks. *Good lord, I really can't keep my foot out of my mouth for more than a hot minute. But seriously, she looks real again. Almost alive.*

Maia smiled gently and wrapped Alex in a comforting hug. While her aunt's body was slightly chilly, the hug felt real to Alex. She wrapped her arms around her aunt and wept.

"Alex, dear, we can talk about things later. There are several others here who'd like to congratulate you on your success." Maia stepped back, her cheeks shining with actual tears.

Vinnie strolled into view, absently rolling an unlit cigarette in his fingers as he eyed Alex with approval. "Mia cara. Congratulations on a successful mission. You were a joy to see in action, my dear. My sympathies on the loss of one of the team."

Vinnie's expensive cologne wafted around Alex as he wrapped her in a comforting hug. Fighting tears, she sniffed and cleared her throat, then her heart cracked open. *Heart-family,* she thought, as she wrapped her arms tightly around her uncle and returned his hug.

FIREWORKS BURST IN THE SKY, their magic forming huge lifelike fire-breathing dragons and other supernatural creatures that danced across the night sky. The light from the explosions reflected in the rippling water of the lake. Supernatural children waved multi-colored magical sparklers and laughed as they weaved in and out amongst the sizable crowd. A country western band played on the stage in the field behind the funeral home as couples danced to the lively music.

"I'm thinking Billy the Squid chose the band." Alex grinned at

Conor as they watched the celebrations from the edge of the river-side field.

Conor squeezed her hand and chuckled. "How did you ever guess?"

Alex glanced at the shore and smiled at the sight of Billy, a brand-new cowboy hat perched precariously on his massive head, his colossal form stretched along the pebbled beach. His head bopped to the beat of the music, while his tentacles waved with enthusiasm. "It wasn't hard to figure out," she replied. "I like his new hat, although it looks more than a little too small for him. Just like the one I fried when he helped me find my magic."

"Do you really think they make hats big enough for a 50-foot-long squid?" Conner snorted in amusement.

"Probably not. Still, it looks good, don't you think? The new hat suits him."

Conor jerked his chin at a couple on the edge of the dance area, dancing gracelessly to the music. "Looks like your gendarme Regenerant has met someone."

"You know his name is Leonard. He's asked you to call him that a dozen times." Alex tilted her head and giggled. "Even if I get to call him Leo."

Conor's lips turned up in a small smile. "I remember. I'm just messing with you since you appear to have a crush on the hand-some French police officer."

"I do not!" Alex tugged sharply on Conor's hand, trying to free her own, but with little success. "You know as well as I do that he's a good guy. He infiltrated Talon's scheme and became a Regenerant to help expose Nyx's evil plot from within." She sighed. "He can't help it if he's now stuck on Earth in another's body. He says he wants to help us protect the Crossroads. I believe him."

Conor's eyes twinkled down at her. "So do I, or he'd still be cooling his heels in the dungeon. I told you, I'm just messing with you."

"Good."

"Okay, then."

A comfortable silence settled over the couple as they watched the community celebrate their victory.

"Ooooh look!" Alex laughed as she pointed at a stocky, dark-haired man dressed in a well-tailored suit. She watched with amusement as her uncle climbed the steps to the stage before joining the band and taking the microphone from the lead singer. "Uncle Vinnie wasn't kidding. He told me he was going to sing a Sinatra song tonight, but I didn't believe him."

The band shifted tempo, and Vinnie began crooning a slow song in a surprisingly good imitation of the famous singer.

Conor grinned and drew Alex's attention to an older couple swaying in a slow dance at the foot of the stage. Alex squinted, realizing the couple's identity. Her aunt, Maia, was dancing with her long-time beau, Alan. The attorney's besotted smile as he gazed lovingly down at Maia made Alex chuckle. Her aunt's spirit had reformed with a vengeance. Her desperate fight to remain on Earth had aged her spirit, so she now appeared almost as solid as her good friend, Queen Elizabeth I. Maia had obviously decided it was time to resume her relationship with Alan. Alex hoped her pep-talk with the now-radiant ghost had contributed to her aunt's renewed pursuit of happiness.

Speaking of ghosts, Alex watched as Liz and her fellow ghosts flitted amongst the celebrations, tilting a hat here, pulling a sleeve there. Crazy Jack was swinging from the stage rigging, savagely playing air guitar to accompany the band. The ghosts appeared to be enjoying the party as much as everyone else, even if in their own unique way.

Alex realized she didn't see the trio of Indigo Fae warriors anywhere. She wondered if they'd returned to their own realm. The magical connection formed the night of her aunt's funeral awoke and an oddly familiar voice interrupted her thoughts. *"Merry Meet, Keeper. This is Tyre. We are not at the celebration this evening as your Queen asked us to guard the In-Between so the triune of goddesses could attend the party."*

An image of the gruff and imperious Queen Elizabeth I filled

Alex's mind, and her brows rose in incredulity. It surprised her that the ghostly regent thought enough of the goddesses to make such an arrangement with the Indigo Fae.

Soft, rumbling laughter brought her thoughts sharply back to the Fae currently connected to her mind. With trepidation, she asked, *"Do you ... can you see what I'm thinking, Tyre?"*

After a brief hesitation, Tyre replied, *"When our minds connect like this, yes, I can see your surface thoughts. Don't worry, I won't pry. And I won't connect to your mind without your knowledge."*

The Fae explained the reason for his mirth. *"The Queen of whom I speak is not your ghostly human one, but instead the one you call goddess. Hecate. Our allegiance in this realm is bound to her, at the request of our Fae Queen. I'll sever our mind connection now. If you need our help, you only need to bring us to mind, and I'll open our magical connection."*

Tye's deep laughter echoed inside her skull, before cutting off abruptly as he left her alone in her mind. Alex knew her face bore an expression of consternation. She gave Conor a shaky smile as he peered worriedly at her. "I'm fine. Just finished having a mind chat with Tyre. I, uh, didn't realize that I could call him with a thought. Or that he can read my mind when our minds are magically connected."

Conor's expression cleared, and he burst out laughing. "Oh Alex, I understand how worried you are about others reading your thoughts. Never fear. Those magically connected to you, as Larry and I—and the Indigo Fae are, will always respect your privacy."

"Yeah, right, so if I'm thinking of something I don't want others to know, or experiencing something ... shit, this just isn't going anywhere that won't embarrass the hell out of me." Alex turned her head away to hide the rising heat of her blush.

Conor's laugh softened to a chuckle. "Never fear—"

"What he's going to tell you is complete garbage, Alex." Larry's laughing voice filled Alex's mind as his furry body pressed against her leg. *"Those of us magically connected to you will always have a general sense of where you are and what you're thinking and feeling. We*

won't be rude enough to intrude, though, unless asked. So yes, to answer your unasked question, and complete your total embarrassment, we'll know when you decide to get it on with the hot Barghest."

Alex buried her face in her hands to hide the deep red blush staining her cheeks. "Oh, god."

Larry's snorting laughter mixed with Conor's deep chuckle. Even Grenoble joined in, his low rumbling of amusement adding to her mortification. Larry had obviously shared the mind conversation with them.

To her eternal gratitude, a gruff, almost familiar voice spoke from behind them and interrupted her companion's mirth. "Keeper, why are you not celebrating with the crowd? I expected you'd be in the thick of things. Especially considering how much this celebration is costing you."

Alex sighed in relief at the interruption. She turned around and gazed down at the squat orange-haired river troll. "Hi, Gina. Thank you for allowing us to use the funeral home and grounds for the celebration. Considering your family's recent loss, it was very generous of you to offer. My condolences on the loss of your sister."

A fleeting look of grief colored the river troll's expression before her customary scowl returned. "My sister was a stubborn, pig-headed fool. But I'll miss her, anyway."

Conor adroitly turned the conversation away from Greta's sacrifice and Gina's grief. "I hear you are going to be taking over management of the funeral home now. Your father must have a lot of confidence in your abilities. Congratulations."

Gina snorted derisively. "Well, the old man doesn't want to lift a finger himself, so it's down to me, now, isn't it? I would have helped Greta run things ... before, well, you know. But my sister was a nit-picky perfectionist and preferred to have the place to herself."

Alex smothered a sad smile as she remembered her first meeting with the little troll standing before her. She hadn't realized Greta had a twin until she saw Gina open the door to the funeral home several days before, when she and Conor arrived to help plan tonight's celebration. Conor had to pinch her arm, so she stopped gaping at Greta's identical twin as she ushered them into her late sister's office.

"I'm sure it would please your sister to see how you've organized tonight's celebration, so again, Gina, thank you."

"Just pay the bill on time, Keeper." The river troll sniped her demand, then waved her arm at a server walking by pushing a trolly of food. "Hey, you, if you don't watch what you're doing, the food on that trolly is going to wind up feeding the worms instead of the guests." Gina trotted toward the wincing waiter without a backward glance.

"I wish you'd told me Greta had an identical twin." Alex murmured a soft reproof to Conor. "I almost had a heart attack when I met Gina the other day."

"Sorry. I didn't even think of it. Everyone in the supernatural community knows the two tyrannical troll twin sisters." Conor apologized, wincing as he realized what he'd implied with his thoughtless words.

"It's okay, Connor." Alex smiled in understanding. "I may be a newbie Crossroads Keeper, and a newcomer to Sylvan City, but I'm here now." She squeezed his hand. "I'm home now."

ALEX SAT QUIETLY, drowsing in the comfortable chair near the blazing fire. Hecate had been silent, staring into its depths, ever since she called Alex to the In-Between.

The goddess heaved a sigh and shook off her melancholy mood, before giving her new Crossroads Keeper an approving nod. "Alexandria, your actions in defeating Nyx and her cohorts and saving your aunt's spirit are commendable. You have proven yourself to be the correct choice for Keeper of this Crossroads." A slightly smug smile hovered on the goddess's lips. "It seems I chose well."

Alex shifted from her comfortable slouch and sat up. Her anxious gaze met that of the goddess. "Um, haven't you heard? You know, about me being a necromancer? Won't that, I dunno, mess with my Keeper mojo?"

Persephone's silvery laugh rippled in the air, startling Alex. She thought she and Hecate had been alone. *Perhaps we had been,* she reflected with a shrug. The three goddesses who formed the triune popped in and out of the In-Between whenever they pleased, it seemed.

"I have provided a full report on the battle in the Underworld to Hecate and my mother." Persephone nodded at Demeter, now seated beside her on a couch Alex could swear hadn't been there a moment ago. "They are both aware of the heroism shown by you and your team. They know how you vanquished Nyx."

The three goddesses exchanged a meaningful look, then all three pairs of divine eyes fixed on Alex in approbation.

Alex heaved a deep breath and began, "But—"

"But what?" Hecate queried.

"Well, aren't you concerned that I have necromantic powers? Conor said that I'm unique, and I'm darn sure he didn't mean that in a good way." Alex clenched her hands in her lap before meeting Hecate's calm gaze and giving voice to her fears. "He told me your priestesses, the Crossroads Keepers, always marry human men or other supernaturals. Always."

Alex swallowed, her throat constricting with worry before continuing, her words tumbling over one another in a rush. "He says Keepers never marry mages, as their power is from the gods and is not compatible with the feminine divine power of a goddess. He says it's been that way since the beginning, so that no mage magic interferes with the flow of divine power through the priestess Keepers."

Stumbling to a stop now she'd finally spoken the words she'd agonized over for days, Alex's nervous gaze flitted across the impassive faces of the goddess triune seated across from her.

The three goddesses suddenly burst out laughing. Alex's jaw

dropped and she watched in growing dismay as the divine trio laughed for what seemed like forever. Finally, when their mirth had resolved into merry glances and giggles, Alex dared to speak. "With respect, goddesses, I don't think my predicament is funny. Since my father's magic bastardizes my Keeper magic, I can't be your Keeper anymore. So, now what happens?"

While Alex held her breath and waited for the answer, she recalled her first meeting with the goddess Hecate in the In-Between with nostalgia. Dismayed at discovering her Keeper heritage and at being bound by the goddess to serve the Cross-roads and its supernatural community, she'd rebelled inwardly at the responsibility and spent weeks plotting ways to abdicate her heritage and return to her independent, if lonely, life in Connecticut as soon as possible.

Now, she dreaded being told she couldn't continue as Keeper, couldn't continue to protect the Crossroads and its community, couldn't remain with her heart-family.

The three goddesses exchanged a final mirthful look before seeming to come to a silent agreement. Small smiles still hovered incongruously on their regal faces.

Hecate, her face a picture of condescending pity at Alex's igno-rant questions, spoke first. "Keeper, do you really think that, in the millennia since I created the Crossroads, my Keepers and their mothers and sisters who would bear the next generations never dallied with a mage...or a god or two?" She snorted in derision. "And you believed your Hellhound Barghest when he regaled you with tales of pure priestess bloodlines!"

Persephone's laugh silvered the air. "Alex, Nyx may be an evil crone, but she's right about one thing. I do sleep around." The pretty goddess shrugged. "So does my husband. It doesn't mean we don't love one another."

Demeter smiled indulgently at her daughter before addressing Alex. "What my daughter is trying to say, Keeper, is that the blood-lines of the gods, their supernatural creations, and their priest-esses weave a convoluted path through history." The goddess's intense gaze pinned Alex to her chair as her words stoked a growing hope. "You are not the first Keeper to have mage magic, nor will you be the last."

"Get over yourself, Keeper, and get on with your duties. You are my rightful heir and the chosen Keeper of this Cross-roads." Hecate, the goddess of the Crossroads, gazed at Alex with a mixture of compassion and reproof.

Hecate's frank words filled Alex with joy, but she felt compelled to clarify. "So, you're saying that my mage power isn't a problem, even though it's necromantic magic." Alex shivered. She had yet to come to terms with her father's death. Or his dark magical heritage.

"Why do you think I chose you," Hecate asked softly. "I've known for a long time that Nyx was scheming to leave the Under-world. She's attempted it before." The goddess bowed her head and revealed the rest of the truth. "Fifteen years ago, my seers told me Nyx would soon have a chance at success and that it would involve a rising of undead. I've been watching her for years, as much as I could. Recently, I discovered she was conspiring with your father; I just didn't think their plans were so advanced, or that she'd almost succeed."

The rest of the puzzle pieces fell into place. Alex's jaw dropped as she stared at Hecate in dismay. "You knew my father was a necromancer and that I'd inherited his magic. After his death during the attack on the Crossroads fifteen years ago, you knew he would eventually find his way to Nyx in the Underworld—and that he'd try again."

"I suspected. And I realized that only another necromancer could fight a necromancer in league with a goddess as powerful as Nyx," Hecate replied with a shrug.

"So, that's why my red magic didn't surprise you." Anger sparked in Alex's voice. "But why didn't you tell me? I would have prepared and trained better. Differently."

"No, you wouldn't, Alex." Hecate closed her eyes and sighed before opening them and fixing Alex with a sympathetic gaze.

"You had enough to worry about learning to be a Keeper. This was the only way, dear. I expected your necromantic power to manifest when needed."

Hecate's wise eyes met Alex's confused ones. "Don't you remember your first time here in the In-Between with me, when I bound you to the Crossroads? I hinted then you had more strength and power than you realized."

Tears tracked down Alex's cheeks. She recalled the goddess's words at their first meeting several weeks ago, after her return to the Crossroads. "You knew all this time ...."

Hecate softly stroked Alex's hair. "Yes, child, I knew all this time. I suspected you would grow to be one of the most powerful priestesses of my long line. I realized your bravery and strength would surpass that of the many others who came before you."

"You mean my father's mage magic would make me more powerful ...."

"No, Alex, your father's magic is not you, any more than your Keeper magic is. Your power lies in your large, brave heart, and those you hold close to fuel that power."

"My heart-family."

"Yes, your heart-family." Hecate smiled in agreement. Her gaze narrowed in warning. "You will need them for the trials to come, Keeper, so let your heart embrace them, as well as your power."

Alex's heart sank as she parsed the goddess's words. "What trials?"

Hecate's gaze held weary wisdom. "There is still Nyx's criminal network here on earth to contend with. I'm sure she can still control them, even from the far edges of the Underworld. Your necromantic powers will need honing so you can continue to control your father's Regenerants, and, through them, Nyx." The goddess narrowed her eyes in anger. "And then there's your mother."

"What about my mother?" Alex eyed the goddess warily as a dark memory slithered under a tiny drift of fog remaining in a far corner of her mind. "I thought she gave up her dreams of becoming Keeper years ago."

"A jealousy as soul deep as your mother's never ebbs. She will try again." Considering, Hecate mused. "It wouldn't surprise me if ... no, that's for another time."

"What? Tell me!"

"Careful, Keeper, I'm still a goddess. I'll tell you when the time is right. Now go and see to your pining Barghest. He's waiting for you on the temple steps."

Alex opened her mouth to question the goddess further. Before she uttered a word, she found herself on the temple portico, teetering on the edge of the steep steps. Conor caught her around the waist, preventing a nasty fall.

"Looks like you pissed off the goddess. Again." Conor's deep voice soothed her mind, bringing her thoughts out of their tailspin.

"Well, you *know* I always open my mouth before I engage my brain."

"That you do, Alex, that you do."

CONOR AND ALEX sat on the low stone wall that edged the temple courtyard and watched as the sun set in a fiery farewell to the day.

"So, that's it. That's what the goddesses told me." Alex carefully averted her eyes from Conor's. One hand curved around the edge of the rough stone wall in a white-knuckled grip while the other shaded her eyes from the brightness of the setting sun. "I guess the priestess bloodline doesn't need to be quite as pure as you implied it did."

Alex dreaded Conor's judgmental gaze. Her revelations would shock him. *Well, he'll just have to get over it,* she reflected, *even if my new necromantic powers make him cringe.* They still had to work together to protect the Crossroads, even if a romantic relationship was now out of the question.

Conor's hand landed gently on her clenched one, and he smoothed it as he spoke. "I've known about your mage magic since I first met you at the airport. I didn't realize it was necromantic magic, but I sensed your mixed power."

Alex counted to ten. Then counted to ten again. It seemed she was the only one who hadn't known about her mage magic. "So, when *did* you know that my mage magic was necromantic?"

With a sheepish grimace, Conor told her. "The first time I saw your magic, when you fried Billy's cowboy hat." He shrugged and slanted her an apologetic glance. "Only necromancers have red magic. It's very rare."

A horrible thought made Alex gasp. "Does everyone know about my mixed magic? I mean, the whole supernatural posse?"

"No one knows but the goddesses. Oh, and your Aunt Maia and Uncle Vinnie, of course."

"Of course." Alex ground out her reply. "Every one of my heart-family knew but me."

"What am I, chopped liver?" Larry's snarky voice distracted Alex from her anger and embarrassment at being the last to discover the truth about her necromantic magical inheritance.

Larry hopped up on the wall beside Alex and peered smugly at her from under his poufy topknot. *"I knew the moment we met. But it's not polite to comment on a supernatural's mixed magical heritage."*

"Is there anything else you two haven't told me? Am I also a shifter? Can I turn into a giant squid? Is my hair suddenly going to turn into snakes, accompanied by a gaze that can turn a man to stone?" Alex glared at her Barghest Guardian and poodle Familiar. "Actually, that last one would come in really handy right about now."

"Nope, there's nothing else. At least, not that I know of." Larry assured Alex she was now aware of everything there was to know about her magical heritage. He shook his head reconsidering, before scooting away, eyeing her long, black hair with caution.

Conor laughed and shook his head as he finally freed Alex's hand from her death grip on the stone wall and enveloped her hand with his. "I don't think Medusa is one of your ancestors, Alex."

"But do you know that for sure?"

"Uh, no."

"Didn't think so. So, don't mess with me, either of you, as you have no idea what other magical tricks I have up my sleeve."

Both man and dog gave her a concerned side eye, no doubt reconsidering their assurances that they—or she—knew everything about her magical powers.

Alex burst out laughing. "Got you both!" She jumped off the stone wall, pulling Conor by the hand as she led them all back down the path toward the house. "I'm starving. Let's go see what wonders Henri has cooked up for dinner."

"Now that sounds like a plan. I'm gonna go round up Grenoble, and we'll meet you in the kitchen." Larry pranced ahead, his furry white body disappearing into the gloom.

Conor sped up, loosing Alex's hand with a grin as he took off at a fast jog. "First one to the kitchen does the dishes."

"Oh, no, you don't!" Alex's feet pounded down the path after him.

EPILOGUE

A startled owl flew from the tree at the edge of the clearing, hooting his displeasure at the disturbance to his rest. The leaves on the branch below his former perch still rustled, both from the large owl's wings and from the impact of the rock which had hit the branch moments before.

"See, I told you my aim is better than yours." Conor teased Vinnie with a lazy grin. "If you'd put that damn cigarette away, instead of playing with it, you'd have better luck. You know you can't throw for shit with your left hand."

"Fuck you." Despite his caustic reply, Vinnie realized Conor was right. He slipped the long, thin cigarette back in his jacket pocket and picked up a loose rock with his right hand, scanning the trees in the clearing across the courtyard for a target. He'd be damned if he lost the contest to the annoyingly right Barghest at his side.

Conor grinned knowingly at his friend. "You almost hit your last avian target, which, as we both know, would piss off both Maia and Alex, so I'm glad you're taking my advice. I don't want to have to bury any dead bodies tonight, even if they're feathered ones. Or vampire ones."

Both men sobered, remembering the first time they had a conversation about dead bodies at the Crossroads.

Vinnie took aim at a tall pine tree at the far edge of the clearing across the courtyard, then launched his rock. A heavy branch shivered from the impact, and an irate squawking came from the branch above. The giant barn owl didn't leave his perch, instead screeching his anger at the rocky interruption to his rest. *"Hey, fuck you guys! Can't you see I'm trying to sleep here! How would you like it if I flew over there and crapped on your heads? Huh? You wouldn't like it, would you?"* The owl subsided into angry muttering, finishing with a last insult. *"Assholes."* After a last baleful glare at the two men, the owl lowered his head and closed his eyes to resume his nap.

Conor gave an evil chuckle. "Did you know that bird was a shifter before you threw the rock?"

"Yep. I smelled his shifter form from here. Guess my vampire nose is better than your canine one."

"Fuck you."

Both friends subsided into amiable silence as the sounds of the night resumed. The full moon laid a silvery light over the Crossroads courtyard, revealing nothing but cobblestones, unmarred by blood or body parts. Or bird crap, thought Conor, because no way could that shifter owl swoop low enough, or with enough speed, to poop on either of them. He reconsidered. Probably not, anyway.

Vinnie opened his mouth to speak, then shrugged and lapsed back into silence.

"What?" Conor frowned. "Spit it out, man. What's on your mind?"

With an apologetic grimace, Vinnie queried, "How's the shifting going? Got your control back yet? I ... just need to ask, in case—"

Conor snorted. "No worries, vampire. I'm not about to go feral, so there's no need to plot my demise. I haven't shifted involuntarily since Hecate bonded Alex to the Crossroads. I told you back then that we needed the Keeper found and bonded and my shifts would sort themselves out."

"Okay then. That's good."

"Yup. Sure is."

After a loaded silence, Vinnie spoke the rest of his mind. "You know, if you hurt her, I'll stab you in the heart and make a Barghest-skin rug out of your hide for in front of my fireplace, don't you?" Vinnie was again rolling the unlit cigarette through his fingers. It was a habit he couldn't break. Not that he wanted to. The cigarette reminded him of his lost humanity and kept him connected to his past. It also spoke of the future, smoke-free, but filled with possibilities for both himself and his heart-family.

Conor grinned, his cheeks taking on a rosy hue. He turned aside Vinnie's comment with snark. "You'd have to catch me, first, vampire, and I've got four legs in Barghest form."

"Oh, I'd catch you, you dumbass. Your doggie form is no match for a mature vampire like myself."

"Mature, huh?" Conor gave Vinnie strong side-eye. "Yeah, right, old man."

"You're one to talk, Renaissance Man." Vinnie returned the side-eye. "My comment stands; you break her heart, and I'll break you into little pieces and feed you to Billy the Squid."

Conor placed his hand over his heart and made a promise. "I solemnly swear not to break Alex's heart." Sotto voice, he added, "But what if she breaks mine?"

"So, you *are* falling in love with her." Vinnie shook his head with a knowing smile. "You old dog! There's a first time for everything, I guess."

"Barghests mate for life. I'm now at the age to start thinking about that. At least, that's what my mother keeps telling me." Conor sighed. "Alex being the Crossroads Keeper, as well as a powerful mage, complicates things, though. What if it doesn't work out and we still have to work together for the next century or so?"

"Well, nothing ventured, nothing gained." Vinnie philosophized.

"Thanks for your input, oh wise one, I'll keep it in mind."

Both men lapsed back into silence, each remembering their first conversation about the new Keeper, when the moon last hung full in the night sky.

Vinnie gave voice to their mutual thoughts. "Well, at least she now knows how loved—and needed, she is here."

Conor blew out a breath, his gaze pensive as he studied the night sky. "Let's hope that's enough to keep her here. And make her happy."

Available for Pre-order:

Larry's Familiar Tale -This novella is the Prequel to Book 1 of The Crossroads Keeper series. It tells Larry's tale of heroism, heartbreak and humor and explains how he found himself as a poodle Familiar to a clueless Crossroads Keeper. Click here to purchase.

Readers who sign up for my newsletter will receive a FREE copy of Larry's Familiar Tale once it is released. They'll also get news of upcoming releases, sneak peeks behind the scenes of each book and chances to win some cool swag. Larry has also insisted the newsletter include his blog...

Other Books in The Crossroads Keeper series

Book 2 - Persephone's Problem is available for pre-order

Book 3 - Demeter's Dilemma coming in 2022

WANT MORE FROM SAMANTHA?

Get a FREE eBook of the prequel to The Crossroads Keeper series when you sign up for my VIP Reading Club newsletter. You'll also receive notice of upcoming releases, behind the scenes details about characters, and so much more.

Check out the *Literature and Living with Dogs* Facebook group, which features all things dog, including books that have a strong canine character—or two. Readers are invited to join the group and immerse themselves in canine conversations with me and other like-minded dog lovers.

Available books in The Crossroads Keeper series:
 Larry's Familiar Tale (Prequel)
 Hecate's Heir (Book 1)
 Persephone's Problem (Book 2)

Visit my website at www.samanthablackwood.com for details of upcoming books and new series coming in 2022.

Join the VIP Reader's Group to receive your free eBook of Larry's Familiar Tale and sign up for the newsletter at:
 https://landing.mailerlite.com/webforms/landing/e3b7d9

PLEASE REVIEW MY BOOK
YOU CAN MAKE A DIFFERENCE

Enjoy this book? You can make a big difference.

Reviews are the most powerful tool in my arsenal when it comes to getting attention for my books. Much as I wish I did, I don't have the big bucks to throw at marketing like the large publishing companies do. Not yet, anyway.

But I have something more powerful than that. I have my loyal readers, who enjoy my books and want to keep reading them as I keep publishing them, which I can only do with your help.

Honest reviews of my books help bring them to the attention of other readers.

If you enjoyed this book, I would be very grateful if you could spend just five minutes leaving a review.

Reviews can be left on the site of the retailer where you purchased the book. Reviews on Amazon, Goodreads and other book rating locations are also appreciated.

Links to the most common review sites can be found on my website at www.samanthablackwoodauthor.com.

Thank you for you support!
Sincerely, Sam

ACKNOWLEDGMENTS

My heartfelt gratitude to the tribe of people who contributed their experience, opinions, and support to this book.

First, a huge thank you to the experienced folks @20Booksto50K, as, without their excellent advice, this book would likely be moldering in a dusty desk drawer or on a cobweb covered thumb drive buried in the bottom drawer of my desk.

Second, a virtual hug to my editor, Whitney Morsillo of Whitney's Book Works and to my cover designer Jes of Blackbird Book Covers.

And lastly, thank you to all my supportive friends, to my eagle-eyed Beta Readers and to the members of the Round Rock Writer's Group Virtual Coffee Chat. Without your belief in my ability to pull this off, this book would not be in the hands of whoever is reading this rather boring acknowledgement, lol!

ABOUT THE AUTHOR

Samantha Blackwood lives in San Antonio, Texas with her husband and pack of rescue dogs. She has worked professionally with dogs most of her life and proudly claims the title of 'Crazy Dog Lady.' Her friends and family don't disagree...

Of course, she couldn't imagine not including dogs in her writing, so there's a canine character based on a member of her pack included in each of her book series. She has a lot of fun giving her fictionalized fur-kids magical abilities—and voices. We all know dogs don't really need human words to communicate, but it's nice —and hilarious—to hear them tell us exactly what they think!

For more information, contact the author.
www.samanthablackwoodauthor.com
sam@samanthablackwoodauthor.com

facebook.com/samanthablackwoodauthor
twitter.com/Samanth42715949
instagram.com/samanthablackwoodauthor
pinterest.com/samanthablackwoodauthor

Made in the USA
Coppell, TX
30 November 2021

66781736R00204